# WILLIAM W. JOHNSTONE

# SCREAM
# OF
# EAGLES

**PINNACLE BOOKS**
Kensington Publishing Corp.
http://www.kensingtonbooks.com

PINNACLE BOOKS are published by

Kensington Publishing Corp.
119 West 40th Street
New York, NY 10018

All Kensington titles, imprints and distributed lines are available at special quantity discounts for bulk purchases for sales promotions, premiums, fund-raising, and educational or institutional use. Special book excerpts or customized printings can also be created to fit specific needs. For details, write or phone the office of the Kensington special sales manager: Kensington Publishing Corp., 119 West 40th Street, New York, NY 10018, attn: Special Sales Department, Phone 1-800-221-2647.

ISBN-13: 978-0-7860-2573-2
ISBN-10: 0-7860-2573-5

First Printing: September 1997
Ninth Printing: July 2011

17   16   15   14   13   12   11   10   9

Printed in the United States of America

# THE OLD LOBO WOLF

Jamie took a sip of his whiskey and carefully placed the glass on the scarred bar. "Good whiskey," he told the bartender. "Hits the spot. But it stinks in here," he added. "Smells like outlaw scum to me."

Tom Brewer stood up from the table. "Old man," he said to Jamie's back. "You been doggin' my back trail for more'un two years now. And I'm tired of it. You've killed my friends and even some of my kin. But your killin' stops right here."

Jamie turned to face him, his short-barreled twelve guage shotgun pressed tight against his leg. "I don't think so, Brewer," he said. "I still got a goodly number of you trash to deal with."

Outside the winter winds screamed like angry eagles. "Make your peace with whatever God will claim you, Brewer," Jamie said. "Then hook and draw."

Brewer cursed Jamie and grabbed iron. Jamie lifted the sawed-off and blew the killer all over the back end of the saloon. Then he drained his glass of whiskey and walked out.

"Who in the hell was that?" a salesman from St. Louis blurted.

"That's an ol' lobo wolf name of Jamie Ian MacCallister." The grizzled trapper spoke from the corner table. "The Miles Nelson gang kilt his wife down in Coloradee two year ago. He's been on the prod ever since. And he'll be on the prod 'til he kills ever' one of them."

"You reckon he'll get it done?" the bartender asked.

The old mountain man smiled. "Bet on it."

# BOOK YOUR PLACE ON OUR WEBSITE AND MAKE THE READING CONNECTION!

We've created a customized website just for our very special readers, where you can get the inside scoop on everything that's going on with Zebra, Pinnacle and Kensington books.

When you come online, you'll have the exciting opportunity to:

- View covers of upcoming books
- Read sample chapters
- Learn about our future publishing schedule (listed by publication month *and author*)
- Find out when your favorite authors will be visiting a city near you
- Search for and order backlist books from our online catalog
- Check out author bios and background information
- Send e-mail to your favorite authors
- Meet the Kensington staff online
- Join us in weekly chats with authors, readers and other guests
- Get writing guidelines
- AND MUCH MORE!

**Visit our website at**
**http://www.kensingtonbooks.com**

# Book One

*Till the sun grows cold,*
*And the stars are old,*
*And the leaves of the Judgment Book*
*unfold . . .*

—Bedouin Song

# Prologue

Jamie Ian MacCallister and his wife Kate were both fifteen years old when they were married in the river town of New Madrid, Missouri. They remained married and faithful and true to one another for forty-five years. By the time Kate died in Jamie's arms after an outlaw raid on the Colorado town they helped found, Jamie and Kate had produced a houseful of kids and dozens of grandchildren and great-grandchildren.

Jamie had already lived longer than many men of that time, but somebody forgot to tell Jamie about that. For a man his age, he was still bull strong and wang-leather tough. His hair was gray, but his heart was young. He used eyeglasses to read fine print, but he sure didn't need glasses to shoot.

The loss of Kate hit Jamie harder than anything ever had over the long and tumultuous years. For several weeks after her violent and untimely death, Jamie could not clearly focus on anything except her dying and the lonely grave overlooking MacCallister's Valley. He holed up deep in the mountains and let his grief take control for a time.

Jamie relived over and over each and every memory shared with Kate. The good and the bad. The laughter and the tears. The pain and the pleasure.

The pleasure far outweighed the pain.

After a couple of weeks, Jamie began to realize that Kate

would not want him doing this. All the grieving in the world would not bring her back from the grave. She was at peace now, having climbed the Starry Path to be greeted by Man Above. She would wait there for him.

Jamie looked up at the high cloudless blue of the sky. He sighed and then smiled. "You know what I have to do, Kate. I couldn't live with myself if I didn't do it. Of course," he said drily, "I might not live much longer doing it. But I reckon that would be all right, too. 'Cause then I'd be with you."

Jamie buckled on his pistols. Twin .44s, model 60 conversion. He wiped the dust off his rifle, a Winchester model 68. He tidied up his camp, packed the frame on the packhorse, and saddled up his big, mean-eyed buckskin. One of his grandchildren—he couldn't remember which one, much less the child's name, Kate had always kept track of those things—had named the huge animal Buck.

It was turning colder now, with winter not far off. During the weeks that Jamie had spent wrapped in his grief, those responsible for the attack on MacCallister's Valley, and the death of Kate, the Miles Nelson gang, would have scattered like dust in the wind. Any trail would be as cold as the stars.

"I got a few good years left in me," Jamie muttered. Buck swung his big head around to look at him. "And I'll use them finding you all. My son Matthew talks of book law and justice. That's his way. I'll have justice my way."

He swung easily into the saddle, the movements like a man twenty years younger.

"I'll find you all," Jamie repeated. "And I'll kill you."

Overhead, soaring on the winds, an eagle screamed.

# 1

Jamie topped the crest and looked down at the town nestled deep in the Rockies. Another mining town. A number of buildings with boarded-up windows told him that already the gold or the silver was playing out and the miners were moving on. What made him certain the town was dying was that among the empty buildings were several saloons.

"Let's go find you boys a warm stall and some hay to munch on," Jamie spoke to his horses. "You both deserve a good rest. It's cold this day."

About twenty degrees above zero, with the ground covered with snow. Jamie wasn't sure, but he thought he had passed the new year in a cave, sitting out a blizzard. "That would make it 1870," he muttered, his breath steaming the air. "Kate's been gone almost six months now." And, he thought, the trail I've been trying to find is as cold as the weather.

Almost six months, Kate lying cold in her grave.

No, he corrected his thoughts as he walked his horses onto the wide street, deep-rutted from the wheels of many heavily laden wagons. That is only the shell that contained the flesh and blood of my Kate. Her soul is with Man Above.

Waiting for me.

Jamie stabled his horses at the livery and told the man to brush and curry the packhorse. "Don't touch Buck," he warned. "He bites and kicks."

"I wouldn't touch that big ugly son of a bitch for fifty dollars," the young man said. He jumped back just in time to avoid the flashing teeth of Buck, who was doing his best to take a chunk out of the livery man's arm.

"Don't hurt his feelings," Jamie cautioned him with a small smile. The smiles were coming more often now, but they were still rare. "He's very sensitive."

The young man rolled his eyes and began forking hay into the stall, muttering about horses in general and Buck in particular.

Jamie took his rifle and saddlebags and walked up the boardwalk to the only hotel that was still open in the dying town. He checked in and stowed his gear. The desk clerk froze as still as death when he reversed the book and read the name.

Jamie Ian MacCallister.

The legend himself. In person. In his hotel. My God!

The clerk took in Jamie's size. Big as a mountain. His hair was almost all gray, but the big man moved like a huge puma. The clerk sensed danger shrouding Jamie like clouds on the high peaks.

"I'll have a haircut and a bath," Jamie said. "Where's the barber shop?"

"Just across the street, sir. To your left as you leave the hotel. May I say that it is an honor to have you here, sir. I . . ."

But Jamie was already out the door. The clerk called for one of his swampers and told the rummy to spread the news. Man Who Is Not Afraid was in town.

Jamie soaped and scrubbed and did it again with buckets of hot water. Then he had the barber cut his long hair short. After Jamie had left, the barber carefully swept up the graying hair. There were people who would pay a lot of money for a few strands of the hair of the man many Indians still called Man Who Plays With Wolves. Still others called the living legend Bear Killer.

Others called him one big mean son of a bitch, but never to his face.

Dusk was settling over the mountains as Jamie went into the hotel bar and ordered a whiskey. "From the good bottle," he told the barkeep. He would linger over the amber liquid, savoring the hard flavor, and then have dinner. The menu on the chalkboard was beef and potatoes.

The men who had lined the bar shifted to one side, giving Jamie the entire left side of the long mahogany. Everyone in the West knew the story of the Miles Nelson attack on MacCallister's Valley, the death of Kate, and that Jamie was on the prod.

After ordering his whiskey, Jamie spoke to no one in the bar, and no one spoke directly to him. A man wearing a star on his coat entered the room, looked at Jamie for a short time, then left. He did not leave because of fear, only because he knew MacCallister's reputation and knew Jamie would not deliberately provoke an argument with any innocent citizen.

But the marshal also knew there were a couple of ol' boys in town who thought themselves to be tough, and when they heard that MacCallister was in town, they would brace him in hopes of gaining a reputation. The marshal didn't want to be around when that happened. He knew that while the two so-called "bad men" were strutting around, talking about what they'd do to MacCallister, Jamie would just shoot them and be done with it.

And when the smoke had cleared, MacCallister would go eat supper.

The marshal went home to eat his own supper, and to hell with those two clowns who thought they were tough. In about fifteen minutes, or less, they wouldn't be tough— they'd just be dead. And in two days, forgotten.

Jamie had just lifted the glass to his lips when the front door banged open and cold air swept through the barroom. Jamie did not turn his head to see who it was. He had positioned himself so he could watch the front door by using the long mirror behind the bar.

Jamie sighed as he watched the two young men. Trouble,

he thought. Local toughs wanting to make a reputation. Go away, boys. Go away.

The pair swaggered toward the bar. Both of them were wearing two guns, low and tied down.

Damn! Jamie thought.

The young men bellied up to the bar, and one called for whiskey in too loud a tone.

The barkeep slid a bottle down to them. He was being very careful to stay clear of the line of fire. The knot of men at the opposite end of the bar left to take tables. No one wanted to get shot.

"Howdy there, old-timer. The name's Pullen," one of the young men said. "Jim Pullen. You heared of me, I reckon."

"Can't say as I have," Jamie said, after taking a small sip of whiskey. Jamie was not really a drinking man, but he did enjoy one or two drinks occasionally.

"Oh, yeah? You don't get around much, do you? Well, I reckon a man of your advanced age pretty much has to stay close to hearth and home."

Jamie smiled. There wasn't much of the West he hadn't seen at one time or the other.

"My pard, here, is Black Jack Perkins. I *know* you've heared of him."

"Can't say as I have, boy."

"Well, he killed a man in Black Hawk, he did."*

"I'm sorry to hear that," Jamie said, after taking another sip of whiskey. "Terrible thing, having to kill a man."

"Huh! Well, I killed my share of men, too. I ain't lost no sleep over it."

Jamie said nothing. He placed his shot glass on the polished bar and waited. He had left his heavy winter coat up in his room and wore a waist-length leather jacket over a dark shirt. Dark trousers and boots. Out of long habit, he had slipped the leather thongs off the hammers of his twin Colts before entering the barroom. He waited.

---

*The town also went by the name of Doe for several years.

"You're Jamie MacCallister, ain't you?" Black Jack asked, stepping away from the bar and facing Jamie.

"That's right."

"I been hearin' 'bout you all my life. I'm sick of it. I don't think you done half of what people say you done. I think most of it was piff and padoodle. Now what do you think about that?"

Jamie was growing very weary of the pair of would-be toughs. But he didn't want to kill either of them. He turned to face the young man and smiled. He lifted one hand and waggled a finger at Black Jack. "Come here, boy."

Black Jack strutted up to Jamie, a curious expression on his face.

Jamie hit him with a left that produced a sound much like a watermelon struck with the flat side of a shovel. Jerking one of the young man's guns from leather, and holding the nearly unconscious Black Jack up between himself and Pullen, Jamie closed the few feet and laid the barrel of the gun against Pullen's head. Jim Pullen hit the floor, his lights turned out.

Jamie popped Black Jack again, and Black Jack joined his buddy on the floor for a nap. He took their pistols and walked out back to the privy, dropping the six-shooters down the twin holes. They disappeared forever with a splash.

Back in the bar, the men seated at the tables winced at the power in those big arms as Jamie reached down with both hands and grabbed the sleeping young men by the backs of their shirt collars and dragged them outside, depositing them both in the street.

Returning to the warmth of the bar, Jamie signaled the barkeep for another drink and then turned to the crowd. "Am I going to have any more trouble here tonight?"

The men slowly and solemnly shook their heads.

"Fine," Jamie said, then took his drink into the restaurant and sat down and ordered dinner. Outside, a citizen helped one of the marshal's deputies drag the unconscious young men across the street. The deputy tossed them into a jail cell and slammed and locked the door.

"Damn fools," the citizen said.

"They're lucky MacCallister didn't kill them," the deputy said. "He may be gettin' on in years, but that is still one war hoss, and no man to brace."—

"Reckon how long he'll stay in town?" the citizen questioned.

"As long as he damn well pleases," the deputy replied.

"It's from Pa!" Matthew shouted with a wide grin, waving the envelope the stage driver had handed him. Matthew looked up at the driver. "Where'd you get this, Luke?"

"Another driver give it to me. It's been passed around some, Matt. I figure it's taken near'bout two months to get here."

Matthew sat down on the porch of the Goldman Mercantile Store and carefully opened the envelope. Abe and Rebecca Goldman were long dead, the store now operated by their youngest son, Tobias.

The entire town, more than five hundred people, soon gathered around, waiting in silence as Matthew read the letter.

"Pa's well," Matthew finally said. Matthew was one of triplets—Matthew, Morgan, and Megan—born in 1832. "Pa was in Central City when he wrote this. He's picked up the trail of some of the Nelson gang and was leavin' out for Wyoming next mornin'."

"What's the date?" Matt's youngest sister, Joleen, asked.

"There ain't any. Hush up and listen."

"Don't tell me to shush, you ox!"

"Shut up, the both of you!" Jamie Ian told his brother and sister. "Read," he told Matt.

"There ain't much more."

"Isn't," Joleen corrected.

Matt sighed and returned to the letter. "Pa says to tend

to Ma's grave site and plant some flowers around about. He says if he comes back here and finds the site all grown up with weeds, somebody's butt is gonna be in trouble." He looked up into the faces of his brothers and sisters, in-laws and nieces and nephews and what have you. "That's it."

"I wonder where Pa is now?" Megan said.

"Atlantic City," Jamie read the faded wooden sign, "Welcomes You."

Jamie had bypassed South Pass City, giving it a wide berth and riding on toward Atlantic City. He had heard that several of the men he was seeking were loafing around that mining town, gambling and whoring and making trouble.

Jamie was about to put an end to all that.

The government had recently started building a fort near Atlantic City. It would be named Fort Stambaugh, after a first lieutenant who had been killed by Indians near Miner's Delight. It would be abandoned in eight years.

After the raid on MacCallister's Valley, the Miles Nelson gang had broken up and scattered. The Pinkertons and Wells Fargo detectives, many sheriffs and town marshals all over the West, as well as federal marshals and the U.S. Army, were after them. With the gold and money taken from the bank and the stagecoach, the gang members could live well for a couple of years. By then, the heat would be off them and they could regroup . . . or so they thought.

But they hadn't taken into consideration one Jamie Ian MacCallister dogging their trail, riding with hard revenge burning in his trail-wise eyes.

When the gang had struck MacCallister's Valley, the Nelson gang was the largest in all the West. Actually there were five gangs, each with about fifteen men, robbing and raping and looting and burning from Kansas to California. Miles had pulled them all together for the raid that killed Jamie's wife. Twenty of the gang had been killed, wounded, or captured during the raid in the valley. That left about fifty-five outlaws still on the loose. Fifty-five of the meanest, sorriest, most worthless dredges of humanity ever assembled.

It had taken Jamie about six months to do it, but he had put together a list of men who were part of the Miles Nelson gang. To do so, he had visited with every sheriff and marshal in every town he passed through, looking at dodgers and talking with men in lock-up. A rustler might steal your cattle, but when it came to raping and killing women, shooting little kids down in the street, that was going too far. And most of the men in jail talked to Jamie.

Jamie had a list of fifty-one names, and if it took him the rest of his life, he was going to visit each name. After the visit, he would draw a line through that man's name.

These men had robbed him of the most precious thing in his life.

Kate.

And if it cost him his own life checking off those names, well, so be it. Without Kate he was nothing.

Just . . . nothing at all.

# 2

Army troops were hard at work building the new fort when Jamie rode past. The post would be located a few miles outside the town, just north and slightly east of Rock Creek.

In the spring of 1870, Atlantic City had a population of over two thousand, mostly miners, gamblers, thieves, con men, and whores. Like most boom towns, it was a wild and woolly place, and you took your life in your own hands venturing out after dark.

Jamie stabled his horses, worked out an arrangement with the livery owner to sleep in the loft (the hotels and boardinghouses were all packed full with varying degrees of humanity), and went to see the town marshal.

The marshal knew who he was the instant Jamie stepped into his office. Jamie Ian MacCallister was a true living legend. Books had been written about him, songs had been sung, and several plays on the life and times of Jamie Ian MacCallister had been produced.

"My name is MacCallister," he informed the marshal and his two deputies, closing the door behind him. The bulk of him was huge in the room. "I'll be in your town for no more than a couple of days. I'm here looking for two men. When I've found them, I'll move on. I think you know why I'm here, so there is no need for me to repeat the story. I respect the law; one of my sons is a sheriff down in Colorado.

But sometimes the law just doesn't work. I'm here to see that it does. That's all I have to say. Good day, gentlemen."

Jamie stepped out onto the warped boardwalk and closed the door behind him.

The marshal looked at his two officers. "Stay out of Mac-Callister's way. One of you go tell the undertaker he's about to have some business."

Jamie found the men in the first saloon he entered. They were sitting in the rear, a bottle of whiskey and two glasses on the table between them.

"Hubbie Joiner and Jesse Maxwell," Jamie called. "Stand up and face me, you murdering bastards!"

The distance between the batwings and the rear table cleared in two heartbeats. No one wanted to get caught in the cross fire.

The two outlaws stood up, hands hovering over the butts of their guns. They both had known that Jamie was after them; that news had spread all up and down the hoot-owl trail. But neither one of them had worried much about it. They were in their early thirties; MacCallister's hair was gray, and he had to be knocking on an old man's door. No way he was going to take two men half his age.

Hubbie grinned, exposing tobacco-stained and rotten teeth. "You bes' go on back home, now, old man. Get in your rockin' chair and pull a shawl over your knees."

"Yeah," Jesse said. "Where'd you leave your cane, old man. You bes' find it 'fore you fall over."

Jamie's smile was hard. "You men were part of the gang that raided MacCallister's Valley last year. You killed a number of people, including my wife, Kate. Now hook and draw, you sorry sons of bitches."

The two outlaws would never know that Jamie Ian Mac-Callister was probably the West's first fast draw; had no way of knowing they were facing the man who mastered the technique. Their hands had just closed around the butts of their guns when Jamie's Colts spat fire and smoke and lead.

Hubbie Joiner sat down in the chair he'd just risen out of and died, a very odd expression on his face as he looked down at the hole in his chest. Jesse Maxwell stumbled backward against the wall and dropped his Remingtons to the floor. He slid down until his butt touched the floor. There he died.

Every eyeball in the saloon clicked toward Jamie. The big man holstered his guns and said, "There'll be money in their pockets. It belongs to Wells Fargo and to the bank in Valley, Colorado. Turn the money over to your marshal."

Jamie walked outside to stand for a moment on the boardwalk. Across the street, the marshal and his officers had stepped out of the office at the sounds of the gunfire. They watched as Jamie unfolded a sheet of paper and took a pencil from his vest pocket. He drew a line on the paper, then carefully folded it and returned it to his inside pocket. Then he walked across the street to a cafe and ordered a cup of coffee and a slice of cake.

A miner ran across the street, peeked into the cafe, then trotted down to where the marshal stood and told the men what happened.

"That MacCallister is a mighty cold man," one of the marshal's men remarked.

"That's a man who saw his wife shot down before his eyes," the marshal responded. "Miles Nelson should have had more sense than to attack MacCallister's Valley. Before that man yonder is done, he's gonna leave a bloody trail behind him."

"You blame him?" the miner asked.

The marshal slowly shook his head. "Not one bit."

Eastern newspapers quickly picked up on Jamie's vendetta and assigned reporters to travel west and cover the story. The leading newspaper in Boston assigned a Negro reporter (at his insistence) to cover it. Ben Franklin Washington, unclaimed son of Anne Woodville, whose real name was Anne Jefferson and whose parents were runaway slaves, was determined to stir up a hornet's nest. Ben was high yellow, but Negro nonetheless. He knew his mother had abandoned him at birth; knew his sister had passed for white all her life and was now married to one of Jamie Ian MacCallister's grandkids. Ben knew his real mother, in cahoots with his uncle, had tried to have him killed in Richmond, Virginia.*

Ben Franklin Washington had no reason to love any member of his family. He was going to do his best to upset as many apple carts as he could.

And he was going to love every minute of it.


Ben's mother, now living in San Francisco and going under the name of Andrea Petri, read with much interest the greatly embellished newspaper account of Jamie's hunt for the Nelson gang. She laid the paper aside and shook her head. Kate was dead and Jamie was on the warpath. Incredible. Kate had been a good person; one of the few people in the world that Andrea had respect for. And Jamie . . . well, the man had to be in his late fifties, at least. But Andrea knew that Jamie would be a man to be reckoned with no matter what his age. It was all very interesting. She would follow this bizarre story closely.

Her thoughts shifted to her brother. Andrea had hired private detectives in an attempt to find Ross, but so far, no luck. She wondered where in the world he might be living.


Her brother, Ross, now living under the name of Russell Clay, opened the Denver paper, adjusted his reading glasses, and carefully read the story about Jamie and the manhunt. Kate dead. He shook his head. Hard to believe. She had been such a vivacious woman. So full of life. And a genuinely nice person. The world had lost a lovely flower with her passing.

A real shame.


The dozen or so reporters from back east gathered at Valley, Colorado. They had decided (and it was a wise move) that if they were going to go traipsing around the Wild West, where red savage Indians abounded, there was strength in numbers. Valley now boasted a population of over six hundred (if one counted all the dogs and cats), a nice sized town for the time and the place. It was a little off the beaten path but quite a fine town once you got there. Mining, farming, and cattle and sheep ranching surrounded the area. The town had a weekly newspaper, the *Valley Dispatch,* and the visiting reporters were amazed at how professional the writing was.

They were equally amazed at how damn many MacCallisters there were in Valley. At least half the population had blond hair and blue eyes. Everyone seemed to be related.

The mayor was a MacCallister: Morgan.

The sheriff was a MacCallister: Matthew.

There were five deputies, and three of them were related to the MacCallisters.

Half the town council was related to the MacCallisters.

Jamie and Kate had nine kids living. Each of them had married and had about six or seven kids. Many of those kids were now of marrying age, and they seemed to be having about six or seven kids each, too.

Andrew and Rosanna, both well-known and highly respected musicians and actors, had homes just outside of town, where they spent many summers.

Falcon, who had married a half Cheyenne/half French lady, ranched and owned a large saloon and gambling hall in Valley. He was also well-known throughout the West as being a very bad man to fool with, lightning quick with his guns, and was a very close friend of the notorious Smoke Jensen: a man who was rumored to have killed over a hundred men before his twentieth birthday (a slight exaggeration, but not by much).*

The original log homes of the first settling families had been carefully preserved, thanks to the efforts of Joleen MacCallister MacKensie, who was head of something called the Valley Historical Society.

For about a week, the reporters forgot all about the manhunt, enthralled as they were with the history of Valley and the settling families. The MacCallisters seemed not to have a bigoted or prejudiced bone in their bodies. Falcon had married an Indian princess, one of the sons of Matthew had married So Lin, the daughter of Hop Son, a Chinese man who had settled his family in the valley back in the 1840s, and one of Ellen Kathleen's sons had married Theresa Nunez.

"This has got to be the most mixed-up goddamn family I have ever seen in my life," a reporter from New York City remarked one evening over drinks in the Wild Rose Saloon. The Wild Rose was owned by Falcon MacCallister.

"Don't say that too loud," he was cautioned. "The way I have it figured is that there are approximately three hundred and twenty-four people in this town related to the MacCallisters. Hell, you never know who you're talking with. Look there."

The reporters turned to stare as Falcon walked in through the batwings, dressed in a black suit with a sparkling white shirt and black string tie. Falcon was the spitting image of his father, with wide shoulders and arms so muscular his suits had to be tailor-made for him. Falcon's eyes were a pale cool blue, and his hair was the color of wheat. While in town, he generally wore only one gun, low and tied down. Few people knew about the derringer he carried behind his belt buckle.

"As much as I enjoy the comforts," another reporter said,

---

*The Last Mountain Man*—Zebra Books

"hanging around here isn't getting the story written."

"We found two men who have agreed to guide us. One of them is with Lawrence now, buying the last of the supplies. Hopefully, we'll be out of here mid-morning tomorrow."

"It's going to be a grand adventure!" another said. "Probably the likes of which none of us will ever again experience."

Another opened a map and laid it out flat on the table. "We'll ride to here," he said, pointing to a series of pencil-drawn lines. "Then catch the train to here. Then ride over to this place. That's where some of the Nelson gang is said to hang out."

"Who says?"

"The guides." He looked at the faces around the table. "Does anybody have a better plan?"

No one did.

"What's the guide's name?"

"One is called Hank. I believe he called the other one Newly, or something like that." Falcon had walked on past the reporters and did not hear the man correct himself. "No, not Newly. It was Newby. Yes. That's it. Newby."


From Atlantic City, Jamie had drifted down to Bear River City. Just two years back, it had been a booming town as the railroad pushed through. Now the town was rapidly dwindling. In a few years it would all but disappear. A few more years, and it would vanish. Fort Bridger was located not far from there.

The commanding officer at the fort had been warned that Jamie was heading his way and was on the prod for the man who killed his wife.

The commanding officer filed the dispatch away and decided to stay out of civilian business. Besides, he couldn't fault Jamie one whit for what he was doing.

Jamie was playing a long shot, for the two men rumored

to be holed up in or near the dying town might have left, or might never have been there. But Jamie had time. And he would check out every lead, no matter how shallow it might seem.

A patrol out of the fort hailed Jamie about ten miles from town. The sergeant was a man who Jamie remembered from the recent unpleasantness between the States. Although how the man could advance to top soldier in only a few years was a mystery to him. That got cleared up in a few heartbeats.

"Sergeant Mahony, Mr. MacCallister," the top soldier said quickly. That was not the name he had used in the Confederate Army. He had probably taken the name of a dead Union sergeant toward the end of the war.

"Sergeant Major," Jamie said with a smile. "I don't recall ever meeting you."

The top soldier breathed a lot easier with that. "I seen you one time during a truce when you was heppin' bring in some Union wounded. I remembered you. Reason I give you a shout, Colonel, was they's two men in town waitin' to kill you. They've made their brags about it."

"I'm hard to kill, Top Soldier."

"Yes, sir. I know that for a pure-dee fact."

"These men in town . . . Phil Howard and Fred Allison?"

"That's them, Colonel. I 'spect they're waitin' in the Lucky Lady saloon, havin' a whiskey."

Jamie's smile was more like the snarl of a wolf. "I hope they enjoy their drinks. In a few hours they'll be in hell!"

# 3

The town was quickly dying. As Jamie rode up the street, he could see many buildings that now stood empty. Soon the wind and rain would begin to rot the lumber; a careless match would add to the demise of some of the structures.

Jamie stabled his horses, brushed the dust of the trail from his clothing, and checked into the one hotel remaining. And it wasn't much.

"I want my room swept and dusted clean, freshly washed sheets on the bed," he told the clerk. "Turn the tick. If I find bugs in my bed, you won't be happy with me."

"Yes, sir, Mr. MacCallister," the clerk was quick to oblige. "I'll have that done right now. We also have bathing facilities. Would you like for me to have the water heated?"

"Do that. Stow my gear in the room. I'll be back shortly."

"Yes, sir."

"Is there law in this town?"

"Not no more, sir."

"Fine. That uncomplicates matters."

Jamie walked across the street to the saloon, shoved open the batwings and stepped in, his eyes sweeping the large room. He walked to the long bar and ordered a glass of beer. "Fred Allison and Phil Howard," he said to the bartender. "They been in here?"

"Just left, Mr. MacCallister. When you rode in. Said they'd

be waitin' out in the street for you anytime you was ready to die."

"Suits me." Jamie drained his glass and walked out the back door.

Jamie Ian MacCallister was many things, among them being a very practical man. The opinions of certain unworldly people notwithstanding (a hundred years later, that group would be known as liberal democrats; in Louisiana those types of people are said to have an alligator mouth and a hummingbird ass), he knew there was no such thing as a fair fight. There was a winner and a loser, and that was all. And when your life, the lives of your loved ones, or your property were on the line, it didn't matter how you won, just do it.

Jamie walked the littered alley and stepped out at the edge of town. His hands were filled with Colts, hammers back. About fifty feet from him, two men were standing in the street, yards apart, each of them carrying sawed-off shotguns.

"Taking no chances, huh, boys?" Jamie called.

The men whirled around and fired the shotguns, the heavy charges blowing off chunks of the building where Jamie had been standing.

But as he spoke, Jamie was moving. He hit the ground belly down and fired his Colts. One slug punched a hole in the belly of Phil Howard, doubling him over and setting him down hard in the street. As he sat down, he pulled the trigger to the second barrel of the Greener and blew off all the toes on his left foot. The other slug went high and caught Fred Allison in the throat, tearing a great hole in the back of the man's neck as it exited.

Jamie stood up by the buckshot-torn corner of the building. Both men died within minutes of each other. Jamie walked over to the bodies and removed their money belts.

"The money is stolen," he told the gathering crowd. "It belongs to Wells Fargo and to the bank in Valley, Colorado." He slung the money belts over his shoulder and picked up one of the sawed-off shotguns. It was a good gun; well made. Jamie took that and a sack of shells lying by the body. His eyes found the desk clerk from the hotel. "I'll have my bath now," he told the man, then turned and walked up the street. He stepped into the hotel without looking back at the bloody street and the stunned crowd.


Roscoe, who had changed his name to Ross LeBeau and then to Russell Clay, was shocked right down to the soles of his handmade shoes when he looked up from studying the Denver Hotel's menu to see his sister's child, his own niece, Page Woodville Haywood, walking into the lobby of the hotel, her husband with her.

Great God in Heaven! Ross thought, once his heart resumed its beating.

The handsome couple were seated across the room from Ross, with Page's back to him. As soon as they were seated, Ross left the dining room as quickly as possible, with as much dignity as he could muster under the circumstances.

The world is certainly becoming a smaller place, he thought, as the doorman hailed a carriage for him. Ross would hire a detective to find out what Page and her husband were doing in Denver.

Then he didn't know what he'd do.


Ben Franklin Washington arrived in the West with three other reporters, a photographer, an artist, a man who was gathering material for a book he was writing on the Wild West, the sons of three wealthy industrialists from back east who came along for the adventure of it all (they left their wives behind and brought their girlfriends), a couple of gofers, several valets, two cooks, and four so-called professional mercenaries who were hired as bodyguards.

They brought enough equipment with them to outfit a small army. They rode the trains as far as they could, then bought wagons, teams, riding horses, and hired men to drive the wagons.

"It's all so, well, thrilling and grand!" cooed Miss Evelyn Wadsworth (better known as Fifi the Feathered Fan Lady to a certain segment of New Yorkers who frequented the burlesque houses), as she took in all the sights and sounds (and smells) of the raw frontier town.

"It is that," her companion, Marshall Henry Ludlow, agreed. "What say you, Richard?"

"Oh, quite," Richard Farnsworth replied. Dickie to his friends.

"I must say, it's all rather primitive," Charles Bennett remarked. Chuckie to his friends. "I've never seen so many *guns* in my life."

"I'm awed and overwhelmed and a little frightened," the Brooklyn-born Rebecca Willingham said, with an accent so pronounced a voice coach would have been reduced to tears of despair. Rebecca was better known as Lulu, in that part of the city where at night the glass of the lanterns glowed red.

Dickie put an arm around her waist. "I'll personally see that no harm befalls you, dear."

Dickie couldn't protect a pork chop from a devout Jew, but everybody has illusions.

However, as the three former fraternity brothers were about to discover, the western frontier was no place to put those illusions to the test.

Mary Marie O'Donnell, a flaming redhead with a scattering of freckles across her nose, whose family had come over from Dublin, and who possessed more common sense in her little finger than the others did in their entire bodies, took one look around her and decided that she had made the right decision by agreeing to accompany Chuckie to the Wild West. It was indeed a grand place. "All this fine land for the homesteadin'," she muttered. "New York City, ye've seen the last of this Irish lassie."

One burly teamster that the odd group had hired took a

hard look at his employers just before they pulled out the next morning, and summed up the feeling of the other drivers. "Lord have mercy on my soul!"

It was nearing dark when Jamie topped the ridge and looked down at the small cluster of buildings standing around the larger structure that was the trading post. An army fort had just been constructed not far from the trading post. It had started out as Fort Augur, but recently changed to Camp Brown, in honor of Captain Fredrick H. Brown who had been killed in '66 in the Fetterman massacre. The camp would be abandoned in early '71.

Jamie stripped the saddle and pack frame from his animals and stabled them. He rubbed down his horses and saw that they both had ample feed and water before even thinking about seeing to his own needs.

Jamie had bathed that morning in the cold waters of a creek and, after stropping his razor, had carefully shaved around his neatly trimmed beard and moustache; like his close-cropped hair, the beard and moustache were gray. A few weeks back he had stopped in a Shoshoni village, spent a few days with them, and traded for new buckskins, moccasins, and leggins.

Now he had to resupply, for he was low on some things and completely out of coffee, bacon, and beans.

He entered the low-ceilinged trading post and stepped to one side, as was his habit, carefully looking all about him, sizing up the half dozen or so men sitting at the rough-hewn tables, playing cards and drinking snake-head whiskey. (Some who made their own whiskey actually did toss in a few snake heads during the "curing" process, claiming it added flavor to the brew. History does not record if anyone died because of that practice.)

Jamie ordered a plate of stew from the counterman and sat down at a vacant table. Before his meal arrived, a question was thrown at him, springing out of the darkness of the far smoky depths of the room.

"You be Jamie MacCallister?"

"I am."

"I got a message for you, MacCallister: Call off your hunt."

"And if I don't?"

"You'll not live to see summer turn to fall."

The heaping plate of stew was placed before him, and it smelled good. Jamie tore off a hunk of bread and sopped up some liquid, chewing slowly, savoring the flavor of food not cooked on the trail.

"You hear me, MacCallister?" the unknown questioner asked.

"I hear you. Now leave me alone and let me enjoy my meal."

"Look here, MacCallister," the man persisted. "Most of them boys you're a-huntin' didn't put no lead in your wife."

"They were there," Jamie replied, laying down the unwritten code of the West. "They're all thieves, murderers, rapists, and worse. And I'm going to see that every one of them steps up and shakes hands with the devil. Now leave me alone."

A chair was pushed back, and boots struck the floor. Jamie did not look up from the food as the boots walked to the bar. "Miles Nelson says the killin' of your wife was not done deliberate. It was an accident."

"She's still dead."

"Goddamn you, MacCallister. Cain't nobody reason with you about this thing?"

"No."

"Then stand up and face me, MacCallister!"

Jamie pushed his plate from him. "Were you with the gang that attacked Valley?"

"No."

"Then I have no quarrel with you."

"My name's Jones."

"That's good, Jones. Everybody ought to know their name."

Jones cursed at that. "My younger brother rides with the Nelson gang."

"I see. And you're going to stop me from killing him, right?"

"That's right, MacCallister."

"Is he worth it, Jones?" Jamie asked softly. "Really worth it?"

"He's my brother, MacCallister! Now stand up and face me."

Jamie moved very quickly. Not as fast as when he was thirty, but fast enough. He grabbed a chair and threw it at the man. The man's hands flew up from the butts of his guns to protect his face. Jamie closed the distance between them and slammed a big fist into Jones's face, pulping his lips. He followed that with a left hook that smashed into the man's jaw, then hit him twice more in the face. Jones sank to the floor, blood streaming from mouth and nose.

Jamie jerked the man's guns from leather and laid them on the bar. He looked at the barkeep. "Put those away. Unless you want a killing in this place."

Jamie walked back to the table and resumed his eating. Several men rose to help Jones to his feet.

"I'll stop you, MacCallister," Jones mumbled through mashed and bloody lips. "You'll not bring no harm to my little brother."

"Stay out of it," Jamie warned. "Go on back home and keep clear of me. Your brother is riding with the worst of scum and filth. The Nelson gang has robbed and raped and killed and tortured from Kansas to California. And your brother Lloyd is a part of it. When you take up for him, that makes you no better. Don't you ever cross my trail again."

Jamie finished his meal, bought his supplies, and walked over to the livery. He made himself a bed in the hayloft and wrapped up in his blankets. If anyone came into the livery, Buck would warn him. Jamie could understand taking up for kin, but not when kin was clearly in the wrong. That he could not understand. Lloyd Jones had dodgers out on him from Kansas to California, with charges ranging from rape to murder, and the wanted posters read dead or alive. Every member of the Nelson gang was wanted dead or alive.

Wanted dead or alive by the law.

Just dead by Jamie.

Jamie pulled out before any lamplights or candles were glowing in the trading post or any of the buildings surrounding it. Although he wished it were not so, Jamie was certain he would run into Jones again. The man seemed hell-bent on getting himself killed. All because of his worthless brother. Perhaps the man would come to his senses, but Jamie doubted it.

Jamie headed straight west, crossing over into Utah. He camped along the Bear River for a couple of days, resting his horses, and then moved on toward the Mormon settlements just west of the Wasatch Range, along the Great Salt Lake.

He had no way of knowing there were dozens of reporters waiting there for him.

Ben Franklin Washington among them.

What Jamie did know was that four of Miles Nelson's men were in the area, hanging out somewhere between Ogden and Logan. And he had learned that four more of the gang were hiding out north of there, up in Southern Idaho. They would be next on the list.

A farmer in a wagon whoaed his team upon spotting Jamie and hailed him. "You'd be Jamie MacCallister, sir?"

"I would," Jamie replied with a smile, always surprised that so many people knew his face.

"Whole passel of newspaper writers waitin' for you in town," the farmer told him. "Snoopin' around and askin' a bunch of fool questions. But them thugs that was in the gang that killed your wife is just north and some east of

Brigham City, at a tradin' post. The law won't interfere, Mr. MacCallister. Long as no innocent person gets hurt."

"To the best of my knowledge, sir, I have never harmed an innocent person in my life."

"Good luck to you." The farmer lifted the reins, clucked to his horses, and rattled on up the road.

Jamie turned Buck's head and rode north. He had no wish to see a bunch of reporters.

But Jamie was news, and reporters could smell out news like a bloodhound on a scent. And a little money spread out here and there to locals never hurt.

When Jamie stepped Buck out on the road that led to the trading post, the reporters, the adventurers, the photographers, the painters, and the hangers-on were waiting for him.

# 4

Only a few of the reporters were sympathetic toward Jamie's manhunt. Even in the 1870s, there were reporters calling for some sort of pistol control.

When Jamie saw the saddle horses and buggies, he muttered, "How in the hell? . . ." Then he saw Jones, staring hate at him. Jones must have ridden two or three horses into the ground to get ahead of Jamie. However he did it, it was done.

But how did he know where Jamie was going?

Then it came to him: Jones's kid brother must be with the gang members here in Utah, or with the bunch up in Southern Idaho. That's the only thing that made any sense.

"Taking the law into your own hands again, Mr. MacCallister?" a reporter yelled.

"Hell with you," Jamie muttered, then wheeled his horse and headed back into the timber.

A few on horseback might try to follow, but even that was doubtful; for these were city folks, and without their guides, they'd be lost as a child in ten minutes.

Jamie rode straight east at a trot, weaving in and out of the timber, letting Buck pick his own way, the packhorse following. After a couple of miles, Jamie stopped and allowed his horses to blow, then headed north with a smile on his lips.

\* \* \*

"Where'd he go?" Marshall Henry Ludlow demanded, twisting in the saddle.

"Don't ask me where *he* went," Fifi said, sitting her sidesaddle. "I don't even know where *I* am."

"He's pullin' something," Newby, the reporter's guide, whispered to Hank. "MacCallister's got more twists and turns than a snake."

"Let's head for the trading post," a reporter suggested, trying to ease his saddle-sore butt. "We'll wait him out. He has to show up sooner or later."

Later. Much later.


Huddled around a fire, those members of the Nelson gang who were hiding out in Southern Idaho were growing restless and surly. It galled them to the bone to be hiding from one man. *One man!*

"Who the hell does this Jamie MacCallister think he is, anyways?" Rudy Hewitt demanded, throwing a couple of sticks on the fire. "Hell, he's an old man! He's got to be in his late fifties. I could take him with one hand tied behind my back."

Rudy was in his early thirties. He wasn't going to get much older.

"This guy fought in the Alamo," Ollie Brennan said. "Christ, I wasn't even *born* when that happened."

"Yeah," Lloyd Jones said. "There can't be much to him. He's just an old man who thinks he's still tough. Hell, my brother's probably done put lead in him."

Russell Stokes walked back from the spring with a pot of fresh water. He put the pot on to boil. "We're 'bout out of coffee. I ain't gonna stand for bein' out of coffee. I'm tarred of waitin' 'round here, hidin' out like cowards. Goddammit, I ain't no coward."

Cliff Baylock nodded his head in agreement. He rubbed his crotch. "I got to have me a woman. Let's mosey on down toward Utah and find us a farm woman. We'll take turns with her."

"Her husband might have something to say about that," Rudy said.

"Hell, we'll just kill him right off. We might get lucky and find us a farm woman with some daughters. I like 'em young and tender. I 'specially like it when they fight and beg. Makes it better."

Lloyd grinned and pulled at his crotch. "Damn, but you're gettin' me all worked up, Cliff."

"I think you got a real good idea, Cliff," Russell said.

"I'm for it," Ollie agreed.

"Me, too," Rudy added.

"Bad idea." The whisper came out of the brush.

"Who said that?" Lloyd demanded, getting to his feet and looking all around him.

"I didn't hear nothin'," Cliff said.

"I didn't neither," Ollie echoed.

"I could have swore I heard someone whisper from over yonder," Lloyd said, pointing toward the brush.

Russell laughed at the younger man. "You just started thinkin' 'bout women and that caused a roarin' in your head, boy. Settle down and let's plan this here thing out."

Lloyd looked all around him, then shrugged and returned to his spot by the fire. "I been out here in the lonesome so long I'm losin' my mind," he muttered.

Jamie couldn't believe the men had dismissed his whisper as imagination. He stood in the brush and timber and listened to the men plan their evil perversions until he could take no more of it.

"It's still a bad idea." Jamie spoke the words loud and clear as he stepped out of the brush, both his hands holding Colts, hammers back.

Ollie was the first to react. "MacCallister!" he yelled. He grabbed for his pistol, whirled around, and Jamie shot him. Ollie screamed and fell backward, landing in the fire. His clothing ignited, and soon he was blazing.

As Cliff Baylock levered a round into his Winchester, Jamie shot him twice in the chest just as Rudy came up with twin Stars, converted to take cartridges. Jamie ended his out-law days and sent him to the grave with a bullet in his brain.

Cursing like a wild man, Russell faced Jamie and managed to fire once, the slug knocking bark off a tree. Jamie shot him twice while a badly frightened Lloyd made it to his horse and went galloping away, toward the south.

Jamie let him go. There was always another day.

Jamie took the money belts from the men, with the exception of Ollie. There wasn't much left of him. Then he took what ammunition he could use and stretched the men out in a row. He stripped the saddles from their mounts and turned the horses loose.

Getting water from the spring, Jamie doused the fire, and the smoldering remains of Ollie, and then dug a common grave under a huge old tree. Into the tree, Jamie carved the words HERE LIES FOUR KILLERS.

Then he mounted up and rode away. He did not look back.


Four days after the shooting in Southern Idaho, a wild-eyed Lloyd, who was heading south, met the gang of adventurers and reporters and what-have-you on the trail as they traveled north.

"It was awful!" he blurted out his tale of woe. "Me and my pards was just sittin' around the fire, drinkin' coffee and jawin' when MacCallister just stepped out of the brush and started shootin'."

"What's your name?" asked a man who had joined the group along the way.

"Lloyd Jones."

The man spurred his horse close and held up a badge. "I'm Pat Riordan. Federal marshal. You're under arrest for murder, rape, bank robbery, mail robbery, and anything else I might be able to dig up on you."

"*What?*" Lloyd screamed.

"I'll be damned if that's so!" Bob Jones, Lloyd's older

brother, yelled, startling everybody. He jerked a hogleg from under his coat and blew the marshal out of the saddle. "Ride, brother, ride!" he shouted.

The two of them left in a cloud of dust.

"My word!" Fifi said, fanning herself with her hat.

A couple of reporters jumped down to aid the marshal, who had been shot in the side. "I can ride," the marshal said grimly, getting to his feet. "Now maybe you goddamn reporters will understand why marshals and sheriffs out here ain't interfering with Jamie's hunt. Them he's huntin' ain't worth the gunpowder it would take to blow their brains out. Far as I'm concerned, MacCallister is doing the country a favor. Personal, I hope he kills ever' damn one of them. Now get out of my way. I got to ride back to town and find a doctor."

The stunned group watched him ride back south.

"This just might turn out to be a much more interesting trip than we originally thought," a reporter said.

I certainly hope so, Ben Franklin Washington silently wished.

Jamie had vanished.

Not one sighting of him was reported the rest of the summer. After he had buried the four killers, Jamie headed north, riding across the Snake River Plain and into the Sawtooth Range of Idaho. There, he holed up for two months, hunting and fishing and staying low.

As autumn began painting the landscape with multicolored hues, many of the reporters returned to their home cities. There was just nothing to report about Jamie Ian MacCallister. But two of the reporters, those who had taken the time to research the background of Jamie, knew what Jamie was doing: playing the waiting game. Lawrence Douglas and Thomas Connor stayed.

Ben Franklin Washington also stayed. Ludlow, Farnsworth, and Bennett had to stay, too, for their fathers had told them they had, by God, better bring back comprehensive reports on the feasibility of buying property, mining interests, and so forth. Their lady friends remained with them. The photographer, Pendroy, stayed, as did the artist, Bob Mark, and the writer, John A. Bellingham. The valets, cooks, and gofers were dismissed, as were the bodyguards.

The so-called "guides," Hank and Newby, pulled out one morning and were not seen again.

On a quiet Saturday afternoon, September, 1870, Jamie rode into a small settlement in Southwestern Montana. The town consisted of a general store, a saloon, a crude livery, and a combination barbershop, bathhouse, boardinghouse, and cafe. The closest law was nearly a hundred miles away.

Jamie was looking to resupply, enjoy a hot bath and a shave (his beard was really beginning to itch), and have a meal prepared by someone else. He had no way of knowing that some of the Miles Nelson gang had the same thought.

He gave no name as he rented a room at the boardinghouse, and was asked for none. He was told by the woman who rented the rooms that supper would be ready at five-thirty and served no later than six-thirty.

Lounging in a huge tub of hot soapy water, Jamie passed the time reading newspapers that were anywhere from three weeks to three months old. But it was still news to him. Since he had left his valley, Wyoming had given the vote and the right to hold office to women. Two months later, Utah Territory did the same. Five years after the Civil War, Texas was readmitted to the Union. He was about to close up the newspaper when he noticed a small article in the back section of the Boston paper. The reporter's name was what caught his attention: Ben Franklin Washington.

He carefully read the article.

It was about Jamie's manhunt, and the dateline was three weeks back in Salt Lake City.

"Paper got here quick," Jamie muttered, as he stepped out of the tub and began drying off.

While he bathed and had a shave and a haircut and a beard trim, he had a woman from the boardinghouse brush off and air out and then iron his spare set of go-to-town clothes. They were hanging just outside the bathhouse. Jamie dressed and walked over to the saloon for a drink and to listen to some talk from the locals.

There were a dozen men in the saloon, most of them ranch hands by their look, and a couple of tired-looking Soiled Doves. All heads turned as Jamie walked to the bar, for he was a stranger in town and got a good once-over from the locals.

"I'll just be damned!" one older cowboy muttered, quickly dropping his gaze.

"You know that man?" his partner asked.

"Yeah. I shore do. That's Jamie MacCallister. I rode through his valley some twenty years ago, whilst I was scoutin' for the army. He treated us right nice. Him and his pretty wife. Hell, the whole valley of folks was friendly and nice."

"Then it was his wife the Miles Nelson gang? . . ." The cowboy trailed that off.

"Yeah. And that ol' war hoss over there is on the prod for them. I hear tell he's already killed eight or ten of 'em. I wouldn't want that man on my trail."

"Did he really fight at the Alamo?"

"He damn shore did."*

"And when he was just a tadpole, he was kidnapped and raised by Injuns?"

"Yep. Shawnees. They named him Man Who Is Not Afraid."

"Hell, Davy. That man's a *legend!*"

"Shore is."

Jamie sipped his whiskey. It was the first drink he'd

*Eyes of Eagles*—Zebra Books

had in a couple of months, and he enjoyed the warmth of it.

The barkeep walked back to where Jamie stood and faced him, the bar between them. "Say, I know you. You're Jamie Ian MacCallister!"

"That's right."

"Well, Bless Pat! It's a pleasure to serve you, Mr. MacCallister." He pushed the coin Jamie had laid on the bar back toward him. "No charge, sir. That one's on the house."

Jamie smiled and thanked him. One by one, the men in the saloon rose to walk over to the bar to shake Jamie's hand and have a moment of conversation with him. This would be something they could brag about the rest of their lives.

All but one.

The grim-faced and unshaven man sat alone at his table and glared open and undisguised hate at Jamie. Some years back, one of MacCallister's boys, Matthew was his name, he thought, or it might have been Falcon, killed his brother over a dispute involving cards during a game of draw poker.

Now would be a real good time to settle that score. He reckoned one MacCallister was as good as the next one. The man poured another drink of courage and swallowed it down, then pushed back his chair and swept back his coat, clearing the butt of his gun.

"No trouble in here, Finlay!" the barkeep said sharply.

"You go right straight to hell," Finlay said. "I got me a score to settle with that man yonder. Turn and face me, MacCallister."

Finlay? Jamie thought. The name meant nothing to him.

"I said turn around and face me, MacCallister!"

Five men had just ridden into the tiny town and reined up at the crude livery.

Jamie turned around slowly, the glass of whiskey in his left hand. His right hand hung close to the butt of his Colt.

The five men, all wearing long dusters, began their walk to the saloon.

"You got a problem, mister?" Jamie asked the man.

"Yeah, I do. One of your cotton-headed bastard sons killed my brother. Now I'm gonna kill you."

"Killed him over what?" Jamie asked easily.

Ten boots clumped against the rough boardwalk. Ten spurs jingled and jangled.

"He shot him dead durin' a card game in a minin' camp."

Falcon, Jamie thought with a smile.

"You think that's funny?" Finlay demanded.

"I'm sure your brother didn't," Jamie replied, the old wild recklessness rearing up strong within him.

The five outlaws stood outside the batwings of the saloon, brushing the trail dust from their clothing and loosening the guns in their holsters.

"What the hell do you want me to do about it?" Jamie asked, a hardness to his tone. "Raise him from the grave? I can't do that. Now why don't you just sit down and be quiet. You'll live a lot longer."

"I'm gonna kill you, MacCallister."

"Oh, I don't think so. Somebody might, someday. But I've got things to do and places to go before that happens. Now sit down, Finlay, before your ass overloads your mouth."

The batwings were pushed open, and the five outlaws stepped into the bar.

"Draw, MacCallister!" Finlay shouted, his hand closing around the butt of his gun.

*"MacCallister!"* one of the Miles Nelson gang yelled.

The saloon erupted in lead and gunsmoke.

# 5

Jamie dropped the glass of whiskey and pulled his left-hand Colt, drilling Finlay first. The bullet took the man in the center of the chest and knocked him backward against the wall. Turning toward the knot of outlaws at the batwings, Jamie began thumbing back the hammers of his guns and pulling the triggers.

Cowboys were hitting the floor to escape the ever-growing hail of lead that whistled and howled above their heads.

Jamie dropped to one knee to present a smaller target as the gang members began spreading out along the front wall.

Jamie put two outlaws on the floor in the first five seconds of the gunfight. The saloon was filled with thick gunsmoke as a third joined his buddies on the barroom floor. The two remaining members decided the best thing for them to do was get the hell gone from there.

One jumped through the big window in the front of the saloon, and the other nearly tore off the batwings in his haste to depart the scene.

Quickly reloading, Jamie ran out the back door and circled around, coming out ahead of the men. One was on the boardwalk in front of the saloon, the other standing by the hitch rail in the street.

Jamie recognized Curly Mack by the long scar running down the left side of his face.

Jamie added a bullet hole to that disfiguration, and Curly Mack's outlawing days were over.

Carter Boyd cussed Jamie wildly and began pouring the lead his way from both guns. Jamie went down to one knee, carefully took aim, and fired, the bullet striking Carter in the center of his forehead. Carter dropped like a rock, falling face forward into the street.

Stillness enveloped the tiny town as a gentle breeze began blowing away the gunsmoke. Jamie rose slowly to his boots and began reloading his Colts.

The saloon emptied, the cowboys and locals crowding the boardwalk to stand and stare. The two Soiled Doves took that time to rifle the pockets of the dead and dying outlaws lying on the saloon floor. They had just begun frantically tearing at the thick money belts when Jamie walked in.

"Take what's in their pockets," he told the whores. "Leave the money belts alone. That's stolen money."

The Doves stood up and backed away.

Jamie looked over at Finlay. The man was still alive, but not for long. He was blowing pink bubbles, and that was an accurate signal he was lung shot. Jamie walked over to him and knelt down.

"My brother always did think he was foolin' people when he cheated," Finlay gasped. "But he wasn't worth a damn at it. I should have left well enough alone, I reckon."

"You know any of those men who jumped into our play?" Jamie asked.

"Two of 'em. Boyd and Curly Mack. Did you get them all?"

"Yes."

"You're good, MacCallister. I'll give you that much." He coughed up blood. "Do me a good turn?"

"If I can."

"You can. You kilt me. You owe me that much. I got money sewed into the linin' of my left boot. Inside. You see to it I get planted proper?"

"I will. You have any kin you want me to notify?"

But Finlay couldn't reply. He was dead.

Jamie stood up and stared down at the man for a few seconds. How many dead men had he looked at who were made that way by his hand? He had stopped counting a long time back. And how old had he been when he killed his first man? Not very old, he recalled.

"You all right, Mr. MacCallister?" a local softly inquired.

Jamie looked at the citizen. "All right? Yes, I'm all right." He pointed to Finlay's left boot. "He has money sewn in there. He wanted a proper burying."

"He'll get it. How about the others?"

Jamie shrugged his shoulders. "I really don't give a damn what you do with them."

It was late September when the reporters learned of the shoot-out in Montana. By now they were wising up and made no plans to travel there; Jamie would be long gone. Much to the chagrin of Russell Clay, the reporters had shifted their base to Denver, where there were telegraph and rail services around the clock—and more social activities available.

Russell Clay was now virtually a prisoner in his own home. Not only did he have to worry about his niece, Page, recognizing him; now he had Ben Franklin Washington, his nosey, snoopy nephew, to worry about.

Because Russell had paid informants scattered around the growing city, he knew what was going on almost before it happened. He knew that Lloyd Jones and his now outlaw older brother, Bob, were hanging around Denver's seedy section. He sent one of his most trusted men to arrange a meeting. Russell had made up his mind on how best to deal with the problem of his sister's half-breed children.

In San Francisco, Page's mother, presumed dead but very much alive and well and living under the name of Andrea Petri, read the reports from her hired detectives and at first had smiled. The smiles quickly changed to frowns as she read on.

Her daughter, Page, and her husband, James William Haywood, the grandson of Jamie MacCallister, had settled in Denver and were well and happy. What brought on the frowns was that her brother, Roscoe, was also living in the city and living under the name of Russell Clay. Andrea knew her brother well, and was well aware that if he felt threatened, he would not hesitate to kill to protect his identity. To make matters worse, Page's nappy-headed brother, Ben Franklin Washington, was also in Denver, snooping around and asking questions. It was only a matter of time before he put everything together and went public with it. That would ruin Page's life.

Andrea couldn't have that.

Would not have that.

She should have killed the nigger-looking brat at birth. She had long regretted that she hadn't done just that.

She sent for some of the thugs she kept on her payroll. She would take care of this matter once and for all.

Permanently.

*Mid-October. Valley, Colorado.*

"Pa's struck again," Matthew said, holding up the week-old newspaper. "Listen." He read the account of the Montana shoot-out to his brothers and sisters and nieces and nephews and what-have-you.

Falcon smiled as his brother finished the reading. "Pa ain't slowed down a bit, has he? Took out six in one whack. That ol' he-coon is still a war-hoss."

"Well, now, that's a hell of a way to talk about your father," Jamie Ian, Jr., admonished his younger brother.

Falcon shrugged his heavy shoulders. "Wasn't no disrespect meant, brother. Anyway, I meant to tell y'all, I'm fixin' to take me a ride to Denver. Keep an eye on Marie and the kids while I'm gone, will you?"

"That goes without asking, stupid!" his sister Joleen told him.

Falcon grinned at her and jauntily tipped his hat.

Joleen stuck out her tongue and took a swipe at him that Falcon easily ducked.

Laughing, Falcon left the living room of his brother's house and pulled out for Denver within the hour.

Jamie's arrival in Elko, Nevada, didn't turn many a head—not at first—but the sheriff noticed him riding in, as did the town marshal. Both of them headed straight for the telegraph office.

The Central Railroad had reached Elko in '68, and the town fast became a drop-off and pick-up point for all the freight coming in for the region's mines. The area boasted large cattle ranches, and sheep were also being introduced, herded by Basque sheepmen. Before the two factions learned to coexist, and they would, eventually, a lot of blood would be spilled on both sides.

But Jamie was not interested in local squabbles and had no intention of getting involved in them. He was looking for three men he had been told were hanging around the town: Red Johnson, Waddy Keeton, and Bob Perlich.

Jamie's hunt had been going on for months now, and the outlaws were well aware they were being hunted, and knew that Jamie had killed about fifteen of their gang. That news was making many of them surly and very, very edgy. To a man, they'd all had detectives from Wells Fargo, the Pinkerton's, bounty hunters, county sheriffs, and federal marshals after them, but no one had ever followed them with the bulldog tenacity of Jamie Ian MacCallister.

It was downright irritating.

The county sheriff and the town marshal both had dodgers on most of the men in the Miles Nelson gang, and they knew that the names of Red, Waddy, and Bob were among those wanted posters. Trouble was, the dodgers didn't have a drawing of the men, the men weren't going by those names, and none of the three had caused any trouble in Elko.

Law enforcement officers were much more practical back in those days when it came to dealing with trash and thugs and ne'er-do-wells. Standing outside the telegraph office, the marshal and sheriff talked it over.

"Hell," the town marshal said to the sheriff, after a brief discussion about the situation. "Maybe MacCallister will take care of the problem for us."

"That is a thought," the sheriff replied. "Tell you what, it's an unusually warm day for this time of year. Why don't we take off and go fishing?"

"Damn good idea," the marshal replied. "I'll get my pole and meet you down on the Humbold, right there where the river bends and it's quiet and shady."

"I know the spot. 'Bout three miles west of town?"

"That's the place."

"See you there."

The sheriff told his wife, "Stay in the house and off the streets."

The marshal told his wife, "Stay in the house and off the streets."

After registering at the hotel, and having the desk clerk's eyes bug out at the name on the registry book, and after a bath and shave and change of clothes, Jamie asked directions to the toughest and seediest saloon in town, and it was pointed out to him.

Jamie checked his guns, worked them in and out of the holsters a couple of times, and headed for the saloon.

Before taking off to go fishing, the marshal had told a couple of notorious gossips about Jamie being in town and what he and the sheriff were going to do, and the word had quickly spread. The stores on either side of the saloon were closed and so were the stores across the street. The wide street in front of the saloon was deserted when Jamie reached the batwings and shoved them open, stepping inside. He walked up to the bar and ordered a whiskey. Outside, the wind picked up as storm clouds began gathering. A dust devil spun crazily up the street. A few drops of rain suddenly splattered against the ground, sending up quick puffs of dust and pocking the dry earth. Lightning licked across the sky.

Jamie took his drink and moved to a rear table, sitting down with his back against the wall. He picked up a worn deck of cards and began a game of solitaire. He had just laid out the cards when the batwings flew open and a man stood there, his eyes wild and his hands over his guns.

Jamie drew his right-hand Colt and kept it out of sight, by one leg of the chair.

"Damn your eyes, Jamie MacCallister!" Red Johnson shouted. "I ain't runnin' from you no more." His hands closed around the butts of his guns, and he started his pull.

Jamie's pistol roared, and Red went stumbling outside, the front of his shirt blossoming crimson. He fell off the boardwalk and died in the dust. A few raindrops glistened on his face.

Jamie laid his pistol on the table, took a sip of whiskey, and resumed his card game.

Moments later, the sounds of galloping horses reached those in the saloon. All eyes turned to Jamie. Jamie smiled and said, "That would probably be Waddy Keeton and Bob Perlich. I guess those boys just don't have the stomach to face me. Another time, I reckon." He looked over at the barkeep. "You got anything to eat in this place?"

"Y . . . Y . . . yes, sir," the man stammered. "Got a stew my old woman just fixed. And some hot bread."

"Bring it. And a big glass of water."

"Yes, sir. Right away, sir."

Jamie took his pocket watch out of his vest and snapped it open. But he was not checking the time. Inside the cover, there was a picture of Kate, frozen in time, smiling at him, her golden hair shining and her blue eyes sparkling.

Jamie smiled at the picture and closed the watch, returning it to his pocket.

"You kilt a mighty fine man just then, MacCallister," a man said in a rough voice.

"I killed a piece of scum and totally worthless trash," Jamie corrected the man just as his food was placed in front of him. "Now shut up and leave me alone." Jamie started eating with his left hand, his right hand close to the pistol on the table.

The local wanted to say more, but friends of his hushed him up and started to lead him outside.

"Leave the body alone," Jamie called. "He's probably wearing a money belt filled with stolen money. The money belongs to the bank in Valley, Colorado, and to Wells Fargo."

"What are you going to do with it?" the big-mouthed friend of Red Johnson questioned, turning to face Jamie. "Take it for your own self?"

Jamie smiled at that. If the truth be told, Jamie was probably one of the richest men west of the Mississippi. He was worth millions of dollars. Ever since first settling in the valley, Jamie had been working gold mines, many of them lodes his grandfather had discovered in the latter part of the last century—when he first came out with the mountain men—and all during the eighteenth century, until his death in 1844. He was buried along the same ledge as Kate, high up, overlooking the long valley.*

The local just wouldn't turn it loose. "You find something funny about that, MacCallister?"

"Let it alone," Jamie warned him. "Just let it alone."

"Come on," the citizen's friends urged him. "Let's get out of here, Max."

But Max had worked himself up into a killing mood. He shook off the hands that held him and stalked over to Jamie's table. He put both hands on the tabletop and said, "Stand up, MacCallister. I think I'll kill you!"

*Dreams of Eagles*—Zebra Books

# 6

Jamie sighed. He did not want to harm this man. He didn't come to Elko to do harm to locals. But what puzzled Jamie was why this citizen was so worked up over the killing of a murderer and rapist.

"I said get up, you son of a bitch!" Max hollered.

Jamie rammed the edge of the table into the man's belly, doubling him over as all the air was forced from him. Jamie rose from the chair with an easy movement and popped Max on the side of his jaw, sending the man tumbling to the floor. He then reached down and took the man's pistol from the holster and tossed it on the table, out of reach. Cursing, Max crawled to his boots, his big hands balled into fists.

Jamie hit him three times in the face, right, left, right, the blows coming together so fast they sounded as one. Max went down for the second time and didn't get up.

"Jesus Christ!" someone in the crowd muttered, looking down at the much younger man who was lying unconscious on the floor, his nose busted and his lips pulped.

Jamie picked up Max's gun and walked over to the bar, handing the pistol to the barkeep. "Give it back to him when he cools down."

"Y . . . y . . . yes, sir," the man stammered. "I'll hide it away right now."

Jamie paid for his drink and food and walked outside. He ripped open Red's shirt, removed the money belt, then walked over to the bank to make arrangements to have the money sent to the bank in Valley.

Jamie had put five miles behind him before the sun rose the next morning.


Falcon sat in his hotel suite in Denver and carefully read all the newspapers he'd bought: papers from New York City and Boston and San Francisco and St. Louis. The article in the Boston paper, written by somebody named Ben F. Washington, particularly disturbed him. The reporter, while not coming right out and openly saying he hoped Jamie would fail in his manhunt, came damn close to it.

Falcon folded up the newspapers and tried to put the article out of his mind. He'd never had much use for big city newspaper writers; seemed like they wanted a perfect world but didn't have enough sense to realize the world was populated with imperfect people.

Falcon decided that if the day came when he ran into this Ben F. Washington, he just might jack his jaw a time or two—maybe that would knock some sense into the man.

Falcon dressed carefully and went down to the lobby, checking to see if James William and Page had replied to the message he'd sent upon arriving in Denver. They had not. Falcon shrugged that off. Could be they were out of town. But he'd go see for himself. He had the doorman hail him a carriage and smoked a cigar on the ride over to James William's house.

Falcon dismissed the carriage and stood for several moments looking at the darkened home just at the edge of town, in a very fashionable neighborhood. The homes were set some distance apart, with lots of shrubbery and trees in the well-kept lawns. He saw the lantern lights of another carriage approaching and stepped behind a tree, although why he felt he had to do that was a mystery to him. Habit, he guessed.

He stood in the shadows and watched a man step from

the carriage, pay the driver, and dismiss the carriage. In the darkness, Falcon could see that the man was dressed in Eastern garb and looked to be in his mid to late twenties. But Falcon couldn't be certain of that.

Falcon froze as still as granite when the man whispered, "You've done well, sister. Very well for yourself. Not bad at all for a quarter-breed nigger gal. It's going to be amusing to watch your make-believe white world crumble all around you."

Falcon let the stranger get a block ahead before he fell in behind him. Following him was easy, for Falcon, like his dad, was a woodsman. He followed him right back to his own hotel. When the man was inside, Falcon approached the doorman.

"That fellow who just walked in, I could swear I know him, but his name escapes me."

"Why, that's the Boston reporter, sir," the doorman replied. "Ben F. Washington."

"Do tell?" Falcon said, slipping the man some money. "Well now. I guess I didn't know him after all."

"The West is getting crowded, sir."

"That it is. That it is."


Waddy Keeton and Bob Perlich had taken out to the east, and that's the direction Jamie took. He had him a hunch they were going to try to link up with that part of the Nelson gang hiding out in Utah Territory.

The more of them I catch together, Jamie thought, the sooner I can finish this thing and return to . . .

What?

Back to the home that he and Kate had shared for so many years?

No. Jamie didn't want to live in that house without Kate. Too many memories.

He made up his mind right then and there to give the home to one of his grandkids and build him a little cabin up in the High Lonesome, overlooking his valley; maybe not too far from Kate's burying place. That way he could walk down there and tend to the grave and sit and talk with Kate from time to time. Until his moment arrived to join her on the Starry Path.

To tell the truth, he just didn't want to live without Kate.

Was that why he was on this manhunt? Did he have some sort of death wish?

Maybe. Maybe that was a part of it.

The thought of another woman never entered his mind. Jamie was a strong, healthy, and virile man. But another woman? No. There could be no other woman in his life. Not ever.

Not even the grave could separate him from Kate.

Jamie looked up at the blue of the sky. "I'll be along soon enough, old woman," he said, speaking in the Shawnee tongue. "You just wait a time. We'll be together. And then we'll never be apart."

Soaring on the currents, high overhead, an eagle screamed.

Falcon followed Ben around Denver for several days, determined to get to the bottom of Ben's whispered comments in front of James William and Page's house.

He didn't learn much, except that it seemed to him that Ben had surrounded himself with fops and fools and, with the exception of a redheaded, green-eyed young lady named Mary Marie O'Donnell, shady ladies. Even before he introduced himself, Falcon had taken an instant liking to Mary Marie. The Irish girl had a tongue on her that could be as sharp as a Bowie knife and didn't mind at all using it. On several occasions, when she was away from the group, Falcon had managed some lengthy conversations with Mary Marie. But he was very careful to make it clear right off that he was a married man and not looking for romance, just conversation. He never told her his last name, and she never asked.

No, sir, she was not the girlfriend of Chuckie. But Chuckie wanted the others to think she was. It was all a game of pretend.

Ben F. Washington? A man who had an axe to grind and someone's ox to gore, she told Falcon. A troubled man, she thought.

Did he ever talk about himself?

No. As a matter of fact, whenever someone would bring that up, he would change the subject. But, she added the last time they spoke, he did let slip one time that he had ties to a family that used to live around Richmond, Virginia.

"Falcon is going to stay longer in Denver than he first thought," Joleen told her brothers and sisters one afternoon, after the stage had dropped off the mail. "Something's come up."

"What?" Megan asked.

"He didn't say."

"Probably a blonde," Matthew said with a grin, cutting his eyes over to Marie Gentle Breeze.

She smiled. "He knows better," she said.

Everybody there knew that sure was the truth. The Cheyenne/French lady had her a temper that could cause a cougar to think twice. Falcon walked the line at his house. He could play cards all night long at his saloon if he wanted to, and sometimes did. He could have a night out with the boys occasionally. He could go off hunting or fishing and stay gone a week if he wanted to. But when he came home, Marie ran the house. Period.

As the old mountain man, Preacher, put it one time, that Gentle Breeze could turn into a tornader faster than you could spit!

Snow covered the ground when Jamie rode into the Mormon controlled area that Brigham Young called The Place.

It was then called Deseret, and a short time later, Utah. Jamie had always gotten along well with the Saints, simply because he respected their ways and did not condemn them for their practices. But he did not want to do anything that might bring the Danites, the enforcement arm of the Mormon Church, sometimes called the Avenging Angels, down on him.

But he need not have worried. The Mormons he encountered were friendly and for the most part totally sympathetic toward Jamie and his manhunt. He learned that the Mormons had driven out the members of the Nelson gang who had been hiding in Northern Utah. They were believed to be somewhere around the Fort Bridger area.

Jamie found an old trapper's cabin that was in pretty good shape and decided to stay there for a time. He rechinked some of the logs, cut an ample supply of firewood, and then went hunting, smoking and jerking some of the meat and making pemmican. If he had done nothing else during the first year of his manhunt, he had broken up the Miles Nelson gang and put the outlaws on the run.

He had detectives from San Francisco, Denver, and St. Louis working to find Miles Nelson, but the outlaw leader had vanished, going into deep cover.

As the days grew colder and the snow deepened, Jamie sat snug in his warm cabin, before his fire, and talked to the dancing flames, occasionally glancing at the picture of Kate he carried inside the face cover of his watch.

"I'll find you all," he whispered. "You can't hide forever. You've got to surface someday, and when you do, I'll be there. And I'll kill you!"


Marshall Henry Ludlow, Richard Farnsworth, and Charles Bennett each received an identical wire from their fathers back in New York City. They were ordered to stay in Denver and open an office. Come the spring, they were to begin traveling Colorado Territory in search of land and mining operations that might prove profitable to the corporation.

At the end of the telegrams were these words: YOUR WIVES DUE TO ARRIVE NEXT TRAIN.

That threw everybody in the group except Mary Marie O'Donnell into a panic. She found it hysterically funny. Chuckie did not share in the humor and kicked her out of the hotel, putting her on the street very nearly penniless.

Falcon found her on the curbside, sitting on her luggage.

"Can you sew?" he asked.

"Are you daft? I'm Irish," she popped back at him, emerald-green eyes flashing. "Of course I can sew. What's sewing got to do with farming?"

Falcon blinked a couple of times. "I beg your pardon?"

"Farming. You hitch up the horse to a plow and turn the ground a time or two. Then you plant the seeds. Then—"

Falcon held up a hand. "I do know something about farming, Miss Mary."

"I want a piece of ground to call my own."

"Who's going to farm it for you?"

"Who? Me! Who else? Saint Pat?"

Falcon smiled and wrote a short note on the back of an envelope then hailed a carriage and began putting Mary's luggage in the rear boot.

"Where are we going?" Mary Marie questioned.

"We're not going anywhere," Falcon told her. "But you're going to Valley, Colorado."

"I am?"

"You are. Now get in. I'll see you to the stage."

"If you think I'm going to be a kept woman, you are out of your mind!"

"Get in the damn carriage and hush up. Did I say anything about you being a kept woman?"

The driver was finding all this very interesting.

"No, but . . ."

"The MacCallisters own Valley. And everything around it

for miles and miles. One of my brothers will sell you a piece of land. You can sew at my sister's dress shop until you save some money to get you started. Now stop arguing and get in the carriage."

"MacCallister?" Mary Marie whispered. "You're? . . ."

"Falcon MacCallister. Jamie Ian MacCallister is my father."

"Damn sure is," the driver said. "Looks just like him."

Ben F. Washington had exited the hotel and was standing just outside the doorway, listening to the exchange.

Mary Marie was rendered speechless for a moment, and for an Irish girl, that was quite a feat.

Falcon picked her up as if she weighed no more than a butterfly and deposited her in the carriage, then climbed in after her. "The stage depot," he told the driver. He looked at Mary Marie and smiled. "I have a nephew named Jamie Ian the Third. I'll make a wager that he'll take one look at you and start walking into trees. By the time I get back to Valley in the spring, I'll wager that you two will be planning a summer wedding."

"Hah!" Mary Marie snorted. "The day I marry some damn tightwad Scotchman, leprechauns will play the 'Star Spangled Banner' on the pipes."

Falcon smiled as the carriage pulled away from the hotel.

"How interesting," Ben F. Washington said.

Ben paid no attention to the three burly men standing across the street, watching him intently.

# 7

Restlessness gripped Jamie, and he could not winter in the cabin. He headed for Fort Bridger.

"They've been here and gone, Mr. MacCallister," the commanding officer of the fort told Jamie. "Six of the hardest-looking men I ever saw. They bought enough supplies to last the winter, loaded them on packhorses, and left. I heard one of them call another Waddy."

"Which way did they go?"

"Straight north. Into the mountains. Give it up until spring, Colonel," the officer urged, addressing Jamie by his old military rank. "This winter is shaping up to be a bad one."

The officer fought away an urge to back up at the sight of Jamie's grim smile and those cold blue eyes. "I'll give it up when they're all dead."

Jamie rested his horses for a day while he resupplied, and then pulled out, heading north.

Jamie found an old campsite on his third day out and spent some time reading sign. When he finished, he knew a lot more about the men he was after.

After studying the ground for a time, Jamie could now recognize their horses' hoof marks anywhere. There were six men, and one of them walked with a limp. None of them appeared to be very concerned about personal hygiene. They had tried to hide the campsite, but either weren't very good at it or had made only a half-hearted effort to do so. He found part of a burned envelope with the name Terry recognizable. That would be Slim Terry, he was sure.

Jamie hit the saddle and continued north. He put the Muddy behind him and stayed on the west side of Commissary Ridge, heading for the trading post on the Hams Fork. He was closing the distance between them by several miles each day.

His friends among the Indians had spread the word about his hunt, and he was not bothered by them. He did wake up one morning to find a new set of buckskins lying beside his bed, and a fine tomahawk with the buckskins.

The Utes, he was sure it was them, were leaving the outlaws alone—leaving them for Jamie.

Jamie sighted the trading post and swung down from the saddle. He took his field glasses from his saddlebags and studied the place for a moment. The long, half-open lean-to that served as a stable was filled with horses.

He had found Slim Terry and his bunch.


Ben F. Washington had not noticed the men trailing him, but Falcon had. He'd spotted them several days before. After seeing Mary Marie O'Donnell off on the stage for Valley, Falcon returned to the hotel and sat in the lobby, pretending to read a newspaper. As shadows began to creep silently over the city, signaling that dusk was about to turn the day into night, Ben walked through the lobby and out to the street. Falcon laid his paper aside and followed him.

Falcon had learned that James William and Page had taken the train to New York City the very day that Falcon had arrived in Denver. They would be gone for a month at least, maybe longer.

And maybe that was a good thing, Falcon thought. That would give him time to get to the bottom of whatever the hell was going on here.

Ben was taking his nightly walk before dinner. Falcon

knew the route he would take, for Ben had never deviated from it. Staying across the street and half a block behind Ben, Falcon spotted the three toughs when they swung in behind the reporter. Falcon quickly crossed the street and closed the distance just as the three thugs—nicely dressed, but thugs nonetheless—reached Ben and dropped a bag over his head and shoved him into a darkened alley.

Falcon picked up a broken wheel spoke from the gutter and ran into the alley, swinging the hard wood. He didn't want to shoot unless it was absolutely necessary, for he wanted some time alone with Ben, without the police.

Falcon's attack came as a surprise to the thugs. The heavy spoke rang off of noggins, splitting the skin, sending the blood flying, and dropping the goons to the dirty and trash-littered alley floor.

Falcon jerked the hood from Ben's head and slammed the reporter up against a brick wall, a .44 stuck up under Ben's chin.

"My name is Falcon MacCallister, mister." Falcon whispered the words to a very scared Ben F. Washington. "James William Haywood is my nephew. Now, you've been snooping around, muttering some damned odd words. You and me, Mr. Washington, are going to have a long talk. And you're going to level with me about what the Billy-Hell is going on around here. And you're going to be truthful with me. For if I think you're lying, I'm going to blow your god-damn head plumb off. You understand all that, city boy?"

Ben managed to nod his head, the muzzle of the .44 cold against his chin.

"Fine," Falcon said, easing the hammer down. "I just knew you'd see it my way."

Jamie rode up to the trading post from the rear, reining up behind the stable. He broke open and filled the twin barrels of the sawed-off shotgun with buckshot loads. At close range, the Greener was a fearsome weapon, capable of taking out two or three men with a single blast from both barrels.

Walking around the stable, Jamie paused as the front door to the trading post opened and two old gray-bearded men stepped out. Trappers, from the looks of them. Men whose time had come and gone, but who were still hanging on to a way of life that advancing civilization had forever destroyed.

The old mountain men spotted Jamie and walked up to him. "They's a smell of evil in yonder, MacCallister," one told him, jerking a thumb toward the trading post. "Fairly stinks, it does. They's six of 'em and they's waitin' for ye. You need airy hep?"

"No," Jamie said softly. "But I thank you for the offer."

"Knowed your grandpere," the second old mountain man said, a touch of French accent in his words. "And I knowed ol' Robedeaux what took up with the Cheyenne and bred forth the woman who's the mama of Gentle Breeze. Your son treatin' her rat, MacCallister?"

"That he is."

"Figured he must be. The Cheyenne would a-never a-stood for it if he wasn't a good man." The old man, who Jamie figured must be eighty if he was a day, looked at the Greener in Jamie's hands and smiled. "That's two men a-sittin' at a table just to your rat as you step in the door. Two more facin' the door, backs to the rear wall. The other two is along the bar. That'd be to your lef' as you walk in. Take the two at the right side table out furst, they's the fastest. Waddy Keeton and Slim Terry. They's some other folks in there, but they's moved out of the way. Go in shootin'. Good luck to you, Mac."

"Thanks."

The old mountain men walked to the hitch rail, swung into their saddles, and were gone.

The cold winds off the mountains blew harsh against Jamie's face as he walked to the front door. Pausing for a few seconds, Jamie took several deep breaths. He eared back both hammers to the sawed-off, slammed open the door and went fast and low, turning to his right.

In Falcon's hotel suite, a pot of coffee on the table, Falcon listened with rapt attention as Ben F. Washington carefully recounted the whole sorry and sordid tale of his family's history—as much as he knew.

When Ben had finished, Falcon poured a fresh cup and leaned back in his chair. "Roscoe and Anne Jefferson became Anne and Ross LeBeau, the actors and singers and musicians. I often wondered what happened to them. So Anne is the mother of you and Page?"

"Yes. She passed for white. Obviously, if you have eyes, you can see I could not."

"But you don't know Page."

"No."

"She's done nothing to you personally."

"No. Nothing."

"And she doesn't know she is a quarter Negro?"

"No."

"Then why do you hate her so and want to destroy her life?"

Ben did not reply to that. He leaned back into his chair and stared at Falcon.

"Is it jealousy?" Falcon asked. "Is that it?"

"Quite possibly, that is part of it."

"You know, of course, that I will not allow you to ruin my nephew's life?" Falcon could butcher the English language when he wanted to, and when he wanted to, he could speak with the precision of a teacher.

"How would you stop me?"

"That's easy. I'd kill you!"

Ben's eyes widened in disbelief. "But you just saved my life!"

"Strictly to get information; to find out what in the hell is going on." Falcon stared hard at the man. "I don't sympathize with you at all, Ben. Not one bit. You've got your own life, so why not just live it, and let others live theirs. You have no right to come along and destroy others just because you're angry at the hand life dealt you. If you want to live, just settle down and play your cards."

"I can't believe you'd kill me, Falcon."

"This is a family matter, Ben. And the MacCallister family sticks together. You poke one of us with a needle, we all feel it. I will stop you from ruining two lives."

Ben didn't believe it. He just didn't believe Falcon would kill him. The reporter rose from his chair and walked to the door. He paused, turned around. "Thank you for what you did in that alley. Tomorrow, I shall buy a pistol and learn how to use it. Good night, Falcon."

Falcon sat for a time, staring at the closed door. He knew what he had to do, but damn sure didn't look forward to doing it.

Six men in the trading post grabbed for guns when the door burst open. The other men hit the floor.

Jamie pulled both triggers of the Greener, and Waddy Keeton and Slim Terry got splattered all over the log wall. Dropping the sawed-off, Jamie bellied down on the floor, his hands filled with Colts, and let them bang.

Bob Perlich took a round in the belly and sat down hard on the floor, screaming and cursing Jamie. Willie Evans' lights were forever turned out as a .44 slug punched a hole in his forehead. Lonnie Rayburn and Jed Hudson ran out the back door and made it to their horses.

But they left all their supplies behind.

Jamie got to his boots and walked over to Perlich. He stood for a moment, then knelt down beside the man.

"You're a rotten son of a bitch, MacCallister," Perlich gasped the words.

"I've been called worse," Jamie replied, reloading his pistols.

"Miles will kill you, MacCallister. You'll not get lead in that man."

"We'll see about that."

The other men in the large room were getting up, looking warily all around them.

"It wasn't in our plans to kill your wife, MacCallister," Perlich said with a grin. "We had plans to grab her and as many of yourn and hers daughters and use 'em up 'til we got tarred of 'em."

Jamie fought back his anger and stared at the man.

"See, we had us a plant in your town feedin' us everythin' that went on. How'd you figure out what we was gonna do?"

"A lucky guess, I suppose."

"I'll see you in hell, MacCallister. 'Cause you ain't no better than us'n."

"You may be right, Bob . . ."

"This here one's still alive!" a man called from the bloody, buckshot-blasted corner of the room. "But not for long."

Kicking Perlich's guns away, far out of the man's reach, Jamie walked over to Waddy Keeton and knelt down.

The man had taken a full load of buckshot in the belly and chest. The pale rider on his death horse was galloping hard toward Waddy, and the man knew it.

"You have something to say to me, Waddy?" Jamie asked.

"Yeah," the outlaw gasped through his pain. He spewed obscenities at Jamie for a moment, then had to catch his breath as the pain from his wounds overcame him.

Jamie waited. Glanced over at Slim Terry. Terry had received the second blast as the shotgun was lifting from the recoil and Jamie's body twisting. He had taken the full load in his face and was unrecognizable . . . due to the fact that most of his head was missing.

"Miles Nelson is shore to be hirin' the top guns in the country, MacCallister," Waddy blurted, spitting out blood with every word. "I ain't gonna be around to see it, but he'll git the last laugh."

Jamie had been hearing words to that effect for nearly five

decades. He was still around. He offered no comment. Kneeling there, he watched Waddy die, a curse on the outlaw's lips as he passed over from life to death. Waddy was blaspheming God with his last breath.

"I'd not like to go out cussin' the Almighty thataway," a trapper remarked.

Jamie removed the money belts from the men. They were not as thick as when he first started his hunt, but still held a goodly amount of stolen gold and money.

"The money is stolen," Jamie explained. "I'm sending it back as I find it."

"Drag them heathens out back and plant 'em," the trading post owner told a couple of men. "Do that and I'll zero out your bar bill. Somebody open the door and let this damn gunsmoke out. It's smartin' to my eyes."

"Can I have his boots?" another man asked, pointing to Perlich. "Mine's plumb wore out."

"Hell, I don't care," the owner said.

"How 'bout them pistols?" another man asked. "Them's fine shootin' irons."

"Take 'em if you want 'em," the owner told him. "That all right with you, Mr. MacCallister?"

Jamie shrugged his indifference as to what happened to the personal effects of the dead men. "I'll take their supplies," he said. "And the best of the packhorses. The rest of the animals you can sell or give away. I don't care."

"That's fair," a man said.

"Rat nice of you, Mr. MacCallister," another spoke up, stripping the guns from Willie Evans while another man tugged off his boots. Willie wore no socks, and his feet were filthy, crusted with dirt.

Jamie viewed the scene without emotion. After a moment, he turned away and walked to the bar, ordering a drink of whiskey.

He did not turn around as the bodies were dragged out the back and laid on the cold ground. Jamie lingered for a time over his drink. He finished his whiskey and walked to the stable, to inspect the supplies left behind by the two men who'd gotten away. It was more than enough to last him through the winter. He picked out the best of the horses and repacked what he was taking, which included almost a thousand rounds of .44 caliber ammunition. The blankets of the dead men, although just recently purchased, appeared to have various types of bugs crawling and hopping around in them. Jamie tossed the blankets to the ground.

"You don't want them blankets?" a man asked.

"No. You can have them."

'Preciate it, Mr. MacCallister. I shorely do. You done us a good turn, so I'll do you one. I know where some of the gang is winterin'."

Jamie waited.

"They's a ramshackle ol' minin' town just 'crost the territorial line in Colorodee. It's in the Medicine Bows. Ain't much to it now; there never was no vein. But that's where you'll find five or six of the gang. Gamblin' and whorin', I 'spect. I also 'spect that's where them two that took out of here like their asses was on far went. So you'll probably be up agin eight or so hard cases."

"I thank you for the information."

"Lak I say, you done me a good turn."

Jamie was gone within the hour. He rode for several hours, reining up often to check his back trail. When he was satisfied he was not being followed, he made his camp in a snug hollow, where he and the horses would be protected from the wind, and spent the night.

He would head for Colorado at first light.

"Find him and kill him!" the man now known as Russell Clay told the Jones brothers. "And when that is accomplished, I'll have another assignment for you. One that will take you to the West Coast and just might make you both rich beyond your wildest dreams."

"Now you're talkin' like we wanna hear, mister," Bob said with a smile.

"You betcha. You just consider 'er done," Lloyd told the man who wore a muffler across his face and his hat pulled down low over his forehead. The brothers could see only the man's eyes.

"Fine. You know how to contact my man." Russell turned and walked out of the warehouse. A carriage was waiting for him at the corner.

The brothers exchanged glances, Bob saying, "We do this thing right, brother, we can get that job out in California. Then we'll forever shake the dust of this territory out of our boots."

Lloyd nodded his head in agreement. "Let's go find that reporter and get it done."

"Easy as pie," the older brother said.

Together, the brothers walked out into the cold night, killing on their minds.

# 8

Jamie Ian was the first to spot the little redheaded beauty sitting on the bench at the stage depot in Valley. He walked over to her.

"Could I help you, miss?" he asked, doffing his hat.

"Sure and b'gorra, you could," Mary Marie said, the Emerald Isle fairly pouring from her mouth. "If your name be MacCallister."

"It is. I'm Jamie Ian."

"You'll be Falcon's brother?"

"I am. And you are? . . ."

"Mary Marie O'Donnell." She handed him the note from Falcon.

Jamie Ian read the note, a smile slowly creeping across his lips. Then he laughed. "You can stay with us until we can find you a place." He spotted his son, Jamie Ian the Third, walking up the street and waved him over. "Pick up the lady's trunk, boy, and tote it down to our house."

Jamie Ian the Third stood staring at Mary Marie, his mouth hanging open.

She smiled sweetly at him.

"Did you hear me, boy?" his father asked.

Jamie Ian the Third turned and hit his head on an awning post, putting a knot on his forehead.

"Good Lord!" the father said.

"Falcon didn't tell me you had a son that was addled," Mary Marie said.

"Only at times," Jamie Ian told her, picking up her carpetbag.

Matthew and Morgan walked up. Morgan looked at the red knot on young Jamie's forehead. "You get in a fight, boy?"

"Shot in the butt with an arrow is more like it," Jamie Ian told his brother.

"An *arrow?*" Matthew questioned, leaning over to inspect his nephew's rear end.

"It's a long story," Jamie Ian told his other brother. "You two pick up the lady's trunk. I'll fill you in on the way over to the house." He turned to his son. "Do you think you could find your way home without falling down or running into anything else, boy?"

"Sure, I can, Pa!"

"Then take the lady's arm and let's go."

Jamie Ian the Third took a misstep and fell off the boardwalk, landing in the street in a sprawl of arms and legs.

Mary Marie shook her head. "Poor lad's spastic, too," she remarked.


Jamie sat alone at a table in the rear of the trading post just north of the Colorado Territorial line, slowly eating from a large bowl of stew. The winter winds were howling like banshees, beating furiously against the walls of the trading post. Huge, wet snowflakes were tumbling out of the sky.

Jamie tore off a chunk of fresh-baked bread and sopped up some liquid, chewing slowly. He was very conscious of the four men sitting at a table on the other side of the room, occasionally glancing over at him, then returning to their low talking and whiskey drinking.

Jamie's hair held no more gold among the silver. In the months since Kate's death, his hair had completely grayed, as had his beard, making him look older than he really was.

But he still had most of his teeth. Old-timers knew that Jamie Ian MacCallister still had quite a bite—in more ways than one—but much younger men either did not know the legends about Jamie, or did not believe them. For some younger men, that lack of knowledge would prove to be tragic.

"Ol'-timer," one of the men across the room called. "You sloppin' up that food like a hog at a trough. You 'bout to make me sick."

Jamie said nothing. He continued eating.

The man behind the bar got ready to hit the floor. He had come west back in the '40s and knew all about Jamie Ian MacCallister.

The one man standing by the rough bar said, "You bes' shut your mouth, Woody. 'Fore you stick a boot in it."

"Go to hell," Woody told him.

The man who had offered the friendly warning shrugged his shoulders and picked up his cup and jug and moved as far away from the line of fire as he could.

"I'm talkin' to you, old man," Woody turned his attentions back to Jamie. "What's the matter, are you deef?"

Jamie did not look up. He continued eating, enjoying the meal and the warmth if not the company.

"Hey!" Woody yelled. "Look at me when I talk to you, you old turd!"

Jamie laid down his spoon and cut his eyes to the four men. "Shut up," he said. "You're beginning to bother me."

Woody flushed a deep red. "Old man, do you know who you're talkin' to?"

"No. And I don't care. Now shut your mouth and let me enjoy my meal."

Woody pushed back his chair and stood up. He wore two guns, Remington conversions, Jamie noted.

"Woody," the barkeep said. "That's Jamie Ian MacCallister."

"I don't give a damn who it is," Woody said. "Far as I'm concerned he's just a noisy ol' fart who eats like a hog and probably hasn't had a bath since last summer. Get up, old man, and make your apologies for sassin' me."

Jamie smiled, and then bluntly and very profanely told Woody where to go, how far to venture, in what part of his anatomy he should stick his pistols, and added that he could ram his horse up there, too, for if that part of his behind was anywhere near as large as his mouth, there would be ample room.

"Goddamn you!" Woody finally screamed, after recovering from his shock at being spoken to in such a manner. Back where Woody had come from—Missouri—he was known as a real tough fellow. A man who liked to hit women, fight smaller men, and strut around on Saturday nights, showing off his fancy guns. "Make your play, you old bastard!"

Jamie lifted the sawed-off 12 gauge with his right hand and pulled the trigger. The buckshot took Woody in the center of his swelled-up chest and knocked the man off his boots, flinging him backward to land on the table he'd just left. The legs of the table collapsed and pinned one of Woody's pals to the floor. The other two jumped out of the way and grabbed for iron.

Jamie fired the other barrel of the Greener and then added his left-hand Colt to the fracas. The whole thing had taken about five seconds.

"DearJesusChristAmighty!" the thug pinned under the table and Woody's leaking body bellered. "Don't kill me, I'm out of this!" He cut his eyes first to one of his friends lying mortally wounded to his left, and then to the other friend, lying as dead as a hammer to his right, his face unrecognizable from the heavy blast of buckshot.

The man who had stood at the bar and warned Woody shook his head. "I told you, boy," he muttered. "MacCallister is a ring-tailed tooter."

Jamie opened the shotgun and pulled out the empties, loading up full. Then he loaded up the Colt's cylinder and laid both weapons on the table. "I'm tired of punks and hooligans woolin' me around," he said. "I'll not take no more of it. Not from this day forward. Goddamn young people nowadays have no respect for their elders."

"You want some more stew, Mr. MacCallister?" the barkeep asked in a nervous voice.

"Halp!" the thug pinned under the table and Woody's body hollered. "Halp!"

"Shut up," Jamie told him. "You're getting on my nerves, boy."

"Yes, sir," the trapped thug said weakly. "Whatever you say, sir."

Jamie walked over to the wounded man, lying to the left of the thug with the table and the body on top of him. Jamie had fired just as the man was turning, and dusted him, the bullet going in one side and blowing out the other.

The man blew blood bubbles and gasped, "Guess we made a . . . real bad mistake, didn't we, Mr. MacCallister?"

"It certainly appears that way."

"I really don't want to die, Mr. MacCallister."

"I never met anybody who did."

"Maybe I won't. Maybe I'll get better."

Jamie stood over the young man and watched him close his eyes. A few seconds later, he slipped quietly beyond the veil. Jamie looked over at the barkeep. "You know these fellows?"

"They been driftin' in and out of here for about six months. They don't never work. I don't know where they get their money. Steal it, I reckon."

"That's about right." Jamie shoved Woody's body off the busted table and then lifted the table off of the pinned man.

"Oh, Lord," the young man said, getting to his hands and knees.

"You reckon He knows you, boy?"

The young man looked up, fear stark in his eyes. "He will from now on, Mr. MacCallister. And that's a promise."

"Take a little more time in choosing your friends in the future," Jamie advised him.

"Count on it, sir. Can I go now?"

"I'm not holding you."

The man struggled into a coat and without a look back at his dead friends ran out of the trading post, into the bitter cold and howling winds and blowing snow.

"Ground's too damn frozen to bury these fools," the barkeep said. "We'll just stack 'em out in the shed and they'll freeze soon enough. We'll plant 'em come spring."

James William and Page returned from New York, and both were surprised and pleased to see Falcon. Falcon gave them a day to get settled in, then went over to their house for dinner and brought them up on all the news from home.

"Something is really gnawing at you, Uncle Falcon," James William said, over cigars and brandy in the front room that faced the street.

"Yes," Page said. "You seemed to be preoccupied all evening. What's wrong? Do you have news of Grandpa Jamie?"

"Last we heard from Pa, he was going strong in his hunt. He's nailed over a dozen of the bunch who killed Ma."

"Do you have any idea where he is, Uncle Falcon?"

"No. He might be up in Canada." Falcon sighed heavily. He knew he should tell Page about her brother. He should warn her about what her brother was going to do, and Falcon was certain that Ben was going to spill the beans. But was it his place to tell the couple? Moreover, did he have the right to do it? What would be Page's reaction? Hysterics? Shock? Fainting? And what would be James William's reaction? Would he pick up a gun and go after Ben F. Washington? He was a MacCallister, and MacCallister blood could run hot. There were a lot of things that had to be considered, and Falcon had spent many an hour going over them in his head. But all the hours of ruminations hadn't done a thing to make this moment any easier.

Falcon drained his brandy glass and got up to pour another. He lingered by the table for a moment, sat down on the sofa and looked at the young couple. "This is about the hardest thing I have ever tried to do," Falcon said, his voice low.

Page smiled strangely at him, reaching over to take the hand of James William.

"Just come right out and say it, Uncle Falcon," James urged. "Whatever it is, there is no point in allowing it to fester."

"There is a man here in town who wants to cause a lot of trouble for the both of you," Falcon said quickly. "He's a reporter, from Boston. I've spoken at length with him, trying to talk some sense into the man. But I don't think I got through to him."

"Ben F. Washington?" Page said, that strange smile on her lips.

Falcon stared at her. "Yes. But how? . . ."

"Page told me all about her family history before we got married, Uncle Falcon," James William said. "I am well aware that she is a quadroon."

Falcon stared for a moment more. "But? . . ."

Page laughed, and it was a good, hardy, lusty laugh. "I grew up on a plantation, Uncle Falcon. In the deep South. Like my mother, I am somewhat of a sneak. I may even be better at it than she is. When I was just a little girl, I used to slip out of bed and make my way down to the colored quarters at night and eavesdrop on conversations. I've known I have Negro blood in me since I was about eight or nine years old. Probably the best job of acting my mother ever did was in telling Jamie that ridiculous story about how insanity runs in our family, and how I had a brother who was a monster and who was confined in a mental institution back east. And how I must never have babies. All piffle and flap-doodle, of course. I know all about Uncle Ross and all about my daddy. And everything I know, James William knows. I hid nothing from him."

Falcon sat silent for a moment. Then he rose and hit the brandy bottle again—hard. Seated, he looked at the young couple and said, "Well, I'll just be goddamned!"

Both of them burst out laughing. Falcon soon joined them, and their laughter rang free, carrying outside to the street.

Standing in the cold shadows, Ben F. Washington stood and listened to the merriment, wondering what in the hell was so funny. It filled him with sudden rage. What right did they have to be so happy?

He turned away and began his walk back toward the hotel. As he walked, his hot anger faded, to be replaced by a cold, calculating anger. Now, he thought, would be a good time to start that book he'd had formulating in his brain. A book about the plantation days in the South, prior to the Civil War, about incestuous relationships and cruelty to slaves and white masters bedding down high yellow Negro wenches, and quadroon and octoroon babies. It would be about a half-Negro woman who passed for white and about her daughter, and about her son that she betrayed and gave away at birth. And a lot more. He would detail his mother's rise to power and how evil she was, and her brother, too. Both of them were filth. And he'd write about the oh-so-haughty Page and her passing for pure, lily-white, and her marriage to the grandson of the famous Jamie Ian Mac-Callister.

Ben hated the MacCallisters. All of them. Despised them. Especially Colonel MacCallister, that high-and-mighty hypocrite, who preached treating all people fairly but fought for the Confederacy. Hypocrisy, pure and simple.

Ben would make them pay. All of them. He'd grind them down with words. Rub their rich noses in dark and evil family secrets.

He picked up his pace.

He couldn't wait to get started.

# 9

On the evening that Page was astonishing Falcon with her knowledge of her family's dark—in more ways than one—history, and Ben was wallowing in his cold and vindictive anger, Jamie was riding into the no-name and nearly deserted mining town in the Medicine Bows. He stabled his horses and carefully rubbed them all down while they were feeding. The hotel clerk was so delighted at finally having a customer who could pay with cash money, he magnanimously gave Jamie the finest room in the hotel . . . guaranteed to have clean sheets with no fleas or bedbugs.

Jamie ordered a bath and lingered long in the hot water, scrubbing the trail dirt from him and washing his hair. Then he trimmed his beard and hair until he felt he was looking almost human again.

The dining room of the hotel had been closed for some time, so Jamie walked across the street to a small cafe and ordered his supper. Venison and beans and bread cooked and served by a man who wore his surly indifference like a badge of honor. The venison was tough, the beans undercooked, and the bread as difficult to chew as hardtack.

"As a cook," Jamie told the man, after paying for the meal, "you'd make a fine carpenter."

"You don't like the grub, go somewheres else and eat in the mornin'."

"There is no other place to eat."

"That's right, ain't it?" the counterman replied with a nasty grin. *"Mister MacCallister!"*

Jamie stared at him for a moment, his eyes narrowing in suspicion; then he stepped outside. He quickly cut to his right, moving swiftly toward the dark alley. There had been something in the counterman's tone that set his teeth on edge and made him very wary.

Just as he left the awninged walk in front of the cafe, a rifle barked from across the street, the slug knocking a huge chunk of wood from the corner where Jamie had just exited.

"Sharps," Jamie muttered. "Take your damn arm off with that thing."

The rifle boomed again, and Jamie guessed it to be a .50-70, or maybe even a .60 caliber. One thing for sure, he didn't want to get hit with that damn round . . . or any others if he could help it.

Jamie ran down the dark alley and rounded the corner, turning left. He remembered that the building he was now behind was empty and boarded up. He tried the back door and found the doorknob turned in his hand. He stepped out of the snow and wind and into the quiet of the empty building.

Jamie knelt down and removed his spurs, slipping them into his jacket pocket. He let his eyes adjust to the darkness before moving toward the front of the building. He could see through the ice-frosted front windows of the building across the street, one lamp burning in the street-side window.

A shadow passed in front of the lamp-lit window: a man on the warped boardwalk. A man carrying a rifle. Behind him a few yards, another man, also carrying a rifle. Jamie recognized the shape of the weapon: a Sharps rifle.

But he couldn't be sure these were the men who had fired at him. He was certain in his mind they were hunting him, but they could also be two men returning home from hunting game for the supper table.

Jamie tapped on the window with the barrel of his pistol and then hit the floor. The window exploded, and shards of glass flew as the night was filled with gunfire.

"No doubt about it now," Jamie muttered, belly down on the cold floor.

He crawled to the nearest corner of the room and peeked out through what remained of the frosty glass. No sign of the two men.

Then he heard a boot scrape on the boardwalk, followed by a soft curse.

"That wasn't him in the building," a voice sprang out of the night, coming from the other end of the boardwalk. "May have been an owl beatin' agin the winder. MacCallister wouldn't make no mistake like 'at."

Jamie silently stood up, both hands filled with Colts and said, "He damn sure wouldn't." Then he cut loose with both pistols.

The man on the boardwalk, standing not two feet from Jamie, took the slugs in the chest and fell silently to the frozen street, his rifle clattering on the icy ground.

Jamie ran through the building and exited out the back door, running hard toward the far edge of the short block. He stopped, listened, and could hear the sounds of cursing. He slipped up the dark alley to the street and paused. A few dogs were barking, but only a few. Most of them had enough sense to find a warm place on this freezing night and stay put.

A man suddenly jumped out of the shadows and began his run across the street. A man carrying a Sharps rifle. Jamie stepped out of the alley and shot the running man, the impact of the bullet turning him around several times and finally dropping him to his knees in the street, the Sharps falling from his hands.

Jamie walked up to the moaning man as a crowd began to gather.

"Asa Pike," a man said. "He's a gun for hire. You better

hunt you a hole and pull the ground in over you, mister. Asa's got a whole passel of kin, and they'll all be comin' after you."

Asa fell belly down on the frozen street and moaned. "You're a dead man, MacCallister," he gasped.

*"MacCallister!"* another citizen said in a shocked tone. "Jamie MacCallister?"

"Yes," Jamie told him.

"I don't know this one over here," a man shouted, standing over the man sprawled by the edge of the boardwalk. "But he's deader 'an hell."

"Is there a doctor in this town?" Jamie asked, looking down at the badly wounded Asa Pike.

"Are you jokin', mister? There ain't fifty people left in this dump, and I'm gettin' out first warm spell. 'Sides, what do you care about Asa? He tried to kill you."

"I don't care about him. I was just curious. He took one in the side and might make it with proper care. Of course," Jamie said reflectively, "if he does, I'll probably have to shoot him again some day."

"You ain't gonna live that much longer, MacCallister," Asa groaned out the words. "My kin will be on your trail hard. You'll never shake them loose."

"Somebody hired you to kill me," Jamie said, staring down at the man. "Who was it?"

"Go to hell!" Asa said.

But Jamie already had a good idea: relatives of the Saxons, the Newbys, the Olmsteads, and others. That blood feud had been going on for nearly five decades.

Jamie reached down and took Asa's pistols from leather and handed them to a man standing close. "Keep these until I'm out of here. Then if Asa's still alive, return them to him."

"Yes, sir."

"I'll be alive, you bastard," Asa promised. "And I'm comin' after you."

"You know what?" a man mused. "I just thought of something. Tomorrow's Christmas."

Falcon returned to Valley, gathered all his brothers and sisters around him and told them about James William and Page. Ben F. Washington took the train back to Boston before the Jones brothers could move against him. But Ben had made up his mind to return to Colorado in the early spring. He was going to travel over to Valley and begin his book there. Ben was a good reporter with a genuine talent for writing, and he was slowly coming to his senses about his sister, and feeling ashamed of himself.

Jamie rode into Denver one cold day in early 1871, and after stabling his horses and making sure they would get the best of care, he headed for the finest hotel in Denver and immediately created quite a stir.

Dressed in buckskins and looking like the wrath of God, Jamie was, at first, refused admittance into the hotel by the doorman.

"Either you get out of my way, or you're going to be wearing your ankles for a necklace," Jamie told the man.

The doorman wisely stepped aside.

Jamie stomped through the lobby and up to the registration desk. He was still a handsome man, and in better physical shape than most men thirty years his junior. He turned many a female head on his walk from the street to the desk.

The painter, John A. Bellingham, was staying at the hotel, and he immediately grabbed up a menu and began sketching Jamie on the back of it.

The hotel detective rushed up to see what all the commotion was about and came to a very abrupt halt when he spotted the elder MacCallister. The detective, a man who was western born and reared, quietly turned around and beat it to the kitchen. He had absolutely no desire to tangle with the man the Indians called Man Who Is Not Afraid, Bear Killer, and Man Who Plays With Wolves.

"I want the best room in the place," Jamie told the desk clerk. "I want a hot bath and a barber, and when that's done, I want a tailor standing by. You got all that?"

"Yes, sir! And, sir, our finest suites have the bathroom adjoining."

Jamie stared at him. "You mean, right there close to where you sleep?"

"Yes, sir!"

Jamie shook his head. "I personally find that disgusting, but all right. If that's the best you've got."

The sheriff of Arapahoe County, Dave Cook, chose that time to enter the hotel to see why such a large crowd had gathered in front of the establishment. Dave was a brave man and an excellent law officer, but he was no fool. When he spotted the bulk of Jamie Ian MacCallister standing at the front desk, Dave simply turned around and walked out of the hotel. No way was he going to tangle with that old mountain lion. Especially since Dave was well aware of Jamie's manhunt. Dave also knew that if you scratched one MacCallister, about thirty would feel the itch. Just the thought of thirty MacCallisters invading Denver made his blood run cold.

Dave went to his office and told his deputies to leave Jamie alone.*

Jamie lingered long in the huge tub of hot soapy water, until he was sure he'd gotten all the trail dirt from his body and hair. Standing in his long underwear, Jamie allowed the tailor to measure him for several suits and shirts and then had the barber go to work.

*Dave Cook was sheriff for several terms. He formed the Rocky Mountain Detective Association, a network of law officers that stretched from Wyoming to New Mexico, and was a thorn in the side of outlaws for years. He was a lawman, in one capacity or another, for forty years, and during that time, Dave and his association arrested thousands of criminals and solved several hundred murders.

Jamie had his beard cut off, leaving only a moustache. While that was being done, he had his suit coat brushed and aired and the wrinkles ironed out. Before he slipped the jacket on, he tied a wide sash around his waist and shoved his pistols into the sash, butts forward for a cross draw should he need it.

Jamie walked down the steps to the lobby, looked things over for a moment, then walked into the dining room. Conversation stopped, the clink of silver ceased, waiters stopped serving, and heads turned as the tall, well-built, handsome, and very erect man was escorted to his table by a very sissy-looking maitre d'. Everything was fine until the fussy little man tried to spread the napkin on Jamie's lap.

"I wouldn't do that," Jamie warned him. "I really wouldn't."

The effeminate-acting man quickly backed away, bowing and apologizing.

Jamie picked up the menu and frowned. Damn thing was printed in French. Sighing, Jamie folded the menu and waggled a finger at the waiter.

He closed the distance quickly to stand nervously by Jamie's table. "Sir?"

"I can't read this damn thing. Bring me a steak, a large one, rare, and some bread and whatever else you have."

"Some veggies, sir?"

Jamie looked at the man. "What the hell is that?"

"Vegetables, sir."

"Oh, yeah. Some of those. Whatever you have. And bring me a drink of whiskey, too."

"Right away, sir."

Conversation resumed in the restaurant after that, but it was somewhat subdued. Jamie was conscious of eyes furtively shifting his way all during the meal, but he was used to that. He'd been a living legend for most of his life and understood that many people were fascinated by that type of person.

The diners respectfully waited until Jamie had finished

his meal before they began approaching him for his autograph. He obliged them graciously, but was glad when the last one had come and gone.

Jamie had a brandy, then decided to step outside for a leisurely stroll and a cigar.

He stood in front of the hotel for a few moments, then lit his cigar and started his stroll, speaking to the passersby as they spoke to him, doffing his hat to the ladies and politely ignoring the batting of eyes and swishing of bustles as they flirted with him.

That amused him. Here I am, Jamie thought, a sixty-year-old man and ladies half my age, and less, are openly and brazenly flirting with me. Incredible. What is this world coming to?

He hadn't gone two blocks before a wild, cursing shout scattered the strollers and spun Jamie around. A man stood in the middle of the street, his coat swept back, giving him easy access to his guns. All traffic had stopped.

"MacCallister! Hook and draw, 'cause tonight you die, you bastard!"

# 10

Jamie held up his left hand to caution the man, his right hand hovering over the butt of his Colt. "There are innocent people on the streets. Let them get clear. Let's don't have a lot of blood spilled here needlessly."

"To hell with them!" the man shouted in a hoarse voice. "I'll kill twenty of them just to get to you."

"I don't know you, mister," Jamie said, stalling for time as the pedestrians began scattering out of the line of fire. "Who are you?"

"The man who's gonna kill you and become famous, that's who I am."

"Have I ever done you a harm?"

"That don't make no never mind."

"What's your name?"

"Boots Lowery. Enough talk, MacCallister."

"You really don't want to do this, Boots. It isn't worth it. Whatever you're getting paid, it isn't worth dying over."

"Old man, I think you're a damned coward!" Boots hollered. "I don't think you got no sand no more. I think you're yellow. Now, draw, goddamn you!"

"After you, Boots," Jamie called. "It's your play."

Boots was fast, and he did clear leather first, but as so often happens, he missed his first shot, the bullet whining off the bricks of a building.

Jamie had turned sideways, to present a smaller target,

and his shot was true. The bullet struck Boots in the center of his chest. The man lowered his gun arm as his fingers suddenly turned numb, his pistol clattering to the street. He looked down at the bloody shirt front, then lifted his head to stare at Jamie.

"You've killed me!" he whispered. "This ain't the way it's 'posed to be."

"But that's the way it is, kid," Jamie said. "You wanted to dance, now pay the band."

Boots tried several times to pull his left-hand gun. His fingers fumbled at the butt until he finally got it clear of leather. He tried to cock the weapon but could not. The pistol slipped from his fingers, and Boots sat down hard in the middle of the street. He finally toppled over on one side.

Jamie walked over to him and looked down. "Who paid you to try this, boy?"

"Go to hell, MacCallister," Boots whispered the words.

Several police officers arrived, one of them saying, "I'll take that pistol, mister."

Jamie looked at him and smiled, then stuck the hogleg back behind his sash. He turned and walked away just as the first few bits of snow began falling. The gathered crowd parted silently, to give him room.

"They'll get you, MacCallister!" Boots managed to shout the words through his pain. "Your life ain't worth a cup of spit."

Jamie kept walking.

"Sir!" another policeman called. "You can't just walk off. You shot this man!"

"The man in the street shot first," a citizen told the policeman.

"But I have to make a written report," the policeman protested. "Stop, sir. Or I'll be forced to place you under arrest."

Jamie stopped and turned around. "All right. Then just write down in your pad that Boots Lowery missed and Jamie

Ian MacCallister didn't." Jamie turned and continued his walk up the street.

The policeman put away his pencil and pad. "Oh, to hell with it," he muttered. Then the name registered. *"Jamie Ian MacCallister!"* he hollered, his voice registering his shock.

Jamie turned the corner and disappeared into the cold night.

"Mama!" Boots Lowery said weakly. "It hurts, mama!"

A doctor pushed his way through the crowd, knelt down beside Boots, and opened the man's coat and shirt. He inspected the wound. A moment later he looked up at the police and shook his head. "Better call the undertaker for this one. It won't be long."

Boots started hollering.

"Lay still," the doctor told him. "And make your peace with God."

"MacCallister!" Boots squalled. "This ain't right. You're an old man. I'm young." He coughed up blood. "It's 'posed to be you here in the street."

"Well, it isn't," the doctor said, standing up. He looked down at the young man. "You actually tried to kill Colonel MacCallister?"

"Yeah."

"Damn fool!"

"He got lucky, that's all," Boots gasped, the words no more than a whisper. He closed his eyes for the last time.

"Maybe so," a policeman said, looking down at the body. "But you're still dead."


"Pa's in Denver," Morgan said, stepping into his sister's house, waving the week-old newspaper. "He killed a man on a downtown street."

Matthew was somewhere out in the county, chasing down a horse thief.

"Then he might be coming home for a time," Little Ben

Pardee said. He and his wife, Kathy, Ellen Kathleen's daughter, were over for a visit.

"I doubt it," Morgan said. "Told me 'fore he left he'd rather not look again on Ma's grave until she was fully avenged." He held up the newspaper. "According to this, the man who braced Pa was a paid assassin."

"Those damn Saxons and Newbys and Olmsteads again," Joleen said, laying aside her sewing.

With the exception of Ben Pardee, everyone in the large room was blond-haired and blue-eyed. Ben said, "Hard to believe the colonel's been gone near'bouts a year and a half. I wonder when he'll come back."

"When it's done," Megan said.

Jamie stood at the bar, one boot on the railing. He was dressed to the nines, wearing a new tailor-made dark suit, sparkling white shirt with string tie, and a new dark hat with a silver band. His boots were polished to a high shine. He wore both Colts in leather, low and tied down. He was clean-shaven now, except for a neatly trimmed moustache. His hair was trimmed short. Jamie stood alone at the bar, at the far end, facing the front door and batwings.

The bar was one of many located on Holladay Street, a four-block area known as the "Street of a Thousand Sinners." The four blocks were filled with saloons, whorehouses, and gambling houses. It was said that those four blocks contained more wickedness than any other four blocks west of the Mississippi River.

Any outlaw who hit town immediately gravitated to Holladay Street.

Jamie waited at the bar. He'd heard that three of Miles Nelson's gang were in town, and knew that sooner or later, they'd surface, and he would be waiting and ready.

There were outlaws in the saloon, but Jamie left them alone. They were not the ones he sought.

Jamie sipped his drink and waited.

A man dressed in rough and stained clothing left a table and walked to Jamie's side, placing his mug of beer on the bar. He was very careful to keep his hands away from his guns. "I ain't never done you a harm, Mr. MacCallister," he spoke in low tones. "And I ain't never been in Valley, Colorado, nor anywhere's close to it. I've rid the hoot-owl trail more'un once, but I ain't never harmed no woman nor child. And I can't abide a man who would. The three you're lookin' for is up to Belle's House of Pleasure. Soon as they get done with the Doves, they'll be here. Son Hogg, Jim Aarons, and Glen Anderson. Nice talkin' to you, and I'm gone."

Jamie nodded his head in acknowledgement. The outlaw downed his beer, set the mug on the bar, and walked out.

Those seated at tables close to the long bar began seeking other places to sit, getting out of the line of fire. Obviously, the outlaw who had warned Jamie was known to many of them, and they probably had discussed it among themselves.

Jamie waited with the patience of a born hunter.

In Boston, the editor of the paper accepted Ben F. Washington's letter of resignation with a great deal of reluctance. Not only was Ben a fine reporter, but he was a friend of the family.

"Not to worry," Ben assured the man. "I have money. I've got to go back to the West. I have to resolve this personal issue."

The editor leaned back in his chair. "I think you're underestimating this Falcon MacCallister, Ben. He's a known gunfighter and a bad man to fool with. If he says he'll kill you, I believe he means to do just that. Ben . . . let sleeping dogs lie. What you plan to do is pure vindictiveness . . . it won't help you. And it's so unlike you."

Ben sat down and looked at his boss and friend. "It was vindictiveness, at first. I will readily admit that. And as Falcon pointed out, jealousy. But since I've been back east, I've had a chance to think things through and realize how silly and petty I've been about this matter." He shook his head. "I really behaved as a fool. Oh, hell, Frank! I'm not going to write a book that would ruin my sister's life. Our parents won't even be in the book. I want to write a book about Jamie Ian MacCallister. Not a Penny Dreadful. But a real book about the man, factual. Jamie Ian and Kate. They're both legends, Frank. Real legends. And somebody needs to chronicle their lives. But Frank, my sister needs to be told of her background. If she becomes pregnant and gives birth to some nappy headed breed . . . *that* would destroy Page and her husband."

The older man nodded his agreement. "But do you have the right to do it, Ben?"

"Since I've come to my senses, I've been giving that considerable thought. I don't really know what to do about the situation. Well, that's not correct. I know *what* to do. I just don't know how to go about it."

"Ben, I'm going to put this resignation in my personal safe. No one else will know about it. In the meantime, I want you to continue working for us. Send in a story every now and then. When your manuscript is ready, I can get your book published. What do you say?"

Ben smiled and reached across the desk, hand extended. "I accept."

"Good, good. When are you planning on leaving?"

"In the morning."

"Going back to Denver?"

"For a time. Then I plan on taking the stage for Valley."

The editor smiled. "Going to jump right into the thick of things, huh?"

Ben returned the smile. "That's the only way, Frank."


The men met in a hotel suite in Washington, D.C. They were the sons and grandsons and cousins of the Newbys, the

Olmsteads, the Saxons, the Layfields, and the Bradfords. And they all, for various reasons, hated Jamie Ian MacCallister. Some of them hated him because their fathers had hated Jamie. That was the sadness of a long-running blood feud: the reasons for the hatred obscured in the mist and shadows of time.

"Now is the perfect time for us to rid ourselves of Jamie Ian MacCallister," a Newby said. "That bastard has bounty hunters all over the West looking for him. A few more men, on our payrolls, won't even be noticed in the hunt."

"Take him alive and torture him," a relative of Kate said. "It's common knowledge he's got gold hidden all over the mountains around Valley. Now that Kate is dead, the gold belongs to the family she deserted down in Kentucky, when she run off with MacCallister back in '25 or '26. It's only right, and I won't be cheated out of my share."

"MacCallister killed my Uncle Henry down the Big Thicket country," a Bradford said. "I want him dead. And I don't need to hire no damn bounty hunters. I got five big, strappin' boys that I can cut loose any time. They'll take care of MacCallister."

"Anybody here know a man name of Grover Ellis?" Olmstead asked.

They all shook their heads.

"MacCallister run Grover out of his valley right after the war. Then Grover got killed a couple or three years later over on the Bearpaw. 'Fore he died, he claimed MacCallister done it or had it done. Well, his kin come out to avenge him, and there was a big shoot-out. MacCallister had gotten together some old mountain men and a couple of Injuns and the like, and they fairly whupped a whole army of men. Well, this Grover Ellis has got more kin just achin' for revenge."

"Just like I'm aching for revenge for my uncle," Layfield spoke up. He grimaced. "Who lies rotting in that damnable insane asylum."

"I personally feel we won't have to do anything," Olmstead said. "Jamie Ian MacCallister's string is just about played out. Let's start our legal actions against the Mac-Callister clan's claim to own all that land. I've got a couple of federal judges in my pocket, and they're ready to go."

"Sounds good," the men all agreed.

"It's over for you, MacCallister," Newby muttered, pouring himself a glass of whiskey. "After all these years, our good name will be avenged, and my kin can rest easy in their graves."

The men in the cigar-smoke-filled room did not take into consideration that Jamie just might have something to say about that.


Jamie waited patiently for over an hour. Finally, his persistence paid off. Three roughly dressed and unshaven men swaggered through the door. Their guns were loose in leather, and they were ready for action. Jamie had no doubt that they had been tipped off to his presence.

"You've been damned lucky this far, MacCallister," Son Hogg said. "But tonight is when your luck runs out."

Son stood staring and sneering at Jamie. A big man, as big as Jamie. Jamie knew that a man Son's size could soak up a lot of lead before going down.

"Could be, Son," Jamie said, then shifted his eyes to Jim Aarons. "You want to flap your big stupid mouth about anything, baby killer?"

Aarons flushed darkly under his unshaven face but kept his mouth closed.

Jamie looked at Anderson. "How about you, child raper? You have anything to say?"

Anderson was suspected of brutally raping at least three young girls during his criminal years.

"I say it's time for you to die, you washed-out, used-up, old son of a bitch!" Anderson flung the words at Jamie. "What do you have to say about that?"

"Then drag iron, baby raper," Jamie told him. None of

the three could see that Jamie had already drawn and cocked his right-hand .44. "What the hell do you want from me, an engraved invite?"

The three outlaws exchanged glances. Even though they had Jamie three-to-one, none of them were all that anxious to mix it up with him. Jamie was still a very dangerous pistolero . . . a hard fact that all three were well aware of.

"Old man," Son said. "They's three of us."

"I learned to count a long time before your mother crawled under the porch and whelped you, Hogg," Jamie said, offhandedly implying the man was a son of a bitch.

"Damn your eyes, MacCallister!" Hogg yelled, his face darkening with rage. "Fill your hand, old man!"

"Oh, it's already filled, Son," Jamie told him, then lifted his pistol and shot Son Hogg in the belly.

Hell broke loose in the saloon.

# 11

Son stumbled against the bar, but didn't go down. "Kill that bastard!" Son hollered, one hand over the bleeding hole in his belly.

Jamie felt the hot tug of a bullet as the lead tore a hole in his new suit coat and blistered the flesh of his upper left arm, the bullet cutting a slight groove there. He turned sideways and shot Jim Aarons twice just as the edge of the bar was splintered by a bullet from Glen Anderson's Remington .44. Jamie turned again just as another bullet from Glen's .44 burned his leg.

The saloon was rapidly filling with gunsmoke, stinging the eyes of the combatants as Jamie shot Anderson in the chest. Glen toppled backward, falling into Son Hogg just as Son was leveling his pistol at Jamie. The shot went wild, blowing a hole in the ceiling and bringing a yelp of fright from a man on the second floor who was being entertained by one of the red-light ladies.

Jim Aarons was down on his knees on the floor, mortally wounded but still game. He managed to lift his Remington and cock it before Jamie turned out his lights with his left-hand Colt. A muscle spasm pulled the trigger on Aaron's Remington and blew yet another hole in the ceiling.

Then it was Jamie and Son Hogg facing each other, about twenty feet separating them.

Upstairs, several of the district's "brides of the multitudes" were screaming bloody murder, and men were cussing and shouting, fumbling for pants and boots.

No one noticed the painter, John A. Bellingham, sitting in a far corner of the saloon, sketching furiously as the gunfight was winding down to its bloody conclusion.

Son Hogg was standing on his own now, legs spread wide apart, seemingly oblivious to the bloody hole in his stomach. He cursed Jamie and lifted both his guns.

Jamie began firing and cocking with both .44s. One long, thunderous roar in the saloon. Son shuddered with each bullet's impact but did not go down. He fired, the bullet striking Jamie on the outside of his left leg, causing him to stagger and lean against the bar for support.

Son was now hanging on to the bar with his left arm, his face and chest bloody. He was still cursing Jamie as he lifted his pistol one last time.

Jamie drilled him in the center of the chest, and Son's gun slipped from numb fingers to clatter on the floor. Son clung to the bar with a death grip, a macabre smile on his bloody face. "Damn you, MacCallister," he gasped. "Damn you to the fiery pits of hell for this."

"You should have stayed out of my town," Jamie told him, leaning against the bar.

"Hell of a time to tell me that," Son whispered. Then he died with his eyes wide open and staring at nothing the living could see.

Jamie stood erect, ignoring the pain in his arm and leg. He reloaded carefully, first his right-hand Colt, then his left-hand Colt.

Bellingham was sketching as fast as he could, squinting against the thick clouds of gunsmoke.

"They was wrong for what they done in Valley, and you was right doing what you did, Mr. MacCallister," a man spoke from the gaming tables. "But you got to give Son his due: he was game to the end."

"That he was," Jamie said.

Son's dead fingers still clung to the edge of the bar, holding him there.

The front door opened, for a moment allowing the cold, late winter winds to blow away the gunsmoke. James William stood there. "Grandpa!" the young man said, moving quickly to Jamie, carefully stepping over the two dead men sprawled on the floor.

"Hello, boy," Jamie said. "I was going to look you up when this shootin' party was over."

"Let's go home, Grandpa," James William said. "I'll get the doctor."

"Sounds good to me, boy."

Jamie and his grandson moved toward the front of the saloon and walked out into the cold night.

"I've seen some shoot-outs in my time," an outlaw said, walking to the bar to stand next to the dead Son Hogg. "But that one was about the best I reckon I've ever seen." He looked into the dead eyes of Son. "You ain't no prettier dead than you was alive, Son. Why don't you just close your eyes and give it up?"

Son's muscles relaxed, and he fell to the floor.

"Well, I'll be goddamned," the outlaw said in amazement. "You reckon he heard me?"


Telegraph wires had finally reached Valley, and the morning after the wild shoot-out, James William sent a telegram to his parents, Ellen Kathleen and William: GRANDPA STAYING WITH US FOR A TIME. SLIGHTLY HURT IN GUNFIGHT. HE'S ALL RIGHT. TAKE THREE MORE OFF THE LIST.

"How many does that make?" Morgan asked Matthew.

"Twenty-one, I think," the sheriff of the county said.

His wife, the former Ginny Hawkins, opened her purse and took out a pad. "Twenty-two," she corrected.

"Well," Falcon said. "Pa's got near'bouts half of them. If he keeps this up, another year and a half and he'll come ridin' back into the valley."

Morgan walked to the window and looked out. "I'm bet-tin' spring will come early this year. All the signs point that-away. Soon as possible, I want flowers planted on Ma's grave. She was always partial to violets." He looked at his sisters. "You reckon you could get violets to grow up yonder, girls?"

"Three or four different kinds, Morgan," Joleen said. "We'll cover her grave with them."

"All different colors?" Morgan asked wistfully.

"All different colors, Morgan," Megan said softly. "White violets, blue violets, and yellow prairie violets."

"Ma would like that," Falcon said. "But the bloomin' time is short. Maybe we could mix in some heart's delight and pussy paws with them. They're right pretty. And I know where they grow. I'll get some come early spring."

"Black-eyed Susans and kittentails, too," Falcon's wife, Marie, said. "And perhaps some paintbrush. I will gather those and sage."

She looked at Falcon, a twinkle in her eyes. "And late this summer, we will have another child."

Falcon stared at her. "*Another* one?"

"Someone needs to tell you how that happens, brother," Matthew said with a laugh.

"Somebody better get you a bundlin' board, brother," Joleen said.

Ellen Kathleen sobered up everybody, real quick, when she held up the telegram from James William. "I didn't read you all of this. Page is with child."

"Damn!" Falcon summed up the feelings of all.


"So you knew all along," Jamie said to Page.

The three of them were sitting in the parlor, overlooking the street, having coffee and cake. Jamie's wounds had been minor, at best, and had healed. He was a hundred percent, but hesitant to leave, since he found he enjoyed Page's com-pany. The young lady had a lot of spunk.

"Since I was a little girl back in Virginia. And James knew long before we were married."

"I just didn't see a problem with it, Grandpa," James William said.

"Well, I think the odds are on your side that the baby will be born white," Jamie said. "But I'm no expert on that subject. I don't know that anyone is. Have you leveled with your doctor, Page?"

"Yes," she said quickly. Then she smiled. "You met him."

Jamie nodded his head. "Yes. Rufus LeBlanc. He has a gentle hand."

"He's Creole, from New Orleans," Page said. "He's Negro, French, and Spanish . . . and maybe some Indian. He isn't sure. He married pure white from around Natchez. They have three children. No problems yet."

Jamie chuckled. "My word, what a mixed-up family the MacCallisters are. Kate and me sure never dreamt of anything like this. But she would be pleased everything turned out so well."

"Have you been back to her grave site, Grandpa?" Page asked softly.

"No. I won't 'til she's avenged. I told her that whilst she was on the Starry Path. She understood."

Which was more than James William and Page did, but they kept silent on the subject.

"When are you due?" Jamie asked Page.

"Late this summer."

"If possible, I'll be back for the birthing," Jamie said. "But don't count on it 'til you see me."

Jamie looked at the young people, first at James William, then at Page. "If the baby is, ah, not white, you know that you have a home in Valley. Little things like that don't cause much of a stir there."

Tears sprang into Page's eyes. She leaned forward and kissed Jamie's cheek. "Thank you, Grandpa."

\* \* \*

On an unusually warm day in late February, Jamie rode out of Denver. James William and Page were sorry to see him go, but not the authorities. They all breathed a collective sigh of relief when Jamie saddled up and pulled out.

Jamie traveled east and slightly north, heading for a small community on the South Platte River, about thirty miles south of the Nebraska line. It had started life as a trading post, and now was a small town of about four hundred souls. Fort Sedgwick was only a few miles from the town; but it was in the process of being deactivated as a military garrison, and most of its troops were gone, having been assigned to other forts. Fort Sedgwick was established in 1864 and abandoned on the last day of May, 1871, when the federal government decided, incorrectly, that all Indian trouble in that area was over.

But it wasn't Indian trouble that was coming toward the quiet little town.

It was Jamie Ian MacCallister.

Jamie Ian the Third was courting Mary Marie O'Donnell with all his might. It had taken him some time to convince the Irish lass that he was neither retarded nor spastic, but after that misunderstanding was corrected, the two were very nearly inseparable.

On the late winter afternoon that Jamie Ian the Second and his wife, the former Caroline Hankins, found the couple groping each other in the hayloft, both of them red-faced and breathing like hard-run racehorses, a wedding was promptly planned.

"Disgraceful," Caroline said. "I don't know what this younger generation is coming to."

"The next thing you know, ladies will be smoking," Jamie Ian the Second said.

"Pitiful," Caroline agreed.

The wedding was planned for March, 1871. And it was a very good thing it was, for Mary Marie gave birth to twins, a boy and a girl, exactly five months after the wedding.

"We'll just say the babies were slightly premature," Dr. Tom Prentiss said drily.

*"Premature!"* Falcon blurted. "Hell, the babies weigh damn near ten pounds each!"

That got him a dirty look and a thumb in his ribs from his wife.

"Right," Falcon got the message. "Premature. Lucky we saved them. Touch and go all the way."

"Red hair and blue eyes," Joleen said with a smile, looking down at the twins.

It would be months later before Jamie learned that he was a great-grandfather . . . again.

Jamie's horse woke him with a soft nicker about an hour before dawn. Jamie could just make out the sounds of walking horses from his camp under a bluff on the north side of the South Platte. He rolled out of his blankets and pulled on his boots. Picking up his rifle, he slipped over to his horses and petted them, quieting them. Then he moved closer to the river and squatted down.

Four mounted men and two packhorses. The men carried their rifles at the ready. Jamie moved closer to the river in an attempt to catch any bit of conversation.

"How much further is this place?" the sound drifted to Jamie. "I'm tarred and want some sleep."

"Quit your grousin', Coots," was the reply. "It ain't far. Where the Pawnee runs into the Platte's only a few miles ahead. I figure we're two days ahead of him. Ample time to rest and set up the ambush. Now be quiet."

The four men rode on, and Jamie returned to his campsite. He didn't figure there were too many men with the last name of Coots, and Coots rode with the Miles Nelson gang. If the information his detectives had supplied him with was correct, Coots always teamed up with Cal Myers, Mario Nunez, and Cuba Fagan when the gang wasn't working at their nefarious trade.

And Jamie had no doubts about who the ambush was for. Him.

Jamie had stopped off in Fort Morgan about a week back and had been certain he was recognized by a couple of hard cases loafing outside the saloon. Those drifters had passed the word along the hoot-owl trail.

Jamie waited for a time, then checked the slight breeze. It was blowing north to south, so the smell of coffee and frying bacon and pan bread would not be picked up by those riding east. Jamie fixed his breakfast and then packed up and pulled out. He headed north for a few miles, then cut due east at a steady, distance-covering gait.

Coots and his buddies wanted an ambush, did they? All right, he'd give them one.

But it wouldn't be the kind they had in mind.

Ben F. Washington lingered for a few days in St. Louis, a few more days in Kansas City, and finally arrived in Denver. After renting a small house, he made arrangements to see James William and Page.

Page was in the yard when the carriage let him out in front of the house. Ben saw that his sister was with child, and he sighed heavily.

"Oh, Page," he muttered. "Do you realize what a chance you are taking?"

James William came out of the house to stand by his wife's side. Both of them stood silently, looking at the young man standing by the side of the road.

Ben approached the handsome young couple slowly, not at all certain what his reception was going to be. James William was the son of a MacCallister, after all, and his temper just might be volatile.

MacCallisters were not known for their gentle, loving ways when angered.

As Ben approached the couple, Page smiled and held out a hand. "Welcome, brother. What took you so long?"

Ben stopped cold in his tracks, too stunned to speak.

# 12

Jamie crossed the Platte southwest of the junction with the Pawnee and found a quiet and secluded place to picket his horses. There was plenty of graze and water, and they could eventually break loose should he not return.

And that was always a possibility.

He removed his boots and slipped on moccasins, laced up his leggins, then packed him a small bait of food and slung his canteen over one shoulder. He picked up his rifle and headed out. He did not have to check his ammo belts, for out of long habit he always kept the loops filled.

He smelled their smoke before he had walked two miles.

They obviously felt safe against being detected, for the wind was blowing out of the south-southwest, carrying the smell away from travelers coming from that direction.

The outlaws were anything but safe.

At that very moment, almost two thousand miles away, in New York City, the editor was studying the sketches of John A. Bellingham. Bellingham had redrawn them to size before sending them east by train. The editor decided to use them as an example of how frontier justice and the code of honor worked in the Wild West . . . with an editorial, of course, about how the West needed to be tamed and how guns should be banned (a hundred and twenty-five years later the same newspaper—and several hundred other liberal rags—would still be blathering and blithering about those awful, terrible, dreadful guns).

The drawings were excellently done, and they were very dramatic, depicting the barroom gunfight just as he actually witnessed it happening: Jamie standing at one end of the bar, both guns blazing. Two men down and dying on the dirty saloon floor, and Son Hogg dying but still trying to shoot as he leaned against the bar.

The editor frowned in thought, then smiled as he leaned back in his chair. He knew just how to caption the drawing: THE CODE OF THE WEST.


Jamie worked his way down a wash, his moccasins making no sound as he moved ever closer to the outlaw camp. He personally knew none of these men he was stalking, but he knew them all well by their foul reputations.

Of these four men, Cuba Fagan was the worst . . . by far. Cuba was wanted by every marshal and sheriff west of the Mississippi River. There was no deed so dark he wouldn't do or hadn't done. And the man who called himself Coots was just about as bad. Mario Nunez had killed his first man at age twelve, his father, and hadn't stopped killing since. Cal Myers was both a murderer and a rapist . . . many times over.

For a man to have come from such a highly respected and refined family, and to be himself so well educated, Miles Nelson had gathered together some of the most odious and evil men in all the country.

Miles Nelson and his various gangs might have gone on to become as well-known (and among some both loved and respected) as the James or Younger boys. But he had made one terrible mistake: he and his gangs had attacked Valley, Colorado, and killed Kate MacCallister.

Jamie had sworn to wipe the Miles Nelson gangs from the face of the earth . . . and he was saving Miles for last. Dessert, you might say.

When Jamie had the outlaw camp in sight, about three hundred yards away, he paused and drank from his canteen. Then he wiped the dust from his guns and levered a round into his rifle, easing the hammer down. He bellied down on the ground and began crawling toward the muted sounds of conversation and food smells.

In his mind, Jamie had reverted back to his boyhood, when he lived with the Shawnees, learning the Warrior's Way. He became one with the earth as he inched his way toward the camp. His eyes were blue and watchful, unblinking flint.

During the next hour, the men in the camp looked in his direction a dozen or more times, but never saw him as he worked his way across the flats toward the wallow where they were. Like so many others, the outlaws looked, but did not see.

For his size, Jamie could move like a huge snake, making no more sound than a gentle breeze across the land.

Jamie had closed the distance to less than fifty feet when he decided that was close enough. He could smell the unwashed bodies of the four men, and wondered how they could stand themselves. The white man talked about the dirty Indians, but the Indians Jamie knew were careful about hygiene, many times breaking the ice in a stream to bathe. In their wickiups and tipis, fragrant sage or other incense-like dried plants were always burning. They aired their robes and bedding, and their personal needs were taken care of away from the camp.

The four men that Jamie now looked at, unknowingly sitting and squatting and lying so close to their graves, were a disgrace to the human race in general.

Jamie decided to do something about that.

Right now.

He stood up and eared back the hammer of his rifle.

"You boys waiting for me?" he called.

The man called Coots jumped up. "MacCallister!" he screamed, and clawed for his pistol.

Jamie shot him in the belly, doubling him over and dropping him to the dirt.

Cal Myers managed to reach his rifle before Jamie dusted him and knocked him to one side.

Mario Nunez got off one shot that went wild before Jamie put a .44 round in the man's chest.

Jamie had been walking as he waged war, levering and shooting his Winchester.

Cuba Fagan jerked both his guns from leather just as Mario fell against him, knocking him off balance. Both of Cuba's shots missed their mark, and Jamie shot him twice, belly and chest. Cuba sank to his knees, cocked both pistols, but could not bring them up. He pulled the triggers and shot himself in both legs. He fell over on one side and died with a scream on his lips.

Jamie walked into the camp, shoving rounds into his rifle as he went. He stood over Coots and kicked his pistols out of reach.

"You got to be the luckiest man alive." Coots gasped the words through the searing pain in his belly.

Jamie grunted his reply and turned to Nunez. The Mexican was fading fast. He spoke in rapid Spanish, the blood spraying from his lips, calling Jamie some really bad names.

Jamie smiled at him—a hard curving of the lips.

Mario reached for a derringer behind his belt buckle, and Jamie kicked the little over-and-under belly gun away. Mario Nunez died with a curse on his lips.

Cal Myers had been shot through and through, from left side to right side, and his eyes were bright with pain, his lips bloody with a pink froth. "You gonna bury us proper-like, MacCallister? Say a word or two over us?"

"I might do that for you," Jamie told him, squatting down and picking up a tin cup. He rinsed it out carefully with water from his own canteen before filling it with coffee from the battered and blackened pot which had been sitting on the rocks around the outlaw fire. He took a sip and grimaced. It was awful. Jamie threw the foul liquid away, cup and all.

"I wush to hell I'd never heared your name," Cal said. "You a goddamn devil, that's what you are. You come straight out of hell, MacCallister."

"That's an area you're going to be very familiar with in a few minutes, Cal."

Cal cussed him.

"Where is Miles Nelson?" Jamie asked, rinsing out the coffeepot and making fresh coffee.

"You go to hell, MacCallister," Coots gasped.

"Yeah. Go to hell, MacCallister," Cal said.

"You boys sure have a limited vocabulary. Ten minutes of conversation with you would put me to sleep." He looked at Coots. "And ten minutes is about all the time you have left."

"You're the meanest bastard I ever seen," Coots groaned out the words. "Here we is dyin', and you sit there makin' coffee and insultin' us."

"What the hell do you want me to do, kiss you?"

"You got any laudanum?"

"You'll be dead by the time it took effect. Then you won't hurt anymore. So quit worrying about it."

Cal cussed him again, long and hard. The outlaw abruptly ceased his cussing and took a ragged breath. Then he slumped back and did not move.

"He's dead, ain't he?" Coots asked.

"Either that or awfully relaxed."

"You the coldest man I ever seen in my life."

"Not as cold as my Kate is, you sorry lowlife no good goddamn son of a bitch!"

The venom behind Jamie's words widened the outlaw's eyes. He forgot his pain for a moment. "He's in Canada," Coots said. "But I don't know 'xactly where."

Jamie cut his eyes. "Miles?"

"Yeah. He has him a fine home up there somewheres. But

I'm tellin' you the truth 'bout me not knowin' where up yonder it is. Is it gettin' dark around here, MacCallister?"

"Yes," Jamie lied to the dying man. "Storm's coming, I reckon." The sun was shining brightly, and there were only high, wispy clouds in the blue sky. "Does he go by his Christian name up there?"

"Sort of." The outlaw spat out a mouthful of blood. "Goes by the name of Nelson Miles. He thinks . . . that's funny. He's supposed to be some sort of big, important man up yonder. I can't see, MacCallister."

"I'll give you a proper burial, Coots."

"Thanks. More'un I deserve, I suppose."

"You have anyone you want me to write?"

"No. Not nobody that would be interested. I burnt my bridges a long time back."

The water in the old pot was beginning to boil, so Jamie dumped in grounds and then added a dash of cold water to settle the grounds. He poured two cups of coffee and placed one on the ground by Coots.

"Thanks, that's right decent of you. But I don't think I'm gonna have time to drink it. It's so awful dark. MacCallister?"

Jamie looked at the man.

The outlaw's eyes were looking up at the sky, seeing things that he alone could see. "I . . . oh, hello, Daddy," he said dreamily. "How you been? Yeah?" Coots grinned in a macabre sort of way. "Well, I guess you was right about me, Daddy."

Then he shuddered, closed his eyes, and died without saying another word.

Jamie wondered what Coots' father had said to his son before the boy had left home?

"Probably that he'd never amount to a hill of beans," Jamie muttered.

Jamie sat for a time, drinking his coffee, looking around the camp for a shovel. There was none, so he walked back and got his horses. Unlashing his spade, he dug a hole wide enough for the four of them and deep enough so the varmints wouldn't dig them up and eat them. Before planting the outlaws, Jamie took their ammunition and what money they had on them . . . which wasn't much. The cash money and gold taken from the robbery back in Valley was almost gone.

Before he shoveled the dirt over them, he noticed that the clothing of the men was ripped and torn and patched, and their boots weren't anything to write home about.

"The glamorous life of an outlaw," he muttered.

He buried the four men and stood for a time, then removed his hat. He knew he should say something, but he just couldn't find the words.

"Lord, if I knew anything good to say about these men, I'd say it." He put his hat back on his head. "But I don't. Amen."

# 13

"I'm simply flabbergasted," Ben said, setting his coffee cup on the chair-side table. "You knew all along."

"Ever since I was old enough to understand," Page replied. "Oh, I don't blame mother for hiding it. Had the knowledge leaked out, she would have been ruined. Negroes couldn't own property. But you must remember this, Ben: our mother and uncle are very ruthless people. There is no doubt in my mind but what they tried to kill you . . . several times. And now that they know you're back in Denver, and have been to see me—and they will know all that—my life is in danger as well."

Ben gave that some thought. "You're right about that. What are your plans?"

"To stay here," James William said quickly. "If we possibly can."

"That hinges on the child?" Ben was very quick.

"Yes," his sister told him.

"Well," Ben said, standing up. "I won't visit again. I will not be responsible for upsetting any more apple carts."

"You can visit whenever you like, brother," Page told him.

Ben shook his head. "No. But thank you. I shall stay here in Denver for a time; then I'll go to Valley. I want to start my book about Jamie and Kate MacCallister. Theirs is a story that must be told."

"Have you a title yet?" James William asked.

"Yes. I think I shall call it *Rage of Eagles.*"


"I don't want trouble in my town, MacCallister," the marshal told Jamie.

Jamie had just left the saddle when the marshal, the mayor, and several townspeople approached him.

He turned to face them. "If the men I'm looking for are here, there will be trouble, and you won't run me out of town, either. Not unless you want the streets to run red with blood . . . and most of it won't be mine."

The men exchanged glances, uncertain as to what to do next. After all, this was Jamie Ian MacCallister, a man of whom countless stories had been told from coast to coast and border to border, and all of them true.

"Mr. MacCallister," the marshal said, softening his tone and becoming much more respectful. "Two of the men you're looking for are in town. Reed Dunlap and Alonzo Barton. But they aren't wanted by any law around here, and I have no dodgers on them. They've rented a small house on the edge of town, and have caused no trouble."

"They attend my church," a tall, skinny man all dressed in severe black with high collar said. "They have found the Lord."

"They're damn sure going to meet Him," Jamie told the preacher. "A hell of a lot sooner than they imagined."

"You are not God's avenging angel," the preacher said. "You have no right to do this."

"And Reed and Barton had no right to attack my town, killing a dozen people, including my wife, and wounding twenty more, and that includes small children. Now get the hell out of my way. I want to stable my horses, take a bath, and have something to eat."

"I'll call the federal marshals," the mayor threatened.

"You do that. By the time they get here, I'll have settled

my score and be a hundred miles away." He looked at the marshal. "You just get the women and kids off the street."

No man could be a coward and be the marshal of a western town. And the marshal was no coward. But he did have his share of common sense. "When I heard you were on your way here, I sent those two men out of town. They'll stay gone until you leave."

"No, they won't," Jamie told the man. "They'll be slipping back in the dead of night to ambush me, kill me while I sleep, or back shoot me. Or they might decide to face me in the street. The rest of you men might not realize that, but the marshal does. A skunk don't lose its stripe just 'cause it gets tired of it, preacher. You ought to be worldly enough to know that."

"The Lord will punish you for this, Jamie Ian MacCallister," the preacher predicted.

"Then that's between me and Him, isn't it?" Jamie took his saddlebags, bedroll, and rifle, and pushed his way through the knot of townspeople. "Excuse me," he said, and walked toward the town's single hotel.

Reed Dunlap and Alonzo Barton were wanted for murder in Texas and Louisiana. They had robbed and raped and killed for more than ten years, and now they had both changed their evil ways and were big workers in the church?

Sure. Right.

But Jamie decided he'd better shave and bathe quickly, for he had him a hunch that word would get to the pair of outlaws shortly . . . and it just might get there through the preacher or some of his flock.

Jamie bathed with his guns close by the tub and then shaved himself instead of seeking out a barber shop. He did not want to be stretched out in the barber chair with a hot towel over his face when Reed and Barton decided to make their play.

It was mid-afternoon and warm when Jamie stepped out of the hotel and took a seat on a bench under the awning over the boardwalk. School was out, and the word had spread about his being in town. Kids began to gather to his left and right and in a bunch across the street, gawking at him.

The marshal ambled up and took a seat on the bench beside him. He took off his hat and wiped his forehead with a red bandanna. "Gettin' warm early, ain't it, Mr. MacCallister?"

"Seems that way. Marshal? Was I you, I'd tell the women to get these kids off the street. A carelessly thrown bullet doesn't care who it hits."

"Reed and Barton won't be comin' in, Mr. MacCallister. They have changed their ways."

"They'll be here, Marshal. And they'll come shooting."

The marshal was thoughtful for a moment, then waved one of his men over and told him to shoo the kids home. He turned to Jamie and asked, "Did you really know Jim Bowie and Davy Crockett?"

"For a few days. They were good men. Every man there was a good and brave man."

"The fight at the Alamo seems a long time away, Mr. MacCallister. I was just a small boy back in Missouri when all that took place."

"Been a lot of changes since then, for sure."

"The coming of law and order for one thing, Mr. MacCallister," the marshal said softly.

Jamie smiled. "Reed and Barton are wanted all over the West, Marshal. For rape, robbery, and murder. And you know it. Why don't you arrest them and notify the authorities?"

"Because they are not wanted here, Mr. MacCallister. And they have broken no laws here. Men can change, sir."

"Yes. They can. But there is a little matter of punishment for past sins, don't you agree?"

Jamie had the marshal with that one, and the marshal knew it. He offered no response to the question. He could only shake his head.

The marshal rose to his boots and looked up and down

the now nearly deserted street. He let out a long sigh. "Well, it's on your head, then, Mr. MacCallister. And the blood spilled will be on your hands."

"I wash my hands several times a day, Marshal. And they'll be clean when I ride out of town."

"*If* you ride out of town, Mr. MacCallister. Have you given that any thought?"

Jamie's only reply was a smile. His eyes had already picked up two riders coming in from the east. "I'll give you odds those riders are your good and decent Reed and Barton, Marshal. And they're coming in loaded for bear. Would you like to take that bet?"

The marshal's eyes were bleak. "You gave them no choice, Mr. MacCallister. You know how people in the West feel about a coward."

"I know how I feel about murderers and thieves and rapists. And as a lawman, you should feel the same way."

The marshal gave no reply to that. He turned and walked away, his boots clumping on the boards.

The two riders were now clearly recognizable as they reined up in front of the livery and stepped down from the saddle. Jamie watched with amused interest as Reed and Barton took rifles from the saddle boots.

The outlaws began walking up the center of the wide, wheelrutted, and dusty street. They stopped directly in front of the hotel to turn and face Jamie, who had risen to his feet, his Colts loose in leather.

The minister, the marshal, and the mayor were standing about fifty feet away, to Jamie's right, in front of a general store with a crudely carved wooden Indian on guard out front.

"How nice to see you boys," Jamie said. "It's always a pleasure to see men who have made such a drastic change in their lives and accepted the Lord and been washed in the blood of the lamb. I reckon you boys have given up your drinking and whoring and thieving and raping and murdering, right?" The sarcasm fairly dripped from his mouth.

Reed cussed Jamie, the vile words springing from his mouth. The minister stood and gawked in disbelief as the filth rolled over the outlaw's tongue.

"My, my, my," Jamie chided the men. "That is no way for a good Christian man to talk. Aren't you ashamed of yourself?"

It was Barton's turn to cuss, and cuss he did, tracing Jamie's ancestry all the way back to the trees and caves, the route liberally sprinkled with profanities.

"My word!" the gangly minister blurted.

"Tsk, tsk, tsk," Jamie said. "I'm plumb ashamed of you boys. You ought to have your mouths washed out with soap. The minister yonder had such high hopes for the both of you."

"I am deeply offended," the minister said to the pair of outlaws.

Barton told him to stick his Bible where the sun don't shine, and Reed added that there might be room there for his buffalo-butted wife, too.

Jamie cut his eyes and had to laugh at the expression on the minister's face. He looked as though someone had just goosed him with a hot branding iron.

"You think this is funny, you son of a bitch?" Reed yelled at Jamie.

"Mildly amusing, yes. You sure pulled the wool over these folks' eyes. How much of the money you helped steal from the Valley Bank and the stage line do you have left?"

"Enough to buy some whoors and celebrate and get drunk after we kill you, MacCallister," Barton said.

"Well, then, you got a mighty big mountain to get over, boys. So why don't you start climbing?"

Jamie's eyes were on the faces of the outlaws; all else was ignored. He heard the minister begin praying, but the words were indistinct. The mayor was saying something, but his words were garbled in Jamie's ears. Time seemed to stand still. The marshal was urging the men to give it up; they'd get a fair trial. If dogs barked, birds sang, or horses whinnied, the sound did not register on Jamie. His concentration was all on the outlaws standing in the street.

Then their expressions changed, and Jamie knew they were going to make their play.

Reed's rifle came up, and Jamie palmed his Colt and fired, the bullet taking Reed in the chest, knocking him to his knees. As soon as he fired, Jamie shifted positions, taking several steps to his right.

Barton's rifle barked, the bullet slamming into the awning post. Jamie fired, the lead hitting Barton about two inches above the belt buckle, the impact turning him in the street.

"We should have burned your damn town to the ground!" Barton hollered. "After we had our way with your females."

Jamie's .44 roared again, and Barton joined his buddy in the dirt, sitting down hard and losing his grip on the Henry rifle.

Reed lifted his pistol and fired, the hot lead burning Jamie's shoulder. Jamie ignored the burning pain and the wetness of blood oozing from the wound and shifted his Colt and pulled the trigger. Reed stretched out full-length in the street and did not move.

A photographer's flash pan popped off to Jamie's left, and the muted mini-explosion almost got the picture taker shot, Jamie holding back at the last instant.

"I'll see you in hell, MacCallister!" Barton yelled, lifting his pistol.

"Say hello to your buddies when you get there," Jamie calmly and coldly told him, then drew his left-hand Colt and fired both pistols, the twin bullets striking the outlaw in the chest.

Barton said no more. He died sitting up and remained that way for a few seconds before toppling over in the dirt. Jamie reloaded and stood for a moment, looking at the bodies in the street.

To his dying day, Jamie could not explain why he did it, but as he stood on the boardwalk that afternoon, the gunsmoke lingering all about him, he let the hammers down on his Colts and spun them a couple of times before sliding them back into leather.

Just as Jamie spun the heavy Colts, the photographer's flash pan popped again. That picture would be shown from coast to coast and border to border. The tall, gray-haired, but still very handsome man, spinning his twin Colts seconds after leaving two outlaws dead in the street.

Jamie Ian MacCallister would forever be epitomized as the stereotyped western gunfighter. From the moment the picture was shown, hundreds of young men began dressing like Jamie, wearing their guns like Jamie, cutting their hair like Jamie, trimming their moustaches like Jamie, and doing their best to be just like him in every way possible.

Jamie turned and walked into the hotel, cutting to his left toward the bar. A very nervous bartender served him whiskey, from the good bottle usually reserved for the mayor, the banker, and rich ranchers in the area.

Jamie took a piece of paper from his jacket pocket and carefully unfolded it. Taking a pencil, he drew a line through two names.

The bartender heard him mutter, "Twenty-eight down, twenty-seven to go."

That muttered phrase, and the pictures and later hundreds of drawings of them, would blast out of the small northeastern Colorado town, scattering like birdshot in all directions.

While Jamie lingered over his whiskey, the bodies of Alonzo Barton and Reed Dunlap were carried off the street and to the undertaker, to be measured for a close coffin fit and planted the next day.

Jamie returned to the hotel and told the desk clerk to send up pen, ink, and paper, and retired to his room. He spent the rest of the afternoon writing letters, leaving them with the front desk to be posted as soon as possible.

Jamie told the marshal to use the money found in the pockets of the dead men to pay for their funeral and maybe hire several mourners and wailers for the service. Jamie knew he had recovered all of the stolen money he was likely to find. After almost two years at the hunt, that money would be spent.

Just before the stores closed for the night, Jamie bought supplies for the trail, checked on his horses, and then went back to his room. He was gone when the town awakened the next morning. Not even the night constable had seen him leave, and no one had any idea where he might have gone.

Exactly as Jamie had planned it.

# 14

The small Nebraska town just north of Julesburg was not known for being any haven for outlaws during the growing period of the West. Perhaps that was the very reason that three members of the Miles Nelson gang chose the town to reside in for a few months during the spring of '71.

But it wouldn't do them much good.

The three outlaws had taken up residence in the abandoned cabin of a homesteader who couldn't make a go of it and had gone back east. Roy Bellar, Carl Dews, and Jack Moore rustled a beeve every now and then—but never, if they could help it, from the same rancher or farmer—and in general kept a very low profile, going into town only occasionally for beans, salt, bacon, flour, tobacco, and what not.

When the marshal of the town saw Jamie ride in one sunny mid-morning, he wisely decided to make himself as inconspicuous as possible. The marshal was by no means a coward, just a very prudent man who had a wife and several kids to look after. And after seeing Jamie MacCallister ride into town, he quickly reached the conclusion that it would be very difficult to take care of one's family from the grave.

The lawman returned to his office, made a fresh pot of coffee, and waited for Jamie to pay him a visit.

It was not a long wait.

The marshal had never seen Jamie up close, just heard

stories about him all his life. When Jamie opened the door, the marshal winced at the size of the man. He was about sixty years old, the marshal accurately guessed, but still one hell of a man, and not one the lawman would want to tangle with.

"Just thought I'd stop by and howdy and shake with you, Marshal," Jamie said.

"Pleasure is all mine, Mr. MacCallister. I've been hearin' about you all my life. Have some coffee—it's fresh made— and sit."

Coffee poured, Jamie sat down and came right to the point. "You've got three outlaws living outside of town, Marshal. Part of the old Miles Nelson gang."

"Really?"

"Yes."

"You want me to go arrest them?" the marshal asked, with about as much enthusiasm as a man facing the prospect of an impacted wisdom tooth.

"I want you to keep the peace in town and let me handle the outlaws."

"Be my guest," the marshal quickly agreed to the suggestion. "You'll not get no interference from me."

"Fine," Jamie said with a smile. "What's the best place to eat in town?"

"Rosie's. Right next to the hotel."

Jamie drained his coffee cup and stood up. "Thanks for the coffee, Marshal. I'll see you around."

"I 'magine."

Jamie paused at the door and smiled. "But not if you're lucky, you're thinking."

"Nobody blames you for your hunt, Mr. MacCallister. At least, not nobody I ever talked to. The Nelson gang hit North Platte 'bout three years ago, robbin' and killin.' It was just after the railroad had pushed through. There ain't nobody 'round here gonna shed any tears if you kill three or a hundred and three or three hundred and three of that gang. But I do worry about the women and the kids."

"When it comes time, you'll know to clear the streets, Marshal. I'll make sure of that."

"Fair enough. You enjoy your meal, Mr. MacCallister. There's a bathhouse right behind the Chinaman's laundry. Lots of hot water, and the towels are clean."

"Thanks."

After his bath, while his good clothes were being aired and then ironed, Jamie sat in his hotel room and carefully cleaned his guns, then rubbed oil into the pockets of his holsters. He knew it would not be long before word of his arrival reached the three outlaws.

But this time the outlaws didn't brace Jamie—they ran.

Shortly after the photograph of the shoot-out taken in the small town just outside of Fort Sedgwick began circulating, several events occurred that would, in time, alter the lives of the residents of Valley, Colorado. The three young men from back east, Marshall Henry Ludlow, Richard Farnsworth, and Charles Bennett, left their wives (and their girlfriends) in Denver, hired a guide and several bodyguards, and ventured off into the wilds of Colorado, heading for Valley. They had heard about land for the taking around there, and their fathers had ordered them to check it out and if it looked promising, buy it or make arrangements to lease it from the government.

The second event, this one directly affecting Jamie, involved the kin of Bradford, Newby, Layfield, Olmstead, and several other men whose families had been involved in the hunting of Jamie and Kate decades back. Most of these men had not yet been born when their ancestors were chasing Jamie. Those original family members were buried in graves that stretched from Kentucky to Colorado.

And now their distant relatives had taken up the hunt.

As Morgan MacCallister said when he heard the news, "Seems like these people would learn to leave Pa alone after a while."

The third event that would affect both Jamie and the people in Valley was the arrival in town of Ben F. Washington. The first impression that settled in Ben's brain when he stepped out of the stagecoach was that he had never seen so damn many blond-haired and blue-eyed people in all his life, all mixed in with Chinese, Negroes, and people of Indian and Spanish descent.

But they were all friendly and courteous and helpful, pointing out the hotel and the sheriff's office and the office of the local newspaper.

Ben checked into the hotel and then went to the sheriff's office. It did not surprise him one whit to learn that a Mac-Callister was the sheriff of the county, for in previous research he had discovered that the MacCallisters were the controlling power in not just this county, but also in several counties surrounding Valley.

Ben knew that he would have to walk light until the people learned that he was not here to upset any apple carts, but to write the true and unbiased story of Jamie and Kate MacCallister.

When Ben stepped into the sheriff's office, he pulled up short at the sight of Falcon MacCallister, sitting at a desk, smiling at him.

"Hello, Ben," the gambler/gunfighter with the cold pale eyes said. "We've been waiting for you."


When two days had passed uneventfully, Jamie saddled up and headed out in the country. He asked questions at each farm and ranch house and soon began piecing the puzzle together. He rode over to the old homesteader's shack and found the signs of three men—three men who had very recently and very hurriedly packed up and hauled their asses. Their tracks headed north, toward the North Platte River. Jamie memorized the horses' hoofprints, rode back to town and checked out of the hotel. A few minutes later he was on the outlaws' trail.

A few days later, Jamie knew where they were heading: to the trading post on the North Platte, west of Chimney Rock and just north of the Wildcat Hills area. It would be years after the coming shoot-out at the trading post before the area would be settled, blocked out, and known as Scottsbluff.

On the third day out, Jamie reined up and swung down, studying the tracks. Three more men had joined the trio, riding up from the south.

"Six at one pop," Jamie muttered to the warm winds of spring that blew gently around him. "This will be interesting."

Jamie built a small fire and put water on to boil. He went to his pack and took out the derringer he'd taken from Mario Nunez and checked it out, firing it several times. It was accurate up to about twelve or fifteen feet; after that, there was no telling where the bullet might go. He loaded both barrels and tucked it behind his sash.

Jamie fried bacon and made pan bread, then took his time eating and drinking the strong coffee. The North Platte River murmured a few hundred yards away.

Jamie wondered what month it might be, and decided it must be April . . . or maybe early May. He'd lost track of time. One thing he did know for sure: the remaining members of the Miles Nelson gang were getting panicky. In about eighteen months, Jamie had cut their gang size by nearly half, leaving a trail of blood and bodies behind him. Those remaining were running scared.

With damn good reason, Jamie thought darkly. Without realizing it was happening, his face had hardened and his eyes turned cold at his thoughts.

Jamie was reaching for the coffeepot when he heard the whisper of moccasins on grass. He threw himself to one side, grabbing up his rifle on the roll.

"Whoa, now!" the voice called. "Just take 'er easy, big feller. I'm friendly. Smelled your coffee a-bilin' and your meat a-cookin'. I don't mean no harm to no man."

"Come on in. But sneaking up on me is not the healthiest thing to do."

As the man led his horses into camp, his age was difficult to guess. Jamie thought he might be anywhere from a badly used sixty to a well-preserved ninety.

Jamie pointed to the coffeepot, and the old man squatted down with a grunt and poured a tin cup full, then sat back and sipped and sighed contentedly.

"Help yourself to some bacon and bread," Jamie told him. "I can always cook more."

"Right nice of you, MacCallister. Neighborly."

"Do I know you?"

"You look just like your grandpa. I knowed him in his declinin' years, boy . . ."

Jamie smiled. He hadn't been called "boy" in years.

"Then years 'fore you and your family come west, I went out to Californee. Got married to a Mex woman and was happy right up 'til the day she passed over. That were . . . oh, 'bout 1840, I reckon. Then I come back to the mountains. I been to St. Louie this time, for the last time, I reckon."

"You don't plan on going back?" Jamie squatted down and refilled his coffee cup.

"Nope. But I do plan on dyin'. Hell, I'm *old,* boy. I were borned 'fore the turn of the century. 1785, I think it was. That would make me . . . what year is this, anyways?"

"1871."

"Well, then, let me see. That would make me eighty-six year old, boy. Don't you think it's 'bout time for me to see the elephant?"

"You going to pick your own time and place, huh?"

The old man smiled. He didn't have a tooth in his mouth. "Something like that." He tapped his chest. "Bad ticker. Docs say I could go anytime. But I'll make it back to the mountains. Even as much as I loved that Mex woman, I always missed the High Lonesome."

"I know the feeling. You have a name?"

"Shore. Ever'body's got a handle. Mine's Jefferson Washburn. Ain't that a mouthful? But I been called any number of names. I'll answer to near'bouts anything."

"How did you manage to slip up on me, Jeff?"

The old man cackled. "Son, when I furst come out here, there *wasn't* no other white man that I knowed of where I was. Hell, Bridger wasn't even born when I come out here. Your grandpa was out here, but me and him didn't cross trails 'til some years later. Man had to be able to slip up on folks to stay alive. But, I'll be truthful with you. My horses was down yonder in them river trees, and I was takin' me a snooze when them outlaws met up with three other bad-lookin' ol' boys. They done some real ugly talkin' 'bout you. You know where they's headed, don't you?"

"Trading post by the bluffs."

"That's right."*

The old man made him a bread and bacon sandwich and wolfed it down with no difficulty . . . despite his having no teeth. He poured another cup of coffee, settled back, and put his old wise eyes on Jamie.

"How old are you, young feller?"

Jamie chuckled at the "young feller" bit. "Sixty, I think."

"And you're going to tackle all six of these hombres by your lonesome, hey?"

"That's my plan."

The old man grunted. "They readin' about you in all the big cities, boy. Some folks is callin' for the government to send people in to arrest you. Some of them newspaper writers, they writin' articles that say you're wrong in doin' what you do. They say what you're doin' is barbaric and you ought to be stopped. What do you think about that?"

"I really don't give a damn what others think about it."

The old man chuckled at that.

"My own son tried to lecture me about law and order,"

*Scotts Bluff National Monument is named for Hiram Scott, a fur trapper and explorer.

Jamie said. "Just a few hours after his ma was shot and killed by these very highwaymen and trash."*

"Well, that don't surprise me none. This younger generation is goin' to hell in a hand basket. No respect for their elders. Why, hell, I seen a woman smokin' a cigarette in St. Louis." The old trapper stood up with an ease that belied his age. "I'm fixin' to cut south now, boy. Head for the Lodgepole, cross the Grasslands and on into the mountains. Thank you kindly for the coffee and the grub. Good luck to you, MacCallister."

Jamie lifted a hand in farewell.

The old man turned and looked at him. "One of them bastards you're chasin' is Hulon Nations. He's got a big, bushy black beard. And he's a bad one, boy. Lightnin' quick with them guns. 'Bout half crazy, I think. He's been around awhile. He ain't no spring chicken. I heared another one called Tim and the third one was called Ray."

"Tim Sandberg and Ray Reynolds."

"I reckon that's them. But I know one thing for certain: they're all lowlifes and scum and trash. Fifty years ago, we used to hang people like that right on the spot. This civilization and progress people jaw about just ain't what it's cracked up to be, boy. And to my way of thinkin' it's just gonna get worser and worser. I'm glad my string is just about played out. I think this nation is doomed to fall like the Roman Empire."

Jefferson Washburn turned and walked off toward the river. Jamie lingered over his coffee until the old trapper had emerged from the trees and was riding south. He did not look back.

Jamie carefully doused his fire and rinsed out the coffeepot and frying pan. As he swung into the saddle and pointed Buck's nose toward the Bluffs, he recalled an old line about the number six.

"Kill 'em all 'cept six. Save them for pallbearers."

* *Talons of Eagles*—Kensington Books

# 15

"And I own a small cabin on the edge of town that you can use just as long as you like," Megan told a very stunned Ben F. Washington. "I think the story of Ma and Pa is one that should be told, honestly and truthfully."

Ben cleared his throat and found his voice. "I will have to interview all of the children extensively. And that will take some time. And I will have to have access to all of your parents' papers and notes."

"You can talk to us all you want," Morgan said. "But you'll have to have Pa's permission to read all the letters and diaries and such. And Ma kept a record of everything that went on from the time she first met Pa, back in Kentucky, I think it was."

"Yes," Joleen said. "That was right after Pa and Hannah escaped from that Shawnee village where they'd been held prisoner."

Ben leaned forward, his eyes alive with excitement, pad and pencil ready. "Tell me what you know about that," he urged. "I want to get everyone's perspective on everything."

"That's gonna take some time," Falcon said with a grin, cutting his eyes to Joleen. "Especially when she starts runnin' her mouth."

Joleen smiled sweetly. "And I have a few things I can tell Mr. Washington about you, too, brother."

"Oh, hell," Falcon muttered.

"I'll make fresh coffee," Megan MacCallister Johnson said.

"Well," Jamie Ian the Second said. "I think Pa was seven years old when the Shawnee attacked . . ."


Jamie sat his saddle and gave the trading post a good eye-balling. There were half a dozen horses tied up at hitch rails in front of the place. The doors to the stable were open, and it appeared to be about half full.

Jamie lifted the reins and said, "All right, Buck. Let's go see what we've found."

Jamie stripped the saddle from Buck, relieved the pack-horse of its burden, and rubbed them both down. He was sure he'd been seen riding up, but no one had as yet left the main building to see what he wanted. Jamie broke open the sawed-off twelve gauge and shoved shells into the twin barrels, snapping it closed.

He checked both his Colts. He usually carried the hammer over an empty chamber, but on this day he loaded them up full. He carefully wiped them clean of dust and checked the action, then slid them back into leather.

Jamie walked toward the closed door of the long and low-roofed trading post on the North Platte.

He passed by an open window and caught the smell of fresh-burned gunpowder. Past the window, Jamie hunkered down low and ran past the closed front door and around to the rear of the building. He checked the rickety, old two-hole outhouse. Empty. He pressed up against the back of the post and put an ear to the door. He could hear no sound. Then: "He rode up," a man said. "Goddammit. It was him. Where is he?"

"I bet you he's standin' by the front door, listenin'," another said.

"That old gray-headed bastard is tricky," yet another voice was added.

"He ain't that old," a fourth voice said calmly. "He

may be sixty year old, but he's still one hell of a man. Don't let him get them hands of hisn on you. He's bull strong."

Jamie smiled.

"You sorry piles of buffalo droppin's," another voice came to Jamie. "There wasn't no need to kill Clay. He didn't do you no harm."

"Shut up, storekeeper," a new voice said. "We thought he was goin' for a gun."

"Well, he wasn't. Me and him been pards for years. Now he's dead for no good reason. I hope MacCallister kills ever' one of you trash bags."

The sound of a hard blow came to Jamie, then a thud as a man hit the floor, followed by: "Now keep that blowhole of yourn closed, old man."

"Don't hit him again!" a woman screamed.

"You can shut up, too, you ugly old bitch," the outlaw said. "You just be glad you're as ugly as a hog's butt, or we'd have you in that back room doin' some pumpin' and humpin'. Now drag that bastard behind the counter and don't say no more."

Jamie lifted the latch string and eased the door open just wide enough for him to slip inside. But this time fate worked against him.

"Oh, hell!" a man yelled, spinning around in the center of the room, spotting Jamie and lifting his pistol.

Jamie blew a hole in him with the Greener, shifted the weapon and cut down a second man who was lifting a rifle. Jamie jumped behind some stacked crates and hauled out his pistols, earing back the hammers as the lead really started to howl and the trading post filled with arid gunsmoke.

Jamie jumped from one spot to another, trying to get a clean shot. He could see only a man's leg from where he squatted, so he shot the outlaw in the knee.

The kneecap shattered, and the leg crumpled under the suddenly screaming outlaw. "Oh, my God. I been ruint."

"Where is he, dammit? I can't see nothin'."

Jamie loaded up the Greener and eared back both hammers. He waited.

"Who's down?" a commanding voice called.

"Sandberg and Reynolds is dead. Bellar's down with a busted knee."

"Oh, God," Bellar hollered. "I ain't never had nothin' pain me so."

While they talked, Jamie moved again, silent in his moccasins as he crept toward the wall that separated the large main room from the storage area. Jamie picked up an empty wooden box and slung it toward the back door. A half second after the box smashed into the door, a man stepped into the archway, both hands filled with pistols and both pistols smoking.

Jamie gave him both barrels of the sawed-off and very nearly blew the man in two. He quickly shifted positions, the thick gunsmoke hiding his silent move.

"So much for Jack," the calm voice spoke from the other side of the wall.

"Let's git out of here, Hulon!"

"Naw," Hulon Nations said. "I'm tarred of runnin' from this bastard. You hear me, MacCallister. Let's finish this thing right here and now."

Jamie waited.

Hulon suddenly giggled like a girl. Jamie recalled Jeff Washburn telling him that the man was about half crazy.

"Kill 'em all, Mr. MacCallister!" a woman's voice shrieked. "You kill ever' black-hearted one of 'em, you hear?"

"Shut up you, you crazy old bag!" Carl Dews hollered.

"I got to have some re-lief," Roy Bellar said with a groan. "I'm tellin' you, I'm in pain."

A pistol roared, and Roy Bellar was silent.

"Good God, Hulon!" Carl yelled. "You done kilt Roy!"

"I's tarred of listenin' to him whine. I never did like him no how. Come on, MacCallister. Let's stand up face-to-face and hook and draw. How about it?"

Jamie waited.

"I'm out of here," Carl said. "I'm like . . . *gone!*"

Jamie heard boots strike the boards and then a wild scream.

"She stobbed me!" Carl bellered. "That old bag stobbed me, Hulon. Oh, God, come pull this thing outta my belly. I'm on far, Hulon."

"Shoot her," Hulon said.

"I can't see her! Where's she gone to. Oh, shit! She's got an axe!"

A flat, smushing sound filled the room, and what was left of Carl Dews hit the floor with an ugly sound.

"Old woman," Hulon said, "I'll deal with you when I git done with MacCallister."

Jamie stood up and stepped into the doorway, both Colts blazing. Hulon started soaking up the lead. The big man had been taken by surprise by Jamie's sudden move. Even with half a dozen bullets in him, the big, black-bearded man lifted his guns and started smoking. Jamie felt the tug of a bullet tear through his jacket and burn his arm. Pain exploded in his head as a hot chunk of lead cut a groove in his scalp. Another bullet creased his ribs as Jamie turned and took careful aim with his right-hand Colt. He let the hammer fall, and the .44 round hit Hulon Nations in the center of the forehead. The big man's boots went flying out from under him, and he stretched out full-length on the boards, fingers still clutching both pistols.

It was over.

Jamie retrieved his Greener and loaded it up, then saw to his pistols. The woman was bathing her husband's bruised and battered face with wet cloths.

"Vilest people I ever encountered in all my years," the woman said. "There's a young girl in the back room. Thirteen or fourteen years old. Homesteader's daughter from the look of her. They brung her with them. Said they grabbed her two days ago, after they killed her parents. They been usin' her somethin' terrible. In all sorts of unnatural ways. I don't know if the poor thing is dead or alive. She stopped screamin' about an hour 'fore you got here."

Jamie stepped over and around the bodies and pushed open the door to the bedroom. A young girl, wearing nothing but what she'd been born with, sat huddled in the center of the bed, her eyes wild with shock. Her thighs were streaked with blood.

"It's over," Jamie told her. "They won't hurt you anymore." The girl started weeping.

"See to the child, Marybelle," the trading post owner said, just as Jamie stepped back into the room. "She'll be needful of a woman's touch."

Jamie began the job of dragging the bodies out the back door.

"I just finished diggin' me a new privy pit," the man said. "Got the new outhouse built. Just shove that old relief station over and drop them bastards down in the shit and whatnot. It's a fittin' place for them."

"I couldn't agree with you more," Jamie replied.

He dragged what was left of Jack Moore out the back door and over to the privy. Jamie shoved the privy over and let it crash to the ground. The impact tore it apart. He tossed the body into the pit as the blood from his bullet-grooved head dripped onto his jacket. The post owner was digging a hole for his partner.

When the six outlaws had been deposited into the pit, Jamie looked at the trading post owner. "You want to say anything over them?"

"Yeah," the man said. He looked down into the dark and odious pit. "Burn in hell, you bastards!"

Jamie spent several days at the trading post. The owner's wife saw to his wounds, and Jamie helped the couple get the place cleaned up and the floor mopped free of blood.

The young girl, who had lost her entire family to the

mindless, ruthless savagery of the outlaws, quickly agreed to stay with the couple and help run the trading post.

Four days after the shoot-out, Jamie saddled up, heading north for the Dakotas. Earlier, at a town with a telegraph, he had wired his detective agency, and they had responded the same day.

There was a trading post of sorts up on the Rapid River, just to the east of the Black Hills, and Jamie had received word by wire that two or three of the men he sought were hanging around up there.*

Jamie forded the Niobrara and then crossed the White, riding past the place where, in March of 1874, the army would build Fort Robinson. Jamie had no way of knowing it, but he would return to this same area in a few years.

The Cheyenne River was running low, and Jamie forded it easily, heading due north. Days later, he crossed the Battle and the Spring. He saw many bands of Indians, but they left him alone.

Jamie had heard that the Indians were on the prowl in this area, due to a few white men coming in to search for gold in the sacred Black Hills, but the word had been passed from tribe to tribe about Jamie; the bands of Indians only watched in silence as Jamie made his lonely way north.

Inside the trading post, Lonnie Rayburn and Jed Hudson, the two thugs who had escaped the shoot-out in the trading post on Hams Fork, had decided they weren't going to run any farther. Lonnie and Jed were just about at the end of their string. They were down to their last few dollars, and their nerves were ragged and raw from the nearly two years of relentless pursuit by Jamie Ian MacCallister. Gary Crane, who had ridden in about a week back with hard news, was in just as bad a shape. But he, too, had decided he would run no more.

The owner of the trading post, who had fought both Indians and outlaws during his long years on the frontier

---

*Rapid City would be settled as a town in 1876.

(and who knew all about Jamie MacCallister), watched with amused eyes as the three men grew more and more jumpy. MacCallister was coming, and the outlaws knew it. They sat and talked in low tones, the trading post owner catching only a word now and then: Ambush. Back shoot him. Run.

The owner knew that these dregs of society would never ambush that wily Ol' Wolf MacCallister, and odds were against them ever getting into position to back shoot him. They'd made their brags that they would run no more, so that left them only one option: stand and fight.

It was going to be right interesting when MacCallister did ride up. For a few minutes at least.

Then the man looked up, and Jamie Ian MacCallister was standing in the doorway, lookin' like an Avengin' Angel, holding that sawed-off Greener in his hands. He must have picketed his horses some distance away and Injuned up on silent feet.

Lonnie, Jed, and Gary were all hunched over a back table, whispering and conjuring up dark and evil plans that none had the courage to see through, totally unaware of Jamie's presence.

The trading post owner signaled to his squaw to stand clear. The Crow woman slipped silently into the storeroom and hunkered down behind some crates.

Lonnie Rayburn felt eyes on him, and looked up, the color draining from his face. "Oh, my God!" he screamed. He jumped to his feet, knocking the chair over as he frantically clawed for his pistol.

Jamie lifted the sawed-off with one hand and pulled the trigger, the buckshot blast striking the outlaw in the upper chest and face and slamming him against the side wall.

Gary Crane managed to jerk out both pistols before the second blast caught him full force in the belly and knocked him to the floor.

"I yield! I yield!" Jed screamed, holding both hands high in the air. "Don't shoot, MacCallister. I give it up."

Jamie had his right-hand Colt out, hammer back. He stood and stared at the outlaw. "You would complicate my life by turnin' yellow on me, boy."

"I got a witness!" Jed yelled. "I ain't grabbin' no iron. I'm surrenderin'. You won't shoot no man with his hands in the air."

"Aw, hell, shoot the son of a bitch, MacCallister," the trading post owner said. "The nearest army post is a hundred miles to the northeast, man. It ain't even got a name yet. The 17th Infantry is there."*

"Shut your mouth, you old fool!" Jed bellered. "I'm surrenderin'."

"I'd take a bullet over hangin', boy," the older man said. "Think about it."

Jamie cut his eyes. "Get his guns and hold him 'til I can get shackles from my saddlebags. I'll not shoot no man with his hands in the air."

Jed Hudson was so relieved to hear that, he wet his pants.

"Shit!" the trading post owner said. "A lot of fuss and bother, you ask me."

Jamie got heavy handcuffs and ankle shackles from his supplies and chained Jed down tight. "I'll drag the bodies out," he told the owner. "Where do you want to plant them?"

"Wherever you've a mind to. I ain't diggin' no holes for the likes of them."

"That ain't decent!" Jeb yelled.

"You're a fine one to talk about decent," Jamie told him. "You'll dig the holes. Move!"

"I wet my britches," Jed muttered.

"You'll do more'un that when they hang you," the trading post owner said. "I hear tell you dump a full load when the rope tightens."

"God*damn* you!" Jed screamed.

Jamie found a shovel and tossed it to Jed, who awkwardly

---

*Named Fort Bennett in 1878. Abandoned November 1891.

caught it with his shackled hands. "Out back," Jamie told him. "I'll resupply while you dig. Then we're gone."

"Foolishness, you ask me," the trading post owner mumbled. "I'd just shoot him and be done with it. Moon Woman!" he hollered. "Fetch us somethin' to eat. I be's hongry around my mouth."

# 16

Jamie pulled out at dawn, with the shackled Jed Hudson in tow. Now that the certainty of what faced him had sunk home, Jed was at first angry and then fell into a sullen mood . . . which suited Jamie just fine. He didn't have time for a lot of chitchat, for he was traveling at a steady pace, putting a lot of miles behind them. It was late afternoon when Jamie called a halt and rubbed down the horses and picketed them on good graze, close to water. Just before dark, he would move them closer to the camp. The Indians wouldn't harm Man Who Is Not Afraid, but it would be a good joke on him to steal his horses.

"They's Injuns out there." Jed finally broke his sullen silence.

"They won't bother me. They might take your hair, but they won't bother me."

"I guess you think that's funny."

"No. Just stating a fact."

"That old man back yonder at the tradin' post—he'd have shot me out-right, wouldn't he?"

"Without giving it a second thought."

Jed ate his beans and bacon and bread in silence for a time. After taking a sip of coffee, he said, "I didn't have no choice, really. I had to become an outlaw."

"Is that right?"

"Yeah. You see, my daddy whupped me a lot."

Jamie smiled. "Obviously, he didn't whip you enough."

Jeb ignored that. "And I always wanted me a paint pony like the boy down the road had. But Pa, he said we didn't have the money for one."

"So you stole one."

"Huh! How'd you know that?"

"Call it a lucky guess." Jamie's reply was decidedly dry.

"Well, it ain't right for some to have more than others."

"Someday, someone is going to come up with a word to cover that kind of thinking."

Jamie wasn't aware of it, but that person was born in 1818. His name was Karl Marx.

"Are you goin' to make me sleep with these shackles on my ankles and wrists?"

"All night long."

"That ain't right, neither. 'Pose I give you my word I won't try to run away?"

"You have to be joking."

Jed smiled. "It was worth a try, weren't it? Hey, it don't bother you a bit that I'm gonna hang, do it?"

"Not a bit."

"Why? You don't know me. I can tell you for a fact it wasn't me who shot your wife."

"I suppose now you're going to tell me you didn't shoot anybody that day down in Valley . . . or in any of the other fifty or so towns the Nelson gang has raided? Or you never harmed a soul on a stage or a train? Or you never took part in any of the foul deeds done to women and young girls at lonely farm and ranch houses?"

" 'Pose I say I'm sorry about them things?"

"Tell it to a judge and jury."

"I will. And they'll believe me, too."

Jamie smiled and took a dodger out of his jacket pocket. "Thomas Jed Hudson," he read. "Wanted for murder and rape and robbery in Missouri, Kansas, Colorado. Wanted for cattle rustling and murder in Texas and Arizona. Wanted for rape in Arkansas. You helped torture a woman to death in Louisiana." He looked up from the wanted poster and stared at Jed in the fast-fading light. "You want me to go on?"

"I reckon not."

"Then eat your supper and shut up."


Federal Marshal Pat Riordan had stopped at the army installation for food and rest. He was just about ready to leave when scouts reported back to the commanding officer that Jamie MacCallister was on his way in with a man who was shackled in the saddle. The marshal smiled and decided to delay his departure.

Inside the post compound, Jamie jerked Jed out of the saddle and asked for the commanding officer.

"No need for that," Pat said, walking up, his badge pinned to his coat. He stuck out a hand. "Pat Riordan. United States Deputy Federal Marshal."

Jamie shook the hand and then jerked a thumb at Jed. "You want this yahoo?"

"Oh, yeah. I sure do. Let's stick him in the stockade and go get something to eat and drink. Then you can bring me up-to-date on members of the Nelson gang you've found, so I can scratch them off my list."

"MacCallister ain't no law-dog," Jed said. "He didn't have no proper authority to arrest me and shackle me like a wild animal and haul me all over the country. I got rights, you know?"

"Shut up, Hudson," Pat told him. He turned to Jamie. "I just got me a notion, Mac, that a hundred years from now, enforcin' the law is gonna be a real problem."

"A hundred years from now," Jamie replied, "what the hell difference will it make to you and me?"

Laughing, Pat took Jamie's arm, and together they walked off to get something to eat.

Jed Hudson was still cussing when a burly sergeant hauled

him off to the stockade, slammed the door and locked him in.

It was mid-summer and hot as Jamie rode into Abilene, Kansas. After stabling his horses, Jamie checked into the Drover's Cottage. He was unaware that the town marshal, James Butler Hickok, better known as Wild Bill, was also staying at the Drover's Cottage. Wild Bill had taken over as city marshal in April of '71, shortly after the death of Thomas Smith, also known as Bear River Smith.

When Jamie checked in, the desk clerk told him, "Wild Bill don't allow no pistols to be toted inside the city limits, Mr. MacCallister." He looked into the cold eyes of Jamie and quickly added, "But he might make an exception in your case."

Also in town were Jesse and Frank James, John Wesley Hardin, Ben Thompson, and Phil Coe. The James boys had done Wild Bill a favor back in Missouri, and the marshal allowed the pair to hide out in and around Abilene as long as they caused no trouble.

After a long hot bath, a haircut and shave, his boots blacked, a white shirt laundered and pressed, and his suit aired and ironed, Jamie stuck one .44 behind his sash and took a stroll around the town.

He hadn't gone a block before Wild Bill stepped out of a store and the two men came face-to-face on the boardwalk.

Hickok was tall, but not as tall as Jamie or as heavy. The men howdied, and then Hickok whispered, "Al Stone and Rod Totton usually hit the Alamo Saloon about dark."

Jamie nodded his head, and that was the only exchange ever known to have occurred between the two men. Hickok walked on and so did Jamie.

Jamie ate an early supper and wandered over to the Alamo Saloon just before dusk. John Wesley Hardin, the volatile and totally unpredictable gunfighter, was sitting at a table near the back, drinking whiskey and playing solitaire.

Hardin, a native of Texas, born in Bonham of God-fearing and hard-working parents (his father was a Methodist circuit preacher), held in high esteem the men who fought and died at the Alamo, and held in particularly high regard the legendary Jamie Ian MacCallister.

"They'll be along shortly," he called from his table. "They've been runnin' their mouths about killin' you. Don't worry about your back, I'll watch it for you."

Jamie turned and nodded his head in thanks. Hardin resumed his card playing, and Jamie nursed his drink of whiskey.

Hickok saddled up and rode out of town, to visit a lady friend who lived a few miles outside of Abilene. Wild Bill was totally sympathetic with Jamie's manhunt, and wanted to give him all the free rein possible in dealing with Stone and Totton.

Word had gotten to Stone and Totton that Jamie was in town. The two outlaws had no choice in the matter. They had boasted all around town about what they would do if MacCallister ever showed up in Abilene. Now they had to back up their words, or be branded cowards and leave town. The outlaws propped up their courage with whiskey in Ben Thompson's Bull's Head Tavern and, just at dark, headed for the Alamo Saloon.

They walked into the saloon with guns drawn.

"Why, you cowardly bastards!" John Wesley shouted, upon seeing the men openly heeled.

But Jamie was already moving. He snaked his .44 out of his sash and drilled Al Stone through the heart. Stone fell against Totton and took the bullet meant for Jamie. Jamie stood and took aim and fired. His bullet struck Totton in the chest and knocked the man back against a wall. Totton lifted his second .45, and Jamie fired again, the .44 round striking the outlaw in the belly. Totton slid down the wall, coming to rest on his butt on the floor. His guns slipped from numbed fingers.

"Damn your eyes, MacCallister!" he managed to gasp.

"You don't never give a man breathin' room. You just kept on comin'. But you'll meet your match when you brace Judy. Judy will kill you for shore."

Totton died with his eyes wide open, staring death in the face.

"Will Judy," John Wesley said. "He's a bad one, Mac. Don't sell him short."

And that was high praise indeed, coming from John Wesley Hardin, perhaps the fastest gun alive.

Jamie carefully reloaded. He turned to John Wesley. "This Will Judy, you know where he is?"

John Wesley shook his head. "That, I don't know, Mac. But he likes the high country and rides with a no-good name of Tom Brewer. And Brewer ain't no man to take lightly."

"Nice meeting you, John Wesley," Jamie said.

"I assure you that pleasure was all mine, Jamie Ian Mac-Callister." He lifted his glass of whiskey and said, "Long live the memory of the Alamo and the men who fought and died there."

"I'll drink to that," Jamie said, and lifted his glass in salute to bravery and freedom.

Jamie then walked out of the saloon and into the night. John Wesley resumed his lonely game of solitaire.*

Fall was blowing cold when Jamie rode into the little two-by-twice town on the Colorado/New Mexico border. He'd picked up the trail of three men nearly six weeks back and had dogged them all the way. They had tried every trick they knew to shake Jamie off their trail . . . nothing had worked.

Sam Woodson, Art Adams, and Ramsey Wicks were at

*In 1895, John Wesley Hardin, while drinking and playing dice in the Acme Saloon in El Paso, was shot in the back of the head by John Selman. Selman was killed the next year by lawman George Scarborough in an alley outside a saloon in El Paso.

the end of their string and all played out when they hit what was left of the tiny town that would soon vanish into the folk-lore of western history. It had sprung up just after the Civil War, flourished briefly, and then began to die. Now there were only a saloon, a general store, and a blacksmith/livery remaining. The other buildings were fast beginning to decay. Soon there would be nothing left. It was never really determined whether the town was located in Colorado or New Mexico. And by the time the last building collapsed in the early 1880s, the town having been abandoned for more than ten years, nobody gave a damn.

The blacksmith looked at Jamie in the fading light and shook his head. "If you be Jamie MacCallister, and I think you are, them hombres you been doggin' is in the saloon. They said for me to tell you they ain't runnin' no more."

"You build caskets?" Jamie asked.

"Well, yeah."

"Then build three. You're going to need them."

The smithy stared in silence as Jamie took a rag and wiped the dust from his sawed-off, then broke it open and loaded it up.

"Ever' time I pick up a newspaper, they's something about you in it," the smithy broke his silence. "Six months old, a year old, two weeks old, it don't make no difference, you and your damn manhunt is in all of them. Do you even know how many men you've killed, MacCallister?"

"You mean, of the Nelson gang?"

"Yes."

"Thirty-nine, to date. I think. It'll soon be forty-two."

The smithy was shocked. He stood with his mouth agape for a moment, then shook his head and whispered, "Thirty-nine souls you've sent wingin'."

"Sent winging right straight to hell," Jamie said, his voice cold. He wiped off his Colts, working the action, then checked the loads, filling up the sixth chamber on each Colt, and finally snapped closed the cylinders and slipped the pistols back into leather.

"How old are you, Jamie MacCallister?" the smithy asked.

"Sixty-one, I believe. I've never been real sure about that."

"You don't look it. 'Ceptin' maybe the eyes."

Jamie turned to go.

"What do you want done with your horses and gear if you don't come back for them?"

Jamie paused and looked at the man. "Instructions are in my saddlebags."

"I would wish you luck, 'ceptin' I don't believe in what you're doin'."

"I don't believe in luck," Jamie told him. He walked across the street and pushed over the batwings, stepping into the saloon.

# 17

Ben F. Washington sat on the front porch of the small house and watched the sun sink over the mountains. He was at peace with himself and the world. He had never known such inner peace. Ben stuffed his pipe with tobacco and fired it up, filling the air with the fragrant scent. A young couple strolled past, and they smiled and spoke to Ben. Ben returned the greeting warmly and watched the handsome couple until they were out of sight; both of them blond-haired and blue-eyed.

A man rode by on a fine bay animal, smiling and touching the brim of his hat with his fingers. Ben waved in return. With a sigh and a contented smile, Ben, right then and there, made up his mind as to his future. He had made a tentative offer to the aging editor and owner of the local newspaper, and the man had accepted. Ben would see him tomorrow and firm up the deal.

"Yes," Ben muttered to the cool winds blowing off the snowcapped mountains all around him. "I am home."


The bartender slid a bottle and a glass down to Jamie and then hit the air, exiting out the back door of the saloon. The half dozen other patrons and one henna-haired, worn-out, and used-up-looking Soiled Dove took tables close to the wall.

Sam Woodson, Art Adams, and Ramsey Wicks were standing up at the far end of the saloon, hands over the butts of their guns.

"Now you hear me good, MacCallister." Sam was the first to speak. "I'm tarred of you doggin' my back trail. This here is gonna end tonight. You hear me?"

Jamie, using his left hand, poured a drink and sipped it. He held the Greener in his big right hand. He said nothing, only smiled.

"It ain't right what you been doin'," Art took it up. "We's human bein's. What's done is done, and you ain't gonna change it."

Jamie bluntly and profanely told the trio to go commit an impossible act upon their persons.

"God*damn* you!" Ramsey screamed, and reached for his guns.

Jamie lifted the Greener and blew a hole in Ramsey, some of the buckshot striking Art in the arm and bringing a yelp of pain. Ramsey slammed against the wall and slid down, coming to rest on his butt, still alive, but not for long.

Yelling his rage, Sam Woodson grabbed iron and cleared leather, tossing a wild shot in Jamie's direction. But Jamie was no longer there. After firing the first barrel, he had dropped into a crouch and duck walked behind the bar, reloading the sawed-off as he went.

"Where the hell did he go?" Art yelled.

Jamie stood up behind the bar. "Right here," he called, and pulled both triggers of the Greener.

Art took the full load of buckshot in the chest and was flung off his boots, both his guns flying from dead fingers. The pistols discharged upon hitting the saloon floor and blew holes in the front windows, sending the spectators leaping for the floor. The Soiled Dove, no lightweight, landed on top of a traveling man and drove the wind from him. He thought he'd been shot and, when he caught his breath, commenced to bellering to beat the band. While he was doing all that, the Soiled Dove lifted his watch and chain and wallet.

Jamie dropped the Greener and hauled iron just as Sam Woodson shifted his weight and brought up his guns. Jamie gave him two .44 rounds in the chest and belly and added a third slug for good measure. Falling backward, Sam pulled the triggers and blew two holes in the ceiling of the saloon.

"Jesus H. Christ!" screamed a wandering cowboy who was trying to get some rest in a room on the second floor, as the bullets tore through the floor and a chunk of lead whined off the iron bedpost. The other slug blew a hole in the chamber pot under the bed.

Jamie returned to the end of the bar and his drink, reloading the sawed-off on the way. He took a sip of the whiskey and peered through the acrid screen of gunsmoke that hung thick in the saloon. Satisfied that no more lead was going to come in his direction, Jamie took out a creased sheet of paper and a stub of pencil and drew a line through three more names on the list.

The bartender opened the door to the storage room and peeked inside. "It is over?" he inquired.

"You offer food here?" Jamie asked.

"Sort of. Stew and bread is all we got."

"Then I'll be back in an hour. Have some hot for me." Jamie finished his drink and walked out into the gathering night. He stood for a moment, breathing deeply of the cold air, then stepped off the boards and returned to the livery to wash up for supper.

The smithy stood in the open double doors of the stable, a hammer and saw in his hands, carpenter's apron tied around his waist.

"How many coffins?" he asked.

"Three," Jamie said. "Just like I told you."

"They got any money on them?"

"I have no idea."

"Well, I guess their guns will be worth something."

"And their horses," Jamie added.

"True." The smithy watched as Jamie took off his jacket and rolled up his shirtsleeves. "You gonna pray now and ask the Lord for forgiveness?"

"No."

"You ought to. Terrible thing, taking a man's life. What are you gonna do?"

"Wash my hands and face and have supper. I'm hungry."

Jamie dropped out of sight for almost six weeks after the shoot-out in the dying little no-name town. No one saw him except Indians, and they were not exactly on speaking terms with most whites. When he again surfaced, it was in eastern Nevada, in a wild and wooly town called Pioche. It was an isolated place, the closest town of any size being Hamilton, almost a hundred miles away to the north. One rumor had it that of the first one hundred people to be buried in the local cemetery, none died of natural causes.

Before Jamie pulled out, two more would be added to that dubious list of honor.

Jim Levy, perhaps the fastest gunslick ever to belt on pistols, but curiously the least known (some claim he was even faster than John Wesley Hardin), watched as Jamie rode up to the livery and swung down from the saddle.*

*James H. Levy, born in Ireland in the early 1840s, of a Jewish father and Irish mother, killed his first man in Pioche, Nevada. It is rumored that he had to borrow a pistol to do that! In his decade-long career as a gunfighter, gambler, and guard for various mining operations, the tough little Jewish/Irish immigrant is credited with killing at least sixteen men (some say the total is twice that), in stand-up, face-to-face gunfights. Levy roamed all over the Southwest, several times traveling as far north as Wyoming, where he killed at least one man outside a saloon in Cheyenne. In Tucson, Arizona, in 1882, after a faro dealer made some disparaging remarks about Jim's ancestry (and Jews in particular), Jim told the man to meet him outside, then left for his hotel room to get his gun. The faro dealer gathered up several of his friends, and they hid along the street and ambushed Jim, emptying their guns into him. When the marshal inspected Jim's bullet-riddled body, he found the man was unarmed. His killers were never brought to trial.

"Going to get interesting around here," Levy muttered, then turned and walked into one of the town's many saloons.

After a well-needed bath and shave and haircut, Jamie dressed in his best suit and had the first meal in many weeks that he hadn't had to cook himself over an open fire.

By now, thanks to a gabby and very excited desk clerk, every man, woman, and child within the city limits (if indeed there were any known city limits) knew that Jamie was in town and on the prod.

And so did Barry Herman and Skip Beech, the two members of the Miles Nelson gang that Jamie had tracked to the town.

Herman and Beech were exhausted and very nearly at wits' end. They had been on a hard run for more than two years, not daring to stay in one place for any length of time, for Jamie Ian MacCallister was always just a step or two behind them.

Newspaper accounts and the writers of various Penny Dreadfuls would claim that Barry Herman went insane that night in Pioche, Nevada, driven into madness by the relentless pursuit of Jamie. But in later years, writers with less wild flights of fancy (mainly one Ben F. Washington) would do some research and find that Herman just drank too much Who-Hit-John in an attempt to screw his courage to the sticking place and called Jamie out.

Jamie obliged him.

"You son of a bitch!" Herman yelled from the end of the street. "I'm gonna end this right here, right now, this minute."

"Then make your play, tinhorn," Jamie called.

The edges of the street and what boardwalks there were in the raw town were filled with spectators.

"You think I'm afraid of you, MacCallister, you damned old buzzard?"

"I think you're a two-bit, back-shooting, woman-killing punk," Jamie said, his words cutting into Herman like a knife.

Barry Herman screamed his rage and jerked iron. Stepping into the center of the street, he began wildly banging away. His shots kicked up dirt in the street, busted windows along both sides, sent two dozen men and women scrambling for whatever cover they could find, and finally hit a traveling dress-and-corset salesman in the butt, causing the rather portly gentleman some discomfort for several days.

Jamie calmly drew his pistol, took deliberate aim in the murky light of dusk, and shot Barry Herman right between the eyes.

"Now face me," said a much more sober Skip Beech from the darkness of an alley. Then he lifted his pistol and pulled the trigger.

The cartridge misfired, the action jammed, and that was all the time Jamie needed. He lifted his .44 and drilled Skip in the belly, doubling the outlaw over in hot agony. Cursing and screaming, Skip dropped the useless pistol and hauled another gun out of his waistband. Jamie fired again, the bullet striking Skip in the hip and spinning him around.

Still game and still on his boots, the outlaw lifted his pistol and cocked the hammer. The last words to leave his lips were curses, all directed at Jamie.

Jamie plugged him with a well-placed shot to the heart.

Skip Beech dropped like a stone.

Jamie holstered his pistol and walked back to his room. Come the morning, Pioche, Nevada, would see the last of him.


*Christmas day, 1871.*


"I hear tell MacCallister kilt two more men down in Nevada 'bout two months or so ago," the old trapper broke the silence in the saloon.

Two unshaven and roughly dressed men seated at a corner table looked up at the words. They uttered silent sighs and exchanged glances at the news.

"More of the Nelson gang?" the bartender asked, polishing a glass with a towel.

"Yep. Some gunslicks name of Herman and Beech. Ol' Mac never flinched. Just stood out tall and tough and plain in the street and gunned 'em down like the dirty bastards they is—or was, I should say."

The front door to the saloon was pushed open, and for a second, the bitter winds of Montana winter howled inside, flakes of snow briefly landing on the floor, quickly melting and puddling. All heads turned to stare at the tall and rugged-built man who stood there.

"Goddammit!" one of the two men at the table muttered under his breath.

The tall, erect, and powerfully built man with the gray hair and moustache, deeply tanned face, and cold, piercing eyes removed his heavy winter coat and hung it on a peg, brushed back his hip-length coat, exposing twin Colts, and walked to the bar, his spurs jingling. "Whiskey," he said.

The trapper took his drink and moved away from the bar, as did the cowboy at the far end of the bar. They both knew who the tall stranger was and had absolutely no desire to get caught by a stray bullet.

Jamie Ian MacCallister. And the old lobo wolf was on the hard prod.

Jamie took a sip of his whiskey and carefully placed the glass on the scarred bar. "Good whiskey," he told the bartender. "Hits the spot. But it stinks in here," he added. "Smells like outlaw scum to me."

Outside, the wind howled in a mindless fury.

"Damn!" the other man at the table muttered. "I knowed it had to come someday," he whispered to his friend.

Tom Brewer stood up from the table. "Old man," he said to Jamie's back. "You been doggin' my back trail for more'un two years now. And I'm tired of it. You've killed my friends and even some of my kin. But your killin' stops right here."

Jamie turned to face him. It was then that Brewer noticed the short-barreled twelve gauge shotgun that Jamie had been holding in his left hand, pressed tight against his leg. "Is that a fact?"

"That's a fact, MacCallister." But there was a very sick feeling in the pit of Brewer's stomach.

Will Judy slipped away from the table and edged along the wall until coming to the storeroom door. He opened the door and stepped out into the cold winds and blowing snow, heading for the livery across the street. If Tom had just used his head, they could have double-teamed MacCallister and taken him out. But Tom had allowed his hate to overcome logic.

Will hated a fool.

He and MacCallister would meet on another day.

"I don't think so, Brewer," Jamie was saying. "I still got a goodly number of you trash to deal with." He had let Will Judy leave. There was always another day.

"Why, you beat-up buzzard! You ain't half the man you used to be. You just think you are, you gray-headed old son of a bitch!"

Jamie, standing tall and unbending in the Montana saloon, smiled at the killer. Outside, the winter winds screamed like angry eagles. "Make your peace with whatever God will claim you, Brewer. Then hook and draw."

Brewer cursed Jamie and grabbed iron. Jamie lifted the sawed-off and blew the killer all over the back end of the saloon. He broke open the Greener and pulled out the empties, loading it up fresh. Then he drained his glass of whiskey and walked out of the saloon, retrieving his coat from the hook.

"Who in the hell was that?" a salesman from St. Louis blurted.

"That's an ol' lobo wolf name of Jamie Ian MacCallister." The grizzled trapper spoke from the corner table. "The Miles Nelson gang kilt his wife down in Coloradee two year ago. He's been on the prod ever since. And he'll be on the prod 'til he kills ever' one of them."

"You reckon he'll get it done?" the bartender asked.

The old mountain man smiled. "Bet on it."

# 18

Winter still locked the high country in a blanket of cold white when Jamie pushed open the door of the trading post located just outside of what was left of Fort Phil Kearny, which had been abandoned in 1868, on the east side of the Bighorn Mountains. Jamie was as rough-looking as his horses, wild and uncurried.

Will Judy threw his cards on the table and shouted, "Son of a *bitch!*" He pushed back his chair and stood up as the others in the room scattered for cover. "Goddamn you, man, why don't you give this up and let people alone?"

"Because I made a promise whilst standing over the grave of my wife," Jamie replied. "And I always keep my promises." Jamie kept his eyes locked on the eyes of Will Judy.

"You can't beat me, MacCallister," Will said. "I'm younger and faster than you."

"We'll see," Jamie said calmly, his eyes never leaving Will Judy's.

As soon as Will's eyes narrowed, Jamie drew, stepping to one side as he did, preparing to fire across his chest. Will was indeed fast with a gun, but Jamie's sudden move threw the outlaw's aim off just enough. Instead of the bullet striking Jamie in the center of the chest, it hit him in the left arm and immediately numbed the arm all the way to his hand. But Jamie's shot was true, the bullet striking the gunfighter/outlaw in the chest and knocking him backward, but not down. Jamie recovered and fired again; this time Will Judy went down hard and stayed down, losing his grip on his pistol.

With blood dripping from his wound, Jamie walked over to the dying man and kicked his pistol away.

"I never thought it would be this way," Will gasped, looking up at Jamie.

"Nobody ever does. Miles Nelson? Is he still up in Canada?"

"No. I won't die with a lie on my lips. I'm gonna . . . have a hard enough time . . . convincin' St. Pete to let me in as it is. You reckon I got a chance of doin' that, MacCallister?"

Jamie started to reply and then closed his mouth.

Will Judy was dead at his feet.

"I know somethin' about doctorin'," a man said, walking to Jamie's side. "Come over to the light and let me take a look at that arm."

Jamie took off his jacket and shirt and peeled his underwear shirt down to his waist. The men in the bar all sat in silence and stared at Jamie's heavy musculature. It was the build of a man twenty years younger.

The bullet had passed through Jamie's arm, tearing a hole as it exited out the back, just above the armpit.

"You're lucky," the man said, after cleaning out the wound, pouring whiskey front and back, and then bandaging the arm and shoulder. "If it had hit that big bone, it might have broken your shoulder or deflected off and wandered around in your chest. But you'll live. You're in marvelous shape for a man in his late forties, MacCallister."

"I'm sixty-one years old, mister," Jamie told him.

"Jesus Christ," one of the men watching muttered. "I hope I'm so lucky."

"You won't be," his partner told him. "You ain't built up that good now!"

\* \* \*

Jamie lounged around the trading post for a week, allowing his wound to start its healing and to rest his horses. While he waited, he went through Will Judy's personal papers and found an envelope. There was no letter inside, but the envelope had been posted from Kansas City, Missouri, and on the back of the envelope, the initials Rev. M.N., Church of the Enlightenment.

"Yeah," Jamie muttered. "You could probably get away with that." He knew that Miles Nelson was the son of a Methodist minister, and a highly educated man, having taught school before turning to a life of depravity. "I'll just save you for last, Nelson. I might just shoot you down in front of your congregation, after I expose you for what you are."

As so many men had learned the hard way, over almost five decades of frontier living, there was no back-up and no quitting in Jamie Ian MacCallister. If he said he'd do something, he did it.

Jamie headed south until he hit the railroad, then followed the tracks east until coming to a town. There, he sent a telegraph to his sons and daughters in Valley: START BUILDING ME A CABIN ON THE RIDGE OVERLOOKING YOUR MA'S GRAVE. BEDROOM, LIVING ROOM, KITCHEN, AND A PORCH IN THE FRONT SO I CAN SIT IN THE EVENING AND LOOK DOWN AND SEE YOUR MA'S GRAVE. I'LL BE HOME BEFORE THE NEXT SNOW FLIES. PA.

He sent another telegram to his detective agency and waited for a reply. When it came, only a few hours later, he smiled and went for supplies. He had a hard ride ahead of him.

Weeks later, Jamie swung down from the saddle and led his weary horses into a livery in Bismarck, in the northern part of the Dakota Territory. North Dakota was still about seventeen years away from achieving statehood. Bismarck was first called Edwinton, then renamed Bismarck after the German chancellor.

And it certainly was not an outlaw haven. Those people settling there were solid family folks, farmers for the most part. When gold was discovered in the Black Hills in 1874, the town boomed, becoming an important stopover for stagecoaches and wagons heading for the Black Hills. Camp Hancock was also under construction when Jamie arrived. The military garrison was there to protect workers on the Northern Pacific Railroad.

Jamie had solid information that there were three outlaws who did live in the country a few miles from the town.

But if Jamie had his way, they wouldn't be living for long.

Jamie was certain he was not that well known in this part of the country. His name was, but not his face. He made arrangements to sleep in the loft of the livery. After a bath, Jamie was standing talking to the smithy when a wagon rolled by, two caskets in the bed.

"Three hoodlums tried to rob Olenmeyer," the smithy said. "But Olenmeyer has four big, strapping sons. And they can shoot, too, by golly. Killed those two hoodlums at the farm, and the third lies dying over yonder in that building. Come to find out they was all part of that terrible Miles Nelson gang. The ones that gunfighter, MacCallister, is hunting."

"Do you know their names?"

"Judd, Moore, and Gentry."

"How about that," Jamie muttered.

Jamie rested himself and his horses for several days and then pulled out, heading south. At a trading post at the confluence of the Bad River and the Missouri, in what would soon become Pierre, South Dakota, Jamie overheard some movers talking about the last of the Miles Nelson gang. He listened without joining in the conversation.

"Vic Taylor and Jordan Keller tried to hold up a bank

down in Texas," one of the men said. "They got shot up pretty bad, I hear tell. But they'll live to stand trial and hang."

"Yep. Thirteen steps and the hangman is gonna cheat ol' Jamie MacCallister out of finally gettin' them all. I hear tell they ain't but two of the gang left: Miles Nelson hisself and some young punk named Lloyd Jones. Miles Nelson has probably buried hisself so deep nobody will ever find him— he's a rich man, I heard—and that Jones boy will try to pull something and get hisself kilt, I betcha."

"Yep. You be right, I reckon."

Jamie bought his supplies and rode away.

Several weeks later, in a crossroads post that would later become Sidney, Nebraska, Jamie learned that Miles Nelson, going under the name of Matthew Nallin, and posing as a preacher, had been discovered by federal marshals, and there had been a wild shoot-out inside the Church of the Enlightenment, in Kansas City. Miles Nelson had escaped.

"You'll show up someday," Jamie muttered. "And I'll be there waiting."

"You say somethin', mister," the counterman asked.

Jamie smiled and shook his head. "Just talking to myself."

"I do it, too. Gets lonesome at times. But they's people headin' west by the droves. I sometimes see four or five new faces a day. It's 'bout got me wore plumb down to a frazzle. Never seen nothin' like it. More coffee?"

"Thanks. Tastes good."

"You look like you've been on the trail for quite a spell."

"I have for a fact. But now I'm going home."

"Home. Sounds good, don't it?"

"It sure does."

"You got far to go?"

"A piece." Jamie packed his supplies and headed out. For Colorado.

It was over.

In mid-July of 1872, the longest and bloodiest manhunt

in the history of the West came to a close. Jamie Ian Mac-Callister had tracked down and killed some forty-four men of the Miles Nelson gang. Later, writers of Penny Dreadfuls would claim that he killed several hundred. A new play was soon written about the life of Jamie, and the gunsmoke behind blank cartridges would sometimes obscure the stage.

Jamie stopped in at the new town of Colorado Springs for a bath, a shave and haircut, a change of clothing and a meal and a bed. Then he was back in the saddle, heading for Valley.

In September, Jamie turned Buck's head and looked down the long main street of Valley. Two minutes later, the whole town had turned out, men, women, and children applauding and cheering. Little Ben Pardee found his harmonica and was playing "Dixie," much to the amusement of the new owner of the newspaper, Ben F. Washington.

Jamie's daughters, granddaughters, and great-granddaughters wept at the sight. His sons swallowed back sudden lumps in their throats.

Jamie Ian MacCallister, Man Who Is Not Afraid, Bear Killer, Man Who Plays With Wolves, and known now as the Silver Wolf, had come home.

Before he left the saddle to stand amid the throngs of people, Jamie looked up to the ridge overlooking the miles-long valley, to the flower-covered mound that was Kate's grave. "Howdy, old woman," he whispered. "My God, I miss you."

# BOOK TWO

*It is well, I die hard, but I am not afraid to go.*
—Last words of George Washington
December 14, 1799

# 19

The whole town had pitched in, and Jamie's cabin, on a ridge overlooking Kate's grave, and the grave of Jamie's grandfather, was up in no time and waiting for Jamie's return. The cabin was a snug one, with large rooms and oversized doors so Jamie would not bump his head entering or leaving. And the cabin had been completely furnished and stocked with food for him.

Andrew and Rosanna had left the past month, for an extended tour of Europe. Their children, now all grown, were either married and living away or still in college, both in America and Europe.

For the first afternoon and night back, Jamie's kith and kin left him alone, to relax and to visit Kate's grave. Before visiting the grave site, Jamie bathed and shaved and dressed in clean clothing. Then he went down to sit by Kate's grave and talk to her.

He talked for more than an hour, telling her all the places he'd been since her death. When he was done talking, Jamie went to his cabin and fixed his supper, then sat in a rocking chair on the front porch and drank coffee and smoked his pipe.

As the shadows lengthened, Jamie began to chuckle as he rocked. He'd stick around for a time, maybe a few weeks, just to get reacquainted with his grandkids and great-grandkids, but damned if he was going to wile away his years sitting and rocking and just let the world go by. No . . no, he was still too young for anything like that. He still had some good years left in him, and by damn, he wasn't going to waste them.

His mind made up, Jamie knocked out his pipe, finished his coffee, and then went into the cabin and turned up the twin lamps by his chair. He found his reading glasses and read the last ten weeks of the Valley newspaper (somebody had left them by the chair) before his eyelids started getting heavy. He blew out the lamps and went to bed. He didn't bother locking the doors. Nobody in Valley locked doors. The last time anybody entered a home uninvited in the middle of the night, with devilment on his mind, he got blown all over the living room. Jamie had heard tell that some folks in the cities were putting bars over their windows to keep intruders out.

When Jamie had heard that, he asked, "Why don't the homeowners just shoot the bastards and have done with it?"

"Can't do that back east, Mac. Criminals have rights back there."

"Sorry damn state of affairs, you ask me. Decent people have to live like they're in jail. That'll by God never happen here."

"Don't bet on it, Mac."

Jamie slept long and well and lingered under the comforter for a time, but before dawn, he was up and had coffee ready, biscuits in the oven, oatmeal in the pot, bacon sliced to fry, and eggs ready to bust and cook.

His belly full, Jamie took his cup of coffee and sat for a time in the coolness of early morning, watching the town below wake up.

When it was full light, Jamie stuck a .44 behind his belt and walked down to the town. The walk would help settle his meal, for as usual, whenever he cooked, he ate too much. Kate had always watched that closely, preparng an ample amount for the both of them, and no more.

"If I'm not careful," Jamie muttered as he walked, "I'll end up with my belly hanging over my belt."

My, but the town has grown, Jamie observed, stepping onto the main street and looking up and down. Then, briefly, waves of sadness washed over him as he thought back to how it had been when those first few wagons had rolled onto the valley floor. Swede and Hannah, Moses and Liza, Sam and Sarah, Juan and Maria and all the children. Now all the adults who had come west with him were dead. Jamie was the last one.

Jamie smelled fresh coffee and looked around him. Damned if there wasn't a new cafe in town. He followed the smell of coffee brewing and biscuits cooking and pushed open the door, standing by the counter until the cook looked up and saw him.

"Just sit down anywhere," the cook called. "I'll be with you in a . . ." Then it dawned on him who the big man was. He'd seen dozens of pictures of Jamie. His mouth dropped open, and he almost hurt himself getting out of the kitchen and into the dining area. "Mr. MacCallister!" he blurted. "I'm sorry I didn't recognize you right off. Please, have a seat, sir."

"Relax," Jamie said with a smile. He stuck out his hand, and the cook took it.

"Tom Donovan, sir. I am proud to shake your hand."

Over coffee, the two men sat and chatted for a time, Tom bringing Jamie up on all the news and events that had taken place while he'd been gone. Tom Donovan had arrived in Valley just a few weeks after Jamie had pulled out on his manhunt, and opened the cafe. His wife was one of the teachers at the new school.

"New school?" Jamie questioned.

"Down on the other end of town. It's a fine one, too. Got six rooms."

"Six rooms? What for?"

"Separate the grades. My wife says students learn bette when they're with kids their own age."*

"Time is sure moving too fast for me," Jamie said. "Passing me by."

Jamie took his mug of coffee outside and sat on a bench watching the town come alive for another day. Jamie's oldest, Jamie Ian the Second, walked up and sat down beside his father. He studied his pa's face for a moment.

"You're not going to stay for long, are you, Pa?" he finall asked.

Jamie shook his head. "I'll stick around for a few weeks then I think I'll ramble."

"The girls will be disappointed."

"They'll get over it." Jamie sighed. "There is nothing her for me, boy."

"Your family is here, Pa!"

Jamie looked at his firstborn. Hard to believe the boy wa almost forty-five years old and a grandfather several time over. Jamie never could remember whether Jamie Ian o Ellen Kathleen was born first that day back in the Big Thicket country of East Texas. He'd always relied on Kate for birth dates and such.

"I guess I might as well be the one to tell you the news Pa. Ben F. Washington bought the *Valley Dispatch.* Do yo know who he is?"

"I know all about him, son. How is he doing?"

"Just fine. He's a likeable fellow and damn good writer He wants to do a book about you and Ma."

"It would be real nice if some writer would get the fact straight," Jamie said drily. "That would be a nice change."

"He wants permission to look over Ma's notes and letter and diary and such."

"Let him look at them. It's all right with me. But I don'

---

*By the time Colorado became a state, in 1876, Valley was recognized a having the finest school system in all the state. A private fine arts colleg was established there in 1900 and is still flourishing.

ant the book published until after my death. I want that
nderstood up front."

"Ben said you would probably say that. He's agreeable to
."

"Then tell him if he wants to talk to me, he'd better get
racking. I aim to pull out before the snow flies."

"Falcon's got a surprise for you, Pa."

"Is Marie pregnant again?"

Jamie Ian laughed. "No. That'll probably happen next
ear. She says she wants ten children."

"Good God!"

"And so does Mary Marie O'Donnell MacCallister."

"That's a mouthful, boy. I bet you can't say that fast three
imes in a row. What's Falcon's surprise?"

"He found a horse for you. Said he knew it was for you
he minute he saw it. Damn thing was so mean its owner was
oing to kill it 'til Falcon offered to take it off his hands."
Ie stood up. "Come on. Let's hitch up the buggy and take
ride out to Falcon's ranch."

"Buggy? You goin' soft on me, boy?"

"It's easier on the butt, Pa."

"You are gettin' kinda ample back there, boy. Easy livin',
reckon."


The stallion was the biggest horse Jamie had ever seen.
t was the color of dark sand and had yellow killer eyes.
amie Ian went on into the house, leaving his father lean-
ng against the corral rails.

"Love at first sight," Falcon said, looking at his father
hrough the kitchen window.

"You name him yet?" his brother asked, pouring a cup of
offee and snagging a hot biscuit from the platter. The
ouse was noisy and full of kids.

Before it was all over and done with, the nine living chil-
lren of Jamie and Kate MacCallister would have conceived
ifty-two children. Those fifty-two would produce three hun-

dred and twelve offspring. Many would be a mixture of Chnese, French/Indian, Irish, German, English, Swedish, anSpanish . . . among other nationalities.

"Sundown," Falcon replied. "But he won't answer to mHowever, I'll bet you a hundred dollars within a week Pa wihave him gentled down. For his touch only."

"No bet. Hell, brother! Look. Pa's done got him eatinslices of apple out of his hand."

"That big bastard took a finger clean off of the man I gohim from."

Marie popped Falcon on the butt with the end of a towe"Watch your language around the children."

One of the most dangerous gunfighters in the Wessmiled and said, "Yes, ma'am!" Then he picked up the baband went outside to jaw awhile with his dad.

Jamie went into town every day for coffee and converstion. The rest of the time he worked with Sundown. Withia week, the monster horse was following him around like puppy, nuzzling him and begging for a slice of apple or bit of sugar.

Jamie put Buck out to stud; the horse had earned a lonrest in the pasture, pleasuring the mares at Falcon's horsranch.

Jamie got reacquainted with all his kin and very quietlmet with attorneys and went over land deeds and other certificates of holding, making certain every *i* was dotted anevery *t* was crossed. He had been advised by his private detectives that powerful forces were working to lay claim tmuch of what he owned.

"If they get to crowdin' me too much, I'll put a stop towith guns," he warned his lawyers.

Which made the lawyers very nervous, for they knew thaJamie did not make idle threats, and would do exactly whahe said he would do. And written law be damned.

"I have no patience with schemers and connivers," Jami

arned them. "I'll put a bullet between their eyes faster than
hey can blink."

"We're certain that all this can be handled without vio-
ence, Mr. MacCallister," one of the attorneys was quick to
ay.

"It damn well better be," Jamie replied.

Jamie gave the cabin that he and Kate had called home
or so many years to the Valley Historical Society. The head
f that group, Joleen MacCallister MacKensie, immediately
et about making the place a museum . . . which amused
amie.*

Jamie said his goodbyes and packed up and pulled out in
he fall of '72. He headed east. He wanted to see the Big
'hicket country one more time, and to visit the grave of
3aby Karen, who was killed at five months of age in '29, dur-
ng an outlaw raid.

Jamie rode Sundown, and he had to admit that out of all
he horses he'd ever had, the dark sand-colored animal was
he finest horse he had ever ridden, standing several hands
aller than any other horse Jamie had ever seen.

But Jamie was the only one who could touch the animal.
Anyone else who attempted it would either get bitten or
icked or both.

Jamie stopped in Pueblo City for a night. The town on
he Arkansas had started out as a trading post, then as a
Mormon settlement for a couple of years back in the mid-
orties. The town itself was laid out in 1860.

Jamie ate early in a nearly deserted cafe and then retired
o the loft in the livery. He certainly wasn't hunting trou-
ole, and didn't want trouble to find him.

Several hours before dawn, he put the darkness of the
own behind him.

Jamie and Kate's home was turned into a visitors' museum and was open
o the public for years, before being returned to the MacCallister estate.
t was completely restored in the late 1960s, and one of Jamie and Kate's
reat-great-great-grandsons and family now live there.

Days later, he had crossed the Huerfano, Apishapa, Purgatoire, and the Two Butte rivers before riding onto the grasslands of southeastern Colorado. Then he crossed the Cimarron and rode into the panhandle of Oklahoma Territory.

He was completely out of supplies when he reached a tiny settlement in the northern part of the Texas Panhandle. There was no hotel, but there was a combination dentist/barbershop/undertaker's place with a roughly boarded area to bathe out back.

After his bath, he had his hair cut, a shave and went to eat in the cafe, which was a part of the general store. He had beef and beans (which was pretty much standard fare those days). But the bread was fresh baked and good, and the dried-apple pie was delicious.

Standing outside, under the front awning, Jamie wondered if this town would last much longer. (It wouldn't. Within ten years the tiny settlement would be just another ghost town. Ten more years, and not a trace of it would be left.)

Jamie rode out before dawn, heading south and slightly east. Sundown ate up the miles effortlessly, and the pack horse Falcon had chosen kept up without strain.

Jamie avoided towns whenever possible, often making his own trails. But the farther east he went, the more difficult that became, for the area was filling up—at least the way he saw it—with farms and ranches and little settlements. He stayed west of Dallas/Fort Worth, and after stopping overnight and resupplying at Hillsboro, Jamie rode straight east.

After he crossed the Trinity, Jamie began seeing familiar landmarks, and the memories flooded back . . . both the good and the bad; but mostly the recalling was filled with pleasure.

Jamie spent a night in Palestine, and overnighted again in Nacogdoches. My, but the town had grown since Jamie had last seen it, with fine homes and schools and a univerty. Jamie recalled that Texas' first newspaper was published here: the *Gaceta de Tejas*. And Jamie learned that the first oil well ever drilled in Texas was drilled just a few miles outside of town by a Mr. L. T. Barret.

After his bath and a change into fresh clothing, Jamie stood in front of the barbershop and carefully took in all about him. Something was wrong. For the past week, Jamie had been experiencing an odd tingle in the center of his back. Somebody was dogging his back trail, but staying well back.

Problem was, it could be anybody. Might be some of the kin of those who'd ridden with the Miles Nelson gang looking for revenge. Might be some reputation-hunting young punk. Might be any one of a hundred enemies from the past.

But it was becoming slightly more than a nuisance.

It was getting downright annoying.

# 20

After spending an hour erasing his tracks, Jamie reined up in a thicket along the Attoyac Bayou. Once he'd picketed his horses, he took his rifle from the boot and his field glasses from his saddlebags. On the crest of a knoll, just at the edge of the timber, he bellied down in the grass. He had waited until mid-morning, when the sun would be to his back—and in the eyes of those trailing him—and would not reflect off the lenses of the field glasses.

Jamie waited patiently, in his mind becoming one with the earth, his very being reverting back to his Shawnee training. The minutes ticked past, marching into an hour, then two. Jamie waited. Movement far in the distance caught his attention. He lifted the long lenses and adjusted for range. He counted twelve men, but they were too far away for him to pick out a face among the crowd.

One man did, however, seem vaguely familiar.

The men dismounted and appeared to be discussing something; probably what to do next. They broke apart and began circling all about, searching for the lost sign.

"Oh, come on, fellows," Jamie muttered. "A six-year-old Shawnee boy could find that sign in two minutes."

Jamie had no way of knowing if the men found his sign or not, but something warned them off. After several minutes of standing around, talking and pointing in his general direction, the men mounted up and headed off to the north, soon disappearing from view.

"They're definitely after me," Jamie said to the gentle wind that blew cool around him. "But I have no idea as to the who or why."

He returned to his horses and pulled the picket pins, then stood for a moment, thoughtful. "Miles Nelson," he mused aloud, then shook his head. He didn't think so. He shrugged and swung into the saddle.

Jamie crossed the bayou and headed east; he was getting close to his old home now. Then he came to a road that sure hadn't been there when he and the others had pulled out. And it was a well-traveled road, too.

There was a weathered sign that read CARTHAGE. An arrow under the name pointed the way.

"I'll be damned," Jamie muttered, as he walked his horses across the rutted road. "Progress has sure come to this area of Texas."

The cabin was gone. Not a trace of it remained. Kicking around, Jamie found some old charred wood and wondered if the fire had been accidental or deliberate. It took him the better part of an hour to find the grave of Baby Karen. He spent the rest of the day pulling weeds and carving a new marker. Then he lined a square area around the grave with rocks. The marker read: KAREN MACCALLISTER B 1829 D 1829.

Jamie camped that night near where the old cabin had stood. He did not tarry long the next morning. After saddling up, he sat for a time, looking at the tiny grave site. "Goodbye, Baby Karen," he said. "I reckon you're with your mother now. And I envy you that." Then he turned Sundown's head toward the south and rode away without looking back.

\* \* \*

No one really knows for sure how Beaumont got its name. It might have been named for the agent who sold the original acres, or for the slight elevation called *beau mont* in French. But it sure had grown since Jamie had last seen the town.

In 1901, Beaumont would become a boom town with the discovery of the Spindletop oil field.

Jamie stabled his horses and rubbed them down, making sure they had ample feed and water, then checked into a small hotel and called for a bath.

After he left Beaumont? . . . He didn't have any idea where he might go. He just didn't want to return to Valley. Kate wasn't there.

Jamie wandered around town for a day, but while he appeared to be just strolling about, he was also keeping an eye out for anyone who might be following him. He could spot no one and pulled out early the next morning, heading west.

He entertained the thought of veering a little south and visiting the Alamo, but decided against it. Too many memories associated with that bloody old mission.

It was a hundred-mile ride over to Navasota, and it was uneventful. Navasota was one of the earliest Anglo-American towns in Texas, settled in 1822 by families from Louisiana. It was also where the explorer La Salle, while attempting to find the mouth of the Mississippi River, was murdered by his own men. La Salle was just a tad south of his objective.

There had been no further sign of those men who had dogged Jamie's back trail in East Texas. Jamie was riding easier, but very much alert for trouble. And he knew once he got in West Texas, he had better keep his eyes wide open if he wanted to keep his hair, for that was Comanche and Kiowa country. In Navasota, Jamie spent the night in a boardinghouse and was on the move early the next morning, heading for Austin.

Jamie knew he was piddling, just wasting time. But he was

without direction, drifting. He just didn't know what to do with the rest of his life. For almost forty-five years, the center of his existence had been Kate. Now there was a great empty void in his being.

The reporters from back east who had been sent out into the Wild West to cover Jamie's life and times had long since returned home. Trying to catch up with Jamie Ian Mac-Callister was like attempting to get a firm grip on smoke.

The young men who had been sent west to buy property and check out other investments had visited Valley. The trio were quickly wising up to the ways of the West, and it didn't take them long to realize that anybody, *anybody*, who tried any shady deals in and around Valley would not last long, and would probably end up shot or hanged, or both. They told their fathers to forget that area of Colorado . . . unless they had a death wish.

During Jamie's brief stay in Valley, he had talked with Ben F. Washington every day, at length, with Ben taking careful notes. And after going through Kate's diaries and journals, he had given the young man most of them. A few were just too personal, and those he had placed in a lockbox. Ben worked on his manuscript for at least an hour every day. There was no rush, for he had given his word that the book would not be published until after Jamie's death.

Those shyster lawyers hired by Newby, Olmstead, Bradford, Layfield, and others to horn in on the MacCallister holdings had hit a stone wall that they could not go around, through, over or under. It had come in the form of one Ulysses S. Grant, President of the United States of America, a good Republican and a man who admired Jamie Ian Mac-Callister.

With the intervention of the president, those schemers and plotters quietly backed off. But they didn't go away. They would bide their time and wait, for their hate ran deep and dark, passed from father to son.

In Austin, Jamie stabled his horses and checked into a hotel. Austin was the state capital, but it still had its wild and woolly places, and was also the home of the gunfighter Ben Thompson. Ben hadn't been out of the state pen long, having served his time for shooting his brother-in-law (after the man had beat up Thompson's wife) and threatening to kill a local justice of the peace.

Jamie wanted no trouble, and breathed a little easier when he learned from local gossip that Ben was raising hell up in Kansas.*

Jamie rested his horses, then provisioned up and put Austin behind him as he continued on west. At Fredericksburg, a town settled by Germans in 1846, when it was right on the edge of the western frontier, Jamie was warned that the Comanches and Kiowa were on the warpath. But there were wagons filled with supplies gearing up to head west for El Paso in a couple of days. It would be a prudent move on Jamie's part to join them. The wagons would be accompanied by a detachment of cavalry heading for Fort Bliss.

Jamie hunted up the wagon master. After the man had recovered from his shock at meeting one of the West's most famous men, he quickly agreed to Jamie coming along. It would be an honor, he said.

The young cavalry officer in charge of the detachment of soldiers (as yet mostly untrained and untested in battle) was clearly in awe of Jamie and for two days followed him around like a lost puppy. The young lieutenant, a recent graduate of West Point and who, until his trip to the Point and this grand adventure out west, had never been more than ten miles from his home in New Hampshire, amused Jamie, and he decided to take the young officer under his

---

*Ben Thompson returned to Austin in 1875, and the next year killed two men in the Senate Saloon. Despite being a convicted felon, Ben was elected city marshal of Austin in 1881, but resigned the next year, after killing several men. Ben Thompson became an alcoholic and in 1884 was killed by Joe Foster and William Simms while watching a show at the Vaudeville Theater in San Antonio. Although he had been shot nine times, Thompson still managed to get his pistols out and put lead into Joe Foster before he died. One of Foster's legs had to be amputated, and he died three days later.

wing, so to speak, and try to teach him enough about the frontier to keep him alive.

"I'm to be posted here for three years, sir," Lt. Cal Sanders told Jamie. "Then I'm going to request duty somewhere in Montana or Wyoming."

"Is that right?"

"Yes, sir. I'm told the Cheyenne are the most magnificent Indians to be found."

"One of my sons married a Cheyenne princess."

"Oh, my. I didn't realize that. And you're friends with the Indians?"

"I've been friends with them and fought them on occasion. But mostly I'm a friend with the Sioux, the Cheyenne, the Nez Perce, the Ute, the Arapaho. I don't know much about the Apache and Kiowa and the Comanche . . . except they're great fighters, and don't get captured by them."

The young lieutenant didn't have to ask why Jamie said that. He had already heard horror stories about what happened to men, and women, too, who were unfortunate enough to be taken alive by the savages.

"It would be a great honor to have you ride along with my detachment, sir," Lt. Sanders said. "I mean, beside me, sir. Not back with the . . ." The lieutenant got all flustered. "You know what I mean, sir."

Jamie laughed. "Relax, Cal. You're going to do just fine out here."

"I'm looking forward to an encounter with the hostiles."

"Not after the first one you won't be," Jamie muttered, as the lieutenant walked away. "If you live through it, that is."

But the Indians obviously thought the wagon train, some twenty-five wagons long, with both civilian guards and soldiers, was too strong for them. Much to the disappointment of Lt. Sanders and the great relief of all the others, the trip to El Paso was uneventful.

Scouting around, Jamie picked up a lot of Indian sign, but saw no Indians, although he was sure they had seen him.

Jamie did his best to pass along to the young lieutenant

at least some of his knowledge about the frontier. By the time the wagons reached El Paso, in the dead of late winter, 1873, Lt. Sanders knew a little something about survival on the frontier.

Jamie lounged around El Paso for a few days, trying to make up his mind where he wanted to go next. He did not want to strike out alone across New Mexico and Arizona, for the Apache nation was at war with the whites—a war that would continue until the surrender of Geronimo, in 1886.

On a cold morning in February, Jamie and five other men, all of them well-seasoned (which meant in the vernacular of the West, they were all gray-beards), rode out of El Paso, heading west, into New Mexico Territory—statehood was still years away: January, 1912.

In Las Cruces, two of the men decided to drop out of the group. That left Jamie, Red Green, an old mountain man who was called Logan, and a retired army sergeant named Canby.

Jamie's eyes were amused as he looked at his new friends, who now sat around a table in a saloon. "Boys," he said, "I reckon between the four of us, we've got about two hundred years of Indian fighting. I aim to see me some new country 'fore I cash in. I have ample money and can get more. What say you we provision up and head into country few white men have seen?"

The three "well-seasoned" men exchanged glances, and all of them smiled.

"Why the hell not?" Logan was the first to speak. "We damn shore ain't gettin' no younger."

"Suits me," Canby said. "Why not? But let's just make damn sure we got enough ammunition to ward off some Injun attacks. 'Cause sure as God made little green apples, we're gonna have to fit some fights."

Red Green nodded his head in agreement. "I like you boys' company, for a fact. I generally shy away from folks, but you boys is different. We get along. And you boys is trail wise and don't jibber-jabber nonsense all the damn time.

But you bes' understand somethin': Odds are that some of us, maybe all of us, won't be ridin' back. 'Paches is about the most notional of all Injuns. I've lost good friends to the 'Paches. And on the other hand, I've made friends with some 'Paches. A few. This ain't gonna be no Sunday school picnic."

Canby looked at him. "You all done preachin'?"

"Shore."

"Then let's ride," Logan said.

# 21

The four men, average age sixty-two, rode out and headed north, each trailing a packhorse. Most of the townspeople thought they were crazy, but kept that opinion to themselves. They were heading into the Caballo Mountains and a trading post located on the hot springs, about sixty miles north of Las Cruces.*

Each of the men wore two pistols belted around them, and two pistols on holsters located on each side of the saddle horn. They all carried lever-action rifles and long-bladed Bowie knives.

Whether the four men had angels riding with them, or if the Apaches were just looking the other way when they rode by, was not known. But whatever the reason, Jamie and his compadres rode from Las Cruces to the springs without incident. The owner of the post shook his head in wonder.

"It happens," the old man said. "Apaches is like rattlesnakes. I've walked a foot from a damned rattler and he didn't even raise his head to look at me. Other times they'll start rattlin' and strikin' if you get within fifty feet of them. 'Paches is the same way, I reckon. But if you see one, don't

---

*After the town was laid out, it was named Hot Springs and remained that way for years. On the tenth anniversary of the radio program "Truth or Consequences," the town accepted an offer to name itself after the show.

hesitate, just blow the damned dirty heathen right off his horse. I hate ever' damn one of them."

"Caused you some grief, have they?" Jamie asked.

The old man spat a stream of brown tobacco juice into a spittoon. "Grief? I should say so. I tried to make friends with them when I furst come out here. I'm still carryin' the arreyhead in my side for that trouble. Then I tried agin. That time they burned down my cabin, killed my wife, and stole my horses. Shot me in the process. For the last ten years I been shootin' ever' goddamn one of 'em I could. We gonna have to wipe 'em all out one of these days. Might as well get on with it, I say." He poured them all drinks and gave them a good look. "You fellers is all past your prime, I'd say." He looked at Jamie. " 'Ceptin' you, maybe. I can't figure you. You boys just wanderin'?"

"Seein' the country," Red told him.

"Yeah? Well, all I can say is good luck. 'Cause you're shore gonna need it."

Days later, the four men found themselves pinned down on the east bank of a tiny creek in what would years later become the Gila Primitive Area.

During a lull in the fighting, Red Green asked, "You reckon them's Apaches?"

"They ain't your grandmother's tea party," Logan told him, shifting his chew of tobacco from one side of his mouth to the other.

Red ignored the sarcasm and asked, "Where's Jamie and Canby?"

"They're in good positions in the rocks. Jamie's to the right and Canby's to the left. Horses is safe to our rear under the bluff."

"They made a mistake attacking us here," Jamie called. "And I think they'll soon realize it."

Canby was too far off to the left to hear the comment, but Logan did. "Yeah, you be right, I'm thinkin'. We got cover and water and a good field of fire in front of us. But you and Canby best watch keeful to your flanks come the night."

Logan had roamed and trapped all over the Northwest and worked at various jobs all the way down to central Texas, but he was new to this country. "I thought Apaches never attacked at night."

"Shit," the old mountain man replied. "Some do, some don't. Depends on whether their medicine's strong enough."

One small brown object had appeared in Jamie's line of view. He lifted his rifle, took careful aim, and fired. There was a short scream of pain as the bullet shattered a kneecap.

The Apaches came in a rush then, darting from rock to rock, bush to bush, until they were right on the edge of the clearing. Then they seemed to vanish into the earth.

"Excellent," Jamie said. "They've learned very well the Warrior's Way."

"They didn't have to larn it so damned good," Logan groused. Then he tensed for a few seconds, jerked up his rifle and fired. They all heard the ugly sound of a bullet striking flesh. A young Apache, looking to be in his late teens, stood up in his moccasins, his chest bloody, and then fell face forward on the rocks. He did not move.

"That one didn't learn it so good," Red remarked, as Logan thumbed another round into his rifle.

The fight continued all that afternoon, without either side inflicting any more damage to the other. As the shadows began to lengthen, Jamie softly called, "Now it gets real interesting, boys. Canby? Slide back and make up a big pot of coffee, brew it strong. Do it before it gets full dark and let the fire die down to coals; just enough to keep the coffee good and hot. We're going to need it. If you sleep tonight, you die."

"What a cheerful thought," Canby replied.

Darkness soon covered the land, and Jamie could taste moisture on his lips. He looked up. Clouds had moved in, obscuring the stars. Rain was not far away, and that was not good for the four defenders. As soon as the rain started, the

Apaches would attack, the falling drops covering any sound they might make.

Jamie did not have to tell the others that. They knew.

Lightning began licking the sky, and thunder rumbled high above the Mimbres Mountains. There was a searing and sudden flash of lightning, and the eyes of the men widened as they caught sight of the warriors coming across the creek, the lightning catching them on the rocks and in the water.

Four rifles crashed and boomed in a deadly crescendo, as fast as the men could fire and lever. Three Apaches made the crossing and leaped onto and then behind the rocks. Logan fired point-blank into the chest of one Apache, the bullet nearly stopping the warrior in mid-air. The mountain man stepped to one side and let the lifeless form fall to the ground.

Canby deflected the swipe of a knife with the barrel of his rifle and brought the butt around with all his strength. It thudded solidly against the Apache's head, followed instantly by the sickening sound of the man's skull being crushed.

Meanwhile, Jamie wrestled a smaller and younger man to the ground and kneed him hard in the groin. The Apache's mouth opened in a silent rush of agony, and he relaxed his hold on Jamie's arms. Jamie closed one big hand around the Apache's throat and crushed the larynx, twisting his hand as he did. The Apache thrashed about on the sand and the rocks as he fought for breath that would never come again.

Jamie picked up the warrior and threw him out into the clearing.

"Anybody hurt?" Jamie called.

No one was.

The night grew quiet as the rains came.

"Get ready for another charge," Logan said, wiping off his rifle and thumbing rounds into the tube. "It ain't over."

\* \* \*

Hundreds of miles to the north, the residents of the town of Valley were relaxing after a day of work and a good supper. The cafes were preparing to close and clean up. Card games were beginning in Falcon's Wild Rose Saloon and Gaming House. Cowboys and miners were drifting in for a drink and some talk. Mothers were putting small children to bed. Older kids were studying textbooks and doing homework. Ben F. Washington was working on his manuscript. Falcon knocked on Matthew's front door and stepped inside.

"What's the matter with you?" Matthew asked, taking a look at his younger brother's face.

Falcon handed him the telegram he'd just received from a friend of his in Kansas.

Matthew opened the single sheet of paper and read: ASA PIKE AND GANG LEFT HERE SEVERAL DAYS AGO STOP. RIDING FOR NEW MEXICO TERRITORY. STOP BELIEVE YOUR FATHER AND SEVERAL FRIENDS HEADING FOR ALBUQUERQUE. STOP. ASA PIKE HAS AT LEAST TWENTY-FIVE MEN WITH HIM. STOP SWORN TO KILL YOUR FATHER. STOP. BEST LUKE.

"Who the hell is Asa Pike?" Matthew asked.

Falcon shrugged heavy shoulders. "I don't know. One of Pa's enemies, I reckon. I think I'll take me a little ride south."

"I'll get my gear together, and—"

"Forget it, Matt," Falcon said, holding up a hand. "You're the sheriff here. You can't just up and leave. Big brother Jamie sure can't go; he's gettin' too fat in the butt. Long ride like that and he wouldn't be able to walk for a month. Morgan's tied down with all his business interests; more so now since he owns controlling stock in the bank. I'm packed up and ready to ride. I've said my goodbyes." He held out a hand, and his older brother shook it. "I'll get word to you when it's over."

Matthew stood on the front porch and watched Falcon ride away into the dark. His wife, Ginny, came to his side. "I overheard. Falcon will always be riding off, won't he?"

"I'm afraid so." Matthew put an arm around her waist. "He's just like Pa. The wilderness calls to him."

"And the wildness," she added.

"That, too."

"He's lucky to have a wife like Marie."

"Ma liked her. In the short time she got to know her, she really liked Marie."

Within minutes, the rest of the MacCallister clan had gathered at the house. Matthew handed them the telegram, and they read it, passing it around.

Joleen asked the question that was on everyone's mind: "Who is Asa Pike?"

No one knew.

"I feel really bad about not going with Falcon," Jamie Ian the Second said.

His wife, Caroline, smiled and patted his arm. "When was the last time you sat a saddle for weeks at a time, love?"

Morgan laughed. "The same time I did, Caroline. And it was a few years back."*

Megan turned to her husband. "Hitch up the buggy for me, Jim. I'm going out to spend the night with Marie. She's had time to do her crying and get done with it. Go on, now." She turned to face the group. "The rest of you can go on home. There is nothing we can accomplish by standing around with long faces. Besides, we'd better get used to Falcon riding off. You all know he's just like Pa when it comes to that."

She had no way of knowing it, but her statement would prove to be prophetic.


The Apaches had carried off their dead during the rainy night and then vanished. They had tested the four men and found them worthy opponents.

*Talons of Eagles*—Kensington Books

"They've cleared out," Jamie said, after spending some time scouting around the area on foot.

"Which way did they go?" Red asked.

"West."

"Then lets us head north for a spell," Logan suggested.

"That just might be a right good idea," Red agreed. "I allow as to how we've pressed our luck pretty hard this go around."

The men started packing up and were gone within the hour, heading north and slightly east. Days later, they rode into Socorro, on the Rio Grande. At the same time, Falcon was checking into a hotel in Santa Fe. Asa Pike and his band of kin and cutthroats were riding into The Meadows, better known as Las Vegas, New Mexico Territory.

One of the strangest and wildest shoot-outs in New Mexico history was only days away from exploding.


Seated in a small cafe on a side street in Socorro, Jamie felt eyes on him and turned his head. A young cowboy was staring at him, but not in an unfriendly way. The cowboy rose from the counter stool and walked over, his big Spanish spurs jingling. He squatted down beside Jamie's chair.

"You're Mr. MacCallister, ain't you?"

"That's right."

Red, Logan, and Canby had stopped eating, listening.

"I got some news that might interest you, sir. I just rode in from the northeast. Been up to Kansas lookin' around. I didn't care for the place; wind blows all the damn time. You know a man name of Asa Pike?"

"I've met him."

"Well . . . he's put together a band of his kin, and they strutted around up yonder for a time, talkin' 'bout what all they was gonna do to you if they ever caught up with you. And none of it was what I'd call right pleasant."

"That is interesting." Jamie studied the young man's face for a moment. "What's your name?"

"Rick. Rick Hanes. My grandma used to talk about you, Mr. MacCallister."

Jamie moved his chair over a bit and said, "Pull up a chair and sit down. Do I know your grandmother?"

"You probably don't remember her, sir," Rick said, sitting down. "But she knew you when you was little, back in Kentucky. She was married to a man named Caney. Her daughter, my ma, married a man name of Hanes."

"Caney," Jamie mused. "Sure. I remember Mr. Caney. He was one of the few men who stood up for me when I was living with Sam and Sarah Montgomery, after Hannah and me escaped from the Shawnee village."

"That's him."

Jamie let his eyes drift over the young man's attire. Down on his luck, Jamie thought. "You eaten today, Rick?"

"Ah . . . well . . . no, sir, I ain't. I just come in here 'cause it smelled good."

Jamie smiled and waved the waiter over. "Bring this young man some supper." He turned to Rick. "Now, let's talk about Asa Pike . . ."

# 22

Several half-drunk cowboys from local ranches came into the cafe, took one look at the four "well-seasoned" men sitting with the much younger rider, and wisely decided to leave them alone. The four older men had the look of Curly Wolf written all over them. The cowboys—all western born—had learned at an early age that older men could and would kill you quicker than you could blink. And there was something about that big, solid-looking man with the pale eyes and the huge hands that spelled trouble . . . to those with enough sense to read it.

The cowboys ordered their supper and kept any sarcastic remarks they might have had to themselves.

Not so one young man who strolled in just as the cowboys were being served their meal. He took one look at Jamie and his group and said, "What is this? A old-folks' convention?"

The cowboys exchanged glances and began eating their supper. They wanted to be through before the fireworks started. And they were, to a man, certain there would be trouble if the loudmouth didn't wise up . . . and do so quickly.

Jamie, Red, Logan, and Canby all chose to ignore the young trouble hunter.

Rick started to rise from his chair, but Jamie's hand

stopped him. "Forget it. He isn't worth the effort to swat him," Jamie said in low tones.

"Did you say something about me, old-timer?" the young punk pushed.

Jamie expelled breath in a sigh.

"Don't push them men, Larado," the counterman warned the young man. "Leave it alone."

The young man who called himself Larado looked at the cafe owner. "Shut up, Charlie. Mind your own business."

"Suit yourself, Larado. It's your funeral."

"You think!" he sneered.

Jamie sipped his freshly filled cup of coffee, then added more sugar to it. When he could get real sugar, he liked his coffee hot and black and sweet.-He smiled, remembering what his old and dear friend Moses Washington had once told him about some of his antics before he married Liza. He said he liked his women the same way.

"What the hell are you smilin' about?" Larado shouted, startling Jamie for a moment.

One thing Jamie had learned about himself as he grew older was that he was less and less inclined to take a bunch of crap from a certain type of the younger generation. He turned in his chair. "Shut up, boy!"

Then he turned around, picked up his fork, and began eating his piece of pie. Good pie.

Larado was stunned into silence for a moment. Then he started laughing. "Charlie! Did you hear what this old buzzard bait just said to me?"

"Yeah," Charlie said. "And was I you, I'd heed that advice. I just now figured out who that man is. That's Jamie Ian Mac-Callister."

"Oh, Lord!" one of the cowboys whispered.

"MacCallister!" Larado roared. "Why, hell. He must be near'bouts a hundred years old." He carelessly slapped both his tied down holsters, a move that in some parts could get him instantly dead, and then looked all around the cafe. "Where'd you park your cane and your crutch, old man?"

Jamie almost told the mouthy young man that if he had a cane and a crutch, he knew where he'd like to park them. But he kept his peace and ate his pie.

"Larado," a nicely dressed middle-aged man, sitting with two other men, spoke up. "MacCallister just got off of a two-year manhunt. He killed some fifty-odd men during that time. Doesn't that tell you anything?"

"I don't believe none of that," the young punk said. "I don't believe half of what-all's said about MacCallister." He moved closer to the table and leaned down, bent over at the waist. When his mouth was about a foot from Jamie's ear, he said, "Did you hear me, old man. I said I don't believe none of them things that's said 'bout you. I don't believe you fought at the Alamo. I don't believe you're no fast gun. But I do believe you're a big bag of wind. I think you made up all them things yourself. I think you're a liar. I think—"

Jamie brought his right elbow up and around—fast and hard. The elbow caught the punk flush on the mouth, the impact producing a sound like someone's boot slowly stepping on a very large roach. Two teeth popped out and bounced on the floor as the blood sprayed, and Larado's hands flew to his ruined mouth. Jamie stood up and snatched both of Larado's guns from their holsters, tossing them on the table.

Then he proceeded to beat the shit out of the big mouth.

Jamie hit him with short, chopping punches, lefts and rights to the face. Larado's nose was flattened against his face. Both eyes were soon closing. One ear was dangling by a thin strip of flesh. Then Jamie started working on Larado's belly and ribs. The scene was ugly, and the sounds of the blows landing were sickening.

It was all over in less than two minutes. Larado lay on the cafe floor, unconscious. Jamie reached down and stripped the gun belt from the man, tossing it on the table. Then he picked up Larado and threw him out the door. The punk olled butt over elbows off the boardwalk to land in the usty street.

Jamie returned to the table, sat down, picked up his fork, nd began eating the remainder of his pie.

"Jesus Christ!" one of the cowboys muttered.

A man wearing a badge ran up to the unconscious Larado nd knelt down. One of the businessmen rose from his able and walked outside, speaking briefly to the deputy. he deputy nodded his head, then motioned to several nen lounging nearby, and they picked up Larado and toted im away.

The businessman returned to his table, and the deputy valked away.

Jamie pointed a fork at the twin guns on the table. "Rick, hat pistol of yours is so old I wouldn't want to be around vhen you fired it. Take those guns. Larado won't be need-ng them."

The pistols were brand spanking new Colts, army model, aliber .45.

"If you're going to ride with us, you need to be well rmed," Jamie added.

The cowboys finished their meal and very quietly left the afe. To a man, they were hard ol' boys, accustomed to loing brutal work from sunup to sundown, and there wasn't nuch they hadn't seen and damn little they would back up rom. But they had never seen such an emotionless and uthless beating administered in such a short time.

The fight in the cafe in Socorro would be talked about or years to come.

But not as much as the gunfight that was only days away rom erupting in the streets of Albuquerque.

"You get enough to eat?" Jamie asked the youngest and newest member of the group.

"Oh, yes, sir," Rick said. "My belly's about to pop. I thank ou for it."

"Stop calling me sir. My name is Jamie." He smiled at the

young man. "Let's find us a place to sleep. We'll pull ou
early in the morning."


Several months after the birth of their child, William and
Page Haywood left Denver and moved to Valley, where
William hung out his shingle and started his practice of law
The baby was dark-haired, blue-eyed, and fair-skinned
much to the relief of all concerned.

Russell Clay was more than delighted to see the young
couple leave Denver; now he could get on with the rest of
his life without fear of bumping into his niece every time
he stepped out of the house. But there was still the matter
of his sister to be resolved. Russell knew that she had hired
detectives to find him, just as she knew that he had hired
detectives to find her. A showdown between brother and sister was inevitable. It was just a matter of time.

Both Russell Clay and Andrea Petri had hired detectives
to travel to Valley, to find out what her son and his nephew,
Ben, was up to. Both were horrified to learn that he going
ahead with his plans to write a book about the MacCallister
family and everyone connected with them over the past
fifty years.

Each of them, without the other knowing it, started making plans to rid themselves, once and for all, of Ben F. Washington. And each other, if the opportunity should present
itself.


Jamie and his little group pulled out of Socorro at about
the same time Asa Pike and his bunch left Las Vegas and Falcon rode out of Santa Fe.

Asa could have saved several days riding time by cutting
across country, but that would have been a dangerous route
due to the Indians. Instead, they followed the stage route,
a winding, curving road that went first to Santa Fe before

tting south. That move put Falcon well ahead of them.
e arrived in Albuquerque one day before his father.

Falcon could get along in Spanish—just like his pa—so
 gravitated to Old Town and got himself a room above a
ntina. The plaza in Old Town would remain the center
 the town until the railroad arrived, in 1880. After that,
e center of the growing community would evolve around
e railroad.

Falcon told the owner of the hotel to reserve a block of
oms; he had some friends coming in.

The younger MacCallister had no way of knowing which
rection his pa would be coming from, but on a hunch, he
de out to the southern edge of town to a cantina. There,
 bought a bottle of tequila and sat outside, under the
vning. His hunch proved correct on the second day.

Falcon heard riders coming and looked up. He smiled.
here was no mistaking that monster his pa rode. Falcon
ood up and stepped out to the edge of the road. He didn't
now any of the men with his pa, but with the exception of
e young man, they were well-seasoned, looking like they
ouldn't be afraid to tackle an angry grizzly.

When the dust had settled, Jamie looked down from the
ddle and said, "Boy, what the hell are you doing down
ere?"

"You fellows light and sit," Falcon told them. "There's big
ouble just around the bend."

"Do tell," Jamie said, swinging down from the saddle.

"I don't have to ask who this is," Red said, eyeballing Fal-
n. "Boy looks just like you, Mac."

"For a fact, he do," Logan said. "And 'pears to be right
pable, too."

"I bet you he's hell with the ladies," Canby remarked.

"Not no more, he isn't," Jamie said. "Marie would cut his
ingus off if she found out about any dallying on his part."

Falcon stood with a smile on his lips, letting the older
en rib him a bit.

"I'm Rick," the young rider said, holding out a hand.

Falcon took the hand. "Where in the hell did you me
up with this disreputable bunch of old codgers."

The others hooted and cawed at that while Falcon's ey
sized up the three older men with his pa. They fairly br
tled with guns and knives, and Falcon sensed they all kne
how to use them, and would. He guessed the older men
be in their sixties, at least. But there was a spring in the
step that many men half their age did not have.

Seated at a table inside the coolness of the cantina, Fa
con handed his pa the telegram he'd received. Jamie hel
the paper out at arm's length but still couldn't make out th
damn words until he put on his reading glasses.

"At least you can read words," Logan said. "I never larne
how myself."

"How long have you been out here, Mr. Logan?" Ric
asked respectfully.

"Not *Mister*, just Logan," the old mountain man correcte
with a smile. "I was twenty year old when I crossed the Mi
sissippi in . . . oh, let me see . . . it were 1829, I think."

"Asa Pike," Jamie said, taking off his reading glasses an
putting them in a hard case. "I remember him. I put lea
in him up in . . . oh, up in the Medicine Bows. Little no
name mining town that was nearly deserted. That was oh
two years ago." He looked at the four men with him. "Thi
isn't your fight, boys."

"Hell it ain't," Red contradicted quickly.

"Yeah," Logan jumped in. "You think you're gonna hav
all the fun, Mac, you got another think comin'."

"We're pards, ain't we?" Canby asked.

"You done me a good turn," Rick said. "I'm stayin'."

"Six-to-one odds, at least, boys," Jamie reminded them.

"Makes it all that more interestin'," Logan said, downin
his tequila and grimacing. "I never *did* like this stuff! Giv
me plain ol' American whiskey any day."

\* \* \*

Falcon led the group into Old Town and to the hotel. The men cleaned up and put on their best, be it buckskin or broadcloth, and went into the cafe for supper. They had just ordered when two men wearing badges approached the table.

"You boys just passin' through?" one of the lawmen asked.

"Just passin' through," Jamie said, filling and rolling up a warm tortilla. He took a bite and smiled up at the deputy. "Something on your mind?"

"Avoiding trouble."

"I've always found that to be a good practice," Jamie said agreeably. "Personally, I'm a peace-loving man."

"Mr. MacCallister," the other deputy said. "We don't want trouble here in Albuquerque. And for the last two and a half years, everywhere you've been there was trouble. Who are you hunting here?"

"No one," Jamie said. "Now someone may be hunting me. But I'm not looking for anyone. Me and the boys here are just seeing some country and trying to keep our hair in the process."

The deputies laughed. "We do know what you mean about that. Gonna be in town long?" one asked innocently.

"Couple of days to rest the horses and resupply, and then we're gone."

They both exchanged glances; then the older of the two said, "See you around."

"You bet." Jamie waited until the men had left the cafe, then said, "They know something's up. The law must be in touch with each other."

"They got them talkin' wires all over the damned place when the Injuns ain't cut them," Logan pointed out. "Which they do regular. But I don't know ifn they got 'em here, or not."

"What do you have in mind, Pa?" Falcon asked.

"Minding my own business, son. I'm not looking for trouble. But neither will I run from it."

"Then you didn't really lie to those deputies, did you, M MacCallister?" Rick asked.

Jamie smiled. "Not exactly."

Logan chuckled. "You can bet they're gonna have the peepers peeled on us."

"Let them look," Red said. "There ain't no law again drinkin' and eatin' and sittin' around jawin'."

"That is a fact, isn't it?" Jamie asked. Then he finished o his tortilla and grinned, the smile wiping years from his fac

# 23

Indian trouble pulled the deputies and a large posse of civilians out of Albuquerque on the third morning after Jamie's arrival. One hour later, Asa Pike and his bunch rode in.

Jamie had hired a couple of young Mexican boys to watch the roads and report back to him when they spotted any large groups of men riding in.

Ten minutes after Asa and his bunch rode in, Jamie knew it. He gave each of the boys some money and told one to watch the men and to report back to him once they left the hotel. He told the other one to warn the citizens around Old Town to get ready to seek cover at his signal.

The residents of Old Town knew all about Jamie Ian MacCallister. Knew he treated every person the same, regardless of color. Knew some of his grandkids had married into Mexican families. Since they had arrived in Old Town, Jamie and the men with him had been respectful and polite to the Mexican community.

The residents of Old Town began doing some planning on their own.

Asa Pike and his men cleaned up and got something to eat; then they returned to their hotel rooms and slept the remainder of the night. Just as dawn was cracking open the cover of dark, and the residents of Albuquerque were beginning to stir, Asa and his men left the hotel and began their walk to Old Town. They each carried at least two pistols—some had spare pistols tucked behind their belts—and all carried rifles.

"Thirty-two of them, counting Asa," Falcon told his pa.

"They must really be a-feared of us," Logan said, draining his cup of coffee and standing up to stretch his muscles and pop his joints. "I've fought off more Injuns than that by my lonesome a time or twice."

The men checked their pistols, and each shoved two spares behind his belt. Jamie loaded up his sawed-off while the others checked rifles; all made certain the loops in their ammo belts were full and they had plenty of cartridges in their pockets.

Jamie looked at the two bright-eyed boys he'd hired. "Pass the word, boys. Everybody inside and keep their heads down."

"Si, señor!" they said, and were gone.

What Jamie and his compadres did not know was that at that moment, the men of Old Town were sharpening knives and machetes, the women were boiling pots of water to throw on the intruders, and young boys had gathered lots of nice-sized rocks to throw.

Jamie rose from the bench. "You boys ready to crank up the band?"

"I been ready," Canby said.

"Let's get this over with so's we can eat," Logan told him. "I've done developed a likin' for this Mexican food."

"What you've developed a likin' for is that fat cook Isabella at the cafe," Red said with a grin.

"I does like 'em ample," the old mountain man admitted. "More to love, and they's warm on a cold night."

"So's a bear," Canby said. "But I don't want to snuggle up to one."

Falcon grinned at Rick Hanes. "You all right?"

"I been down this road before," the young man said easily. "I ain't no cherry when it comes to gunhawkin'."

Falcon slowly nodded his head. "I got you pegged now.

ook me a time, but I knew it would come to me. You faced
our men in that saloon over in El Paso a couple of years
ack."

"They got lead in me," Rick replied.

"But you killed all four of them."

"For a fact," the young man said.

Jamie looked at the pair. "And before that, a bully braced
ou in Fort Worth and you dropped him. Yeah. I know who
ou are now. How come you were so down on your luck
vhen we connected?"

"I got all those damn Kermit brothers and all their kin
nd such out of Arkansas after me," Rick said. "I can't hold
 job long enough to get ahead none. I get a job, they show
p. And they's about a hundred of them."

"What'd you do to them?" Logan asked.

"Well," Rick said, wiping a speck of dust from the action
f his right-hand .45, "I was hangin' around Little Rock a
vhile back when this pretty little golden-haired lady started
 attin' her eyes and swishin' her bustle at me. We ended up
 on a blanket down by a crick under a tree. Hell, I didn't
 know she was married. And I shore didn't know she was
 narried to Herman Kermit. He called me out later on that
 night." Rick shrugged his shoulders. "He missed and I
 lidn't. I been dodgin' all them damn Kermits ever since."

Jamie and the others laughed at the hangdog expression
 on the young man's face. Jamie said, "That sounds like
 omething Falcon used to do."

"Aw, Pa!" Falcon protested, his face red.

"Don't 'aw, Pa' me. I recollect that time you was all snug-
 gled up to that Sadie Lovington woman, and her husband
 caught you both bare-assed in the barn."

"I kept tellin' you and Ma, I didn't know she was married!"

"I thought I was gonna have to shoot Clyde Lovington,"
 Jamie said, chuckling. "That was one of the funniest sights
 I ever saw. You as naked as the day you were born and your
 Ma two steps behind, swingin' that quirt. She'd connect on

your bare ass, and you'd jump about three feet in the a
and squall like a puma."

"You sure have a good memory," Falcon mumbled, :
laughter rang out all around him.

"How old were you?" Rick asked, wiping his eyes.

Falcon mumbled under his breath.

"You were not," his pa corrected. "You were fifteen, an
Sadie would never see thirty again. That woman sure like
to spread her charms around. Course, I will have to say tha
when you were fifteen, you looked twenty-one."

"Thank you for that," Falcon said.

"But sometimes acted like you were ten," his pa added.

"Shit!" Falcon muttered. "Can we drop the subject?"

"Jamie Ian MacCallister!" The shout echoed around th
buildings of Old Town. "I be Abraham Pike and I'm her
to avenge my kin. Step out here and face me."

"Well, here we go," Jamie said. He cocked both hammer
to the Greener and stepped around the corner of the build
ing. He walked toward the man, standing tall and straigh
in the center of the block. "Your brother tried to kill me
Pike. Tried to bushwhack me."

"You're a damn liar, MacCallister. My brother weren't n
back shooter."

Jamie was closing the distance fast. His eyes had alread
picked out the spot where he was going to jump after he
fired the Greener.

"Draw, damn you!" Abraham yelled.

Just then a rock came flying out from an alley and struck
Abraham on the back of the head, just under his hat brim
The man dropped like a brick, his guns still in leather.

"What? . . ." Jamie muttered. Then he realized what a vul-
nerable position he was in and quickly moved to one side
pressing up against a building. Abraham Pike had not
moved. He was out cold. Jamie slipped into the alley. He did
not see two small boys run out of a nearby building. One
pulled Abraham's pistols from their holsters, and the other
grabbed up his rifle, leaving the man defenseless. Then

ey both jerked off Abraham's boots, leaving him barefoot
the street. The boots were tossed into a watering trough,
d the boys vanished.

Jamie heard a hideous scream from somewhere in the
aze of buildings that made up Old Town. Someone had
ssed a pot of hot water on one of Asa's men.

Falcon peeked around the corner of a building in time
see a woman lean out of a window and smash a club
wn on a man's head. The man dropped to the street, un-
nscious. Two boys raced out and grabbed his weapons
d boots.

"What the hell? . . ." Falcon muttered with a grin.

Logan slipped down an alley and ducked into a recessed
oorway when he heard the scrape of a boot on bricks.
hen he heard a thud, a moan, and the sound of a man hit-
ng the alley floor. He peeked out and grinned at the sight:
o boys were removing the man's guns, boots, and trousers,
aving him bare-butt naked from the waist down.

"Now that's about the ugliest sight I ever did see," the old
ountain man said under his breath.

Rick froze still as a wild scream cut the early morning air.
hen he heard the pounding of boots and a lot of painful
ssing. He watched a man come staggering out into the
reet, both hands holding his bleeding buttocks. Someone
ad slashed the man deeply with a machete across both
heeks. The man limped painfully up the street, hollering
r someone to help him.

Canby heard an ugly snap, followed by a scream of pain.
Oh, God, my ankle's broke!" The sound wound around the
visting streets. "I done stepped in a bar trap. Help me!"
hen the man fell silent as he drifted into unconsciousness.
So far, not a shot had been fired.

"What are you doin', MacCallister?" a man yelled. "Why
on't you stand and fight, you yeller-bellied bastard!"

" 'Cause I can't find anybody to fight, you idiot," Jamie
uttered.

"Yowweee!" one of Asa's men squalled, as hot water was

dumped on his head from a woman on a balcony. His ha
saved his face from being badly burned, but his shoulder
and arms were scalded.

Red watched a man stumble up the street, both hands t
his bleeding face. A heavy rock had smashed his cheek
knocking out several teeth and putting a large gash in h
face. "What the hell's goin' on?" Red muttered.

"Where's my goddamn pants?" The shout drifted aroun
the street. "Somebody stole my pants!"

Logan had to stick a fist into his mouth to suppress h
giggling as the pantless man used his hat to cover his pr
vates. Then couldn't resist calling, "But your ugly ass
hangin' out in the breeze!"

The bare-butted man whirled around and around, tryin
to locate the source of the taunt. "Ifn I had a gun I'd ki
you!" he shouted to the seemingly empty alley.

"Ooowww!" a man yelled, as a small boy put an arrow int
one cheek of his ass, the point embedding deeply. "Ma
Callister's got Injuns workin' for him!" he hollered. "Oh .
my ass is on fire, I tell you. I can't reach the arrey to pull
out." He limped away, groaning with each step.

"Fall back, fall back!" Asa yelled, the shout repeated se
eral times. "They's too much trickery here. Back to the hotel

The unconscious men were located and dragged off. Th
jaws of the bear trap were sprung, freeing the trapped mar
Someone found a serape and handed it to the half-nake
man.

"You cowardly bastards will pay for this!" one of Asa
men yelled in retreat. "You ain't seen the last of us. And tha
by God, is a promise." An arrow came whizzing out o
nowhere and embedded itself in the man's leg. Th
wounded leg buckled under him, and he went down, fallir
on his face in the street.

Jamie and his group had not fired a shot.

The next dawn would bring that bloody day.

\*　　\*　　\*

One by one the men began gathering in Valley, Colorado. Two groups of five each. One group had been hired by Andrea Petri, the second group by Russell Clay. To each other, hard cases are as easy to identify as skunks, and within hours, the men were gathering and talking.

"Them folks that hired us is quality," one said. "So how come they're so interested in one nigger?"

"Sure more here than meets the eye," another reflected. "We talk about this long enough, might figure out a way to make us some money."

"Might," the others agreed, one saying, "If we can figure out what the hell's goin' on."

"Them folks that hired us, they want the paper burned down and the man's house burned. Why? I went over the back issues. There ain't nothin' in there about nobody in San Francisco. You went over the same papers, Jeff; you didn't find out nothin' bad writ about anybody in Denver. So what's goin' on? I think it's something else. I think this editor has something the folks want destroyed."

"What could it be?"

The thug shrugged his shoulders. "I don't know. But I betcha I'm gonna find out."


"Damnedst gunfight I ever been in," Red said, after draining his glass of beer.

"These folks here in this part of town is nice folks," Logan said. "But they played a dangerous game. These kids could have been hurt real bad."

"I've passed the word for the people to stay out of it from now on," Jamie said. "They've agreed to do so unless Asa and his people bother them." Jamie smiled. "But it was funny."

"I make it seven hurt to one degree or the other," Falcon said. "Three of them with knots on their heads."

Logan shook his head. "I dislike fightin' a person I can' put a name to. Not countin' Injuns, o' course."*

"Names or no names," Canby said, "they'll be back, we can bet on that. And this time, they'll be comin' in loaded for bear."

"Well, I can't get no readier," Logan said. "But what I can do is amble over to the cafe and get me somethin' to eat."

"You mean," Rick said with a smile, "you're going over to see Isabella."

The old mountain man grinned. "That, too, boy."

---

*Many on the frontier did not consider the Indian to be part of the human race. The hatred was so strong the Indian was regarded as a subspecies.

# 24

Having become irritated at the Jones brothers' inability to carry out even the simplest of assignments (the brothers were not exceptionally swift in the brain department), Russell Clay had told them to hit the road months back. After committing a series of petty crimes (and two badly bungled and unsuccessful holdups), the brothers arrived in Albuquerque on the afternoon of the aborted shoot-out. After hearing all the talk about the blood feud, the brothers decided to pitch their lot with Asa Pike and his kin.

"Why?" Asa sourly asked the pair.

"I owe Jamie MacCallister," Bob said. "And me and my brother here aim to put lead in him."

"Then you're welcome to join us," Abraham said.

Lloyd looked at the bandage on the man's head. "What happened to you?"

"I would rather not discuss it," Abraham said. Abraham was very touchy on that point, ever since he'd been told he was conked on the noggin by a rock thrown by a ten-year-old.

"When do we take them?" Bob asked.

"Dawn, tomorrow," Asa said. "I've sent them word."

"Why don't we just go on down there now and shoot them?" Lloyd asked.

"It's a matter of honor," Asa told him.

"Oh."

\* \* \*

"Man shore loves the crack of dawn," Logan said, after receiving the word.

"I've got to say that these ain't the smartest ol' boys I've ever run up on," Red added. "Ever' one of them 'pears to be 'bout two eggs short of a dozen."

"But they've got guns and know how to use them," Rick said.

"That do make up for being a tad stumpy in the brain department, don't it?" Canby agreed.

"It'll be no fun and games come the dawning," Jamie said. "They'll be moving in for the kill. The whole thing is stupid and pointless, but none of us can allow that to override hard facts. It's kill or be killed. I wish they'd just ride on and leave us alone. But they're not going to do that, so how many options does that leave us?"

Dusk was settling over the land. Somewhere close a man was playing a guitar and singing a love song in Spanish. The air was filled with soft music and the good smells of supper cooking. It was hard to bring into the picture that in a few hours, the air would be filled with gunsmoke and the thick odor of blood.

"We haven't had much of a chance to talk, son," Jamie said to Falcon. "What's been happening back home?"

"It's been quiet, Pa. Babies being born. The town's got two new businesses. Valley is now officially the county seat of government . . . course we all knew it would be. Big brother Jamie is gettin' fat in the butt from all that easy livin'. It's awful hard for me to believe that he's pushin' fifty. Don't seem possible."

Jamie smiled. It didn't seem possible to him, either. "Jamie Ian is . . . forty-six, I believe. I never was much good at dates; I always left that up to your ma. Lord, where have the years gone? I'm an old man, son. A old man."

"You ain't neither, Pa. You're stronger than most men and can ride as good as ever. You might have some years on you,

ut you're a long ways from being an old man. 'Sides, I've
een the way women look at you."

Jamie shook his head. "Never be another woman in my
ife, son. The only woman I ever loved was your ma. She's
a constant with me." Jamie took out his watch and opened
he lid, gazing for a moment not at the ever-moving hands
of time, but at the tiny picture of Kate. "I can't tell you how
much I miss her."

Jamie stood up and stretched. "We'd all best get something to eat and turn in early. Come the dawning, we're all
gonna be right busy."

Old Town was buttoned up tight.

The occasional chicken or dog or cat wandered the
streets; but no horses were visible, and no citizen left his
home. There was no wind, but the day was cool.

Jamie stood under an awning and finished his after-
breakfast coffee. He set the empty cup down on a bench and
picked up his sawed-off shotgun, loading both barrels.

Falcon was across the street, his tailored suit coat swept
back to reveal his twin pearl-handled pistols. Another pistol was shoved behind his belt, and he carried a .32 caliber
short-barreled pistol in a shoulder holster rig.

The old mountain man, Logan, was about fifty yards away,
lounging in front of a closed general mercantile store. He
picked up his rifle and waited.

Canby stood to Jamie's right, in the mouth of an alley.

Rick was leaning up against a hitch rail.

Red was waiting on the stoop of a saddle and gun shop.
The shop would not open for business until the shooting
was over.

"They come, señor!" one of the boys hired by Jamie
called, pointing.

"Fine," Jamie told him. "Now you and your friend go
home and stay there."

"Si, señor!" The boys took off at a run.

"This time I don't wait for them to come to me," Jamie muttered. He stepped out into the street and started walking toward the edge of Old Town. Falcon walked over and fell in step with his father.

Logan and Canby stepped out and followed, one on each side of him in the street, just slightly to Jamie's rear. Rick and Red stayed close to the storefronts.

A bearded man stepped out of an alley. "You dishonored our family name, MacCallister!" he shouted.

"You're an idiot!" Jamie told him, and never stopped walking.

"Now you die!"

"Not this day," Jamie said. He lifted the Greener and gave the man one barrel from about thirty feet. The heavy charge caught the man in the chest and lifted him off his boots, flinging him backward. He landed in the street in a puff of dust.

Jamie kept on walking while he pulled out the empty and shoved in a fresh round.

Suddenly the street was filled with men, all of whom held pistols at the ready.

"Separate!" Jamie yelled, as he began running for cover.

Falcon dropped behind a watering trough and let both his guns start to bang. Four Pikes went down in the first few seconds.

Rick, standing in a doorway, lifted his .45 and drilled a man in the chest. Canby lined up a man in his rifle sights and dropped him in an alleyway. Logan brought one down, then shifted positions and drilled another one. Red, a pistol in each hand, stood in front of a closed dress shop and brought down two more.

Just as Asa yelled, "Retreat, boys, retreat!" Jamie fired both barrels of the Greener at two men who had just stepped into the daylight and were lining up Falcon in their sights. The twin barrels roared smoke and rusty nails and screws and buckshot, leaving a big mess on the side of the building the men were hurled against.

As the gunsmoke began drifting away, thirteen men lay sprawled in the street, dead, dying, or badly hurt. The gunfight had taken about two minutes, from beginning to end.

Jamie walked over to a dying man and looked down. "Did I ever do a hurt to you?"

"Can't say as you have," the man gasped, his eyes bright with pain. "Not 'til this day anyways."

"Then what is the point of all this death and suffering?"

"Kin. You understand that."

"I don't understand it when Asa was clearly in the wrong by attacking me a couple of years back."

"He's still kin. And blood is thicker than water."

"Well, that makes you a fool," Jamie told him.

"And a dead one at that," Logan said, looking down as the man closed his eyes and slipped behind the veil.

"This one over here's gonna make it, I think," Red called, squatting down beside a fallen man.

Jamie walked over.

"You'll have to kill us all," the man whispered. "And the mountains back to home is filled with Pikes and kin."

Jamie said nothing. Canby called, "Got another one over here that might make it."

Jamie walked over and looked down. The young man was about Rick's age.

"This one ain't hurt bad," Falcon called to his pa. "But he sure is cussin' you for all it's worth."

Jamie stepped over a couple of dead men and looked down. "I hate you damn MacCallisters," the wounded man said. His voice was strong.

"Why?" Jamie questioned. "I never saw you before today."

"Ever'thin' comes to y'all easy."

"What the hell's he talkin' about, Pa?" Falcon asked.

"I don't know."

"Rest of us have to hardscrabble for anythin' we have," the wounded man said.

"I think he must be delicious," Logan said.

"Delirious," Red corrected. "There ain't nothing delicious about this bastard."

"Whatever," the mountain man said.

"Folks like you ought to share with folks like us," the Pike kin continued.

"He's babbling," Jamie said, turning away from the man. "You boys collect all their guns; then we'll see about getting the wounded to doctors."

"Why?" Logan questioned. "They got themselves shot; they can see to ease their own sufferin'."

Jamie smiled. The breed of men called mountain men were the toughest, hardest, and most pragmatic group to ever wander the West.

Just as the guns were being collected and put in cloth sacks, a doctor and several citizens showed up and took over the care and transporting of the wounded.

"Way I got it figured, Pa"—Falcon came to Jamie's side—"we still got about nineteen or twenty to deal with. And I don't figure they'll be inclined to give it up and go on back home."

"No, we haven't seen the last of it. Unfortunately."

"What do you want done with these guns?" Rick called from across the plaza.

"We'll give them to the law. They can do whatever they want with them."

"Ain't no law here now," a citizen said. "They're all out after Injuns."

"They's Fatso Burke," another local said. "He's a constable. Not much of one, but he totes a badge and looks after the jail."

"Go get him," Jamie requested.

"Are you kiddin'? He ain't about to get in between this mess. You boys is on your own 'til the regular law gets back."

"Good," Logan said. "Then we'll handle it our own selves."

The undertaker rattled up in his black hearse and

solemnly looked around at all the bodies. He turned to his assistant. "Go back and get another wagon. And tell Abel to start knocking together some boxes. Make them long boxes; these are tall men. Go on now, step lively."

Jamie and his group backed off and stayed clear . . . but at the ready in case Asa wanted to continue the fight this day. Within minutes, a man stepped into the plaza, unarmed and holding a stick with a white handkerchief tied to it. "I'm not armed," he called. "But I'm kin of these men. I've come to see to their proper burial."

"I hope you've got some money," the undertaker said. "This is going to get expensive."

"We have money. We want a nice service with mourners and wailers and a drum and horn."

"What the hell are they gonna do?" Logan questioned. "Have a dance or a buryin'?"

"Will you please show some respect for the dead," the doctor said sharply.

"Why?" Logan asked. "They damn shore didn't show no respect for us!"

"Let's get out here," Jamie suggested.

The funerals started about mid-afternoon that day. Even from where Jamie and his bunch were seated, in front of the hotel, the sounds could be heard. There were mourners and wailers lifting their voices to the heavens, and a big drum and someone tooting on a trumpet.

Logan walked out onto the side of the street and tried to get a dance step going. The old mountain man was uncommonly spry for his age. "I wish they'd pick up the beat some," he complained. "I can't get no rhythm goin' with that. Least the Injuns got some pep to their drummin'."

"Pa," Falcon said, ducking his head to hide a grin at the buckskin-clad Logan's antics, "I got to say that when you pick men to ride with, you can come up with some characters."

"You'd be hard-pressed to find better men to ride with though."

"I won't argue that." They sat for a time, watching Logan do some dance steps in time with the wailing and moaning and carrying on. "Pa?"

"Uummm?"

"What are you gonna do with the rest of your life?"

"Providing we can get out of here alive, I'm gonna see some country, boy."

"Just wander, Pa?"

"That's about it. Hell, boy, I got more money than I could spend in ten lifetimes. I sure don't need to look for a job. I'm not gonna hang around Valley doin' nothing."

"I think I got it now," Logan said, doing a slow pirouette to the drum and trumpet.

"Well, keep it to yourself," Red told him. "It might be catchin'."

"Mac?" Canby asked.

"Uummm?"

"When we get this here little mess took care of, what say you we head over into Arizona Territory?"

"Sounds good to me. You know anybody over there?"

"Nary a soul. But I always wanted to see the Muggyown."*

"Why not?" Jamie replied, then cut his eyes to Falcon. "And no, you can't come along. You've got a family to look after."

"Never entered my mind," Falcon said with a smile.

"You lie, too."

Rick walked up, looked at Logan for a moment, then shook his head in disbelief and handed Jamie a note. "Little boy just give this to me."

Logan stopped his dancing and wandered over as Jamie opened the folded piece of paper and read: "OLD ABAN-

---

*The Mogollon Rim, named after Juan Ignacio Flores Mogollon, Spanish Governor of the area that would someday become Arizona and New Mexico.

DONED BUILDINGS NORTH OF TOWN. NOON TO-
MORROW." It was signed Asa Pike.

"That's what's left of an old village built back in the late
1700s," Logan told them. "Me and a half dozen ol' boys
camped there one night back in . . . oh, '44 or '45, I reckon
it was."

Jamie stood up. "Let's sorta ease on out there now," he
said. "Find ourselves some good fighting positions and get
ready."

"Why don't we just hide and ambush the bastards when
they come ridin' up?" Logan suggested. "Then we'll have
done with it and can get gone to the Muggyowns."

"You're a sneaky old bastard, you know that?" Rick said.

Logan grinned. "Damn right, I am. And I'm *alive* because
of it! You bes' remember that, boy."

Jamie didn't say anything, but he agreed with Logan.

"Let's provision up," Canby said. "Then when it's over, we
can just head on west without havin' to come back here and
answer a bunch of damn-fool questions."

"Good idea."

The second bunch of funerals were just getting underway
as Jamie and the group checked out of the hotel in Old
Town and rode out.

"Most depressin' damn music I ever did hear," Logan
said. "If you boys has to plant me, I want somebody to whis-
tle a happy tune, and the rest of you do a jig over my restin'
place. I'd hate to have to spend eternity with the sounds of
that sorrowful mess a-ringin' through my bones."

"I'll do a fancy jig right on top of your grave," Red
promised him.

"I didn't say collapse the damn thing," Logan told him.
"Big as your feet is, you'd cause an earthquake. Just dance
around the hole, will you?"

Laughing, the men put the town of Albuquerque and the
funeral music behind them.

# 25

"I haven't seen Mr. Washington all day, Sheriff," the young lady at the newspaper office said. Then grinned and added, "Uncle Matt."

Matthew winked at his niece and looked toward the rear, where the typesetter was busy working. "Paul? You seen Ben today?"

"Not hide nor hair of him, Sheriff. He's never been this late."

"You reckon he's with Lola?"

Lola Dubois, a beautiful mulatto from New Orleans, had come to town one day and within weeks had bought the hotel and started redecorating it. It was the most elegant hotel outside of Denver. She had named it the La Pierre. She and Ben had been keeping company for months; and recently, Ben had proposed to her, and Lola had accepted his offer of marriage.

"No. She was by here looking for him. She's worried sick."

"I don't like this," Matthew said. "Not at all."

"What could have happened to him in Valley?" the typesetter asked.

"I don't know," Matthew said. "But I damn sure plan on finding out."

After carefully searching the town for over an hour, Matthew and his deputies knew one thing for certain: Ben F. Washington had vanished.

The alarm was sounded, and townspeople turned out, armed, mounted, and each man with a three-day supply of food. Matthew sent groups out in all directions. From the saddle, the sheriff looked down into the worried face of Lola. "If he's within fifty miles of here, we'll find him," he assured the woman. "He may have gone for an early morning ride and just got lost. It's easy to do. And we know his horse is missing. We'll find him, Lola."

But Matthew didn't think Ben was lost. He felt certain that Ben had been taken against his will. But why? was the question.

"Well, if this ain't about the dumbest thing I ever saw," Canby said, lowering his field glasses. "Yonder they come, in plain sight and all bunched up."

"Get into position," Jamie told his group. "We're going to settle this thing today, once and for all."

Asa Pike halted his men about three-quarters of a mile from the ruins of the village. Jamie watched through field glasses as the men dismounted and bunched up for a few minutes. Then they picketed their horses and spread out, walking slowly, advancing toward the ruins in a long, straight line.

The men in the ruins looked on in silence for a few minutes, as the Pike group slowly advanced.

"This is nuts, Pa," Falcon said. "They act like they want to get killed."

"Hell, I can't bring myself to shoot at them," Rick said.

"I can," Logan said. "But I want them a tad closer."

When the advancing men were about two hundred yards away, Jamie abruptly stood up and shouted, "Asa! This doesn't have to be. Let's call this thing off and go on about our business!"

"You go right straight to hell, MacCallister!" Asa shouted, then lifted his rifle and triggered off a round. The bullet howled past Jamie's head, and Jamie dropped down behind cover.

"I believe they just opened the dance," Red observed.

"Fire," Jamie said.

The ruins of the village thundered with rifle fire. When the smoke cleared, twelve of Asa's kin were on the ground, and those left were running back to their horses as fast as they could go. They pulled the picket pins, jumped into saddles, and were gone without looking back.

"I have been in some strange tussles in my time," Logan allowed. "But this here has got to be the strangest ever."

"I saw sights just like it during the war," Jamie said, punching rounds into his rifle. "Brave men doing foolish things. Let's go see how many are wounded."

Six men were dead, six were wounded. Rick and Falcon went to get their horses while Jamie and the others saw to their wounds as best they could with what they had. Of the six wounded, two had only minor wounds, three were hard hit, and one probably would not last the day. The badly wounded man died at noon, just as the county sheriff, his deputies, and a doctor were riding up.

"Good God!" the sheriff said, swinging down from the saddle. He looked at Jamie. "You and your men are under arrest, MacCallister. Surrender your weapons."

"Not likely," Jamie told him.

Falcon and the others had spread out, the muzzles of their rifles pointed at the sheriff and his men. At this range, if any shooting started, it would be carnage. Jamie had exchanged his rifle for the Greener. And this close up, that terrible weapon could easily take out two or three men, and not leave much to write home about.

"Mr. MacCallister," the sheriff softened his tone. "Over the past two days, you and your people have killed or wounded twenty-six men—at least. Not counting Indian attacks, this is the worst shoot-out this county has ever experienced. . . ."

"They didn't start it," one of the badly wounded men asped out the truth. "We did."

"Did you hear that, Dr. Ferrara?" the sheriff asked the loctor.

"I did."

The sheriff slowly nodded his head. His eyes found the ackhorses, then looked back at Jamie. "Are you men leaving this area?"

"Today, if possible," Jamie told him.

"Thank God," the sheriff muttered. He cleared his throat and said, "Fine. That's dandy. The best news I've heard in lays. You can leave whenever you like. The sooner, the better. Personally, I hope I never see any of you again."

"You need some help totin' these folks back to town?" Logan asked, a wicked glint in his eyes and a smile on his lips.

"No! Hell, no!" the sheriff quickly replied. "I want you people gone."

"Then we'll be heading for home," Jamie said, conscious of several of the wounded men listening intently, knowing Asa was too much of a coward to face the entire MacCallister family. "Springtime in Colorado is a beautiful sight."

"I'm anxious to see it," Logan said, picking up on the lie immediately.

Falcon produced a badge from his pocket. "I'm a deputy sheriff up in Valley, Colorado. My brother is county sheriff. I want you to tell Asa Pike something for me, Sheriff. If I ever lay eyes on him in Valley, I'll kill him where he stands, and I won't hesitate."

"I'll see he gets the word."

"And I mean what I say, Sheriff," Falcon added.

"I've no doubt of that."

Jamie and his people turned and walked to their horses. Two minutes later they were riding north.

One of the deputies took off his hat and wiped his sweaty face. "That could have got real ugly in a hurry."

"It ain't over," one of the wounded men said. "I can

promise you that. As long as they's one Pike or kin left alive, he'll be huntin' Jamie Ian MacCallister and his kin."

"Then that makes you a family of fools," the sheriff told him.

There was no trace of Ben F. Washington to be found. Matthew's Indian trackers could turn up nothing. Ben had vanished without a trace. Matthew and his weary posse rode back to Valley, and Matthew went immediately to see Lola with the bad news.

She took the news as calmly as possible; Matthew could see she was shaken, but struggling to maintain composure. She waved him to a chair and brought coffee. "It has to be either his mother or his uncle behind this, Sheriff. Or both of them. He told me several times that he knew they were still alive and would someday try to kill him. There have been attempts on his life."

"I know. Ben's told me the whole sorry story. And we'll find Ben, Lola. He's got to be in this area. Every farmer, rancher, cowboy, and trapper in a seventy-five-mile radius is looking. I think they're close, Lola. I feel it. But I don't know where."

Matthew was right. They were close. The men were holding Ben in Jamie's cabin, on the ridge overlooking Kate's grave. But it was just unthinkable to the residents of Valley that anyone outside of the family would dare intrude into the home of Jamie MacCallister.

Matthew went to his office and found several wires waiting for him from various lawmen, some as far away as San Francisco.

The San Francisco wire read: RECEIVED WORD FROM MY STREET INFORMANTS THAT FIVE THUGS ARE HEADING YOUR WAY. STOP. STONE GIBSON BILLY CARNES NATE CLAPTON ERIC ARMER PETE DREW STOP. ALL ARE KNOWN HOOLIGANS AND STRONG ARM MEN. STOP. ALL HAVE BEEN ARRESTED FOR

SUSPICION OF MURDER BUT NO CONVICTIONS. STOP. THEY'RE BAD ONES. STOP. BE CAREFUL WITH THEM.

The wire from Denver read: FIVE LOCAL THUGS BELIEVED HEADED YOUR WAY. STOP. JACK WALLACE MARCUS HINTON STERLING DRAKE JEFF HOOKS CARTER YOUNG. STOP. ALL HAVE CRIMINAL RECORDS AND CAPABLE OF DOING ANYTHING. STOP. BELIEVE THEM TO BE INVOLVED IN SOME SORT OF KIDNAPPING SCHEME. STOP. WATCH YOURSELF.

Matthew removed his spurs, then leaned back in his chair and put his boots up on the desk. It made sense to him that Ben's mother and uncle were in San Francisco and Denver, living under assumed names. And they had to be the ones who hired the men to kidnap Ben.

But where in the hell were they holding him?

Ben was unconscious—again. He was tied to a chair, and his chin rested on his chest, blood dripping from his mouth, numerous cuts on his face, and his nose busted.

"What the hell do we do now?" Stone asked, looking around him. "We don't want to kill him, and he can't take much more beatin' on."

"You're workin' at the wrong end," Eric said. "Nigger ain't got no sense in his head. It's all in his pecker. Threaten to cut his pecker off, he'll tell you ever'thang he knows."

"So would I," Nate said. "And so would any man. Stone? I'm beginnin' to think the darky's tellin' the truth. I don't think he's got anythin' that's a threat to anybody."

"You may be right about that. But we'll hammer on him a little bit more. Throw a bucket of water on him and get him awake."

"You go on up and dust off things in your grandpa's house, Cathy Lou," Joleen told her middle daughter. "And yes, you can ride that paint your Uncle Falcon gentled for you. I'll be up later on."

"Yes, Ma," the fourteen-year-old said with a grin. She liked to go up and be alone at her grandpa's house. The place was filled with so many pictures and old books and pillows with fancy stitching on them that her grandma, Kate, had done. She liked to sit in her grandma's rocker in the big living room and look through the old family Bible.

She threw a saddle on the paint pony and hopped on. She'd ride by that Johnny Scott's house on the way and wave at him. She pinched her cheeks to get a little color in them before Johnny saw her, and rode off at a gallop.

Just a few miles north of the ruins, Jamie and his group hooked up with a bunch of teamsters heading north to Santa Fe. Jamie said goodbye to Falcon and watched as his son rode off with the wagons.

"That's a mighty fine boy there, Mac," Logan said. "How many kids did you say you had?"

"Nine living. Falcon's the youngest. The ages range from forty-six to thirty-four."

"Fever got the others?" Canby asked.

Jamie shook his head. "Bounty hunters looking for me killed Baby Karen when she was about six months old. Down in the Big Thicket country of East Texas. Back in '29."

"I reckon I don't have to ask what happened to them men," Red said.

"No, you don't." Jamie lifted the reins. "Let's ride."

Cathy hopped down from the pony and stood for a moment. She thought she heard something coming from the small barn. But that was impossible; Grandpa Jamie had been gone for months. All his livestock was out at Uncle Falcon's ranch. She shook her head and walked up to the front porch to stand for a moment. Quite a view from up here.

The town of Valley lay peaceful-looking, a few miles away. She could see almost the entire town; could almost pick out her house.

She turned and opened the door. Rough hands grabbed her and jerked her inside. One hard hand clamped over her mouth while the free hand roamed her body.

"Would you just take a look at the titties on this one," the man holding her said. "Man, she is ripe for the pickin'."

Cathy tried to bite the man. Pain exploded in her head as he clubbed her with a fist.

"You just settle down, honey." Her clothing was being torn from her. "I got something you're gonna like."

Cathy's eyes found Ben tied to a chair, his face all bloody and swollen. He was unconscious. She felt herself lifted off the floor and carried into the bedroom and dumped on the bed.

"You scream, little girlie," the man hissed in her ear. His breath was very bad. "And I'll hurt you something awful. You understand?"

Cathy nodded her head while the man was pulling off his clothing.

"That's good. You just lay back and enjoy this."

Rough hands roamed all over her flesh, fondling her breasts, her body, all the secret places.

Cathy could not help herself. She screamed as the nakedness of the man covered her and he tore into her.

A rag was tied over her mouth, silencing the sound.

It was the beginning of a long and painful afternoon for fourteen-year-old Cathy Lou MacKensie.

"They's a trading post up here on the Puerco River," Logan said, pouring himself a cup of coffee. "I figure we're two days' ride from it. Then the country gets rough and wild. But it's some pretty."*

Gallup, New Mexico, would grow from there.

"You reckon what's left of them Pikes will be followin' us Mac?" Canby asked.

"Not if they're smart."

"Smart, they ain't," Red said. "But at least we cut 'em down to size."

"And after that?" Rick asked.

"I was told there is a little cowtown that was settled two/three years ago on the Little Colorado River," Jamie told the men. "It's called Horsehead Crossing.* We can resupply there and then cut south into the Muggyowns."

"And if we're lucky, we won't see another human bein' for days," Logan said. "It's gettin' crowded out here."

The bacon fried, Jamie dumped slices of potato and bits of onion into the grease and watched them sizzle. Bread was ready in another pan.

"That do smell good," Red said. "Gets my mouth to salivatin' something fierce."

The men filled their tin plates with food and their cups with coffee and settled back against their saddles to enjoy the evening meal.

The Wild West was still plenty wild, and would be for several more decades, but Logan was right: settlers were pouring in. Despite the hardships of the land and the warring Indians, people kept coming. Little settlements were springing up all over the country. Many of them would wither and die within a few years, but some would grow and prosper, just like the pioneers who had left everything behind to come west in search of a new life.

"There any gold to be found down in the Muggyowns?" Rick asked.

"I 'spect," Logan said. "But one thing that there's a plenty of is Apaches. We got Hopis and Navajos all around us now. And we'll be ridin' right through Zuni country. The Papagos is way down south, near the Mex border. Havasupai Injuns is over to the west and some north. When I furst

*In a few years, the name would be changed to Holbrook.

ome through here there wasn't *no* white men. I recollect
hat we scared the piss outta some Injuns. They didn't know
hat to make of us; didn't know what the hell we was.
Vhen we farred our guns, them Injuns scattered like the
ind." He looked over at Jamie. "You and me and Red and
Canby, now, we're the last of a breed . . . you know that,
Mac?"

"I've been told. But men like my Falcon and Rick there,
hey'll carry on and travel the trails that we blazed."

"For a fact," Red said. "Reckon how things is back in your
ittle town of Valley, Mac?"

"Oh, all right, I 'magine. Not much happens up there."


At mid-afternoon, Joleen hitched up the buggy and drove
irst to town, to pick up some things at the store. She gos-
iped for a time with some ladies—the talk was all about the
lisappearance of Ben—and then drove up to Jamie's cabin.
Out of long habit, Joleen carried a little .41 over-and-under
lerringer in the side pocket of her dress. Valley had been
ong settled, but there was still the occasional thug or hooli-
;an who wandered through. Although doing harm to a
voman in the West was about the best way known to wind
ip on the wrong end of a rope.

Cathy's paint pony was standing dejectedly at the hitch
ail. "Now why didn't that child put him in the corral?"
oleen questioned.

Joleen walked up to the porch, opened the front door to
ter pa's cabin, and stepped into hell. Rough hands grabbed
ter before she could get to her pistol. She was flung to the
loor, her clothing being ripped off before she hit the
ooards. She started to scream, and a fist exploded pain in
ter head. She slipped into a cloudy haze just as her legs
vere being spread apart.

"Mama!" Cathy cried.

# 26

After having their way with Joleen and Cathy, the outlaws panicked and fled. What sense they possessed had returned to them, and they knew that if found, there would be no trial. They would either be hanged or shot on the spot . . . or worse. In the West, rapists had been known to be dragged to death, stoned, buried up to their chins in anthills, and staked out naked in the sun to slowly die.

The outlaws had tried to set fire to the cabin, but shortly after they rode away, the fire went out. Cathy was naked and unconscious on the bed. Ben was still tied to the chair, swimming in and out of consciousness. Joleen was naked and unconscious on the floor, having been clubbed on the head and left for dead after the men were through with her.

Ben managed to start his chair rocking from side to side until it toppled over. He then struggled toward the open front door and out onto the porch. There, he shoved too hard with his feet and threw himself off the porch, hitting his head on the steps and dropping once more into darkness.

Pat MacKensie got worried when he came home from the fields and Joleen and Cathy Lou were gone. The other kids did not know where they were, but the buggy was gone and so was Cathy Lou's paint pony. Pat paced the floor for a time and then rode into town, heading for Matthew's office. He passed the Scott boy along the way and hailed him down.

"I seen her hours ago, Mr. MacKensie. Headin' up toward er grandpa's place. Then I seen Mrs. MacKensie headin' p that way 'bout two hours or so ago, in the buggy."

"Come on, Johnny. Ride with me. Something's very rong about this."

As soon as Pat saw Ben lying by the front steps, uncon-cious and bloody and tied to the chair, he told Johnny, Ride like the wind, Johnny. Ring the alarm bell and get 1atthew and the doctor up here. Go, boy!"

Pat looked in the house and almost vomited at the sight. Ie quickly composed himself and found blankets to cover he nakedness of the women. He knew better than to try to 1ove them until the doctor arrived. He pumped water and ent to Ben, bathing the man's face until Ben regained con-ciousness.

"Outlaws," Ben gasped. "Joleen and Cathy?"

"They're alive," Pat said grimly. "But just barely."

Pat cut the ropes that bound Ben and got another blan-et to cover him with. The MacCallister boys thundered up nd jumped out of their saddles. Dr. Prentiss looked at Pat nd started to kneel down beside Ben.

"See to the women in the house." Ben pushed the words ast smashed and swollen lips. "They've been used very adly."

Matthew turned to a deputy. "Get a posse together and et on the trail. I'll be along."

Morgan said, "I wish Pa was here."

Matthew looked up at him. "In a way, I'm glad he's not."


The outlaws rode hard for several miles, then cut south-vest, heading for what would someday be called the Four Corners area, where Utah, Colorado, Arizona, and New Mexico meet. They weren't really thinking; just riding in vhat at first was no more than a blind panic to get away.

Back in Valley, no one knew how to get in touch with Fal-con, and they certainly had no idea where Jamie might be.

The posse trailed the outlaws for a week, then lost them i a heavy rain shortly after entering the San Juans. Matthe reluctantly turned back.

Cathy Lou would be all right, with a lot of love from fam ily and friends.

But Joleen lay in a coma.

"I've done all that I can do," Dr. Prentiss told the famil "It's in God's hands now. We just don't know that muc about head injuries."

The family could do nothing but wait.

The stage drivers began passing the word all up and dow the line, leaving messages at relay stations. It might tak months, but eventually Jamie would get the message.

It was a tired and dusty group of men who rode into th newly formed and raw cowtown of Holbrook. Because of re cent Indian trouble, the town was the westernmost stoppin point on the stage line, for the time being.

The stage had not yet arrived, but since it was seldom o time—sometimes it was several days late; when it did arriv it was often peppered with bullet holes and had so many ar rows sticking out of the coach it resembled a large porcu pine—no one gave that much attention.

Jamie and friends stabled their weary horses, rubbin them down and seeing that they had water and food befor seeking comforts for themselves.

The men had their spare clothing washed and irone while they soaked and scrubbed and soaped in tubs of ho water behind the barbershop and then had haircuts an shaves. When they began to once more resemble human be ings, they dressed and looked around for a place to have drink and then get something to eat that someone else ha cooked, served on real plates.

The marshal of the town had spotted the men as the rode in, and gave them time to get cleaned up before h ambled over for a closer look-see at the strangers.

Glass of beer in hand, the marshal took a seat at an adjoining table and asked, "You boys have any Indian trouble on your way in?"

Jamie looked at the man. "Not a bit. We were spotted a number of times, but for whatever reason, they left us alone."

The marshal eyeballed the men for several seconds, thinking: Injuns may be savages, but they ain't fools. This bunch of ol' boys has Curly Wolf stamped on them as clear as a brand. Even the younger one has the look of a bad man.*

"I ain't tryin' to nose into your business, boys," the marshal continued. "But any news 'bout Injuns or road conditions is welcome here."

"The road was all right," Logan said, after downing his whiskey and holding up his glass, signaling the barkeep for a refill. "We did check out some smoke and found a settler's house had been set on fire. But that was a good day's ride east of here. There wasn't a livin' soul about and no bodies. Corral was empty."

"House set south of the road?"

"Yep."

"The Saunders ranch." The marshal spoke the words softly. "They were sure they could make friends with the Indians and live in peace."

"They probably did with the Hopi and Zuni and the Navajo," the old mountain man said. "But not with the 'Pache. I been roamin' the West since rain was wet, and I ain't never seen a more disagreeable bunch of people than them goddamn 'Paches. Hell, I even got along with the Pawnee and the Blackfeet . . . most of the time. But I hate them goddamn 'Paches."

"You're not alone in that," the marshal said drily. "No sign of bodies, hey?"

---

*In the West, a "bad man" was not necessarily a thug or outlaw. It just meant the person was a "bad" man to fool with.

"No," Jamie said. "But they might have been caught in th house when it burned and were buried under the debr when the roof collapsed."

"Better that than taken prisoner," the barkeep said, se ting a bottle of whiskey down on the table. "You boys eve come up on what's left of a man or woman after the Apach got done havin' fun with them?"

"I have," Logan said, his words soft, but his eyes as har as flint. "Eyes gouged out, tongue cut out, privates cut o and the back of their ankles cut so's they can't do nothir but flop around on the ground in agony. Sometimes the last for days 'fore they die. I don't know who in the hell eve come up with this 'noble red man' crap."

The marshal nodded his head in total agreement. Of a the Indian tribes west of the Mississippi River, the Apach was probably the most despised and feared. The residen of the Southwest did their dead-level best to wipe ther from the face of the earth, and came very close to su ceeding.

"I don't mean to stare, mister," the marshal said to Jami "But are you Jamie MacCallister?"

"I am."

"I got a long letter for you over at the office. It come i on the stage last week. The last stage we've seen, by the wa It's been handed from driver to driver for nearly tw months. It's from Valley, Colorado."

Jamie started to get up, and the marshal waved him bac into his chair. "You eat your meal. I'll go over and get th letter and bring it to you. It'd be an honor."

Jamie was just digging into his food when the marshal r turned and handed him the well-worn envelope. He put o his reading glasses and tore open the envelope. As he rea his face hardened. He quickly scanned the letter and the read it more slowly the second time.

"Trouble, Mac?" Red asked.

"Yes. Bad trouble." He explained the contents of the le ter. Everyone in the saloon had fallen silent, listening.

The barkeep was the first to break the silence after Jamie
had folded the letter, put it back in the envelope, and
tucked it away in a pocket.

"If they stay on the trail the posse followed, they'll probably come through here. There ain't jack-shit west of here
for a hundred miles, 'cept maybe some way stations, pro-
vidin' the goddamn Apaches ain't killed ever'body there
and burned the buildings."

On that particular east to west trail through north central Arizona, Winslow would not come into being until 1880,
and Flagstaff in 1881. The Apaches' war with the whites
would continue, off and on, until 1894, when all surviving
Apaches were rounded up and hauled off to Fort Sill, Oklahoma. Geronimo died there in 1909. During his last years,
the great Apache warrior eked out a living selling souvenir
bows and arrows to tourists.

"You want to head for home, Mac?" Logan asked softly.

Jamie shook his head. "There is nothing I can do back
home. But I think I'll postpone my trip into the Muggyowns.
I want to stick around and see if these bastards"—he tapped
the pocket holding the letter—"come through here. I want
to be waiting for them."

Red opened his mouth to protest, and Jamie held up a
big hand. "No, you boys go on. We'll hook up again someday. This is something I have to do myself."

"I do understand," Logan said. "We'll stick around long
enough to rest the horses and resupply, and then we'll be
on our way."

Jamie finished his meal and then left the table to walk outside and sit by himself and read the letter again.

"Are we just going to ride off and leave Mr. MacCallister
here alone?" Rick asked.

"That's the way he wants it, boy," Red said.

"It don't hardly seem right."

The older men smiled at one another, Logan saying, "It's
just something he's got to do by himself, boy."

Rick toyed with his coffee cup. "I . . . ah. Well, it's just th I have this feeling we'll never see him again."

"Maybe so, maybe not," Canby said. "But he'll always  a friend, and that's something to value, right?"

Rick nodded his head. "I reckon."

"Mac's carryin' a load of grief right now, boy," Red sai "Mayhaps he's thinkin' that if he had stayed to home, th awfulness might not have happened. When it comes to far ily, a man gets to thinkin' them kind of thoughts whe tragedy befalls."

Rick looked at Jamie, sitting on the bench in front of th saloon, reading the long letter from home. "He just look well, so *alone.*"

"Sometimes it's best to stand alone, boy," Logan told hin "You think about that when you get a quiet moment." H pushed back his chair and stood up.

"Where you goin'?" Canby asked.

"I'm gonna find me a bottle, crawl up in the loft of th stable and get myself drunk."

"I wonder what Mr. Mac is gonna do?" Rick said.

"What's Mac gonna do?" Logan questioned. "Why, he gonna wait for them trash who hurt his family. Then he gonna kill them. That's what he's gonna do. It's what's e: pected of a man . . . leastways out here, it is."

"Won't be that way for long," Canby said. "I seen tha comin' last post I was on back east. Now they got fanc lawyers and duded-up judges who say a man ain't got th right to deal justice to them who's done him a hurt. The say only the courts has that right."

Logan snorted. "Be a mighty sorry damn day when tha kind of thinkin' takes hold out here."

"Well, it's a comin'. Bet on that."

"I hope I ain't around to see no shame and disgrace lik that. But I'll tell you one thing." He jerked a thumb towar Jamie. "Yonder sits a man that won't pay no attention t such foolishness."

# 27

Jamie wrote a letter to his family back in Valley, explaining where he was and that he had received their letter about Coleen and Cathy Lou MacKensie. The stage finally made it through the day that Canby, Red, Logan, and Rick pulled out, and Jamie gave the letter to the driver, explaining what had happened and asking if he would pass it along.

"I'll do better than that, Mr. MacCallister," the driver said. "I'll have a telegram sent when I get back to New Mexico, telling them you're okay and a letter will follow."

"I'd appreciate it."

"Consider it done. And if you need some help dealing with those bastards, you just holler. They'll be men a-plenty come runnin'."

Jamie smiled his thanks, and the stage thundered out, heading back east.

Jamie waited in the little cowtown.

Back in Valley, Matthew had spread the word to all lawmen west of Valley, and hundreds of dodgers had gone out to marshals and sheriffs. They started appearing tacked onto trees and telegraph poles, and when the rapists and kidnappers came out of hiding and started to move, they began seeing the wanted posters everywhere.

"We got to head south," Stone said.

"There ain't nothin' south 'ceptin' Apaches!" Jack Wallace protested.

"But north, west, and east there ain't nothin' but a han[ man's rope for us," Stone replied. "We'll head for Mexic and wait it out."

"We're damn near out of everything," Billy Carn[ pointed out.

"They's a little cowtown 'bout two days' ride from here Sterling Drake said. "I think it's called Holbrook."

"We'll head for there," Stone said. "Let's ride. I can sme freedom, boys. We're almost clear. I can smell it!"

His nose should have sniffed out another odor.

Gunsmoke.

Jamie sat on the bench in front of a dry goods store an watched the lone rider come into town and tie up in fron of the saloon. The traveler's clothing was mud-splattere[ and his horse was weary. The rider wore two guns tied dow low, which meant absolutely nothing, for a lot of men wor two guns, including Jamie.

But there was something about the man. . . .

Jamie rose from the bench and walked across the stree glancing at the brand on the horse. He did not recogniz it. Deciding at the last second not to enter the saloon, Jami took a seat in a chair in front of an apothecary shop an waited. The rider came out of the saloon after only a fe minutes and took a gunnysack from behind his saddle, the walked over to the general store. He left there with the sac bulging with only enough supplies to last one man about week. Jamie relaxed. Unless the men had split up, and h didn't think that likely, this was just a drifting rider. H watched the man ride out of town.

About an hour later, another lone rider came into town Just as the first rider, his clothing was dirty and muc splattered and his horse weary. Jamie perked up.

The man did exactly what the first rider had done: saloon first, then to the general store, and left with about the sam amount of supplies in a sack.

"If one more rides in," Jamie muttered, "it's the bunch on the run from Valley."

About an hour later, another rider came drifting in, from the same direction as the other two. Mud-splattered clothing, weary horse. He went first to the saloon, then over to the general store and bought the same amount of supplies.

As he was riding out, heading in the same direction the other two had taken, Jamie was saddling Sundown. He waited for a few minutes, then swung in behind the man, staying well back.

Jamie trailed him for several miles, then stopped and picketed Sundown near a wash that still held a trickle of water. He took a drink from his canteen and settled down amid a jumble of rocks—after checking carefully for sleeping rattlesnakes—near the trail and waited.

Jamie had no physical descriptions of the men who had attacked his daughter and granddaughter, only their names. He had to be sure before he confronted the men, and he hadn't worked out in his mind how he was going to do that.

Right now, he would wait.

Russell Clay almost had a heart attack when he finally learned what had taken place in Valley. For several minutes, he actually thought he was going to die. He had to sit down and take several deep breaths and will his heart to stop its wild racing.

He dismissed his trusted manservant and sat for a time in near shock. "Fools," he finally muttered. "Ignorant, redneck fools."

He poured a brandy and drank it down. "Assaulting and raping Jamie's daughter and granddaughter," he whispered. "If he has to, the man will spend the rest of his life tracking you down."

He poured another brandy and looked out the window of his luxurious home in Denver. "I didn't mean for this to

happen. As God is my witness, I didn't. I was only trying t
protect myself."

Then the man who was born Roscoe Jefferson, son of run
away slaves, who became an actor under the name of Ros
LeBeau, and now went under the name of Russell Cla
laughed bitterly. "God?" he whispered. "Don't bring Go
into this, you fool. Not after all that you've done."

Then he thought of his sister. He had not seen her in
years, but he knew she was living in San Francisco under th
name of Andrea Petri. He wondered what her reaction
would be when she learned of the debacle in Valley.


"Rape!" Andrea shrieked at the shyster lawyer wh
brought her the news. "Dear God in Heaven! Did thos
fools go crazy?"

The attorney said nothing. He knew only too well how
volatile the woman's temper was, and if the truth be known
she frightened him. He had never before known such a
ruthless person.

"Jamie Ian MacCallister will track them to the end of the
earth if he has to," Andrea said, lowering her voice. She
faced the lawyer. "And if one of them talks . . ." Her cold
eyes bored into the soul of the man.

"The authorities will trace it back to me," the attorney
whispered.

And you'll blab, Andrea thought. She turned to a table
and carefully chose a bottle, pouring the man a drink. Smil
ing, she held out the glass. "Drink this and calm down," she
said. "And then you must leave."

"Yes, yes. Of course. We must have no further contact for
a time." The lawyer gulped down the brandy, and she
showed him to the door.

"Have a nice day," Andrea said with a smile.

The lawyer nodded his head and hurriedly walked away.
Four blocks later, he dropped stone dead to the street.

"Such a pity," Andrea said, carefully tucking that bottle way. "He was such a useful man, too."


Jamie seemed to rise out of the earth like some demon ut of the pits of hell. The horse reared up in fright, and ete Drew felt himself jerked from the saddle and slammed o the ground. The air whooshed out of him, and his eyes ould not focus. When he could focus, he was looking into e cold eyes of a big man with gray hair. Then he saw the uzzle of a pistol and heard the hammer being eared back.

"Name," Jamie said. "And you better get it right the first me."

"Pete Drew!" the outlaw said. "Lord God, mister. I ain't one nothin' to you."

"You raped my daughter and granddaughter and tried to ill Ben F. Washington."

"It was a mistake!" Pete screamed. "We didn't mean to do at. I'm sorry it happened. It was . . . it was . . . just . . . one f them things that happened."

"You son of a bitch!"

Pete was blubbering, snot running out of his nose. He iled himself, and the stench was awful. "It wasn't my idee!" e squalled. "It was . . . it was Stone's idee. I had to go along ith it. If I hadn't a-humped them women, the rest would ave laughed at me."

Jamie cussed the man for a moment. "You know what ou're going to do next?" Jamie asked, his voice low and old.

Pete shook his head.

"Kiss the devil's hot butt!"

"No!" Pete screamed.

The last thing Pete Drew saw on the living side of the veil as the flame that erupted from the muzzle of Jamie's pis- ol. His final scream echoed over the land.


\* \* \*

Jack Wallace felt the hammer blow in his chest tha
knocked him sprawling. He looked down at his blood
stained shirtfront and wondered, briefly, what the hell ha
happened. Then he lowered his head to the ground an
died.

Billy Carnes jumped to his feet and grabbed for his gun
Jamie's rifle barked again, and Billy's head snapped back
a black hole in the center of his forehead.

Marcus Hinton looked wildly all around him, certain the
were under attack from the Apaches. He began firing hi
pistols in all directions, hitting nothing but late afternoo
air. Jamie's rifle boomed, and Marcus was knocked off hi
boots, hitting the rocky ground hard. He looked stupidl
down at the spreading stain on his shirt.

"Well, I'll be damned!" was the last thing the outlaw sai
before he toppled over and died. He couldn't have uttere
a more apt truism.

Sterling Drake spun around and around like a child's top
firing his pistols until Jamie's bullet cut him down, the bu
let entering one side and blowing out the other side. Ster
ling was still trying to cock and fire his empty pistols whe
death spread its dark cloak over him.

Stone Gibson, Nate Clapton, Jeff Hooks, and Carter
Young made it to their horses and galloped off, toward th
north. Eric Armer stood in the midst of the carnage
screaming and cussing his unknown and as yet unseen
enemy.

"Come out and fight me like a man!" he shouted to th
big empty all around him.

"Over here," Jamie called.

Eric spun around and fired. But there was no one to b
seen.

"How about over here, punk!" Jamie called.

Eric whirled around just in time to catch a bullet in hi
chest. He stumbled backward, lost his footing, and sat dow
on his butt, hollering as the pain reached him.

Jamie appeared at the edge of the camp.

"Damn you!" Eric cussed. He tried to lift his pistols but found he did not have the strength.

"Who hired you to attack Ben Washington?" Jamie asked.

"Go to hell!" Eric gasped.

"What were you looking for?"

Blood began leaking out of Eric's mouth, a pink froth that told Jamie the man had been lung shot.

"You don't have long," he told Eric. "Why not tell the truth for once in your life?"

"I got a right to know who killed me."

"Jamie Ian MacCallister."

"Them women up north? . . ."

"My daughter and granddaughter."

"Bad mistake, wasn't it?"

"You're dying because of it." Jamie walked closer, giving each man a glance to make sure they were out of action.

"You gonna bury me proper?"

"I doubt it."

"That ain't decent!"

"Neither are you." Jamie squatted down beside the dying man.

"Promise you'll bury me so's the varmints can't get at me and I'll tell you what I know."

"You better make it fast."

"A woman in San Francisco hired me and the four I rode with. Man in Denver hired the others."

"They have names?"

"No," Eric said, then fell over on the sand and did not move.

"You dead?" Jamie asked.

"You cold-hearted bastard!" Eric blurted weakly. "You're a devil."

"You got a shovel around here?"

"I ain't never seen no one as hard as you," the outlaw gasped out the words.

"I've heard that before," Jamie said, looking around for something to dig with. No sign of a shovel. "I'll pile rocks on you."

"Thanks."

"The ones who got away?"

Eric gasped out the names. He was just about at the end of his string.

"MacCallister?"

"What?"

"You read some words over me?"

"I'll say something. You have folks that might give a damn about you?"

"No. Pa threw me out of the house years ago."

"Why?"

"I tried to rape my sister."

Jamie shook his head in disgust just as Eric rattled his last breath, stiffened, and then was still.

Jamie dragged the bodies to a wash and collapsed one side of the wash over them, then stacked rocks over that. He climbed back out of the makeshift grave and stood for a time. He tried to think of something to say over the bodies, but could not come up with anything.

Finally, mounted on Sundown, he looked toward the cave-over and said, "You boys must have done something worthwhile when you were alive. I'm sure that will be taken into account. But it wouldn't if I had anything to say about it."

He plopped his hat back on his head and rode off.

# 28

Jamie rode out the next morning and picked up the trail of those who had escaped his attack. They were heading north and slightly east and making no attempt to hide their tracks.

Days later, they crossed over into Colorado and were forced to stop at a trading post on the Animas River. Their horses were just about done in.*

Jamie was two hours behind them and coming on strong.

The ragged and worn-down outlaws staggered into the trading post and up to the bar. "Whiskey," Stone ordered, his voice hoarse.

"You boys got law trouble?" the bartender asked.

"If we do, it ain't none of your concern," Stone told him bluntly.

"Don't sass me, sonny-boy," the older man said. "It's my business if you bring trouble in here." He peered closely at the four men, then cut his eyes to the wanted poster tacked up behind the bar.

The man was reaching for a gun under the counter when Stone smashed his pistol down on the man's head, and Jeff dragged him off and tied him up in a storeroom. "We ain't seen no sign of that bastard trailin' us in days," Stone said. "I don't figure we lost that law-dog, but we got a good two

*Durango would be founded here in 1880.

days on him, way I figure. Time enough for us to swap horses and stock up on food and such. Let's get some grub goin'. I'm half-starved."

Nate stoked up the fire in the stove and began slicing bacon while Carter was rummaging through the stacks of men's britches and shirts to replace their own stinking and filthy clothing. None of the four outlaws even thought about taking a bath.

Their bellies full of hot food, wearing clean clothing, the men relaxed at one of the rough tables in the bar of the trading post, drinking whiskey.

"What happens if someone comes in here lookin' to buy something?" Nate asked.

"Hell, we sell it to them," Stone replied. "Then we shoot 'em!"

The four men thought that to be hysterically funny and roared with laughter. They opened another bottle of whiskey and gave no thought to the "law-dog" who'd been trailing them for days.

The man they assumed to be a lawman had picketed his horses about a half mile from the lonely trading post and was now slipping silently toward the building, coming up on a windowless blind side. Jamie had left his rifle in the boot and was carrying his sawed-off double-barreled shotgun.

The owner of the trading post had regained consciousness. After testing the ropes that bound him and finding them well-tied, he lay still and made no noise. He had lived in the West for more than thirty years, and knew these renegades would not hesitate to kill him if he started kicking up a fuss. He looked up as the back door to the storage room began slowly opening and one of the biggest and meanest-looking men he'd ever seen stepped inside. He recognized Jamie instantly, for the man was a Colorado legend.

Jamie swiftly cut the ropes that held the man and then put a finger to his lips. The man nodded in understanding and held up four fingers, cutting his eyes to the main part of the long and low building.

Jamie nodded and moved toward the curtained archway, earing back the hammers on the Greener as he walked. The post owner lay on the floor and smiled through his headache.

Jamie slipped through the curtains and stood for a moment, looking at the four men who were lounging at the table cussing and laughing and drinking whiskey.

Carter Young was the first to spot the big man standing in the shadows of the room, the Greener in his hands. His eyes widened and his mouth dropped open.

"Ah . . . Stone." He finally found his voice.

"What? Man, you look like you just seen a ghost."

"I wish I had."

Nate cut his eyes and said, "Oh, shit!"

"I can take you back to Valley for a trial and a hanging," Jamie said. "Or we can end it here. Whichever way you boys want it is fine with me."

As if one mind controlled them all, the four men threw themselves away from the table. Jamie's shotgun roared the instant he saw the men tense. Manhunting was something that Jamie was an expert at; he'd been doing it successfully for almost fifty years. Carter caught the full load from one barrel, and Jeff took the second one.

Jamie dropped the Greener and hauled iron just as Nate was filling his own hands and cocking the hammers. Jamie shot him twice, then fell into a crouch and disappeared behind the bar just as Stone's pistols began to bark and snarl. Jamie popped out at the other end of the bar and dusted Stone twice, the slugs turning the man around and dropping him to his knees. Stone snapped off a shot that nicked Jamie's left shoulder, burning and bringing blood. Jamie leveled his right-hand pistol and drilled Stone in the center of his forehead. Stone stretched out on the floor and did not move.

It was over.

"Hot damn!" the trading post owner yelled from the archway. "I've seen some sights in my time, but this one wins the prize. That was some mighty fine shootin', MacCallister."

"You can have their personal belongings and their horses and saddles," Jamie told him. "That'll help ease that lump on the back of your head some."

"Damn shore will. Lemme tend to your shoulder furst. Then I'll drag this trash outta here and drop 'em in a hole. I buried a horse the other day and haven't had the time to shovel in much dirt. I'll dump 'em at the south end; that's where the horse's ass is." He gathered up bandages and a basin of hot water from the pot on the stove.

"That one there," he said, pointing to Stone as he dipped a clean cloth into the hot water, "is the ringleader of this pack of piss-ants. I heard him talkin' 'bout them women they raped. It was disgustin'."

Jamie pulled his scalping knife from its sheath and knelt down beside Stone Gibson. The trading post owner watched unemotionally.

Two weeks later, the residents of Valley silently lined the streets and watched as Jamie rode down the main street. They all saw the scalp tied to Sundown's mane. A young federal marshal stood with Matthew in front of the sheriff's office. He was relatively new to the West and was still appalled by what he considered to be highly barbaric behavior by some westerners.

He grimaced at the sight of the human hair hanging from the mane of the big horse. "Is that what I think it is?"

"It is," Matthew told him.

"Who is that rough-looking old man?"

Matthew smiled. "My pa," he told the young federal marshal. "That, sir, is Jamie Ian MacCallister."

The federal marshal gulped. "And that, ah, scalp, means he got one of the men who attacked your sister and niece?"

"No, sir," Falcon said, walking up. "That means he got them all."

"But acting without authority and certainly without due process," the federal marshal said.

Falcon laughed at the young man. "Hey, Pa!" he called. "Joleen opened her eyes about two weeks ago. She's up and doin' fine."

Jamie reined up and swung down. He stepped up onto the boardwalk and shook hands with his sons, ignoring the young man with the badge pinned to his suit coat. "Cathy Lou?" he asked.

"She'll be all right, Pa," Matthew said. "She just needs a lot of love and care."

"Those criminals you pursued were wanted by the government for mail robbery and assault on a federal officer, MacCallister," the young marshal said. "I'll need a full report from you and I expect it promptly. I also—"

"Shut up," Jamie told him.

The marshal's mouth dropped open. "I . . . ah, I beg your pardon?"

"I said shut up. I was speaking to my sons. Not to you. When I'm finished speaking with my family, which is going to take the rest of the day and a good part of the evening, then I'll get around to you. Meanwhile, just stand aside and be quiet."

The lawman looked down at the badge pinned to his coat. The badge always seemed to impress most folks east of the Mississippi River. But out here in the West, he'd been told on more than one occasion where to take his badge and stick it. Which would have made walking, sitting, standing, or riding very uncomfortable.

These westerners certainly were an independent lot. And uncommonly blunt, too.

Jamie was content to stay close to home after his return, at least for a while. He thought occasionally of Logan, Red, Canby, and Rick, and wondered if they'd made it into and out of the Muggyowns with their hair.

In late 1873, Jamie received a message from the war department in Washington, D.C. An expedition into the Black

Hills of Dakota was being planned and would Jamie like to be one of the scouts?

Jamie wired back, asking who would lead the expedition.

Lt. Colonel George Armstrong Custer.

At first Jamie refused, for he knew Custer from the War Between the States, and did not like the man. Indeed, Jamie considered Custer to be nothing more than a flamboyant fool (an opinion that was shared by many career army men).

Custer had been a general at war's end, but was then reduced to the rank of captain. That didn't last long. In less than a year, he had been leap-frogged over more qualified men and was promoted to lieutenant colonel in the 7th Cavalry, which was being formed up at Fort Riley, Kansas.

Since he had arrived in the West, just after the War Between the States, Custer had been involved in many skirmishes with the Indians . . . not always coming out victorious. And to those who studied such things, and Jamie did, whenever he could get his hands on the manuals, it proved that Custer was a man who possessed a fatal weakness in the area of tactics. And Jamie knew, from long years of experience, that when dealing with Indians, perhaps the greatest guerilla fighters that ever lived, one had damn well better understand tactics.

And Jamie understood that while no one could call Custer a coward, Custer was not always faithful to his men. At the battle of Washita River, it was rumored that Custer left Major Elliot and nineteen of his men to die. While that accusation was never really confirmed, from that day forward, in 1868, Custer never again regained the full loyalty of his officers in the 7th Cavalry.

"Oh, why the hell not go?" Jamie muttered. "I have nothing to hold me here."

Truth was, he was getting bored.

Jamie saddled up and rode down to the telegraph office and wired the war department he would agree to scout for the Black Hills expedition.

Much to Jamie's surprise, Lt. Colonel Custer wired him as soon as he heard the news and expressed great delight that the famous commanding officer and guerrilla fighter in the recent unpleasantness was going to join his command.

"What's this all about, Pa?" Megan asked, during a visit to her father's cabin on the ridge.

"Gold, honey. That's the bottom line. The army says it's going to look for a northern railroad route through Dakota and Montana—and I'm sure they are—but the bottom line is gold."

"But Falcon says part of that area is sacred to the Indians."

"He's right. Especially the Sioux. And when gold is confirmed in the Black Hills, the miners will come swarming like ants to honey."

"And? . . ."

"There'll be trouble. I suspect another reason for this expedition is to locate a good spot to build a fort."

"But don't we have treaties with the Indians about the Black Hills?" Joleen asked.

Joleen had recovered from her experience and was coping. But not so with her daughter, Cathy Lou. Physically, Cathy was fine, but now she seldom smiled and had become withdrawn, rarely leaving the house without company.

"Sure we have treaties," Jamie answered. "But progress is not going to be stopped dead in its tracks by a piece of paper. And the Indians have done their share of breaking treaties, too," he added. He looked at Joleen. "Why didn't Cathy come up here with you, girl?"

"She's not feeling well, Pa. Pa?"

"Ummm?"

"We're thinking of sending her back east. To finish her education at a private girls' school."

"And what does she think about that?"

Joleen sighed. "She really wants to go. She says she hates the West."

Jamie knew all about that, for Cathy had talked to her grandpa at length. "Then send her. Finances are no problem. The family has money a-plenty."

"That's not it, Pa. You know as well as us that if we do that she might never come back."

Megan brought the coffeepot from the kitchen, and Jamie held out his cup for her to refill it with hot coffee. When Jamie was home, his family doted on him—male and female alike.

"Or she might realize that what happened to her could just as easily happen back east. It's her life, girl. She's reached the age where we can't live it for her."

Joleen nodded her head. "When do you leave, Pa?"

"In the spring."

"Then we have plenty of time. We'll talk more about i 'fore you go."

Megan had hung out Jamie's good black suit to air and was now heating the irons to press it. There were some big doings tomorrow: Ben F. Washington and Lola were to be married.

Jamie's birthday had passed; he was either sixty-three or sixty-four years old. He thought he'd been born in 1810, but he just wasn't certain about the date.

But he knew he'd lived a good long time. And he also knew that his age was quickly catching up with him. The past winter had been especially hard on him, his joints occasionally aching something fierce on bitterly cold mornings.

But he could still ride with the best of them and was still uncommonly strong. He had trouble reading anything up close without his glasses, but at a distance, his eyes were as good as any man's. Jamie figured he had two or three good years left in him before he'd have to really put on the brake and think about staying close to the hearth.

He was going to make the best of those years.

"What are you thinking, Pa?" Joleen broke into his thoughts.

Jamie smiled at her. "Oh, nothing of any importance."

After his kids had left, and the cabin was silent, Jamie sat or a time, looking at the pictures of Kate on the mantel and on tables around the large room. "I got me a hunch, Kate. got me a feeling that I'm gonna be seeing you 'fore too much longer. Custer is a fool, honey. And I may be a bigger fool for riding with him. I guess we'll just have to see."

Jamie stepped outside to stand on the porch. He looked up into the impossible blue of the Colorado sky. High above, an eagle soared and screamed.

# 29

Sundown was rarin' to hit the trail when Jamie threw a saddle on him and led him around to the front of the cabin. He was to link up with Custer and his men at Fort Abraham Lincoln in the Dakotas, on the west bank of the Missouri River and just north of the Cannonball River.

Jamie stood for a moment, looking down at Kate's grave on the ridge below him. "You rest easy, old woman," he muttered. "I'll be back, I promise you that." He turned away and swung into the saddle.

Jamie rode down the mountain, packhorse trailing, and then up part of the main street of town. He returned the dozens of waves from friends and relatives (mostly relatives), and then was out of Valley and riding north. The day was uncommonly warm for this time of year, and Jamie felt the years being blown away from him.

This was his destiny. This was his way of life. He was no more cut out for a rocking chair than an eagle was to be confined in a cage. Jamie did not want to die in a bed, with long-faced family members hovering about. This was where he should fight the final fight, out under Man Above's skies.

Only one thing wrong with that: he wanted his bones to lie beside Kate.

A small detail he'd have to ruminate on some.

\* \* \*

"Colonel MacCallister," Custer said, rising from his chair and extending his hand in greeting. "How good of you to join us. What a grand adventure awaits us in the Black Hills."

Jamie smiled and took the offered hand.

"We'll have at least three newspaper correspondents accompanying us," Custer rambled on. "And several prospectors, too."

Jamie's expression did not change at the news of the prospectors, but silently he congratulated himself for being right about the true objective behind the expedition. He would probably never know the entire truth of the matter, but he had figured all along that certain members of congress and some money and land speculators had gambled that if Custer could find gold, the miners would swarm in by the thousands and not leave. They would force the Indians to attack, and the army would then be sent in to put down the rebellion. The Indians would then be accused of breaking the treaty, and could be rounded up and put on reservations. More country would be opened up for pioneers, and the Indians would be put in their place where they could cause no more problems.

Very neat, Jamie thought. Not very ethical, but very neat.

Later that evening, alone in his quarters, Jamie amended his thinking somewhat. He was in sympathy with the Indians, but he also realized that civilization and progress went hand in hand, and many, if not most, of the Plains Indians simply would not accept the white man's way. They were hunters and warriors, not farmers and shopkeepers, ranchers and cowboys and laborers. They were nomadic, not settlers. And they would stubbornly hold on until the end. Jamie also knew that for many, the end was not that far away. For some, it was over.

Out in California, the warring Modoc tribe was forced into surrender, and four of their leaders, including the main leader, Captain Jack, were hanged at Fort Klamath in October of '73.

Out in Nevada, the richest strike to date in the history of

mining had occurred just a few months back, and the miners and prospectors were pouring across the land to get to Virginia City. A vein of ore, both gold and silver, had been discovered that was some fifty-five feet wide.

Also a few months back, silver was dropped as a coin, and gold was made the sole monetary standard. Many called the action the "crime of 1873."

And Jesse and Frank James held up their first train in 1873, killing an engineer and several passengers.

Just the column itself was impressive. One hundred and ten wagons accompanied the 7th Cavalry as they pushed off from Fort Abraham Lincoln in early summer, 1874, heading for the Black Hills, the most rugged and remote part of the Sioux reservation, located in the western Dakotas.

Custer was a happy man: he was back in the field again, and he did cut a resplendent figure, dressed in his buckskins, the sun shining off his long yellow hair. George Armstrong Custer sat a horse well . . . although that was about the only thing he did well. He was unaware up to his death that a few years before, General Sherman had written to a friend, "George A. Custer appears to not have much sense."

The band was playing gaily as the 7th moved out that day, with Custer sure they were heading for fame and glory. His wife, the lovely Libbie, waved her hankie at her man, and Custer's pets howled and barked and whined and carried on. The couple had no children, but Custer did have his pets. Lord, did he have pets! He had a tame mouse and a not so tame wolf. He had a raccoon and an opossum and forty dogs. And a pelican he had captured on the Arkansas River. Custer would, on occasion, carry the mouse in his long, flowing hair (it was sometimes quite a shock to visiting guests to see the mouse running around George's head, occasionally peeking out through the flowing locks). History did not record whatever happened to the mouse, the wolf, the raccoon, and the opossum . . . or to the Cheyenne girl (captured after the battle of Washita) that Custer reportedly kept as his mistress.

Jamie was amused by all the hoopla as the long column snaked its way out of the fort and headed west. Custer was certain his 7th Cavalry would encounter many hostiles during this expedition and return with souvenirs of glorious victories. But Jamie knew something that Custer did not: the tribes that occupied the area around the Black Hills were gone; they were in Montana for their annual summer's reunion.

Jamie kept that information to himself, not wanting to put a damper on Custer's euphoric mood. When George was in a good mood, he was an amusing and charming fellow. When he was in a bad mood, he became petty, demanding, red-faced and sullen . . . and he stuttered.

Despite all that, George Armstrong Custer was a man of undeniable courage; he would, without argument, charge through the gates of hell in pursuit of an enemy.

He just didn't have any common sense.

Jamie scouted far ahead of the long column, choosing the best places to camp for the night and the best places to ford the rivers.

As always, on this expedition George would suddenly leave the column to go hunting by himself. But George had a lousy sense of direction and never strayed too far from the main column. Not since several years back when he had galloped off to go buffalo hunting, but instead of shooting the buffalo he'd found, he accidentally shot his horse in the head, killing the animal instantly. Miles from the column, in the middle of hostile Indian country, he was lost. He finally followed his dogs back to the column. Since that episode, George had become much more careful about straying too far from the dust of his soldiers.

Whenever possible, George would ride with Jamie, and was always after him to relate stories about the fight at the Alamo, his life with the Shawnee, and of the many adventures in Jamie's long years on the frontier. Consequently,

Jamie tried to stay miles ahead of the column and away from Custer. Jamie did not have a very high opinion of the man.

The weeks wore on and the days became a blur. Not a single Indian was spotted. Finally Jamie told Custer that the Indians were gone up into Montana for the summer.

"Drat!" said Custer.

The column pushed on.

Custer didn't find his Indians, but he did find that the area offered the white man timber, game, and thousands of acres of grazing land. And the prospectors riding with Custer found gold.

That find was to be the beginning of the end for both the Indians and for Lt. Colonel George Armstrong Custer, commanding officer of the 7th Cavalry.

In late fall of 1874, Jamie, with permission, left the column and headed south. His work was finished . . . or so he thought. He had no way of knowing that he would ride one more time with Custer.

"There's a man to ride the rivers and the wild and lonely lands with, gentlemen," Custer told his officers as Jamie rode away. "I assure you, I will personally see to it that one day he will ride with the 7th into glorious victory against the hostiles."

Part of that statement would certainly come to be. But not the whole.

More than gold was found in the Black Hills. Silver, beryl, feldspar, and mica were also discovered. The Black Hills was soon called the richest place on earth. When the column finally returned to Fort Abraham Lincoln in late 1874, and the reporters could get their stories out and back to the eastern newspapers, the stampede west began, and the Indians had no choice but to fight. This land had been given to them, promised in writing to be theirs forever and ever. But once again, the white man had broken his word.

Jamie had angled some west, and rode down through southeastern Wyoming. At a trading post near Fort D. A. Russell, Jamie heard a familiar voice and turned to see Red, Logan, Canby, and Rick, sitting at a table in the far corner. Amid whoops and hollers, the men immediately started making plans to get into some mischief.

"I heard you was scoutin' for the army," Canby said.

"I was. One time only. With Custer," he added, smiling at the sudden grimace on Canby's face. "What are you boys up to?"

"Prowlin' around," Logan said. "We got out of the Mug-gyowns in the nick of time, with about a hundred screamin' savages right behind us. Damned unfriendly bunch of hea-hens. Way they was actin' you'd a thought we goosed the chief or humped his wife or somethin' equally awful."

"We heard you caught up with them ol' boys that done them turrible things to your kin," Red said.

"That I did," Jamie confirmed.

"You still got people after your hide, Mr. Mac," Rick said. "That crazy damned Asa Pike and them Jones boys is still prowlin' around makin' threats."

Jamie shook his head. "I can't be worried about that pack of nitwits. But I can guarantee you boys one thing: if they ever show up in Valley, they'll be dead within the hour. My son Falcon doesn't make idle threats."

"Yeah, we sorta got that impression," Red said with a smile.

"Where are you boys wintering?" Jamie asked.

The four men exchanged quick glances. "We thought we'd head down to Texas, maybe," Canby said. He smiled. "Jamie, you 'member Rick here tellin' us 'bout all them Kermit brothers bein' after him?"

"I do."

"Whole pack and passel of 'em is down Texas way. They bought 'em some sort of ranch down yonder. They're a crazy bunch; heavy into thievin' and rustlin'. But they pass themselves off as lovers of the Lord. We thought we'd amble down there and get them off the boy's back and do the sheriff a favor whilst we was at it."

Jamie nodded his gray head. "Sounds good to me. Where in Texas?"

"Some little two by twice town just north of the border. Called Eagle Pass," Logan said.

"Well, hell," Jamie said. "I've never been there."

"Wanna go?" Red asked, a hopeful note behind his words.

"Sure. Why not? Let's provision up and put some miles behind us. That's a far piece from here."

"We got us some gold, Mr. Mac," Rick said softly, his eyes twinkling.

"Hit you a strike down in the Muggyowns, did you?" Jamie asked with a smile.

"Not no mother lode," Logan whispered. "But enough to carry us for a time without worryin' where our next meal was comin' from."

"That's always a good feeling. You boys ready to go?"

"There ain't no moss growin' on my feet," Canby said.

Jamie tossed some coins on the table, and the five men rose from their chairs and hit the air.

"What a crew," a man muttered when the five were safely out of earshot.

"What do you mean?" his riding partner asked.

"Hell, man. You can practically smell the gunsmoke hangin' all around them ol' boys. That big, mean-lookin' one is Jamie Ian MacCallister . . ."

*"Really?"*

"You bet your boots it is. The young one is Rick Hanes. A first-class pistolero. The old scruffy one is Logan, the mountain man. And Red Green is no one to fool around with. Canby was in the army for about thirty years and is still as tough as they come. You can bet that them ol' boys is out to stir the mischief pot some."

"Wanna tag along?"

"Not me. I ain't got no death wish. Way I hear tell, them

l' boys got a habit of goin' where *angels* won't even go. Them's the ones that shot up New Mexico a while back."

"You don't say!"

"I do say."

"I 'member hearin' somethin' about that. Killed a whole bunch of folks down there."

"Yeah. And from the looks of things, they's gonna be ome more get dirt shoveled in their faces." He smiled. "I ure hope I'm in that good a shape when I get their age."

Jamie looked over at Logan, noticing a slight limp as the man walked along. "What's the matter with you, Logan?"

"I got a damn rock in my boot!"

"Well, why don't you shake it out?" Rick asked.

"I's thinkin' 'bout gettin' me a crutch instead," the old mountain man said with a straight face.

Red whipped off his hat, dragged it through a watering rough, then dumped the contents over Logan's head.

Laughing, the men walked on, to fill yet another page of western history.

# 30

The men provisioned up and headed south and slightly west, happy to be together again. As they rode, the older men looked through wise eyes at the progress that was steadily pushing westward in the form of pioneers.

"Damn haybinders." Logan cussed the homesteaders that seemed to be springing up all over the place.

"Wait until that new barbed wire gets out here," Jamie told the group as they were settling into camp for the evening. "Then you'll really see progress at its worst."

"What kind of wire?" Canby asked.

"Man back in Illinois, I think it is, has invented a new kind of wire. It has little bitty sharp spikes on it that'll cut you if you touch it. Calls it barbed wire. It's for keeping cattle in the fields."

"What happens if a human bein' rubs up agin it?" Logan asked.

"Same thing. You get cut."

"That's nasty," Red remarked. "They ought not to allow stuff like that to be sold."

"You can bet the damn haybinders will be stringin' it all over the place," Logan said. "Course, in a way you can't blame 'em. They're tryin' to get by just like the cattlemen."

They pushed on, riding by the ruins of Bent's Fort in southeastern Colorado.

"It was some place in its day," Logan said wistfully.

"That it was," Jamie agreed.

The fort was built in 1833 by the Bent brothers, Charles and William, and it was a magnificent structure. The walls were fourteen feet high and three feet thick. Inside, there was lodging for up to two hundred men at a time. Bent's fort was an oasis of civilization in the midst of the wilderness, where Indian and white could mingle without trouble. The fort had an icehouse, storerooms, a huge dining hall, a carpenter's shop, a tailor shop, and a blacksmith's shop. The fort's cook, Charlotte Green, was a lady of color, and she laid out a table of food that was unsurpassed anywhere between St. Louis and California. Charlotte used to say that she was "the only lady in the whole damn Injun country."

In late 1849, his brother Charles dead, William Bent, irritated at the government's refusal to give him a fair price for the fort, blew it up.

Jamie and the others rode on, crossing into Oklahoma Territory and then into Texas. They camped at the ruins of Adobe Walls, where, some months back, twenty-nine buffalo hunters and one woman held off nearly eight hundred Kiowa, Comanche, Cheyenne, and Arapaho warriors under the command of Quanah Parker and Lone Wolf. It was at Adobe Walls that Billy Dixon made his famous shot with a Sharps .50 caliber rifle, shooting an Indian off his horse at a range of almost one mile. The Indians were so shocked at the accuracy of the rapid-fire Sharps rifles, they finally withdrew. Among the defenders at the Walls was Bat Masterson.*

Shortly after the siege at Adobe Walls, the Red River Indian wars came to a close, as hundreds of Kiowa and Comanche warriors surrendered to the army. Over seventy warrior chiefs were placed in irons and transported to a military prison in Florida. The Indian wars on the North Texas plains were just about over.

The site of the battle of Adobe Walls lies about twenty miles northeast of the town of Stinnett, Texas.

Now the riders headed straight south, through the bitte[r] cold and blowing snow of the North Texas winter, a blu[e] norther that came howling down from Canada, gatherin[g] strength as it slammed over the great plains. They were ru[n]ning out of supplies and half-frozen when they spotted th[e] outline of a trading post, seemingly sitting smack in the mi[d]dle of nowhere.

"Is that for real or is this hell?" Red asked.

"Hell's hot," Canby corrected.

"I'd settle in for about twenty minutes of it," Logan sai[d]

The men stabled their horses out of the wind and saw t[o] the animals' comfort and then walked into the long, lo[w] building.

"Come a fur piece, did you?" the man behind the counte[r] asked.

"What happened to summer?" Rick asked.

The counterman laughed. "When it gets here, you'll b[e] wishin' it was winter agin. Trouble with this country is ther[e] ain't no middle ground. It's either hot or cold. I got coffe[e] and beef and beans, boys."

"Pour it in and dish it up," Jamie told him.

"Whiskey furst," Logan said. "My innards is froze solid.["]

The chill slowly leaving their bodies, the men sat dow[n] at a table to eat and drink.

"Where you boys headin'?"

"Eagle Pass," Canby told him.

The man shook his head. "Maverick County. That's ba[d] country, boys. Even this fur north of there I can tell yo[u] that's King Fisher's country."

"Who the hell is King Fisher?" Logan asked around [a] mouthful of food.

"Started out as a gunslick and a rustler. Now he calls hi[m]self a rancher. He's a bad one. The King runs that count[y] Now I hear he's thrown in with some bad ol' boys name [o]f Kermit."

"Is that a fact?" Rick said.

"Shore is. Was I you boys, I'd fight shy of that area."

"One thing about it," Canby said, "it'll be a damn sight warmer down there than it is here."

"You do have a point, but fired lead's hotter than ice, too."

Since his initial run-in with the Kermit brothers and kin, some time back, Rick had grown a handlebar mustache and had fleshed out some due to eating regular.

"They might not recognize me right off," he told his compadres when they finally reached the outskirts of Eagle Pass. "But it'll come to them sooner or later."

"Damn shore warmer down here than up north," Logan said. "My bones is finally thawin' out. I might just decide to live out the rest of my days down here."

"We might not none of us have no choice in the matter," Red said with a grin. "We might all get *planted* down here."

"You are such a joy to have along," Canby said. "Just full of good cheer and such."

"I just wonder if this King Fisher character is goin' to pitch in with the Kermit boys," Red mused aloud.

"We'll know soon enough," Jamie said, pointing to a road sign that read EAGLE PASS TEN MILES.

"I hope they got a good cafe in town," Logan said. "I'm right hongry."

The others laughed, Jamie saying, "Logan, I've never known you when you weren't hungry!"

In the small border town, the men stabled their horses and then found rooms. After cleaning up, they went looking for a cafe and had an early supper. After eating, they sat on benches in front of the general store and smoked and eyeballed the few riders that came in.

If there was any local lawman, he was either home for the evening or gone out of town, for no badge toter came near them.

"I think I'll amble over to that whiskey shop acrost the

street," Logan said, standing up. "Keep my ears open an
see what I can pick up. I'll be back."

Jamie opened his watch and checked the time. It was
few minutes before five o'clock on this late winter's day, an
the light was fast fading. Logan returned after a short tim
and took a seat.

"This King Fisher person is out of the country, I believe
But the Kermit brothers come into town most evenin's t
have supper. They're usually at the saloon over yonder b
five-thirty, and they'll drink for about an hour and then ea
They have thrown in with Fisher, and from what I coul
overhear, Fisher has this town buffaloed. Not just the town
but the whole damn county and a lot of the surroundin
area. What law there is around here is in Fisher's pocket."

"How many Kermits are there?" Red asked.

"Eight brothers and a whole bunch of cousins an
nephews and what have you," Rick answered. "And they'r
all big and mean and good with a gun."

"Sounds to me like these Kermits plan on hornin' in o
Fisher's play," Canby said.

Jamie nodded his head in the gathering darkness
"Shapes up that way, doesn't it?"*

"Too bad we can't just wait around for them to kill of
each other," Red opined.

"No time left to worry about that," Jamie said, cutting hi
eyes to the far end of the street. "I believe those are the Ke
mit brothers and kin riding in now."

*That power play certainly would have been attempted had not Jamie an
the others forced the Kermit brothers' hand that late winter's night in th
border town and all but wiped out the male members of the Kermit fam
ily. King Fisher continued his lawless ways until about 1883. Then he re
portedly "got religion" and moved his family to Uvalde County and becam
a deputy sheriff. On March 11, 1884, Fisher was attending a show at th
Vaudeville Theater in San Antonio with his gunfighter friend, the Englis
born Ben Thompson. Joe Foster and William Simms, aided by Canada Bi
and Harry Tremaine, suddenly opened fire on the two men, killing bot
Thompson and Fisher. Fisher was shot a dozen times in the head and ches
John "King" Fisher was thirty years old.

"Jesus me!" Canby said in mock horror. "Looks like about o dozen of them."

"Plenty to go around, for shore," Logan replied, after itting a brown stream of tobacco juice into the street.

"I believe I'm gonna see the elephant this night," Red reen suddenly announced.

The others looked at him.

"But I couldn't check out with no better friends around e," Red added.

"What brought all that on?" Canby asked.

"Just a feelin', that's all. But a damn strong one."

"Probably indigestion," Logan told him. "You ate about n pounds of beef."

But Red shook his head. "Nope. Tonight's the end for e." He looked at Rick. "My gold's yours, boy. Take it and uy yourself a spread somewhere. Make somethin' out of ourself. You're young; you got plenty of time to do that."

"I wish you'd quit talkin' like that," Rick told the older an. "We got plenty of trails to ride yet."

Red stared at the thirty or so riders as they rode up and vung down from their saddles. "This is track's end for me. ou know what I'm talkin' about, don't you, Jamie?"

Jamie nodded his head in the darkness. "I know," he oke softly, just as the owner of the store came out and lit e twin lamps out front.

"I could have done without that," Jamie whispered, as the mplight outlined them clearly on the benches.

"You really believe you're gonna cash in your chips night, Red?" Canby asked.

"Yes. And I ain't a-feared of it. All I want is a nice box and headstone. I'm trustin' you boys to do me right."

"You know we will," Logan said.

"And you can dance all around my grave," Red said with smile. "But not on it." Red lifted his eyes to the crowd cross the street. "They sure are givin' us the once-over, in't they?"

"Yeah," Rick said. "I think they recognize me. The one

standing and starin' right at us is Percy Kermit. He's the ol
est of the clan. Surroundin' him is his brothers, Claud
Zeb, Zeke, Samuel, Calhoun, Temple, and Isham."

"You know any of the others?" Logan asked.

"A few of their names. The fat one is called Fat Phil. Th
twins on the right is Dunk and Dink. Next to them is Al
jah and Skinny."

The mob of Kermits and kin suddenly turned and we
into the saloon.

"We better go fetch our spare pistols," Red said, standi
up. "This here shoot-out is gonna be a dandy one."

The men walked back to the small hotel, opened the
bedrolls and saddlebags and dug through their possible
laying aside their spare pistols. They carefully cleaned th
guns and loaded them up full, stuffing their pockets wi
spare cartridges.

"Don't make my tombstone nothin' fancy now, you hear
Red said, as the men walked out of the hotel.

"I swear to God I'm gonna hit you on the head and t
you to a hitch rail if you don't hush that kind of talk," Canl
told him.

"I've played out my string," Red said stubbornly. "A ma
knows when it's time. Y'all just heed my wishes now, yc
hear?"

"I seen one oncet had fat little angels dancin' on it
Logan said.

"I don't want nothin' like that. Just my name and the da
I passed."

"When was you born?" Canby asked.

"Hell, I don't know. I'm 'bout sixty-five years old, or ther
abouts."

"You're gonna live a good long time yet," Rick said.

"Least another hour or so," Red told him. "But by Gc
I'm gonna go out with a smoke pole in each hand, and I
take some of them damn Kermits with me."

Rick looked at him and shook his head. He glanced

mie. "Mr. Mac, did you ever get one of them feelin's like
d's got?"

"No. But I have known men who did."

"What happened to them?"

"They died shortly thereafter."

"Told you," Red said with a faint smile.

Two men stepped out of the alley and blocked the walk-
y. One of them held up a hand. "I be Abijah Kermit and
is here is my nephew, Thalis. If you men has thrown in
ur lot with that filthy wife-stealin', rapin', no-good forni-
tor Hanes, then you can die with him come the morning.
e'll meet you all at the livery. Good night."

"I ain't no fornicator!" Rick yelled. "And I didn't rape no-
dy. That damn woman chased after me, not the other way
ound."

"You lie," Thalis said.

"You damn Bible-spoutin' hypocrites! You go right
aight to hell!" Rick told them both.

"You'll feel the heat from the pits and the sting of the
vil's pitchfork long before us," Abijah said.

"We'll see you all at dawn. Make your peace," Thalis said.

"That works both ways," Jamie said softly.

The two men stared at him for a moment, then turned
ound and stalked off, with Rick giving them both a sound
ssing. The men disappeared into the darkness.

Logan looked at Rick. "Boy, have you been fornicatin'
hen we wasn't lookin'?"

"Not lately," Rick said.

"I'm glad I ain't been," Red said. "I'd hate to go meet my
aker with Him knowin' I'd just been a-fornicatin' some-
in' fierce."

"Boys," Jamie said, "does anybody here really want to wait
l dawn to open this dance?"

The returning smiles told him they did not.

"Well, let's go see what kind of a tune we can play this
ening."

# 31

Those in the saloon who weren't Kermits beat a hasty ex
out the back door when Jamie and the others pushed ope
the batwings and stepped inside the smoky bar and bega
spreading out.

"You men are fools!" Percy Kermit said to Jamie. "I ga
you until dawn to make your peace with God."

"We done that," Logan said. "He tole us to come on
here and kick your ass."

"You blaspheme!"

Logan looked hurt. "I'm just tellin' you what He said. H
said He don't have much use for hypocrites like y'all."

A man stood up from a table. "Permission to spea
cousin?"

"Go ahead, Eli."

"The Lord has delivered our enemies into our camp. I
God's will that we obey the sign and destroy them."

"I do believe you're right, Eli."

"What a bunch of bloomin' idgits," Red said.

"Yeah," Logan responded. "I believe the Lord has deli
ered us into this den of sin for a reason. And I sure wouldn
want to disregard no message from the Heavens."

"My goodness no!" Canby said.

"You'll all burn in hell!" Percy said.

Jamie stared hard at Percy. "This fight doesn't have to b
Rick's a good boy, and we believe he's telling the tru

out what happened. The woman chased him, not the
her way around."

"He's a lying fornicator," another Kermit said, standing
.

"You be right, Ham," Percy said.

"I do believe we've talked long enough," Logan opined.
think it's time to read some from the Scriptures."

Claude Kermit grabbed for his guns, and Logan shot him
the belly.

Then Kermits and kin all jumped to their feet, and the
rroom erupted in a hail of bullets and gunsmoke.

As soon as Logan had fired, Jamie and his group stepped
t of position; for a few precious seconds that move threw
f the aim of the Kermits.

Red put a bullet into the chest of a man just as Jamie
agged iron and dropped Percy with a bullet to the head.
ck lined up Fat Phil and put the pus-gut on the floor, bel-
ing and squalling from the hole in his belly.

Jamie dropped to one knee and put lead into a man who
s aiming at Red. The bullet broke the man's shooting arm
the elbow, angled off and up, and struck him in the jaw,
ocking him down.

Canby stood with a pistol in each hand, blasting away
th terrible results: there were several bodies lying in front
him, some moving, some who would never again move
der their own power.

Jamie saw Red take a bullet in the chest. The big man stag-
red back, smiled, dropped his empty pistols and jerked
ll-loaded guns from behind his belt. "I'm a ring-tailed
oter from way back!" the flame-haired and freckle-faced
an yelled. "And it'll take more than that to put me down,
u damned pack of heathens!"

Red opened up, firing as fast as he could cock the ham-
ers and pull the triggers. The results were devastating.

"I'm hit!" Archie Kermit screamed, just as his cousin,
rnard, took a bullet from Red's guns in the center of his

forehead and fell against him, both men tumbling to th floor.

Jamie felt the whip and sting of a bullet cut a groove i his cheek as yet another bullet took off a small chunk flesh from his upper left arm. Jamie took aim through th smoke and yelling and confusion and ended the days of Ze and Zeke Kermit with four fast rounds from his guns.

Red was down on his knees, his face and chest bloody. H let out a wild yell and emptied one gun into a knot of Ke mits and kin, did a fast border roll, and emptied his secon pistol before falling over to one side, his pistol slippin from suddenly numb fingers.

Enraged at the sight, Logan jumped right into the mi dle of a group of Kermits, his big Bowie knife flashing bac and forth, each slash reddening the razor-sharp blade.

Dunk and Dink went down, eyes wide with shock, gapin holes in their throats.

Jamie took splinters from the bar in one side of his fac and the blood poured out. Ignoring the sting and the we ness, he jerked freshly charged pistols from his belt an began pouring out the lead. Temple and Isham Kermi went down under the rolling and deadly thunderous ba rage just as Canby ended the days of Samuel and Calhoun

Rick jerked the sawed-off shotgun from pegs behind th bar and fired both barrels into several cousins and nephews knocking one completely off his feet and sending anothe two rolling on the floor, chest and belly shot.

Jamie watched through unbelieving eyes as Red staggere to his boots and emptied a six-gun into the chest of Han Kermit. Then the big man turned, his eyes meeting thos of Jamie, his smile bloody. "See you on the other side, Mac, he said, then fell forward, dead.

As suddenly as it had begun, the fight was over. The bar room was filled with thick gunsmoke, the acrid smell min gling with the sharp odor of blood.

Only two of the Kermit kin were unhit and able to stand Gratton and Cornelius. They stood with their hands empt

nd in the air. Their eyes were wide and disbelieving at
hat had just happened in the saloon. The moaning of the
ounded filled the smoky air.

Only two of the eight brothers were still alive, Claude and
emple, and they were badly wounded.

Jamie reloaded, then pulled what splinters he could from
is face and wiped away the blood. "I believe that just about
nds your problem with the Kermits, Rick," he said calmly.

Logan wiped the bloody blade of his Bowie on a dead
an's shirt and said, "Damn shore does."

As King Fisher would later say, "I'm glad I wasn't around
at night. Those old bastards are rattlesnake mean. I'd not
ant to lock horns with Jamie Ian MacCallister or anybody
ho rode with him."

The highest compliment one gunfighter could give an-
ther.

Jamie and his friends looked over at Red. He had died
ith what appeared to be a very faint smile on his lips.
ogan walked over to him and knelt down. With his fin-
ertips, he very gently closed Red's eyes. "Have a good jour-
ey, ol' partner," he whispered. "I'll be along someday. Then
e can ride together forever."

Rick was struggling with his emotions, fighting to keep
he tears from rolling down his cheeks. He lost the battle
nd let the tears flow.

"Well, look at the little baby cry," Gratton sneered.

Çanby closed the distance between them and hit Gratton
cross the jaw with the barrel of his pistol. The sound of the
awbone cracking was loud in the near silence. Canby
urned to Cornelius.

"You got anything you want to say?"

"N-no . . . no, sir. Nothin' a-tall."

"Fine."

Logan looked at the bartender, who had just a moment
efore gotten up from the floor behind the bar and was
usting himself off. "You got airy undertaker in this burg?"

"Yes, sir."

"Go fetch him."

"What about our kin?" Cornelius asked.

Jamie glanced at the man. "What about them?"

"They need a doctor."

One of the wounded Kermits raised up on one elbow an gave Logan a cussing, then made the mistake of pointing pistol at him. The old mountain man shot him between th eyes and said, "That 'un don't no more."

"You foul, evil old man!" Cornelius said.

"Old, I'll go along with, sonny. But foul and evil suits yo more 'un me. Now shut that blowhole of yourn 'fore I tak me a notion to shut it for you."

Cornelius closed his mouth and kept it closed.

Rick and Canby gathered up all the weapons from th dead and wounded and toted them out back, dropping th whole kit and caboodle down the opening of the one-hol privy.

Gratton was getting to his feet, holding his busted jaw when the undertaker and his helper arrived. The under taker smiled and rubbed his hands together at the sight There were dead bodies all over the place.

Jamie pointed to Red. "You do this man first. And you d him right. We'll bring you clean clothes within the hour."

"Yes, sir. Of course. Now, about the headstone . . ."

Red was buried the next morning, a cold, windy overcas day in South Texas. No one knew what his first name wa or if Green was even his Christian last name. After the shor service, the men did not linger long at the grave site. The said their goodbyes to Red and rode out of town, following the Rio Grande north.

Two days later, sitting at a table in a cantina, the mer toasted the memory of Red Green.

"I think I'll head back home," Canby announced. "I don' figure any of my brothers or sisters is still livin', or even i hey was, if they'd want to see me, but I ain't never even seen my parents' graves. I think I ought to do that."

"I think I'll head up to Fort Stockton and hook up with a party that's maybe heading to Californee," Logan said. "Hell, I might decide to spend the rest of my days out yonder. You been out there, ain't you, Mac?"

"Oh, yes. Some years back. The weather's nice year-round."

The group was silent for a time, knowing they were spliting up, probably for the last time.

"Rick," Canby said. "You got Red's gold, and with your hare, that makes a tidy poke. You ought to think about setlin' down. Marry up with a nice woman and stop this here wanderin'."

"What woman would want me?" the young man asked.

Jamie smiled. "Oh, I know a place just full of single gals. Most of them blond-headed and blue-eyed."

"You don't say!"

"Sure do. And I know where there's a nice piece of land for sale to the right person. It's ten sections. Man could raise horses, run some cattle, and have him a nice garden. And I know the president of the bank right well, too. The land could be got for a fair price."

"That sounds good to me," Rick said.

"We'll pull out at dawn, then. It's a long ride."

"Well, I guess it's trail's end, boys," Logan said with a sigh. "But I want to tell y'all this: I ain't never ridden with no better men. Now, I ain't much for mushy goodbyes. So I'll just finish this drink and walk out of here. Nobody needs to say no more."

The men nodded their heads and watched as the old mountain man drained his glass, then stood up and walked out of the cantina.

Canby poured himself another drink, downed it, and stood up. "See you boys around," he said, then tossed them a salute and walked away.

Rick finally broke the silence after Logan and Canby had

left. "I ain't never gonna forget them men," he said, hi
voice husky.

"Nor they us," Jamie replied.

"I used to think all I ever wanted to do was ride the trails
Mr. Mac. But now I realize that a man's got to have a home
something solid to hold on to. Logan's never had that and
neither has Canby—'ceptin' for all them years in the army
I reckon I want more than that out of life."

Jamie nodded in agreement. "I been talking around. It'
about eighty-five miles straight north to a trading post. We'l
make that and provision again there. Then ride on up
through the plains and angle some west. We'll be home
when the mountain flowers are just beginning to bloom."

"That sure has a good sound to me, Mr. Mac. But then
what'll I do?"

Jamie smiled. "You can build you a cabin, hang those
guns up on a peg, and for the most part, leave them there
Then you can go courtin'."

"And I'll have me a home."

"That you will."


Logan rode west, Canby rode east, and Jamie and Rick
headed north. Red lay in his grave just outside of Eagle Pass
But the five of them had broken the back and cut off the
head of the Kermit gang in a shoot-out that would become
legend.

Jamie and Rick rode across the once empty plains that
were not so empty anymore. Pioneers were pushing steadily
westward, building their lonely cabins, with the only company the whine of the wind and the howl of the coyote. In
another twenty-five years, the panhandle of Texas would be
dotted with small towns and settlements.

The two men crossed the windswept and lonely plains
and provisioned at a trading post near the juncture of the
Mustang and Carrizo rivers and spent a day and a night
there, resting their horses and themselves. They crossed

ito Oklahoma Territory, an area that was rapidly filling
ith outlaws on the run and assorted other riffraff and
ropouts from the human race. They had just made camp
nd had the coffee ready when a voice called out from the
athering shadows.

"Come on in," Jamie said, his pistol in his hand, hammer
ack. "But you'd better be friendly."

"I'm friendly if you are. I'm a U.S. marshal, on the hunt
or three murderers." The man stepped into the light and
amie smiled.

"Pat Riordan," Jamie said. "It's been a while since I've
een you."

"Jamie MacCallister!" the federal marshal called. "Well,
ll be damned."

The two men shook hands, and Jamie introduced Rick.
at led his horse in and up to the picket line and saw to its
eeds before seeing to his own. Then he settled down with
sigh and accepted a cup of coffee.

"Who are you looking for?" Jamie asked.

"Twins named Dunk and Dink Kermit, and a cousin of
heirs called Rip."

Jamie smiled. "They're all dead." Then he explained
bout the shoot-out.

"Good," Pat said. "You've got several thousand dollars of
eward money coming, Mac."

"Give it to Rick, here. Have it sent to the Bank of Valley,
Colorado, in his name. He'll be settling there."

"Fair enough." Then he chuckled. "You boys realize you
viped out the whole damn gang! You done something in
ive minutes that we've been tryin' to do for five years."

"We tend to take a more direct course than you boys,"
amie said with a smile.

"I can attest to that, for a fact," the marshal replied drily.
What now, Mac?"

"Home for both me and Rick. At least for a while, for me."

"Well, I can tell you that the army's lookin' for you.
There's trouble in the Black Hills. The government's made

up its mind to settle it once and for all. They're sendin
Custer and his Seventh Cavalry in. Least that's the way
heard it."*

"I may be up to one more ride," Jamie said, not knowin
that with those words, he had sealed his fate.

*The government had just declared Crazy Horse and Sitting Bull an
those warriors who followed them to be hostile Indians. A few months late
they would order all Indians in the Black Hills to be removed to reserv
tions or face military force. When the Indians refused to budge, Lt. Colon
George Armstrong Custer and his Seventh Cavalry would be ordered in

# 32

"It's beautiful, Mr. Mac," Rick said, getting his first look at MacCallister's Valley.

"That's what I thought the first time I saw it, and I still think it is."

"If I could have me a real home here, I don't think I'd ever leave it."

Jamie smiled. "You couldn't find a better place, Rick. Come on, let's go home."

The first thing, the *very* first thing Rick noticed was all the good-looking women, most of them blond-haired and blue-eyed; even the ones with dark or red hair had blue eyes. "Mr. Mac, you and your missus sure had a lot of offspring."

Jamie got a laugh out of that. "Yeah, Rick. We sure did. I guess I'm related to about three-fourths of the town."

Jamie got Rick settled in Lola's La Pierre Hotel, then walked down to the sheriff's office. Matthew had a worried look on his face. After greeting his father, Matthew said, "Pa, don't do it."

"What are you talking about, boy?"

"The army wants to see you, Pa. Right now. There's gonna be war with the Indians. They want you to scout for them."

"The army or the Indians?" Jamie asked with a smile.

"Dammit, Pa! This is no laughing matter. We got all sorts of trouble here in Valley."

Jamie poured a cup of coffee and sat down. "You want t
tell me about it?"

"Some rogue Cheyenne warriors slipped into this are
about a week ago. Kidnapped Falcon's wife. It all starte
about six weeks or so back. Some of her family came to se
her, said she was a traitor for marrying outside her race . .
or words to that effect."

"Where was Falcon while all this was going on?"

"The first time or the second time?"

"Any of them."

"When the family come to see her, Falcon was out in th
county buying cattle. When they grabbed her, he was here
in town. They done it in broad daylight."

"The kids?"

"They're safe. They were over with friends."

"The baby?"

"With Megan."

"Falcon's out looking?"

"Sure. But you know better than any of us, if an India
don't want to be found, they ain't gonna be found."

Jamie sat down and was silent for a moment, deep i
thought. Finally he said, "I know that Marie's mother i
dead. Her grandparents are dead. We're about the onl
family she's got. If Falcon's looking for her in Colorado, he'
wasting his time. Them that grabbed her carried her north
up into the Dakotas or Wyoming Territory. All this was
warning to me, boy."

"To keep you from scoutin' for the army?"

"Yeah."

"What are you goin' to do, Pa?"

Jamie stood up and stretched the kinks from long mile
in the saddle. "After I resupply and let the horses rest, I'n
going to look for her. But don't nobody get their hopes up.

Matthew stared at his father for a moment. "Why do yo
say that, Pa?"

"Because I think she's dead, that's why."

\* \* \*

The next day, Jamie helped Rick buy some land and set up a line of credit at the bank. Morgan was decidedly and openly irritated by his father's seemingly cavalier attitude toward the kidnapping of Marie. After only a few minutes, Jamie set him straight—very bluntly.

"Climb down from behind that pulpit, boy," the father told the son. "I love Marie as if she was my own. But I know things about Indians that you'll never know. If it was Cheyenne that took her, and I strongly doubt it was, they done so without tribal permission. Indians is no different from whites in that they got outlaws and trash among them just like we do. Those that took Marie probably were banished from some tribe a long time ago. They won't dare take Marie back to any village. They'd be killed if they did that. You know damn well we in this valley made peace with the Indians more than thirty years ago. And they don't dare turn her loose for fear that Marie would point them out later. They used her and then killed her, boy. And then scattered to the four winds. They'll never speak of what they done—not among themselves or to anyone else. If the various Indian tribes are gathering for a fight, as the army thinks, them that took Marie will circle around and come in from the north to join up with the other warriors . . . if they'll have them. And they probably will if this is going to be an all-out war."

"Yes, Pa," Morgan said humbly, knowing very well he had been put in his place.

"Now I'm going to go look for Marie. But the odds are I will never find her. Falcon's going to be beside himself with grief, and he'll want to do something real stupid. It's up to you other kids to prevent that. Now tell me what's been happening up the Black Hills."

Ben F. Washington, Matthew, and Jamie Ian the Second had been standing quietly near the door, listening to Jamie unload on Morgan. Ben said, "Thousands of miners have

swarmed into the Black Hills, Mr. MacCallister. They've settled and built a town in a place that some are calling Dead-
wood. And the Indians are going to fight."

"How do you propose for us to keep Falcon here, Pa?
Jamie Ian asked his dad. "Toss a loop around him and
hogtie him?"

"If you have to."

"I got me a mental picture of that," Matthew said. "And
the picture is us gettin' the hell shot out of us. Tryin' to dab
a loop on Falcon would be like tryin' to rope the wind. You
know damn well Falcon ain't gonna listen to but one person, and that's you, Pa."

"Then I'll stick around for a few more days," Jamie said.
He sighed and added, "There is no point in hurrying
things."

"You really believe Marie is dead, don't you, Mr. Mac-
Callister?" Ben asked.

"Yes. I do. And her kidnapping may have been done to
try to provoke trouble between us and the few Indians remaining in this area. But it won't work." Jamie stood up. "I'll
go buy my supplies and get ready to pull out as soon as Falcon shows up and I settle him down . . . or try to. Marie was
the steadying influence in his life. With her gone, I don't
even like to think about Falcon's future."

Jamie went to have lunch with Joleen and family. No one
had mentioned Cathy Lou to him, and Jamie thought he
had a pretty good idea why that was. Joleen confirmed it.

"She's gone, Pa. We sent her back east to school. I don't
think we'll ever see her again."

"That's a mighty cold way of looking at it, child."

Joleen shrugged her shoulders as she worked around the
stove. The girl looked so much like Kate it made Jamie's
heart ache. "You taught us to be honest and to speak our
minds, Pa."

"That I did."

Joleen turned to face him. "If Marie is . . . dead," she stumbled over the word. "What's going to happen to Falcon?"

"More importantly, what's going to become of the chil-
ren?" Jamie countered.

"Oh, you know we'll take them in without hesitation, Pa."

"But can you kids raise them knowing the Indian way?
hat was very important to Marie."

"All we can do is try, Pa. I'm worried about Falcon."

Joleen and Falcon were as close as a brother and sister
ould be. The last two children of Kate and Jamie MacCal-
ster. Joleen born in Texas in '34, and Falcon born in Val-
ey in '39.

"It isn't like me and your ma, girl. Falcon's in his prime.
Ie'll find someone else. He's too young not to."

"You can't be sure that Marie is dead, Pa."

"I'm sure, girl. It's something that can't be explained. It's
he Shawnee coming out in me."

"You going to scout for the army, Pa?"

"Probably."

"Pa, you're sixty-five years old. Don't you think you de-
erve a rest?"

"Girl, I feel no older than fifty. I'm not as spry as I used
o be. I have some aches and pains on cold mornings that
didn't used to have. I can't hook and draw as fast as I once
ould; I got to wear glasses when I read. But at a distance,
can out-see an eagle. And I can still sit a saddle all day long,
nd I am definitely not yet ready for the rocking chair and
hawl."

Joleen smiled at her pa, then leaned over and gave him
 peck on the cheek. "When do you plan on pulling out,
 a?"

"Well, I've wired the army and told them I'd scout for
Custer. Maybe I can keep the fool from getting killed. But
 m not leaving until I can sit Falcon down and talk to him."

"Good luck with that," Joleen said, more than a touch of
 arcasm in her words.

Jamie left her house to walk the boardwalks of the town.
Ie had a strange feeling that he could not shake loose. He
 ad a feeling that he was seeing his town for the last time.

"Silly," he muttered. Then he thought about Red, down in Eagle Pass, and the feeling that had come over his friend on that last evening on earth for him. Jamie finally shoved the strange feeling away and rode back up to his cabin. He sat on the porch until it started getting dark, occasionally looking down at Kate's grave, now covered with a wildly colored profusion of mountain flowers. The same type of flowers were growing on Grandpa MacCallister's grave.

Just before full dark, one of his grandkids—he couldn't remember the boy's name—rode up with supper, all carefully wrapped and sealed in jars and put in a wicker basket. Jamie noticed that the boy—about twelve, he guessed—seemed afraid of him.

"Sit," Jamie told him, and the boy promptly sat. "You want some of this food, boy?"

"Oh, no, sir. I ate already. But thank you."

"Whose boy are you, anyway?"

"Megan's my mama. I'm the youngest. Name's John."

"When were you born?"

"1864, sir. You was off fightin' the Yankees."

Jamie smiled. "Seems like a long time ago."

"I reckon it was, sir. I'll be twelve this year."

Cotton-headed and blue-eyed, Jamie thought. Damn sure has MacCallister blood in him.

"Sir?"

"What?"

"Did you really fight a grizzly bear one time?"

Jamie laughed and the boy smiled. "Well . . . I guess you might say that. I didn't have much choice in the matter, though. He ran me up a tree."

John laughed and laughed as Jamie told him the truth about the fight with Ol' Big Paw, with Jamie only slightly embellishing the tale.

Long after the boy had left, taking the pots and plates and dishes back with him, Jamie sat and smoked his pipe and was lost in memories. Finally, he blew out the lamps and went to bed. He hoped Falcon would ride in soon.

His youngest son returned the next day at noon, looking gaunt and tired and riding with a very short fuse.

Jamie waited for Falcon to come to him. He knew he would.

Jamie pointed to a chair on the porch. "Sit, son."

Falcon sat and said, "She ain't dead, Pa."

"Maybe so, maybe not. But the odds aren't real good on the not. You better start preparing your mind for that."

Falcon said nothing.

"I'm going out to look for her, son. I got eyes and ears out there in the Big Empty you'll never have. If Marie is alive, I'll find out."

"I'll go with you."

"No, you won't, boy. You got kids that need you to be home. They need you more right now than they ever have. And I won't brook no sass on the subject. You understand that?"

"Yes, Pa."

"I'll say my goodbyes in the morning and pull out. Son?"

"Yes, Pa?"

"If what I suspect happened to Marie is true, don't let grief overtake you and turn you down the wrong trail, you hear? It's something you're going to have to fight."

"Yes, sir."

"And don't let the wrong cards dealt too early turn you sour, neither."

"I understand, Pa."

"Fine. I hope you do, son. Now shake my hand and go get cleaned up and get some hot food in you and a good night's sleep. You look like a tree full of owls at the end of forty miles of bad road."

Falcon smiled. "Do I really look that bad, Pa?"

"You do."

Falcon stood up and shook his father's hand. "I'll see you before you leave?"

"I'll see all of you before I leave." One last time, that omnous thought suddenly sprang into his head. He grimace and shook it away.

"Something wrong, Pa?"

"Oh, no. Nothing. I reckon I just ate too much of Megan good cooking, that's all."

"See you in the mornin', Pa."

"Will you be staying out at your ranch?"

Falcon hesitated for a few seconds. "No. I've got a roo at the Wild Rose."

"That's right. I forgot about that. All right. Sleep wel boy."

Jamie put on his jacket, stuffed his pipe, and sat down i his chair on the porch, smoking and thinking.

He looked down toward Kate's grave.

For the last time, that thought once more jumped int his head.

He looked down at the lights of Valley, far below him.

For the last time.

"Damn!" Jamie said irritably, wishing that thought woul go away and leave him alone. He got up and walked out t the small barn. He spoke to his horses and rubbed Sun down's nose. "Want to take another ride, fellow?"

Sundown whinnied and nuzzled Jamie's neck.

Jamie went back into the house and pulled out a trunk He removed two sets of buckskins, buckskins he hadn' worn since Kate's death, and took them out to the porch draping them across the rail, letting the coolness of nigh air them out.

Back in his cabin, Jamie poured another cup of coffee stirred in sugar and sat for a time in his chair, the cabin i near darkness. He wondered what Falcon would do, shoul what he suspected happened to Marie turn out to be true but he didn't wonder long. The boy was just like Jamie, an he would do what Jamie had done. Saddle up and ride. Rid high and wide and lonesome for a time.

The kids would be taken in by the family, and Falcon would return from time to time, but it would never be the same for him.

Jamie drained his coffee cup. With a sigh he got up and blew out the lamps.

Tomorrow he'd ride out of Valley.

For the last time, that thought once more came to him.

"Crap!" Jamie said, and went to bed.

# 33

"Y'all hush all this blubberin' and bleatin'," Jamie told th
women gathered around him. "You kids have seen me rid
off dozens of times over the years. This time is no differen
When, or if, I find out something about Marie, I'll get wor
back to you." Jamie swung into the saddle and lifted th
reins. He waved at his kids, grandkids, great-grandkids, an
many friends, and pointed Sundown's nose north. He di
not look back at the town.

Jamie had no way of knowing that hundreds of miles t
the north and east, Brigadier General Alfred H. Terry, com
mander of the department of Dakota, had received order
from Washington to prepare for military action against th
Sioux and Cheyenne tribes.

The seventh night out Jamie spent with a small band o
peaceful Indians who were not going to take any part in th
upcoming fight—or so they said. But Jamie noticed the
had no women with them and were packed for travel. H
made no mention of that.

"Bear Killer has always been a friend to us," an elder said
"So we will tell him what we know of Marie Gentle Breeze
Bad Indians planned to take her north against her will. Sh
fought them constantly. They killed her. Crushed her head
with a war axe and threw her into the Colored River."*

*Blue River

"Did they rape her?"

"Many times. They thought by taking the woman they would gain much respect from others and be allowed back into the tribe. They were wrong. They are under sentence of death by the council."

Jamie drew a line in the dirt. "Show me where they threw her body into the river."

The elder pointed to a spot. "There." He lifted his eyes and stared at Jamie. "Man Who Is Not Afraid should not ride with the soldiers. Not this time."

Jamie did not push the conversation, for he knew that warning was all he was going to get from the elder. He was gone just after dawn the next morning. For several days, he rode and walked for miles on both sides of the river. He finally found what was left of Marie, and it was not much. What was left of Falcon's wife was wedged in between a log and a large rock just a few feet away from the west bank of the river.

Jamie gathered up what he could of Marie, handling the remains with as much dignity as was possible, considering the condition of the body, and buried her. He piled a mound of rocks over the grave and marked it carefully.

He rode over to the mining town of Georgetown, got himself a room at Louis Dupuy's fancy Hotel de Paris, and sent word to Falcon.

Sitting on the side of the bed in the luxuriously appointed room, with its solid walnut bed, hot and cold water taps over marble basins, and the finest of linens on the bed, Jamie suddenly realized he was tired, and it was only mid-day.

Age is catching up with me fast, Jamie thought, then added this to his thoughts: Well, why not? How many times have I been shot and stabbed? And I was once left for dead with injuries so severe it took months for me to heal. All those things had to have taken a toll on me.

Jamie bathed and dressed in his one set of good clothing he'd brought with him, then walked down to the hotel bar. He was not expecting any trouble, for of all the mining towns in the West, Georgetown was now and always had been the calmest; and in the hotel, Louis would tolerate no trouble of any kind, no matter who started it. Wild Bill Hickok made Georgetown his home for a time back in '72, and even he respected the hotel's reputation as a safe haven.

That was not to say that Georgetown was not a whiskey drinkin', poker-playin' and whorin' town, for it was. It just never saw much trouble.

Jamie enjoyed two slow drinks of fine whiskey at the bar, then Louis came in and motioned him over to his private table. He shook Jamie's hand.

"An honor, monsieur," the Frenchman said. "Your exploits are known world wide."

"Thank you," Jamie said modestly.

"Do you ride north to fight the Indians, monsieur?"

"Yes. With mixed emotions."

"I do understand . . . both sides, I try to tell myself." He shrugged his shoulders. "But can a white man ever understand the Indian?"

"Louis, I have a long distance to travel, and I have a feeling that time is running out." Jamie could not, of course, realize at the time just how prophetic those words would prove to be. "I think my son, Falcon, will be along in a few days." He handed the hotel owner a carefully drawn map. "Would you see that he gets this, please?"

"But of course. Consider it done." He picked up a menu and with a smile said, "Now, if you would do me the honor of selecting your evening meal? . . ."

"Of course."


Jamie rode out of Georgetown before dawn the next morning, heading north. He had told the army he would rendezvous with them on the Yellowstone, where Rosebud Creek flowed out of the Yellowstone.

Actually, he was looking forward to the ride.

\* \* \*

It was one of the many councils among the chiefs of many tribes. Sitting Bull, Gall, Red Cloud, Crazy Horse, Low Dog, and a dozen others. There were various tribes of Sioux represented at the council as well as Cheyenne, Sans Arc, and Blackfeet: Hunkpapa, Miniconjoux, and Oglala. Soon there would be fifteen thousand Indians gathered along the banks of the Greasy Grass River.*

"We will fight and destroy them all," Crazy Horse said. "We will drive them from our lands forever."

"We might win the battle," the more moderate Red Cloud said. "But we will never win the war. Why can't any of you see this?"

"Bah!" Crazy Horse said. "You have talked and talked and talked with the white man. Has he ever kept his word? No. Seven times you have traveled on the iron horse to see the white leaders in Washington. Seven times they promised this and that, and seven times they *lied!* The white man has the tongue of a snake. The truth is not in them. You are the only one among us to hold out, Red Cloud. Your influence is gone. I do not wish to hear your words. They are the words of a frightened woman."

Brave and bold words on the part of Crazy Horse, for Red Cloud was a man who once held a lofty position within the tribe . . . but no more. Crazy Horse had openly helped push along Red Cloud's decline of power.

Red Cloud rose from the circle in the tipi and left. There was great sadness in the man's heart, for he had been east many times, once to speak at the Cooper Institute in New York City, where (not surprisingly) there was much pro-Indian sentiment among those men and women who had never been farther west than New Jersey.

Those in attendance had wildly applauded Red Cloud's words as they were translated. Immediately afterward, the

*Little Bighorn River

idealists drew up a plan, which was never shown to Red Cloud or implemented. Which was fine, for it wouldn't have worked anyway. The idealists (not surprisingly) did not understand what most westerners knew practically from birth: the majority of Indians did not want to be civilized, at least not in accordance with the white man's definition of the word.

On this day, Red Cloud walked away from the council tipi to be alone with his wisdom. "All is lost," the great chief muttered. "All is lost. For we cannot win. Crazy Horse and Yellow Hair* could well be brothers, for while they are brave men, they are also fools. One wants to kill all the whites; the other wants to kill all the Indians. All is lost."

Falcon arrived at Georgetown days after his father had left and was given Jamie's message and map. He immediately set out to find the grave of his wife, unaware that his arrival in, and the quick departure out of, the mining town had not gone unnoticed by a group of men who had just missed Jamie.

The men followed the grieving Falcon from a safe distance. They would strike when the time was right. When it came to being dead, one damned MacCallister was as good as the other.

General Alfred H. Terry had received orders from Washington to pull out of Fort Abraham Lincoln on May 17, 1876, with a massive force of men, including twelve companies of the 7th Cavalry, commanded by Lt. Colonel George Armstrong Custer. General Sheridan had personally drawn up the plan: General Terry would move west to the Yellowstone, Colonel John Gibbon would move east out of Fort Ellis, Montana, and General George Crook

*Custer

ould move north out of Fort Fetterman in Wyoming.

The commanders had been assured they would not do attle with more than five hundred hostiles at any given me.

They were going to be in for quite a surprise. Especially uster. Briefly.

Jamie headed straight north through Wyoming, follow-g an established Indian trail that in the years ahead would ecome a major north/south highway. (The Indian has ever been given credit for finding the easiest route rough difficult terrain.)

By the time Jamie reached the North Platte River, unal-rable events were taking place, occurrences that would nd with tragic results for both the Indian and the white an . . . but much more so for the Indian: the tribes were athering along the banks of the Greasy Grass River in outhern Montana. Thousands of them.

Still, the army commanders were being told again and gain by messenger that they would encounter only a few undred hostiles at any given time, for the Indians had ever banded together under one commander and cer-ainly would not do so now. Be assured of that.

Somebody forgot to tell the Indians that.

Falcon found Marie's grave and sat by it for a time, try-ng to make some sense out of her death. He could not. Fal-on had brought along a heavy hammer and a chisel, and fter looking around for a proper stone, found one, mus-led it into place, and began the laborious job of slowly chis-ling her name into the stone.

He was intent upon his work, but not so much that he ailed to occasionally check his surroundings, for despite all he moves toward civilization, this was still the Wild West. And Falcon had been well-schooled by his father.

Falcon became aware that he was being watched. And no[t] by Indians. Falcon allowed himself a very small smile. H[e] had never seen an Indian this clumsy. He continued h[is] work on the stone, but only after furtively slipping th[e] leather loops from the hammers of his pistols and check[-] ing to make sure his rifle was close at hand.

After concluding that his watchers were at least six stron[g] and probably more, Falcon made several trips to his pack[,] ostensibly for a drink of water, but really to stuff his poc[k-] ets full of cartridges for his rifle and pistols. Then he wou[ld] return to work on the stone.

He worked and waited and wondered.


Jamie continued to ride north, drawing ever closer to h[is] date with destiny.


In Valley, Ben F. Washington, after Falcon let him rea[d] the message from Jamie to his son, sadly prepared the obi[t-] uary notice for Marie MacCallister. Then a sudden an[d] sobering thought caused him to put aside his pencil. H[e] wondered, right out of the blue, if he would ever see Jam[ie] Ian MacCallister again.

He leaned back in his swivel chair and wondered why th[at] terrible concern had popped into his brain.

Ben shook his head and returned to his writing.


"I wish Pa had not gone off on this scout," Morgan sai[d] to his brothers, Jamie Ian and Matthew.

Andrew and Rosanna were touring in the East and woul[d] leave for Europe in late June. Their sailing date was sche[d-] uled for the 26th of June.

"You got a bad feelin', too?" Matthew asked.

"Yeah, just like Ian. A real bad feeling about it."

'The girls are all tore up about it," Jamie Ian said. "Pat
d me Joleen cried all the night."

"That's the same thing Jim told me about Megan."

"Anybody seen Ellen Kathleen?"

"She's holdin' up. But William told me she's wearin' a
e like a thundercloud."

'I worry more about Falcon than Pa," Matthew said. "Pa's
en ridin' with death all around him for almost sixty years
w. Tell you the truth, and it's a hard thing to say, I don't
nk Pa gives a damn anymore. Not since Ma passed. I
nk he's ready in his mind to die. But Falcon . . ." He shook
s head. "Folks better fight shy of him, mood he's in."

Morgan looked at Jamie Ian and smiled. "How's your boy
d Mary Marie doin'?"

Jamie Ian laughed, lightening the somber moment. "That
l keeps him at a flat lope all day long. They've been mar-
d now, oh, four and half years. Expecting their third
ild this fall. Red-haired, freckle-faced, and blue-eyed."

"Way that boy works at the farm, he don't have time to
much else than some nighttime cuddlin'," Matthew said
h a smile.

"Seems like that's about all we done, too," Jamie Ian said.
When you take a look at all the kids in this town."


With the waters of the Blue River softly flowing not far
vay, Falcon heard the men when they made their rush to-
rd him. He turned, dropped to one knee, and drew his
ght-hand pistol, all in one fluid motion.

"We want him alive!" Asa Pike shouted, just as one of his
en pointed a gun at Falcon.

Falcon shot the man in the chest and then threw himself
one side as the men rushed him. He drew his other pis-
l and opened fire; at nearly point-blank range, his fire was
evastating.

The Jones brothers, Lloyd and Bob, were among the first
go down, both of them mortally wounded. Lloyd stum-

bled backward and lost his balance, finally tumbling o⟩ the side of the bank and falling into the river. Bob sat do⟩ hard, both hands holding his bullet-perforated belly.

Falcon had no time to observe what Bob did next; he ⟩ in a fight for his life without having any idea why the m⟩ had attacked him.

The fight was over in less than a minute. The cool mo⟩ tain air was acrid with lingering gunsmoke, mixed with ⟩ faint sounds of a couple of horses galloping away, the mo⟩ ing of the wounded, and the silence of the dead.

Falcon quickly reloaded and, with a pistol in each ha⟩ began warily walking among the wounded, kicking pist⟩ away from the men and out of reach.

Falcon stood over one dying man and asked, "Why?"

" 'Cause you a goddamn MacCallister, that's why," ⟩ man told him, then closed his eyes and died.

# 34

Jamie began seeing bands of Indians, all seemingly headed for the same place, and that slowed his travel, for he did not want to be seen . . . if he could help it. The Indians he saw were carrying war shields, and many carried both bows and arrows and rifles. That meant only one thing: war.

Jamie was forced to alter his route of travel. He cut east for a time, then once more turned Sundown's head to the north. Just north of Pyramid Butte, he was scanning the terrain ahead of him and spotted an army patrol. He left his scant cover and rode toward the patrol, smiling as he drew close enough to be able to pick out features.

It was Lt. Cal Sanders.

"Stars and garters!" the young lieutenant blurted. "Mr. MacCallister. I haven't seen you since El Paso, sir."

Jamie pulled in close and shook the offered hand.

"The men who were riding with you, sir . . . how are they?"

Briefly, Jamie brought the young lieutenant up to date.

"I'm sorry to hear about Mr. Green. He seemed to be a very fine and capable man. Sir, we heard you were going to scout for the army on this foray. But I don't think it's going to amount to very much. We've seen only a few scattered bands of hostiles, and they ran away from us."

"Which direction did they go?"

"West, sir. Always toward the west. But what's odd abo▌
it, is that they always taunted us before they fled."

Jamie cut his eyes to the Arikara scout riding with th▌
party. He noticed a decidedly worried look in the Arikar▌
eyes.

"Did it seem like they wanted you to follow them?" Jam▌
asked the lieutenant.

"Well . . . yes, it did. But we're under orders not to enga▌
the enemy. Just report on their movements."

Jamie looked at the Arikara scout. "What tribe?"

"Lakota."

"Are you with Custer?" Jamie asked the lieutenant.

"Yes, sir. Under Captain Benteen's command."

"That's good." Jamie had heard from several goo▌
sources that Captain Frederick William Benteen despise▌
Custer, considering the man to be no more than a glor▌
hungry fool. "Can you take me to Benteen?"

"Of course, sir. If you can wait until tomorrow. We're o▌
the last leg of this patrol. We were just turning around t▌
head back when you were spotted."

"That'll be fine."

After chatting with Jamie for a few more minutes, L▌
Sanders ordered the patrol to turn back north, with Jami▌
riding for a time with the Arikara scout. "How are yo▌
called?" Jamie asked.

"Jumping Wolf. It is an honor to meet the great Bea▌
Killer."

"The tribes are gathering to make war, Jumping Wolf."

"I know. But I cannot convince any officer of that. I hav▌
spoken with other scouts, Two Whistles, Spotted Setter, an▌
White Man Runs Him.* They have seen with their own eye▌
large bands of Sioux and Cheyenne gathering. But no on▌
believes them."

"I believe them," Jamie said. "I've seen the same thing.▌

"Long Hair is a fool," Jumping Wolf said bluntly. "I thin▌

---

*Indian scouts who fought at the Little Big Horn and survived the battl▌

at many will die, and very soon. He cut his hair short be-
re leaving the fort. Bad sign, I think."

"What about Bloody Knife?" Another Arikara scout who
s Custer's favorite and a man Custer usually listened to.
t not this time.

"Bloody Knife has told Custer that there are more Sioux
thering than his men have bullets to kill them. Custer did
t believe him."

"I do."

"It is good you do. Perhaps you can convince Long Hair
at we are riding toward our doom."

"I doubt I'll be able to do that. How about Lonesome
arley Reynolds?" Jamie asked.

Lonesome Charley was a friend of Jamie's. The two men
d scouted together many times in the past.

"There he rides," Jumping Wolf said, pointing ahead.
sk him yourself."

Jamie and Lonesome Charley greeted each other warmly,
d Charley shook his head. "It's bad, Ol' Hoss. And it ain't
st Custer who's playin' the fool. I been out here for
onths and seen what's happenin' up close and personal.
he Injuns has been gatherin' guns by the hundreds. But
an't convince them brass-buttoned sons of bitches of the
uth. Jamie, I think they's upwards of six to eight thousand
juns gatherin'."*

"Eight *thousand!*" Jamie blurted.

"Yep. At least that."

"More," Jumping Wolf said.

"More?" Jamie turned to the Arikara scout.

"More," Jumping Wolf said stubbornly.

"What the hell are we getting into here, Charley?" Jamie
ked.

"Bad trouble, Ol' Hoss. Real bad trouble."

stimates put the number of Indians at close to fifteen thousand, with
veral thousand warriors; never again would such a large force be as-
mbled.

Jamie sat his saddle, too stunned to speak.

"Even most of the scouts don't agree on any set numbe Charley said. "Most of them put the figure at two, may three thousand, at most." He paused and met Jamie's stea gaze. "I've tried to get General Terry to relieve me, but won't."

"You're that worried about it?"

"You bet I am."

The men quieted as Lt. Sanders rode up, all smil "When we do catch up with the hostiles, gentlemen, i going to be a grand fight."

Lonesome Charley Reynolds looked at the young offic "Yeah," he said drily.

Falcon buried the dead far away from his wife's grave. I did not mark the shallow, mass grave. One attacker who h survived the fight had told Falcon who had led the ambus Falcon had seen to the man's wounds as best he could wi what he had, put him on a horse, and told him to go hon adding, "If I ever see you again, I'll shoot you on the spo

"You'll not see me no more," the man said. "But Asa v be back. Bet on it."

"The man must be insane," Falcon said, then slapped t horse on the rump and sent him galloping.

Falcon spent the rest of the day finishing the marker f Marie's resting place. Then he tidied up the area and sto for a time by Marie's grave. Falcon put his hat on his hea walked to his horse, and rode away without looking ba He did not know where he was going. He was just ridir He headed west, toward Utah. Falcon wanted only to ri away his grief; just be alone for a time and let the wind a the rain help cure the ache deep inside him.

He had no way of knowing at the time that he was abo to become one of the most wanted men west of the Miss sippi River.

\*   \*   \*

The first thing Jamie heard when he rode into the mili-
y encampment was chanting.

Dismounting, Lt. Sanders said, "That doesn't sound like
ppy chanting to me."

"Far from it," Lonesome Charley Reynolds said. "Them's
e Arikara and Crow scouts singin' their death songs."

"Where's Custer?" Jamie asked.

A sergeant who had walked over to the group said, "He
t to meet with General Terry and Colonel Gibbon up on
e Yellowstone. I think there's been a change in plans."

"There better be," Lonesome Charley muttered. "Like a
ll retreat."

It was May 17, 1876.

No one, including General Terry, who was on the stern-
eeler, the *Far West*, anchored on the Yellowstone, had any
owledge that on that day—one month to the day after
rry had left Fort Abraham Lincoln—General Crook, at
e Rosebud River, came into contact with some fifteen
ndred very hostile Sioux, led by Crazy Horse. Crook was
rced to retreat. He suffered ten dead and two dozen
unded. He ordered his men to head south and regroup
Goose Creek.

Crook would not be in position when Custer foolishly
lit his forces and jumped the gun and attacked eight days
ter. Crook and his detachment would be miles south, in
yoming. There were some who tried to place part of the
ame on Crook for the disaster that occurred but that
ame lay squarely on the shoulders of Lt. Colonel Custer.

For several days, Jamie and the other scouts, including a
ench/Indian named Mitch Bouyer, did little except scout
bit and talk.

Custer returned from his meeting on the Yellowstone
d ordered his men to make ready for a march.

"Well," Lonesome Charley said morosely. "Here we go,
ys. Make your peace with God."

The date was May 22, 1876. Noon.

The trumpets sounded, and six hundred men of the 7th Cavalry, in perfect formation, rode past a group of officers, among which was General Alfred Terry.

About a mile away, several of the scouts had gathered, sitting their saddles and watching the scene.

"Real pretty," Mitch Bouyer said.

"Just darlin'," Lonesome Charley said.

Custer's favorite and most trusted scout, the Arikara chief, Bloody Knife, looked at the men and said nothing. But his thoughts were dark. He had already sung his death song.

At General Terry's side was Lt. Colonel George Armstrong Custer, his hair neatly trimmed. He wore buckskins, high boots, and a wide-brimmed hat. He was mounted on his horse, Vic.

All around the men was wilderness. There was no sign of civilization, except for the men themselves.

General Terry consulted his timepiece. "It's time, George," he said.

Vic was prancing in place, eager to be on the trail. Custer had to keep a tight rein on the strong animal.

Colonel John Gibbon smiled and said, "Now don't be greedy, George. There are plenty of Indians for us all. Wait for us."

Custer's reply has been studied and analyzed and debated for over a hundred years. "No," he said, "I won't." Then he rode away, galloping up to the head of the column.

General Terry frowned and glanced at Colonel Gibbon. "Now, what the hell did he mean by that?"

"I don't know, sir."

Moments later, the twelve companies of the 7th, under Custer's command, disappeared from view, riding south toward the Rosebud. Only their dust could be seen. At Custer's insistence, he had refused to take along an additional battalion of troops and a battery of Gatling guns.

"They would only slow me down," he had told General

rry at the meeting on the sternwheeler. "Besides, the 7th
n handle anything the hostiles might throw at us."

As Custer and his column faded from view, General Terry
ook hands with Colonel Gibbon. "Good luck, John."

"Thank you, sir."

Jamie and the other scouts rode out far ahead of the col-
nn, ranging north, south, and west of the advancing troops.
Jamie, as did the other scouts, began to see signs that dis-
rbed him. The signs told him that there were far more In-
ans in the area than the army had thought. Jamie began
wonder if even Lonesome Charley's estimates might be
w. Just before leaving camp, Lonesome Charley had given
s few personal possessions away.

"I ain't comin' back," he told one friend.

"There ain't none of us gonna come back," Mitch Bouyer
d added solemnly.

It was one o'clock on June 22. Custer and some two hun-
ed and sixty-one (that figure has been in dispute for a
ndred and twenty years) other officers and enlisted men
d approximately seventy-two hours to live.

After getting himself a room in the small hotel in a tiny
wn in Utah, Falcon went down for a drink and something
eat. Much of the grief he'd been carrying had left him,
at he was still not wanting company. He took his bottle and
ass and went to a far corner of the saloon.

Two men walked in, one wearing a sheriff's badge, the
her with a federal marshal's badge pinned to his suit coat.
alcon was not interested in them and paid them scant at-
ntion as they walked to the bar (strutted was more like it,
e thought) and ordered whiskey. Falcon returned to his
hiskey and his sorrowful thoughts and ignored all others
the saloon.

But Falcon was his father's son; he could smell trouble,
d the lawmen had it written all over them. To begin with,
ey were both small men, about five-six or -seven, and both

walked like they had something to prove. And the bigg
the man to prove it with, or on, the better.

Falcon was wondering where his dad was and how he w
doing when he heard boots approaching his table. I
looked up into the faces of the two star packers. Very u
friendly faces.

"Stand up," the federal marshal said.

"I beg your pardon?" Falcon questioned.

"Get on your feet, Lucas," the sheriff said.

"My name is not Lucas. It's Falcon MacCallister. And I a
very comfortable sitting, thank you."

"I said get up, you thievin' son of a bitch!" the feder
marshal demanded. "Lucas or MacCallister, it don't mal
no difference. You're still a horse thief and a rustler."

Falcon took a better look at the men. Definitely relate
Probably brothers.

The sheriff pulled a leather-wrapped cosh from his ba
pocket and held it up threateningly. "Get up, you scum. (
I'll pound your head in where you sit."

"That would be a real bad mistake, Sheriff," Falco
warned.

"You makin' threats agin my brother, boy?" the feder
marshal asked.

Falcon was getting mad. He could feel his temper bein
unleashed. "My name is MacCallister. I'm from Valley, Co
orado. I have done nothing wrong. Why don't you gentl
men take a seat and we'll talk about this?"

"Get up, you bastard!" the sheriff hollered. Then he to
a swing at Falcon with the blackjack.

Falcon ducked the swing and grabbed the edge of th
table, overturning it and knocking the two star packe
sprawling on the floor. The federal marshal grabbed for h
pistol, and Falcon kicked it out of his hand and then p
his boot against the side of the man's jaw. The federal ma
shal kissed the floor, out cold.

The sheriff was struggling to get to his feet. Falcon helpe
him, sort of.

He reached down, grabbed a handful of the sheriff's
irt, and hit him on the side of the jaw with a powerful right
t. The sheriff's eyes rolled back into his head, and Falcon
leased the man. The sheriff sighed and joined his brother
the floor.

"Idiots," Falcon said, straightening his coat.

"Run, mister," a customer said. "Run for your life."

Falcon looked at the local. "Run? Why?"

" 'Cause when them two wakes up, they'll kill you for
re. Them's the Noonan brothers. They're both crazy. And
ey're Nance Noonan's brothers, both of 'em."

"Who the hell is Nance Noonan?"

"The he-coon of this part of the territory, son," an older
an said. "And you're in his town. Nance Noonan owns
erything and damn near everybody in this part of the ter-
cory. He owns the N/N ranch."

"He's right, mister," another local said. "Get gone from
re as quick as you can. Pride ain't worth dyin' for. Not in
y book anyways."

"You do have a point," Falcon said.

"I'll saddle your horse whilst you pack your possibles," the
cal said. "Then ride, boy, ride. The name MacCallister
n't mean nothin' to men like Nance Noonan . . ."

The federal marshal stirred and reached for his gun. "I'll
ll you, you son of a bitch!"

Falcon palmed his gun and shot him, the .45 slug punch-
g a hole in the center of the man's forehead.

"Git the hell up to your room and pack, son," Falcon was
ged. "I'll throw a saddle on your horse."

Falcon was coming down the stairs with his bedroll, sad-
ebags, and rifle when Sheriff Butch Noonan rose to his
oots and grabbed for his guns. Falcon lifted the Winches-
r .44-40, thumbed back the hammer, and drilled the man
the center of his chest.

"Oh, shit!" a citizen breathed.

"Ride, MacCallister, ride!" a man shouted. "Ride like Ol'
ick is after you, 'cause he damn shore is!"

# 35

Custer was convinced that no Indian would ever stan and fight. He felt that given the slightest chance to cut an run, the Indian would do just that. Custer was fully awar that he had to have a mighty victory to carry on his militar career, for he was disliked intensely by many, which now i cluded the President of the United States, Grant. Custer ha taken along with him, against orders from Sherman, friend of his, a civilian reporter, Mark Kellogg of the Ne York Herald. Kellogg was to chronicle Custer's victory again the Indians. It was a story he would never get to write.

On the morning of the 23rd, Custer started the march about five o'clock in the morning, and he set a tough pac The day turned hot and dry.

"Look," Jamie said to Lonesome Charley. He pointed the ground, rutted by the lodgepoles dragged by India horses. "I've seen hundreds of those."

"Yeah," Lonesome Charley agreed. "They's so many I juns the grass has been et right down to the roots by the ponies. I'm tellin' you, Ol' Hoss, we're ridin' right straigh into hell."

The men rode on, and became more dismayed by th signs left by the Indians.

"This is not a series of camps we've been seeing," Jami said. "It's one damn huge camp."

"You be right," Lonesome Charley said. "Biggest dam

jun camp I ever saw. Hell, Ol' Hoss, it must stretch for
iles!"

"Maybe twelve or fifteen thousand Indians," Jamie mused.

"Sweet Baby Jesus!" Lonesome Charley breathed in awe.

"Nonsense!" Custer said, after hearing Jamie's report.
uff and piffle. What you're implying is that the Indians
ave banded together, probably under one leader." He
ook his head. "That has never happened and is not hap-
ening now." He dismissed Jamie with a wave of his hand.

Jamie resisted an impulse to deck the man. Angered at
e man's stubborn resistance to the truth, Jamie wheeled
ound and left the tent without another word.

"Well, ol' son, you tried," Mitch Bouyer said to Jamie over
offee. "Up yonder a ways, I found a place where I figure
e Indians held a sun dance. That tells me someone, a chief
robably, had a vision of a great victory for the Indians. If
at's so, there ain't gonna be no holdin' 'em back."

"The Northern Cheyenne is in here, too," Lonesome
harley said. "I wish I could get close enough to their camp
see if they're gonna do the Suicide Warrior's dance. That
ould really tell me somethin'."*

Mitch Bouyer smiled. "If the Northern Cheyenne is in on
is, that means Custer is gonna be fightin' some of his rel-
ives, in a manner of speakin', that is."

The men chuckled. It was an open secret that Custer had
Cheyenne mistress, a very comely maiden named Me-o-
i.

Jamie looked far off into the distance. "The valley of the
ittle Big Horn," he finally said. "Near the bluffs. That's
here they'll be."

"Good water and graze," Lonesome Charley said. "Yep.
hat's where we'll find them."

"And God help us when we do," Mitch said softly.

---

ometimes called the Dying Dance. A dance by boys and young men who
ledge to fight to the death.

*May 24, 1876*

Custer had set a brutal pace that day, the column trave[ing] just over thirty miles through very rough terrain befor[e] Custer called a halt. The troopers were as tired as the[ir] horses, which were exhausted.

When the Crow scouts Custer had sent out returned ear[ly] that evening, Custer made several of the decisions tha[t] would ultimately cost him his life . . . and those decision[s] went against direct orders he had received from the com[-]manding general of the campaign. (1) He ordered his me[n] to prepare for a night march. (2) He was so far advance[d] past any point where Terry might believe him to be, he wa[s] miles out of position. (3) He was going to launch a surpri[se] attack alone and thus claim the victory as his own.

Custer did not know that Sioux scouts were watching h[is] troopers' every move. The only surprise would be Custer'[s.] And that would not last long.

The column moved out just before midnight, the me[n] cussing, the horses whinnying, kicking, and biting. Th[e] men were running into each other in the thick, chokin[g] dust, and the mules were braying to high heaven.

"This is a surprise attack?" Jamie said to Lonesom[e] Charley.

"We're gonna be the only ones surprised," the scout sai[d,] and then added with a dour smile, "Surprised if we wake u[p] in Heaven instead of hell."

Jamie chuckled. "You afraid of dying, Charley?"

"No. But I ain't 'specially lookin' forward to it neither.["]

They marched for ten long miles before Custer called [a] halt for rest and water and food. At seven the next morn[n]ing, they were back in the saddle and put ten more mile[s] behind them.

Ahead of the column, on the eastern side of the Littl[e] Bighorn, on bluffs some one hundred feet high, just a[t] dawn, Lieutenant Varnum and several scouts had just awak[e]

ned from a short nap. They were stunned by what they saw:
n a plain, some miles away, they could just make out huge
erds of horses—thousands and thousands of horses.

"Dear God in Heaven," Varnum said, as much a prayer as
n utterance.

He immediately sent word back to Custer.

Custer was awake and waiting word from Varnum. He had
ressed casually that morning: a blue flannel shirt, buckskin
ritches tucked into high boots. He wore a white hat and
arried two pistols. Custer mounted up on Vic and rode
hrough the camp, giving orders to his officers.

They were on the march moments later.

By the time Custer reached Varnum's observation post,
he day had turned scorchingly hot, and the sky was hazy.
Custer was unable to see the thousands of horses (some
lace the number at twenty thousand), or the Indian en-
ampment.

"It's the biggest Indian camp I ever seen," Bouyer had
old him.

Custer smiled. He did not care how big the Indian camp
vas. Only that it was there. And only that it was his. His mo-
nent of glory was at hand.

He mounted up and waved his cavalry forward, toward
he Little Big Horn.

When Custer reached Ash Creek (later changed to Reno
Creek), he halted the regiment.

It was blisteringly hot at noon on June 26, 1876.

Custer began dividing his command. He ordered one
ull company and squads of men from others to stay and
guard the slow-moving pack train. He ordered Captain
Frederick Benteen to take three companies and scout the
area south of the valley.

Benteen smiled, thinking: Keeping me well out of the
ight, eh, George. How typical of you.

Benteen mounted up and rode off.

Custer ordered Major Marcus Reno to take three com-

panies of men and strike the Indian camp at the souther
end. Custer told him that he, Custer, would take five com
panies and support Reno.

Reno and his men rode off.

"Go with him, Colonel MacCallister," Custer said to Jamie
using Jamie's old rank.

Jamie nodded and swung in behind Reno's column. H
whoaed Sundown for a moment to lift a hand in farewell t
Lonesome Charley Reynolds and Mitch Bouyer. They bot
waved their farewells to Jamie.

Each man in the regiment of the 7th Cavalry carried on
hundred and twenty-five rounds of ammunition. Custer le
behind with the pack train some twenty-five thousan
rounds of rifle and pistol ammunition.

Custer swung into the saddle and headed out, but he di
not ride after Reno. Instead, he turned downstream, ridin
parallel to the river. His officers exchanged glances, wor
dering what in the hell he was doing.

As they drew ever closer to the massive Indian village
Mitch Bouyer said, "If we go in there, we won't come out

Custer gave him a sharp look. "Are you afraid, M
Bouyer? Have you turned coward on me?"

Mitch spat on the ground and refused to dignify tha
with a reply. So far as is known, that was the last exchang
between Lt. Colonel George Armstrong Custer and scou
Mitch Bouyer . . . at least on this earth. Although it i
strongly suspected that just before Custer and his men wer
overwhelmed on a piece of ground that some would ca
Last Stand Hill, Bouyer gave Custer a thorough cussing
surely he was not alone in doing that.

Bloody Knife looked up at the sun and said goodbye t
it, using sign language.

Jamie rode to the head of the column and said to Majo
Reno, "Custer's turned away from us."

"What!"

"He's heading downstream."

Reno considered the situation, cussed for a momen

en shrugged his shoulders. "We have our orders, Mr. acCallister. We must follow them."

"Indeed we must," Jamie replied.

Lt. Varnum and most of the scouts rode up to join Reno's olumn.

"What the hell? . . ." Reno exclaimed.

"Bouyer sent us to join you," one of the scouts said. "He id there is no point in all of us dying this day."

"The man has uncommon good sense," Jamie muttered. But I wonder why he didn't save himself?"

Reno heard Jamie's comments but chose not to reply to em. He twisted in the saddle and looked back at the col-mn, doing some quick arithmetic. He had about one hun-red and thirty-five officers and men, and some fifteen or xteen scouts.

Then, faintly, he heard the first shots of the day being red.

"We're in it now," Reno muttered, not knowing that the hots were not coming from Custer's men attacking the In-ians, but from Indians attacking Custer from ambush.

"Let's water our horses up ahead," Jamie suggested, ointing to the river. "And ourselves," he added. "We might ot get another chance."

Horses watered and canteens filled, Reno and his men orded the river and regrouped on the other side, the In-ian village about three miles away. Reno positioned his en in the classic cavalry line and lifted his arm. "Charge!" e shouted, and the long blue line galloped forward.

The village Reno and his pitifully small detachment were ttacking was a Hunkpapa village, under the leadership of Chief Gall. The Indians started shouting as the cavalry harge became evident, and Crazy Horse, in another village, eard the shouting and leaped onto his pony, racing toward he sound of yelling and gunfire.

"Fall back, fall back to me!" Crazy Horse yelled from his ony. "Let them come on!"

The Indians began running back toward the village.

Reno saw the movement and picked up immediately o what the Indians were doing. He halted the charge.

"It's a trap!" he shouted. "Don't fall for it."

Reno ordered his men to dismount; every fourth ma would hold four horses, and the others would form a ski mish line. He had already lost some men; others had be come scattered as their horses had panicked and tosse them to the ground. Some riders (many of whom were il trained new recruits) could not control their animals an could do little more than try to stay in the saddle until th horse wore itself out.

Reno had about eighty-five men left, including the scout He had no idea where Custer was. One end of the skirmis line was in the timber. The men were standing about eigh feet apart, weapons at the ready.

Reno's charge was halted, and thus, technically, he ha disobeyed Custer's orders. But had he gone on into the vi lage, he and his men would have been slaughtered withi seconds. It was a tough field decision to call, but Majo Reno was right in making it.

"The woods!" Jamie called, and Reno nodded his hea in agreement, having already made up his mind to take t the woods for better cover.

Now, all any man could do was think of survival.

Reno looked around for Custer. But he had no way o knowing that Custer was miles away, across the river, at tacking the village.

"Goddammit!" Reno cussed.

Some of the newer men were wildly firing their rifles even though the enemy was far out of range.

"Cease fire!" Reno yelled. "Goddammit, cease firing!"

As yet, Jamie had not fired a shot. There was nothing fo him to shoot at.

Lonesome Charley Reynolds unexpectedly galloped int the fray, jumping from his horse. "Howdy," he said to Jamie

"Did you just happen by?" Jamie asked with a smile.

"I didn't have no choice in the matter, Ol' Hoss," the

cout replied calmly. "We're nearly surrounded. And them injuns is almighty angered."

"Do you blame them?"

"Cain't say as I do. You got any ideas, Ol' Hoss?"

"Get the hell out of here."

Lonesome Charley pointed to the bluffs. "That's the oniest way we might take."

Reno had already spotted that, and he ordered a retreat across the river and to the bluffs. It was a bad move, for the opposite bank was nearly ten feet high in spots, too high for a tired horse to make it up.

Reno turned to Bloody Knife just in time to witness through horrified eyes the scout taking a heavy caliber bullet in the center of his forehead. It blew his head apart, and Bloody Knife's prediction came to be: he had seen his last sunset. Reno's face and chest were splattered with the scout's blood and brains. For a few moments, Major Marcus Reno lost control of his emotions and was unable to function as a commanding officer.

Yelling, Reno put the spurs to his horse and galloped out of the timber, his men right behind him.

Reno would be condemned for leaving his wounded behind, but actually, he had no choice in the matter—none whatsoever. Had Reno stayed just one more minute in the timber, he and what was left of his command would have been wiped out to the last man, for he was facing a force of Indians that outnumbered him some twenty to one, and growing.

They galloped for about three-quarters of a mile, following the river, then began to ford the river, the Indians right behind them, so close they were pulling soldiers off their horses and smashing their brains out with war axes. The river turned red with blood.

Lonesome Charley Reynolds, a brave man to the end, had his horse shot out from under him as he was fighting a rearguard action, trying to protect the retreating soldiers.

"Damn!" Jamie muttered, seeing Charley fall.

But Charley didn't die easily or quickly. From the number of shell casings later found where he'd fought behind his dead horse, Charley had taken a number of Indians with him.

Reno had lost more than a third of his men, but he had reached the bluffs and now dug in. Except for a few well-hidden snipers, the Indians were gone, galloping away whooping and hollering.

The war chief Gall had heard the shooting downriver and had led his warriors there.

The soldiers on the bluffs heard the shooting and thought that surely Custer was really dishing out the punishment to the Indians.

Benteen, after riding around for an hour and seeing no hostiles, decided to hell with orders and headed back to the Little Big Horn. He was shocked when Reno (he had lost his hat on the other side of the river, and his uniform was torn and bloody from assisting others) ran out of cover and shouted, "For God's sake, Captain. I've lost almost half my men. Help us."

The two men talked for a few minutes, neither of them really knowing what to do. Finally, Reno said he wasn't moving until the pack trains caught up and his men were provisioned with ample ammunition.

Provisions finally arrived, and Reno and Benteen moved out, after sharply rebuking a young junior officer, Captain Tom Weir. Weir had ignored the reprimand and ridden off with his company, in search of Custer. Weir was a great admirer of Custer, Benteen couldn't stand the man, and Reno wasn't too thrilled with him either.

Benteen and Reno reached a high point and could see nothing of Custer.

It was Jamie who pointed out the lodges below them.

"My God!" Benteen breathed, at that moment realizing finally, what they were up against.

The men were gazing at over two thousand Indian lodges.

"Here they come!" Jamie said, lifting his rifle and dust

ag one of the several hundred charging Indians, knocking
ae warrior off his horse.

After a brief fight, Reno ordered all the men back to the
luffs, and there they dug in and got ready for a battle. They
ought the Indians for over three hours—three hours of
ery heavy fighting. Then, as dusk began to fall, the fight-
ag ceased as the Indians pulled back.

Neither Benteen nor Reno had any idea what had hap-
ened to Lt. Colonel Custer.

# 36

Custer had crossed Medicine Tail Coulee and then Dee[
Coulee; then the Indians struck, Crazy Horse attackin[
from the right flank and Gall attacking on the left. Custe[
and his men were forced to retreat, finally making their las[
fight on Last Stand Hill.

A group of Indians led by White Shield was attackin[
Company C, which was commanded by Tom Custer, brothe[
of George. White Shield thought Tom was George an[
pressed the attack until all the soldiers were dead. Tom[
body was then so badly mutilated that he could later b[
identified only by his initials tattooed on his arm.

Boston Custer, a civilian scout, was killed only a few hun[
dred yards from his brother, Tom. Their nephew, eighteen[
year-old Harry Reed, who had come along for the adventur[
of it all, died a few feet from Boston.

From Ash Creek to Calhoun Hill, dead soldiers wer[
being stripped of their clothing and then mutilated so thei[
spirits would not be able to enjoy a final resting place, bu[
would instead be forced to wander forever.

Many Indians put on the uniforms of the dead soldier[
and were then killed by other Indians who mistook then[
for white soldiers.

Custer and his men had now reached what would b[
called Last Stand Hill, the warriors of Crazy Horse and Gal[
all around them.

Benteen and Reno remained pinned down by sniper fire, unable to move.

Mitch Bouyer was shot dead.

The last person to see Custer alive was trumpeter Giovanni Martini. By the time he found Benteen and handed him the hastily sprawled message from Custer, the fight on Last Stand Hill had been long over. The message read: BENTEEN. COME ON. BIG VILLAGE. BE QUICK. BRING PACS.

Pacs meant the packs containing ammunition.

Stragglers were now staggering into the area controlled, more or less, by Reno and Benteen. Some of them were weaponless, some of them wounded; all of them were frightened nearly out of their minds. They told horror stories of scalping and mutilation of the dead.

"Dig in," Reno ordered the men.

"With what?" a private asked, then added, "sir."

"With anything you have, son," Reno told him. "Just do it."

As darkness began spreading a shroud over the land, the men on the bluffs could see huge fires, the flames leaping high into the still-smoky and dusty air. In the flame light, the soldiers could see figures dancing about, jumping and hollering.

"Victory dance," Jamie told the gathering of officers and men. "We're all that's left, I reckon. Everyone else is dead."

"My God, you don't mean that!" Captain Weir blurted.

" 'Fraid I do, boy," Jamie said.

"You can't be certain of that," the young captain argued.

Jamie pointed to the fires and the wildly and joyous dancing of the Indians. "They damn sure seem to be."

"Then . . . we're next." Benteen spoke the words softly in the summer air.

"They'll throw everything they've got at us tomorrow," Jamie said. "But I've been in worse spots."

"Where, for God's sake?" Reno demanded.

"The Alamo," Jamie replied.

Nobody had a thing to add to that.

Earlier that day, just as Rosanna and Andrew were abou
to board ship, Rosanna experienced a panic attack, unlik
anything she had ever known before. She refused to boar
the ship.

"But the tour," their business manager and agent said.

"To hell with the tour," Andrew said, after speaking in pri
vate with his sister. "We'll postpone it for a time."

"Get us tickets on the morning train," Rosanna said. "Al
the way through. We're going home."

Falcon sat by a hat-sized fire, frying his bacon, the coffe
already made and the pot set off to one side on the circl
of rocks. He knew he was in serious trouble, for even though
the two brothers he'd killed back down the trail a-ways had
been no more than worthless bullies, they were still sta
packers. And one of them a federal lawman.

He'd have to stay on the run until this thing got straight
ened out; already he missed his kids something fierce.

He'd have to get word to his brothers in Valley, and they'
hire detectives to come in and ferret out the straight stor
of what had happened. Until then? . . .

Falcon's laugh was void of humor. "I'm an outlaw on the
run," he said. "Probably the richest outlaw in history, bu
on the run nevertheless."

"Crap!" Falcon summed up his mood.

The children of Jamie and Kate gathered at the home o
Jamie Ian the Second. They all had experienced a terribl
feeling that day. And that mood was only deepened when
Matthew held up a piece of paper.

"I got this wire this afternoon. Falcon's killed two mer

ver in Utah Territory. A county sheriff and a federal mar-
hal. He's on the run."

Matthew stood silent for a moment, letting the sudden
abble of voices die down. "I don't have the particulars yet,
ut you can all bet that those lawmen pushed Falcon over
he line. And Falcon is not a man you can push. You all know
ow Pa made us set things up. Falcon's got money a-plenty
nder a different name in a bank in San Francisco, a bank
n Denver, a bank in Dallas, and several other places." He
miled. "We all do. Pa never trusted in organized law and
rder out of a book. He said common sense was the only
ood law; and the folks that don't use good common sense
ill end up with a bullet in them, and society will be better
ff for it. I ain't sayin' I agree total with Pa, but damned if
can disagree much with that view."

The brothers and sisters exchanged glances. Joleen fi-
ally said, "Have you received any codes from Falcon?"

Years back, Jamie had made his kids work out and mem-
rize a code that only they would know. To anyone else it
ould be gibberish.

"Not yet, but he'll get word to us by and by."

"Is there any word about Custer?" Ellen Kathleen asked.

"Nothing. And there probably won't be for weeks. The
earest telegraph wire is a couple of hundred miles from
here Pa was scoutin'. I know we all got a terrible feelin'
his day. But don't none of us know just what it means.
We're just goin' to have to wait."


The Indians attacked just after dawn, several thousand
trong. But with plenty of ammunition, the defenders along
he bluffs threw back attack after attack in fierce fighting.

At about one o'clock in the afternoon, the Indians, for
easons that are still not quite clear, suddenly quit the fight
nd began taking down their lodges and packing up. By
nid-afternoon, they were moving south en mass.

The battle of the Little Big Horn was over.

Jamie slipped away and threw a saddle on Sundown and began his search for Custer. As usual, the Indians had carried away their dead. Just as the dust of General Terry's command was filling the sky, Jamie rode up to Last Stand Hill. He knew what he would find, and it did not surprise him. Scalped and mutilated bodies of men and dead horses lay under the sun. The men were all naked and had been horribly slashed with knives. Privates cut off, eyes gouged out, hands cut off. Custer had been stripped naked, but had not been mutilated in any way. Kneeling beside the body, Jamie discovered two wounds, one in the chest, one in the head. Either one could have killed the man.

Jamie mounted up and rode to meet General Terry. The general visibly paled at Jamie's words.

"George?" he questioned, his voice shaky.

"Dead with his men." Jamie pointed. "Yonder they lie. Benteen and Reno are over there, on the bluff. We held out, but suffered a lot of dead and wounded."

General Terry sighed heavily and took off his hat to mop his sweaty face and forehead. "What in God's name happened here?"

"I reckon no one will ever really know the answer to that, General."

And to this day, no one really does.


General Terry ordered the burying of the fallen men of the 7th Cavalry to begin the next day, June 28, 1876. And it was not a pleasant task, for the sun had already begun its work and the bodies were beginning to bloat and rot and stink. The dead were buried where they fell. Lt. Colonel George Armstrong Custer was later given a hero's burial at West Point.

The only survivor of what has become known as Custer's Last Stand was Captain Myles Keogh's horse, Comanche. Comanche had been badly wounded in the fight, but was nursed back to health. For years, Comanche was featured

7th Cavalry parades, saddled, but riderless. Comanche was twenty-eight years old when he died in 1891.

A year after the battle, Sitting Bull said, "These men who fought with Long Hair were as good men as ever fought."

During the next year, 1877, General Crook would take to the field and push his troops as hard as any troops were ever pushed. They showed no mercy to the Indians, killing them where they found them. They destroyed villages, burned food supplies, and left men, women, and children to die in the cold and snow. Retribution for Custer's Last Stand was harsh.

Major Marcus Reno was accused of cowardice in the face of the enemy. Angered, Reno demanded a court of inquiry. That was convened in 1879. Reno was cleared, for no one would swear that he had seen any cowardice displayed by Reno. Major Marcus Reno died in 1889.

Jamie rode out of the valley of the Little Big Horn on the 30th of June. His work was finished. He was going home.

For the last time.

# 37

Jamie was tired and depressed. A lot of good men had been lost back along the Little Big Horn . . . and that included people on both sides. Jamie knew in his heart that the slaughter of Custer would pull the country together against the Indians like nothing had ever done. The Indians were finished. Oh, there would be pitched battles for another ten or so years, but while the Little Big Horn had been a victory for the Indians, it had, in Jamie's mind, also signaled the end for them.

It was days later, at a trading post on the North Platte,* when Jamie heard the news about Falcon. To the eyes and mind of the new post owner, Jamie was just another rugged-looking old relic of a mountain man, not worth a cup of spit for anything.

Jamie bought his supplies, then had a drink and listened to the men talk. Falcon had killed two lawmen over in Utah Territory, a county sheriff and a deputy federal marshal.

But why had he killed them?

The men at the bar didn't know that, only that he had. Falcon had left the little town riding a horse the color of dark sand—a big horse, for Falcon, like his father, was a big man. His packhorse was a gray.

Riding a horse the same color and approximately the

*The city of Casper would be founded here in 1888.

me size as mine, and trailing a gray packhorse, just like
ine, Jamie mused.

Jamie quietly left the trading post without notice and
nce more headed south. He stopped at Fort Fred Steele
nd told the commanding officer there what had really
ken place at the Little Big Horn. The CO and his other
fficers listened intently as Jamie laid it all out, from be-
inning to end. They had learned about the slaughter, but
new few particulars.

It was there that Jamie arranged for a wire to be sent to
is kids in Valley. He knew that by now they would be wor-
ed sick.

Jamie pushed on toward home. He crossed the Divide
nd felt pretty sure he was in Colorado (boundaries were
ill a bit illdefined), and felt better. He was not that far from
ome. Well, maybe a week's riding.

About a day out of Valley, Jamie was humming an old song
hat Kate used to sing when two hammer blows struck him
n the back, almost knocking him out of the saddle. As he
ruggled to stay on the horse, he thought he heard a shout
f triumph. Sundown took off like a bolt of lightning, the
ackhorse trailing.

When he got the big horse calmed down, Jamie managed
 stuff handkerchiefs in the holes in his back. He knew he
ared not leave the saddle; he'd never be able to get back
n the deck if he did. Through waves of hot pain, he cut
ngths of rope and tied himself in the saddle.

"All right, Sundown," Jamie gasped. "You know the way
ome. Take me to Kate."


Two of Jamie's great-grandsons spotted the slow-walking
orse and the big man slumped unconscious in the saddle.
hey'd been heading down to the creek to fish. When they
ealized who it was, it scared the be-Jesus out of both of
hem. They took off for town, running as fast as they could.
hey ran right down the center of main street, yelling and

hollering at the top of their lungs and pointing toward th
north.

Matthew was the first to respond. He leaped onto hi
horse and headed toward the north road that led into tow
Dr. Tom Prentiss was a minute behind him. As he rode, th
doctor yelled, "Hitch up a wagon and follow me!"

As the two men cut the ropes that bound Jamie and a
gently as possible eased him from the saddle, Doctor Tor
took one look at the hideous wounds in Jamie's back, an
for a second, his eyes touched those of Matthew. Tom shoo
his head.

"Oh, goddammit!" Matthew yelled. "No!"

The wagon rattled up, and the men placed Jamie in th
bed after spreading several blankets. "Take him to th
clinic," Tom told the driver. He looked at Matthew. "Gathe
your kin, Matthew."

Hours later, Tom Prentiss stepped out to meet the im
mediate family. Only Matthew was missing. He'd been tol
there was a wire waiting for him at the telegraph office. Th
street outside the clinic was filled with friends and relative
of Jamie.

"I've made him as comfortable as possible," the docto
said. "He refused any offer of laudanum. I can't dig out th
bullets. They're too deep and I don't know where they ar
I don't see how he made it this far."

"How long . . . before? . . ." Joleen managed to get thos
words out before tears stopped her voice.

"Maybe an hour, maybe a day," the doctor said. He looke
at Jamie Ian the Second. "How old is your father, Ian?"

The eldest son cleared his throat. "Pa thought he wa
born in 1810, Tom. But he never was real sure of that. It ma
have been 1808 or 1809."

The doctor nodded his head. "During a moment of con
sciousness, he asked that one of you kids lay out his goo
set of buckskins. For now, well, all of you can go in for a mo

ent and see him. But he won't recognize you. He's drift-
ig in and out. He's . . . ah, well, he's been talking to Kate."

Matthew stepped into the doctor's outer office, a
legram in his hand. His brothers and sisters turned to
im. Matthew's eyes were bright with anger. He held up the
ire. "This is from a sheriff friend of mine over near the
tah line. Seems as though a posse of men from some
inch called the N/N, and headed by several newly ap-
ointed deputy federal marshals, think they got lead into
alcon. Happened yesterday or the day before some miles
orth of here. What they done was they mistook Pa for Fal-
on."

Joleen said, "There'll be blood on the moon when Fal-
on hears of this."

"For a fact," Matthew said. "My friend is gonna send me
iore information as he gets it. How's Pa?"

"Dying," Ian said, then put his big hands to his face and
ept openly.


Jamie Ian MacCallister, the man called Bear Killer, Man
Vho Is Not Afraid, Man Who Plays With Wolves, died on
ugust the first, 1876, at eight o'clock in the morning. He
as buried that afternoon, beside his beloved Kate and his
randfather, on a ridge overlooking the town of Valley.
Iverhead, circling and soaring high above the ridge, sev-
ral eagles screamed.

Jamie and Kate were together again, never to be sepa-
ited.


The next day, James William Haywood, Jamie's grandson
om Ellen Kathleen and William Haywood, opened Jamie's
ill in front of the family. He had read it the night before,
nd was shocked right down to his boots at the enormity of
imie's wealth.

"Your father," he told the gathering, "was more than likely

the richest man in all of Colorado. He was worth million
of dollars. He drew up this map—" he held up a map car
fully outlined on a large piece of deerskin—"about a yea
ago. It shows all the places where he cached bags and boxe
of gold and silver. During the wanderings of your grea
grandfather, the man called the Silver Wolf, who lies burie
up on the ridge with Jamie and Kate, he discovered a cav
of Spanish treasure. He gave that to Jamie, and now Jam
is giving it to all of you. The location is on the map. You chi
dren of Jamie and Kate MacCallister just might be the rich
est family in all of North America. Now, your father le
some of his wealth to every member of the MacCallister fan
ily. Nieces, nephews, cousins . . . he left no one out. He le
a sizeable sum of money to be used by the town of Valley.
is carefully invested and will bring in a nice return fo
decades to come."

James William sighed and looked up from the pages-lon
will. "I never realized what a complex man Jamie Ian Ma
Callister was. Not until I opened and read this will. He wa
a self-educated man, and he did a good job of it." He lifte
the will for all to see. "We'll go over this document point b
point later on, but for now, does anyone know where Fa
con is?"

"No," Matthew said. "I received a coded wire from hi
last night. I replied, in code, telling him of our father
death. The telegrapher tapped back that it had been r
ceived, but I have no way of knowing where Falcon wa
when he sent the wire. Hell, he might not have sent it. H
might have had a friend do it."

The young lawyer looked at Rosanna and Andrew. "An
you two? . . ."

"We've rescheduled our tour. It's what Ma and Pa woul
have wanted us to do," Andrew said. "Pa used to say that lif
has to go on."

James William nodded. "It's going to be . . . strang
around here without Grandpa Jamie. It's going to tak
some . . . getting used to."

"It will never be the same." Megan summed up the feel-
gs of all the kids of Jamie and Kate MacCallister.

After the initial reading of the will, Jamie Ian met with
atthew in Falcon's Wild Rose Saloon and said, "Now,
other, you want to tell the truth about Falcon?"

"He's in Utah. He's going after Nance Noonan and those
osse members. He's going to destroy the N/N and then
rn down the town. Right down to the last brick and
ard."

"There were federal marshals in that posse."

"You think Falcon gives a damn about that?"

Jamie Ian sighed and shook his head. "I reckon not."

"Joleen summed it up the other day. There's gonna be
ood on the moon before this is over."

The brothers walked out to stand on the boardwalk, look-
g up at the ridge where their mother and father and
andfather lay in peace.

"You think Pa would have done what Falcon is about to
o?" Jamie Ian asked.

"It's *exactly* what Pa would have done."